THROUGH THE HAZEL TREE

By

ANNA KIRKUP

PUBLISHED BY GOLDEN STORYLINE BOOKS

This book was published in the United Kingdom and Internationally by Golden Storyline Books.

COPYRIGHT © ANNA KIRKUP 2023

All rights reserved. No part of this book may be reproduced, distributed, or transmitted in any form or by any means, or stored in a database or retrieval system without prior written permission from the author.

Disclaimer: Although some of the places and locations that are mentioned in this novel do exist, the underground facilities referred to within, are purely fictitious and from the author's own imagination. Any resemblance to real person's past or present is purely coincidental.

PROLOGUE

'The future of Felicia is in our hands, Mara. I simply cannot turn down this opportunity. They asked for me specifically, she needs me.'

Osmond held his wife's slim hands in his, her shaking was becoming increasingly more concerning with each passing moment, her usually olive skin turned deathly pale.

'But I need you! Our children need you… your city needs you!' Mara begged, her voice hushed so as not to wake her young children sleeping only a few feet away, curled up together in a rickety single bed.

'I cannot provide for them here, Mara. There is little need for a warlock of my age, the work will cease without question, and I simply will not let you down in that way.' Osmond tried to conceal the desperation in his voice. His wife didn't need to see him break, she needed him to be strong.

'When I married you, I promised you all of the finer things in life… the most delicately crafted silk bedding to be changed each Sunday, fresh fruit for the children every morning before school, brand new books with hard covers and gold calligraphy for you to read over lunch. I promised you all of that, my dear. I have not yet been able to see it through and I loathe myself for that. I am not the husband you wished for, and I am not the father they deserve.'

His voice finally cracked as he turned to look at his young children. His four year old son was lying against the cracked plaster of the wall with his arm protectively draped across his baby sister's torso. Her black curls spilled over onto the pillowcase, and her dark lashes stood starkly against her pale, hollow cheeks.

'Felicia needs a sense of hope, and Forneus is trusting in my sense of duty. We will be paid handsomely for my sacrifice, and the girl will always have someone who truly cares for her... a father figure and mentor. I have this feeling that she will change our world so greatly. She can solve all of Felicia's problems, I just know it! One day in the future, we will return to our homeland. We will have the room to grow and the space to evolve. No more population crisis, no more homelessness, no more hunger. We can begin again! Start our lives over! Forneus has already promised us a home within the Council, I'll be able to join you there when I am allowed leave. Our children will be happy and most importantly, safe. We cannot deny them of that right, Mara. Please let me do this... for our family.'

Fat, salty tears were pouring down Mara's cheeks. Her face was angular and bony, her shoulder blades pressing uncomfortably against her skin.

'Daddy?'

Archer had sat up in the bed, he was rubbing the back of his hand harshly against his eyes, they were deep blue and sleepy in the faint candlelight.

'Shh, son. Go back to sleep, it's alright,' Osmond whispered, crossing the small distance to his children's bed and pulling the blanket up over both of their shoulders.

Archer laid reluctantly back down, stroking the soft hem of the fabric against his top lip. 'Are you leaving us?' he asked quietly, his voice serious.

A part of Osmond's heart plummeted into his stomach, his cheeks aching with un-shed tears. 'I would never leave you, my boy. But I must go away for a little while, to make a better life for you and your sister. But I promise that I'll come and visit every single month. You're going to be moving with your mother to a wonderful new house… somewhere for you to make lots of new friends. Won't that be exciting?'

Archer nodded silently, tucking his arm back around his sister as his eyes began to close.

Osmond took a deep breath and turned back to his wife. A defeated look lingered in her eyes, her shoulders slumped as she stared at her children.

'I'll miss you, daddy,' Archer whispered as he drifted back into unconsciousness, and the tears finally filled Osmond's eyes.

'I'll miss you most.'

CHAPTER ONE

Elara

The Scottish countryside may as well have been another world.
Though she'd lived there just shy of a month, her new village was already starting to become more familiar. In London almost every corner was packed with people, cultures, and noise, here she could be quiet. Alone and calm in the tranquillity. Her new bedroom wasn't fully decorated yet, but already the large bay window overlooking the forest was Elara's happy place. A pile of brightly coloured cushions and blankets littered the floor, whilst gentle mid-August sunlight bled through the trees and lit up the room. She could sit for hours, reading and painting, or just watching the leaves change and sway.
Elara was due to start at her new college this week. Though the other pupils would also be getting used to the college, it was likely many of them already knew each other. In a village this small, it seemed everywhere Elara went she got funny looks from the locals.
Her mum had been panic-buying college supplies for the last three weeks, despite Elara's protests that she had everything she needed. The house was still a tip, barely any

boxes unpacked, but her mother's main priority had always been Elara's education.

Elara had never understood her mother's obsession with success and learning, she would much rather do something artistic with her life, but her mum was adamant that Elara would become a partner in her law firm by the time she turned 25. A lot of pressure for a 16-year-old.

'Elara, come down here, I want you to look through some textbooks for tomorrow!' Rose Anderson called to her daughter, as she tapped impatiently on the ladder up to her bedroom. Elara peaked her head out over the hatch and smiled down at her mother.

'Mum, I appreciate you getting me all these books, but please, I really don't need to read them all for tomorrow. You know that's what the class is for, right?'

Rose rolled her darkly lined eyes back up at her daughter. 'Yes hon, but you need to get your head start on the course! Let them know you're really invested!' Rose smiled as she handed the books up to Elara, along with a pencil case filled with brightly coloured pens.

'I highlighted the next 3 weeks' worth of reading for you to get started on, make a few notes as well, they'll come in really useful. Tea will be ready in half an hour. I expect you'll be done by then.' Rose blew a kiss to her daughter before disappearing off down the stairs.

Elara rolled her eyes before lying back on her cushions with a groan. Sometimes living with her mother was a full-time job.

After a while of pretending to study, Elara made her way downstairs, seeking out the warm comforting scent of her favourite meal.

'Hey kid,' her dad smiled, glancing up from the TV where Antiques Roadshow was blaring as Elara leaned over the counter, picking at a slice of garlic bread. 'Homemade lasagne, are you hungry?'

'I'm surprised you even have to ask!' Elara joked before settling into her seat at the table, her stomach rumbling so loudly it made her wince. There were candles in the middle as a centrepiece, surrounded by peach-coloured roses and a card leaning up against her plate.

'What's all this about?' Elara asked. 'Did I miss my birthday?'

Her parents grinned at her.

'We're just so proud of how you've managed all this, kid,' her dad said as he sat down at the table across from his daughter. 'It can't have been easy leaving everything you've known behind, all your friends, your school, but you've handled it so well Els. We love you so much.'

He looked like he might cry, so Elara got up and gave him a tight squeeze from behind.

'Thanks, Dad, I love you too.'

Rose scrunched her nose up at her family. 'Alright, enough of the soppiness, let's eat!'

After a night of restless sleep, Elara was woken by a cool breeze drifting through her room.

'Morning El!' her mum said joyfully, already dressed in a crisp white blazer as she plumped a large orange cushion in the window.

'Jesus Christ, you scared the life out of me. Why are you up so early? My alarm doesn't go off for another hour!' Elara grumbled as she pulled her quilt up over her head.

'I want to make sure you're not late, you need to make a good first impression Elara. I picked out an outfit for you as well. Please wear it. I don't want you looking sloppy. Breakfast will be ready in 20 minutes,' she said, climbing back down the ladder.

Elara groaned turning back over to sleep.

'Now El!'

The outfit Rose had picked out for her daughter was certainly professional, way too professional for Elara's liking. She swapped out the blouse for a cropped sage green cardigan, wearing her favourite colour might at least give her a splash of confidence, and in place of the pin-stripe trousers went a black miniskirt. She straightened her hair, only to fluff it back up again and applied some light makeup. At least if her outfit didn't impress her mother, some effort on her face might.

As she made her way into the kitchen, Rose threw an exasperated look at her daughter, her gaze focussing on the sliver of skin between her cropped cardi and high-waisted skirt.
'Who raised you, Elara Hazel?' she asked with a sigh, tossing an apple over to her before disappearing into the conservatory. Likely needing a minute to regain her composure.
'I think you look great,' her dad whispered, kissing the top of her head as he made his way to the front door.
Peter Anderson had led a very busy life back in London working as an IT Manager for a company he hated six days a week. Now, after his sudden, but greatly appreciated redundancy, he was making the most out of his free time with a fresh start in Scotland, the country her parents had always dreamed of living in. Pottery classes were Mondays and Fridays, and beginners art classes the rest of the week.
Chasing his childhood dreams looked good on him, he was more relaxed than ever. Elara only wished her mother would learn from her dad's spontaneity, however working remotely for Rose meant she'd taken on twice the amount of clients at her law firm, alongside being a full-time 'mumager', as Pete liked to call her.
'See you later El, be good!' he smiled, slipping out of the front door with a wide-eyed look to the conservatory

where they could hear Elara's mother counting her breaths. She was a very highly-strung lady.

Elara's new college was only a 5-minute walk from her house. Though in the future this might be a blessing, Elara was desperate for the walk to take hours to hold the day away a little longer. She could already hear the laughter and lilting Scottish accents from down the street and as she rounded the corner onto the main road out of the village, her new college stood tall against the grey sky. Crowds of people were leaning against the main gates, whilst students on bikes and motorbikes circled around like vultures. Elara shifted her rucksack higher onto her shoulder and squared her jaw to stop it from trembling, her teeth clenched tightly. Fake it till you make it, right? She'd been asked to report to the front desk at 9am to pick up her ID card and be shown to her tutor room. All she had to do was make it through this giant crowd of people and try and find the front desk, preferably without crying or causing a scene.

As she neared the gates, students left, right and centre began to turn and look at her, before spinning back around and whispering to their friends. Despite all of her village exploring over the last few weeks, not one of these faces looked familiar. As she walked past a large group of girls, they all began to giggle and point at her rucksack. Elara fought the urge to scowl at them and instead smiled politely as she slunk past, wincing inwardly as the sole of her black boot scraped noisily on the tarmac.

In Scotland, the girls looked different to city girls. Elara had never quite managed to fit in in London either, but at least there they didn't point and stare. Perhaps here, it was the fact that her light blonde hair was clipped away from her face with a black velvet bow that her mother hated that made her stick out from the crowd... or the fact that she wasn't dressed entirely appropriately for the weather. Here everyone wore designer coats, stylish fleeces, quirky shackets. Elara hated to admit that she already felt marginally frozen, but she was certain she hadn't packed anything more substantial than a cropped denim jacket. Many girls here carried tiny, bright shoulder bags or tote bags, very different to Elara's muted black rucksack that her mum had picked out for her, much to Elara's annoyance. She'd already covered it in badges and pins to try and liven it up a bit. She hoped maybe one of them would be a conversation starter.

Lost in her own thoughts, Elara had failed to notice that a group of teenage boys oozing with concerning levels of testosterone were leaning on the handlebars of their bikes and were now blocking the entrance to the college. She glanced up from the ground and smiled wanly, trying to squeeze past.

'My, my, my!' one of the guys grinned, grabbing Elara's arm to stop her from moving. 'You're certainly not from round here, are you babe?' he asked condescendingly, smirking at his friends. 'I'd have remembered a pretty face like that.'

He looked Elara up and down, curling his lip. Elara suppressed a laugh, jerking her arm out of his grip with a sigh. Clearly this morning wasn't going to go as smoothly as she'd hoped. He had a very strong Scottish accent that Elara struggled to understand, and a crowd had begun to form around the whole interaction. Elara shifted her rucksack further onto her shoulder, an uncomfortable prickle beginning to crawl along her skin.

'So does the new girl speak?' another guy leered, 'or are you not from this country, darling?'

Elara cleared her throat. 'Don't call me darling. I'm from London,' she said with a roll of her eyes, moving away slightly from the group, perhaps there was a back entrance.

'Hey, not so fast, Miss London.'

Yet another guy hopped down from his bike and started making his way towards Elara.

'I'm sure there's more to you than that. Come on love, let's have a little chat. What's your name? What brought you to Scotland? What's your bra size?' he cackled as his friends screeched hysterically, all now climbing down from their bikes and surrounding Elara. The crowd behind them started murmuring, some pulling out their phones to record.

Elara had been prepared for a little bit of drama, but this was ridiculous.

'You have to be kidding,' she laughed, 'could you let me past please? I have an appointment at 9, I don't want to be late.' She'd hoped to shrug them off, but in startling clarity she realised they weren't joking. They were deadly serious. It was all she could do not to drop to the ground and weave through their legs to escape. She could feel a pink blush spreading across her chest, up along her neck and over her cheeks. She tried to breathe slowly to calm the redness, but it was too late, the group had already noticed.

'Ooooh, are we getting shy, princess? Do we make you nervous? There's no need for that.' A boy with dark brown hair and piercing green eyes sauntered towards Elara. He lifted his hand up to stroke her cheek with a menacing grin. Elara balled her fists up, ready to punch the cocky bastard, but was stopped short by someone pushing their way to the front of the circle.

'Hey Brandon, what's going on? Who's this?' the guy asked, stepping in front of Elara, and facing the group. Elara backed away slightly, hoping this was her chance for escape, but the circle around them were keeping her in, still recording… likely hoping to be at the forefront of a viral video.

'Yo, Xander! This is our friend, Miss London. She's new here so we're giving her a warm Oakbridge welcome.' The guy Elara presumed was Brandon, the leader of the psychos, peered around and winked at her, his friends chortling away in the background. She looked him up and down, hoping to appear unimpressed with his whole performance as butterflies flocked in her stomach.

'Well, if you want to get to know her so badly, I'm sure polite conversation would do the trick. Though we both know English isn't your strong point, Brandon, so why don't I do the honours?'

Laughter and gasps rang out from the crowd as Elara felt a smirk creep onto her face.

'Hey, I'm Alexander but everyone just calls me Xander. What's your name?' he turned to ask, a kind smile on his face.

'Elara, I moved here a few weeks ago.'

'See Brandon?' Xander turned back around to face the group, his light eyes sparkling mischievously, 'tell me, was that really so hard?'

Brandon's face slowly turned a bright scarlet. He wanted Xander's approval, and this clearly wasn't the way to get it.

'You're right man, I'm sorry. Nice to meet you Elara,' he smiled sheepishly, changing his whole façade in an instant and holding out a hand to Elara.

The group finally dispersed, and Elara checked her watch, she was already two minutes late for her meeting, if her mum found out she'd probably explode from the stress. All that and Elara still didn't know where the stupid front desk was.

As she started walking away, she heard footsteps running after her.

'You're welcome, by the way!' a voice called from somewhere behind her.

Elara rolled her eyes, not slowing her pace, 'I didn't need your help, I can handle myself.'

'Hey, wait,' Xander called, dropping into a stride alongside her, 'you're right, I'm sorry I was only messing. Hey, you came into my family's pharmacy the other day with your mum; I recognise your hair,' he smiled, gesturing to her long, light blonde hair.

'Yeah um, I have nightmares, so I have to take sleep medication,' Elara said, surprised at herself for suddenly dropping that into conversation with a stranger, but shaking the immediate onset of embarrassment out of her head and looking around for any signs that might tell her where she was going.

'Yeah, I saw the prescription.'

Elara stopped, shooting a strange look at Xander.

'Not that I was looking, I just help package orders sometimes.'

Elara raised her eyebrows but carried on walking in the general direction she hoped would lead her to the front desk.

'You want me to walk you to your tutor group?' Xander asked as he checked his watch.

'I need to go check in first, get my ID. I'm already late so I should get going,' she said, beginning to walk away from him again.

'Oh, hey my tutor room is in that direction, I'll walk you there.'

Elara wasn't sure whether she was pleased or annoyed at his insistence.

As she finally arrived at the front desk she glanced at the clock on the wall and realised she was now eight minutes late. Rose Anderson would not be happy.

'Hi, I'm so sorry I'm late, I got held up. My names Elara, I got told to come here for my ID?'

'Late on the first day, Miss Anderson, not the best start, is it?' the receptionist sighed, peering at Elara over her glasses.

Xander cleared his throat, 'Actually, Mrs Michael it was my fault, I was showing Elara round, I'm sorry.' Xander threw a charming smile at the teacher, and she instantly softened.

'Why is it, Alexander Griffin, that you are always at the heart of trouble?' she grumbled, but a warm smile pulled at her lips.

'What can I say Miss, I just attract it,' he grinned, glancing back at Elara with a sparkle in his eye.

'Here's your ID and timetable, Miss Anderson,' the receptionist handed an envelope over to Elara, still smiling at Xander and signing a piece of paper with a flourish.

'I'm sure Alexander can show you to your tutor room, give them this note to explain why you're late. I hope you'll be very happy studying with us.'

Elara smiled before slipping the ID card into her pocket and following Xander to the stairs.

'So, Miss Anderson, what are you studying in this fine institution?' he grinned, putting on a snobby teacher voice.

'Law, politics and art. You?'

'I won't lie, you don't look like the academic type,' he laughed.

Elara stopped dead in her tracks, a few steps behind him. It took a second for him to realise that she'd dropped back, and as he turned around, a sheepish blush had coloured his cheeks.

'Again, I'm sorry. I didn't mean that you look like you're not smart, or that you shouldn't be doing difficult classes because you're a girl- Oh God no not that I was judging you based on your gender, or your appearance! You don't look like anything in fact... wait, no! I- I...' he rambled, stumbling over his words.

Elara tilted her head, an amused frown on her face. He caught her expression and finally smiled, raking a hand through his hair.

'What I'm trying to say is, I'm doing law too, alongside history and English. For the first week or so, I could meet you after your classes? We could walk together so you don't get lost. Can't have you being late again.'

Elara laughed; this boy clearly wasn't going to give up easily.

'Yeah, trust me I'd rather be doing all fun subjects,' Elara grinned, bounding up the couple of steps so that she was face to face with Xander once more, 'but my mum wants me to be a lawyer, so law and politics it is. And sure, that'd be helpful, actually. Thanks.'

He stopped outside a door, before knocking on it loudly.

'See you soon, Miss Anderson.'

Elara's tutor wasn't really bothered by her lateness, in fact she hardly spoke to her at all aside from assigning her a desk. None of the other students interacted with her either, mainly they just stared or ignored her completely. Elara was surprised to find herself looking forward to Xander picking her up and saving her from the awkwardness.

After a dreary half an hour, the tutor group finally let out. Elara seemed to be the only one taking notes on anything Miss Ashcroft had been saying. Maybe that wasn't cool here, but at least her mother might appreciate the effort.

As promised, the second she left the room, Xander was stood waiting for her. She could see him glancing through the crowd looking for her, but already he was surrounded by a gaggle of students, both boys and girls alike. He nodded her over and Elara raised her eyebrows at the sea of people around him. He smirked and began to push his way through the crowd.

'So what, were you like the Prom King of Oakbridge High?' Elara asked with a grin as Xander guided her towards a corridor that looked marginally less busy, and the giggles and gossip slowly faded away into the background.

He laughed widely up at the ceiling with a shake of his head. 'Yeah, right. I had braces and curtains in high school. No one even gave me a second glance.'

Elara stole a peak at him out of the corner of her eye, his eyes were startlingly blue and twinkling under the fluorescents. 'Hey, now. Curtains are back in. You were clearly trendier than you thought.'

Xander raised his eyebrows at her with a smirk as he held open a door for her to duck under, following closely behind.

'Anyway how was the first tutor time? They're boring right? Hardly anyone even turns up to them.'

'Yeah, I don't think Miss Ashcroft liked me. She didn't even smile at me when I walked in, plus no-one in the class seemed at all interested,' Elara said, trying to focus on the route they were taking. She needed to at least be able to find her classes in this mammoth school.

'Nah that's just what the teachers here are like, they don't get paid enough to care. Wasn't your old school like that?'

'No,' Elara replied, trying her best to keep up with Xander's long strides, 'my high school was an academy, not one person in my whole year ever failed a term.'

Xander looked surprised, 'well, that's the North for you Elara, you're gonna love it,' he said with a wink.

After another two slightly dull classes, it was finally time for lunch. Most of her time had been spent playing pointless ice-breaker games and getting used to the structure of the courses. It all seemed unnecessary and increasingly awkward as the day went on, and Elara knew her mother wouldn't be impressed by the lack of education. At least it gave Elara a chance to get used to her new classmates, even if they didn't seem interested in getting to know her. Xander had offered a seat with him and his friends for lunch, and although Elara was terrified at the idea of being forced upon so many strangers, she accepted gratefully. She knew it would be more embarrassing to eat alone on her first day.

The cafeteria was clearly the hub of all student life. There were countless brightly coloured booths and tables, pounding music playing from a stereo in the corner and Elara could count at least five different food stations, all serving slightly questionable looking meals. The amount of people crowded around the tables was alarming, and Elara suddenly found herself very grateful for having Xander at her side to lead her through the jungle. Xander confidently weaved his way through the crowds and Elara followed quickly, trying her best not to get trampled. She found herself at a small table towards the corner of the cafeteria, slightly away from the worst of the noise, yet still there were four people chatting away, who all turned to stare when Xander cleared his throat.

'Hey guys, this is Elara, she's going to be eating with us today,' he said, pulling her forward a little bit, front and centre for all his friends to get a good look.

'Elara, this is Matt, Alfie, Jenna and Natalia.'

Elara knew she would forget half of those names by the end of the day, but it was nice to be introduced. Everyone at the table was looking up at Elara with a smile, perhaps a little reluctant, but a smile none the less, apart from Natalia.

She stood out from everyone else in the cafeteria. Ginger hair was surprisingly common round here, the vibrant hues a refreshing comparison to the girls at her old school who had sleepovers purely for the intent of box-dying each other's hair 'Crimson Fire' that often turned out more like 'Tiger Stripes'.

Natalia's hair was flaming red, the kind of shade that could only ever be natural, and it fell in pretty waves around her face, it contrasted perfectly with her ice-white skin. Her eyes were steel grey, and they directed a searing gaze straight at Elara, making her more and more uncomfortable by the second. Even her clothes were different. Where a lot of college girls seemed to wear trendy, casual clothing,

Natalia looked ready for the catwalk. A short, blue sun dress was matched with a tangle of gold jewellery, heavy black combat boots and over the knee black socks. Natalia reminded Elara much more of the preppy London girls from back home, though, if possible, she looked meaner, and Elara wondered briefly how she wasn't completely frozen from the cool Scottish weather.

Jenna greeted Elara with much more warmth. She had a wide smile that perfectly lit up her dark features and her jet-black hair was flawlessly sleek. A small, red bindi was placed in the centre of her brows that perfectly complemented the deep brown of her eyes. Elara returned her smile happily, a kind face seemed to be hard to come by round here, so she wasn't going to pass up an opportunity to make a good impression.

'Nat, move up please, so Elara can sit down,' Xander said with a pointed look. Natalia huffed and rolled her eyes, moving the tiniest inch along the bench. Elara cleared her throat awkwardly and perched herself on the very end of the seat, dropping her bag to the floor.

'I'm Natalia Stewart,' she purred, holding out a perfectly manicured hand, her wrist jingling with bangles. 'You've probably heard my last name? My dad's own the bar in town,' she purred, her voice was surprisingly soft, her accent light. For some reason Elara had expected her to sound like a fire-breathing dragon.

Elara took her hand gingerly and pumped it limply up and down. 'No, actually. I've only been here a few weeks.'

Natalia scoffed, tossing her hair out of her flawless face.

'I see. Where on Earth did you get that bag from? Looks like you stole it from a charity shop. Or maybe nicked it out a bin. And why all those weird badges? Don't tell me you're some kind of hippy that believes in fairies and reincarnation,' Natalia giggled, looking around the rest of the table with a smirk.

'My mum bought it for me, I didn't really get a choice.'

'Jesus you're posh. Your family 100% voted for the posh pricks who steal money from us commoners,' she cackled, resting her chin in her hand to display her stiletto crimson nails, as sharp as her tongue.

Elara felt her cheeks begin to burn; an angry prickle worked its way down her spine.

'It sounds like you're from Buckingham Palace, do you know the Queen? Doesn't look like you would fit in there,' Natalia mocked, looking Elara up and down.

Xander rolled his eyes. 'She's from London, you div. That's just her accent, I think it's nice.'

Elara blushed slightly, whilst Natalia made retching noises next to her.

'Actually Natalia, I do know the Queen,' Elara cooed as she felt her patience begin to diminish. 'She sent me here to collect you. She heard of your flawless ability to be exceptionally rude and is demanding that you be beheaded. I'm sure that's not a problem for you though, as there doesn't seem to be much going on up there anyway,' Elara smiled sweetly, as Natalia's cheeks turned almost the same colour as her hair.

'You bitch,' Natalia spat, clenching her jaw, 'are you gonna let this freakshow speak to me like that Xander?'

He took another bite out of his sandwich, shrugging carelessly. Elara could see the others at the table struggling to choose between shock and laughter.

Natalia flew up from the table, her face a perfect picture of rage, and stormed out of the cafeteria, practically flattening anyone who got in her way.

'Whoah,' one of the boys breathed, 'Xander where did you find this one? No one speaks to Natalia that way. You're in for a treat this term Elara let me tell you.'

Elara shrugged. 'I don't like people who are disrespectful, and she clearly needed putting in her place. Sorry.'

'No don't be sorry,' Xander was grinning now as he leaned over the table, 'I wish I had half of your nerve. I think there's a lot more to you than you're letting on Elara Anderson,' he said, with a twinkle in his eye.

As predicted, Rose Anderson was not happy with the amount of work Elara had been set.

'Where's all the worksheets? The homework? I'd set out the table so that we could work through it together,' she said, looking disappointed.

Elara could see the line of pens in every colour imaginable taking up half of the dining room table. A glass of water in the centre and a bowl of fruit ready for nourishment. Elara hid a laugh and handed her mother her notebook, watching as she flipped through the empty pages.

'Sorry mum, it was only the first day. They just had us all introduce ourselves, try and make friends, you know?'

'Well why on Earth would you need to do that?' she asked, 'college is for learning, not playing games.'

Elara gave her mum a pointed look.

'Mum it's a local college, not Harvard School of Law. I want to make friends and have fun too, and I'm sure they'll get into the proper teaching soon, don't worry.'

Rose sighed, passing the notebook back over to her daughter.

'Well did you make any friends then? Are the other students nice?' she asked, handing Elara a steaming cup of tea.

Elara frowned, sitting down at the dining room table. 'Actually, hardly anyone was friendly. There was this rude girl who insulted me right to my face. But I met a nice guy. He's called Xander.'

Elara's mum laughed, 'a guy already El? Well, is he cute? When do we get to meet him?'

'It's not like that mum, he just showed me around and invited me to eat with his friends at lunch. I doubt he'll even speak to me tomorrow,' Elara said, taking a sip from her brew.

'Look at your face El! He must be gorgeous to have caught your attention! Come on, find him on social media. I wanna see this mysterious Xander.'

'Xander?' Elara's dad asked as he walked through the front door, flourishing a slightly wonky looking hand-painted mug.

'Elara's new lover,' Rose said tauntingly, winking at her daughter. 'Hi Pete, good day love?'

Elara rolled her eyes but smiled as her dad kissed the top of her head.

'Wow, Elara. First day and you've already got boys falling at your feet. I mean who wouldn't? Look at that angelic face!' Peter said, as he ruffled her hair with a mischievous looking grin.

Elara threw a sarcastic smile at her parents, before grabbing a handful of fresh strawberries out of the fruit bowl and scampering up the stairs to hide the embarrassed redness that was already beginning to creep along her skin.

CHAPTER TWO

Elara

The world around her had turned black. A faint orange glow shone out from the shadows and Elara fought with every single one of her senses to try and figure out what it was and where it was coming from. She started running, her feet tearing up the ground as she went. The closer she got, the feeling that she was being pulled apart became torturous. Almost as though her skin was being ripped from her flesh and taking her identity with it. As she got closer to the orange light, her skin began to prickle painfully with heat. The air around her was getting hotter and hotter, until her body felt like it was on fire. She couldn't tell if it was tears or sweat running down her face as the scene unfolded before her. Suddenly, in bright, blinding light she could see thousands of women and children tied to wooden stakes. Crisp yellow flames licked at their feet and turned their clothes to ash. The sky was red from the haze, and others at the scene were screaming in agony as they tried to untie the ropes that bound the women to the wood. The flames showed no mercy and blistered the hands of anybody that came close.

As Elara ran to the nearest stake, smoke began to worm its way down her throat, clogging up her lungs and choking her. She all but stumbled to the ground as a violent coughing fit shook her body, and she became practically blind in the thick haze. She reached for the stake; she could see the fear in the children's eyes as they begged her for help. Elara tried to reassure them that she would set them free, but it was as though her voice had been taken too and she couldn't say a word, her throat was tight, and her chest screamed for air. She reached out a hand to undo the ropes, her skin already blackened from the ash pouring out of the sky, but suddenly her fingertips slipped straight through the wood, ghostlike. Her mind was screaming at her to pull at the ropes, to grab the children and run, but her body had other ideas and nothing she could do would let her touch the binds that held them down. She screamed out to someone nearby, her eyes flaring with frustration, but barely a rasp made it beyond her lips, and nobody came to help. She watched in agony as the children before her screamed and cried, hot tears burned at her face as she tugged desperately on her hair.

The little girl looked Elara directly in the eye, an understanding smile washing over her young features until eventually, she passed out from the pain. Elara collapsed to the blackened ground with a deathly scream that finally ripped out of her chest. She could hear someone calling her name, but she couldn't respond.

'Elara? Elara it's okay, honey it was just a nightmare. Elara wake up.'

Someone was shaking her. Trying to bring her back to reality but Elara wasn't sure she wanted to be there either. She could feel the sheets from her bed tangled up beneath her legs, her pyjamas were dripping with sweat and her voice was hoarse.

'Elara you were screaming, what happened? What did you dream about?'

Elara broke down into floods of tears, collapsing in her mum's arms as her dad stroked her back.

'The same dream, the dream I have every time. I couldn't save them I swear I tried.'

'I know sweetheart, it's okay it was just a nasty dream. Did you take your medication?'

Elara shook her head, nodding to the small pill bottle on the other side of the room.

'Okay honey, I'll go get you some water and a biscuit. Then you can forget all about this and go back to sleep.'

Her mum disappeared off down the ladder again as her dad sat on the edge of the bed, cradling her as she shook.

'You gave us a fright El! Such a bloodcurdling scream, must have learnt that from your mother!' Elara tried to force a smile, but she was sure it looked more like a grimace.

'Here Elara, wake us if you need anything else sweetheart. Try and get some rest,' her mum soothed, placing the tablet and water down on the bedside table.

Elara nodded, and took a deep breath as her parents left with slightly worried smiles.

As Elara went to take the glass of water, she noticed that the tips of each of her fingers was burned and blistered. She untangled the sheets and saw that her knees were a dirty grey. She'd had the dreams before, but this was certainly a new development.

CHAPTER THREE

Elara

The next few weeks of college went by in a blur. Elara had managed to get into a routine and much to her mother's delight, the college had finally started teaching real classes. Every day she met Xander at the corner of the street just down from the college and they walked together to meet his group of friends. They chatted easily about college and life in Scotland. He asked a lot of questions about her friends from London, who was she closest with? What was there to do on the weekends in the Capital? Would she ever want to go back? It surprised Elara quite how fascinated he seemed to be by her somewhat boring life. She felt as though she'd known him for years, she couldn't believe it'd been less than a month.

She was getting more used to his friends now and their sing-song accents. Natalia still hadn't spoken a word to her since the first day, instead turning her attention wholly to Xander, flirting and joking with him as she doodled along the margins of her notebooks.

At least Jenna seemed to have more patience for Elara, inviting her to come study with her and Alfie on the weekends. They all did politics, so her mother very much approved of this friendship. Though they were all friendly with one another, Elara still sensed that Xander's friends were a little wary around her. She wasn't sure why, but hoped that as the weeks went on, they'd get closer. Xander on the other hand, was completely comfortable to be around, an unusual connection between them that Elara couldn't quite put her finger on. They sat together in law and though Elara had assumed he'd stop walking her to class after the first week, three weeks on he still waited for her every time, greeting her with an easy smile and a new topic of conversation. He always seemed so laid back, whereas she felt like she was suppressing nerves every time she caught a glimpse of him watching her, desperately trying to refrain her cheeks from turning tomato red.

    Each lunchtime, Elara found herself excited to sit with the group, she loved how Xander was around his friends, funny and down to earth, nothing like the other guys she'd met on the first day. Sometimes she'd be talking and feel him staring and goosebumps would emerge embarrassingly across her arms. He'd hold her gaze until she gave in and looked away, a cheeky smile on his face, unapologetically aware of his influence. Often, he'd choose to sit next to her, his arm brushing against hers on the small benches and she'd see the others share a quick glance, before smiling knowingly at her. She would blush as Xander munched away on his lunch, oblivious to his mocking friends. Natalia, however, was certainly not oblivious, her scowl growing deeper by the day.
    She'd made a few friends in her art class now too. She found her three hours of art each week the perfect escape from her busy schedule. Mr Costello was by far her favourite teacher. He chatted amicably to his students, playing music when they asked, letting them move freely around the classroom and checking up on each of them individually. Elara spent her time in her own little world, drawing and

painting fantasy worlds that earned the approval of her fellow students.

'So, Elara. How have you found your first months here in Scotland?' Xander asked one Friday lunchtime, leaning across the table to hold his water bottle out like a microphone, his eyes twinkling with mischief.
Elara shook her head with a grin, 'well Mr Griffin, it has been incredibly cold and rather rainy, but I have to say, I'm a big fan of this little village. Feels like I'm in a fairy tale.' Natalia scoffed, rolling her eyes at Elara. 'Good God,' she huffed, pushing her curly hair out of her face, 'I wouldn't call a close-minded prison a 'fairy tale'.' Natalia narrowed her cool grey eyes harshly, her lips pursed together. Elara felt sorry for the pasta Natalia was eating, it had been massacred in the last 2 minutes.
Xander clicked his tongue disapprovingly at Natalia, which earned a sharp laugh from her as some unspoken conversation flitted between them.
'Ignore her,' he said with a smirk, 'what about the company, Elara… is there anyone you miss back in London?' His question was pointed, a surprisingly guarded look in his eyes. Elara chose to ignore his intended meaning and instead pondered the question for a moment. There certainly hadn't been anyone she was romantically involved with back in London. She messaged her friends every now and then but was surprised to find that she hadn't missed them much. Maybe she was caught up in the business of college life.
'Of course I miss my friends,' she fibbed, 'but I like change. Plus, it's fun to meet new people,' she said, smiling at the others around the table, Xander held her gaze for a moment longer before dropping the water bottle back to the table with a smile and a cheeky wink. Elara could feel Natalia's gaze burning into her temple, as she turned her

attention back towards the plate of chips in front of her, feeling a blush spread across her cheeks.

At the end of the day, Elara was glad that it was the weekend. She was meeting Jenna to study on Sunday, for the second week in a row. She was glad that Jenna was making the effort with her, it seemed genuine.

Just as Elara was leaving through the college gates, she heard someone calling her name. She turned to see Xander crossing the carpark, holding a carrier bag, and making his way over to her.

'Hey,' he called, nodding his head at her, 'you in a rush?'

Elara squinted at him, putting a hand over her eyes to block out the low-lying sun as she shook her head.

'Good,' he smiled, 'remember last week when I asked you which snacks you'd take to a desert island?'

He opened the bag as he neared closer so she could see what was inside. There were a couple of bottles of Diet Coke, a sharing bag of sour Skittles and a punnet of fresh strawberries.

'Should I be worried?' she asked with a laugh, pushing her loose hair out of her face.

'I thought we could take a walk. I've lived in this village my whole life and I'm sure there's some interesting places I could show you,' he said, already walking off without her.

'Umm, yeah sure, that'd be nice,' she said, quickening her pace to catch up with his long strides, 'I need to tell my mum first though; she'll be expecting me back.'

'That's fine, just send her a text,' Xander replied, opening the packet of Skittles and tossing a few into his mouth.

'She doesn't let me bring my phone to college, we'll have to walk via my house. I can drop my bag off then as well.'

'Actually, that's a good idea. You should get changed too. You don't wanna be trailing around the Scottish countryside in that outfit,' he smirked, glancing at her incredibly ripped blue jeans and fresh white Converse.

'You'll either freeze to death or get mauled by sheep. They're notorious for that around here.'

Elara rolled her eyes at him, nudging him lightly with her elbow. She was happy to be spending time with Xander outside of college, but not so happy that she was going to have to introduce him to her mother. She made enough jokes about him as it was.

As predicted, the second Elara walked through her front door with Xander in tow, her mother stood up from the table where she was working on a case and rushed over to them, completely ignoring Elara and holding a perfectly manicured hand out to Xander.

'Wow, you must be Alexander. It's great to finally meet you, I've heard so much about you,' she said with a quick, excited looking glance at Elara.

'Just Xander is fine, it's great to meet you too Mrs Anderson. I just wanted to take Elara on a tour of the village if that's okay. Though I insisted she got changed first.'

His expression was mocking as Elara fought the childish urge to stick her tongue out at him, but Rose's face lit up even more.

'Gosh Xander, the amount of times I've told Elara that her outfits are inappropriate for Scotland, I sound like a broken record! I'm glad you have some sense about you,' she said, with an 'I told-you-so' look at Elara.

'All right that's quite enough bonding from you two, come on Xander, leave the crazy woman to do her work. I'm sure you can chat again later,' Elara sighed, dropping her bag by the door, and heading off to her room. Giving her mother an exasperated look as she went.

'Elara, tell Alexander to ask home if he can stay for tea. We'd love to get to know him better... and set some boundaries!'

'MUM!'

Elara turned and raised her eyebrows at Xander.

'Well, I'd love to stay for tea, thanks for offering,' he said with a cheeky looking smile, as he shrugged his shoulders and pushed past her up the stairs.

'Up there.' Elara pointed to the ladder that led up to her room, and Xander peered up in surprise.

'No way! Your room is in the attic? Like Harry Potter?'

'Harry Potter lived in a cupboard, not an attic. Don't you do English? You should pay more attention Alexander.'

He rolled his eyes at her with a grin before making his way up the ladder.

'Whoah,' he breathed as he popped his head up out of the hatch, 'this is so cool!'

He immediately plopped himself down on one of the giant cushions in the window, looking around at her multiple bookshelves, her bedside table laden with crystals, and the pictures and artwork on the walls.

'Did you paint those?' he asked gesturing to a collection of paintings of one of Elara's friends from back home, each one viewing her from a different angle and combining to look almost 3D.

'Yeah, just a hobby,' she replied, rifling through her drawers for some more practical clothing.

'They're incredible,' he breathed, reaching out to run a finger along the paintwork.

Elara stopped and watched him for a second. Golden hour had struck, and orange sunlight was pouring in through her window, washing across his features and making him look almost like a painting himself. Elara had always just thought of his hair as being brown, but now she could see the streaks of red and gold that sparkled in the sunlight. His blue eyes almost clear, and the faint smattering of freckles across his nose. The harsh shadows in comparison chiselled away at his jaw as he turned back to look at her. Over the past few weeks, Elara had tried to deny to herself just how good-looking he was, but in this moment he was downright beautiful. Nervous butterflies swam through her stomach as he smiled.

'So how else do you spend your time when you're not studying like a madwoman?' Xander asked, shuffling to get comfortable on the cushion.

Elara turned back to the chest of drawers to hide the blush creeping up her chest.

'Sometimes I play guitar,' she nodded over to the light coloured acoustic guitar covered in stickers in the corner of the room. 'My dad taught me when I was younger. I can only play a few chords now though.'

'Oh, cool!' Xander breathed, already dashing over to the guitar, stumming the delicate strings in a way that made Elara wince.

'What are those?' he asked suddenly, pointing to her bedside table.

'Um… Those are- that's my crystal collection,' she said quietly, eyeing up Xander to gauge his reaction. She'd expected him to laugh, but his face lit up in excitement.

'Really? I've always wanted to know more about crystals, they're so fascinating. Do you know all their properties and stuff?'

Elara paused before nodding, a tight smile pulling at her lips.

'How long have you been collecting them?'

'Ever since I was little, though I'm not sure why. I think I just like that they sparkle.'

Xander chuckled, reaching out to pick one up and turn it over in his palm. 'That sounds about right.'

Elara smiled to herself and held up the clothes she'd gathered.

'I'm gonna go and get changed, feel free to snoop,' she nodded at the rest of her room.

After changing into some leggings and a t-shirt, and one of her dad's old fleeces, she and Xander grabbed the snacks, and he began to lead her down a small alleyway at the back of her house that Elara didn't know was there, and eventually it emerged out into a clearing surrounded by woods.

Elara turned, she could still see the roof of her house just a couple of hundred yards back, but here the noise from the street had been completely silenced, and all she could hear was the rustling of the leaves and birds overhead. She looked around in awe, the trees here were so majestic and green, though the tips of the leaves were slowly starting to turn yellow in the Autumn sun.

Elara took a deep lungful of crisp, fresh air. She'd spent so much time recently stressing over classes and trying to fit in, she'd forgotten how different Scotland was to London. Elara had loved her life back in the capital, it was all she'd ever known. It gave her endless opportunities to people-watch with a constant rotation of cultures. She could order Chinese food at three in the morning or go out and listen to buskers on the corner of any street. The noise of the city never faded in her family's tiny flat, and she went to sleep each night with the streetlamps blinking on and off in the light-polluted sky. But Elara knew she had never belonged... always feeling as though she was playing a part and waiting for her own life to begin.

Her friends seemed to grow up so much faster than she did, they couldn't wait to start fake ID-ing their way into nightclubs, chatting up men twenty years their senior, and rushing through life. Elara was growing desperate for time to slow down when her parents announced their desire to move to Oakbridge, a tiny little village on the Scottish borders. Elara's friends had been appalled at the idea, wailing dramatically with the promise that she would always be a 'city girl' at heart. Elara couldn't have packed her suitcase quick enough, practically tasting the fresh air on her tongue.

'Come on, we're not at my favourite place yet,' Xander said suddenly, his voice interrupting her thoughts. His smile was bright, his eyes kind as he beckoned her towards a gap in the trees.

The path was narrow, so Xander lead the way, checking back on Elara every few seconds to check she hadn't disappeared into the thick foliage.

They walked quietly for a few minutes, taking in their surroundings, before Elara finally broke the silence.

'So how come you didn't invite the others to come with us? We could've brought a picnic,' Elara asked.

'Did you want everyone else here?' Xander replied, stopping and turning to look at her.

Elara was still looking at the plants on the ground and nearly walked straight into his chest.

'Oh, sorry. No, I'm happy it just being us, I just thought you might prefer to spend time with your other friends too.'

'I like hanging out with you Elara, plus shouldn't it be my decision how I spend my birthday?'

Elara stopped dead in her tracks, gawking at Xander.

'It's your birthday?! Why didn't you say something? I would've gotten you a gift, or we could've celebrated!' she gasped, hurrying to catch up with him as he carried on trekking down the path, his large strides carrying him metres ahead.

'I don't really celebrate my birthday, plus I'm only 17, not anything special.'

'That is special!' Elara insisted, 'I love celebrating my birthday.'

'Well Elara, I love spending time with you,' he said, turning around once more to look at her. 'I didn't want anyone else here, I just wanted to spend the evening with you, and since it's my birthday, for once you're not allowed to argue. So, shall we carry on to my favourite place? Or do you want me to message Natalia and see if she wants to join us?'

Elara tried to keep the smile on her lips at bay, her chest flooding with heat. 'Oh actually I would love Natalia to be here with us, you're right! Give her some ideas on where to bury my body for when she murders me!'

He shook his head and laughed at her, 'you're something else aren't you, Elara Anderson? Come on, we're almost there.'

He offered out his hand for her to take, a mischievous look appearing on his face as she hesitated. 'I'm not asking you to marry me, I just don't want you to trip!'

Elara scrunched her nose at him, and took his hand fiercely, a daring sparkle in her eye.

He simply laughed and faced forwards once more. Elara was glad he'd turned around as it meant he couldn't see the blush spreading up across her cheeks. Her slim hand looked small in his, her collection of vintage rings sparkling in the last dregs of sunlight filtering between the leaves of the canopy. She smiled as he stroked her thumb gently, guiding her out of the woods.

The view before them was exquisite. They were near the edge of a small cliff that led out onto a river. The edge of the cliff was rocky, strewn with wildflowers and pebbles. The river down below ran fast and loudly, crashing along the spines of the cliffs and out of sight over the crest of a waterfall.

'It's beautiful,' Elara breathed, gazing around, 'how did I not know about this place?'

Xander smiled, settling himself down on to a rock near the edge as he allowed himself a lingering glance at Elara, her blonde hair golden in the early evening sunset.

'Not many people do,' he patted the rock beside him, 'I used to come here all the time with my Grandad. Since he died, I just like to come here sometimes, it's peaceful.'

'Oh, I'm sorry about your Grandad, were you close?' Elara asked, perching carefully on the rock, pulling her fleece tight around her stomach and tucking her hands into the soft folds of the fabric.

Xander noticed with a sly glance out of the corner of his eye, and took her hands soundlessly into his own, rubbing along her fingers until the colour began to flush back across her skin.

Elara nibbled on her bottom lip, letting her hair drop like a curtain in front of her face.

Was Xander making her shy? She certainly wasn't accustomed to feeling shy. In fact she was certain her mother wished her only daughter could be a little more bashful, ladylike. But Elara scolded herself inwardly and tossed her hair out of her face, forcing herself to concentrate and ignoring the gentle roughness of his hands as they brought heat to hers.

'It was a long time ago now, but yeah we were. He taught me how to ride a bike, or he'd take me on walks when I got sick of my brothers,' he smiled, 'you would've liked him,' he said, looking across at Elara, a slight sadness in his eyes.

Elara shifted slightly closer to him and leaned against him gently. 'I'm sure I would,' she replied as they settled into a comfortable silence and Xander somewhat reluctantly released her hands, turning looking out at the view.

They sat for a while, talking and laughing. Elara began to pick at the daisies that surrounded them.

'Here, for you. Happy birthday,' she said, as she handed him her freshly made daisy chain.

He laughed, Elara had never noticed before but now she was sat close to him, there was a faint dimple in his left cheek when he smiled, it was sweet. He turned to say something to her and saw her staring.

'What's up?' he asked.

'No, nothing. Sorry.'

'You don't have to apologise, Elara. I'm not complaining,' he said with a grin, as he leaned closer to her slightly. Elara wasn't used to someone being so confident in themselves. It shouldn't have surprised her, it was clear his popularity got him far in school, but he made no attempts to hide the way he felt about her.

He brought his hand up to her cheek and she leaned into it, his hand warm on her cold face. He smiled, stoking her bottom lip gently with his thumb.

Elara was just about to close her eyes, enjoy this perfect moment, when she saw faint movement in the treeline behind Xander, she waited for a second, perhaps it was the shadows playing tricks on her.

Xander pulled away, a confused look on his face.

He was about to say something, but Elara shushed him, still watching the trees. Then again, she saw it. A dark figure moving slightly out from behind a tree, then they slipped straight back behind it.

'Xander, there's someone watching us from the trees, don't look too quickly,' she murmured, looking down at the daisy chain in Xander's hands.

Xander glanced back slowly, his gaze immediately focussing on the dark figure. The sky was starting to darken now too, the late September sunshine dipping below the horizon.

'I don't like this,' Elara murmured, moving closer to Xander.

'Me neither, come on let's get going, I know another way back,' he said picking up the bags whilst keeping an eye on the trees.

As soon as Elara stood up, the figure emerged from the tree line for just a second, and Elara caught a glimpse of short silver hair, a wiry slim build, and black non-descript clothing. Elara went to call out, but the man turned and fled before she could say a word.

'Come on, let's get you home,' Xander said, putting an arm around her shoulders and leading her back into the woods.

Back at the house, they were greeted with warm air from the fire and the delicious smell of Rose's cooking. Elara's dad was sat on the couch, skimming through an 'art for dummies' magazine, though the second they walked through the door he stood up to greet them and Elara knew he hadn't been reading it at all, mainly because it was upside-down.

'Hi sweetheart, good day? This is Alexander I presume?'

'Yeah Dad, this is Xander. Xander, this is my dad, Peter,' Elara said, stepping into the kitchen to grab cutlery.

'Mr Anderson,' Xander said, throwing him one of his winning smiles, 'It's a pleasure to meet you sir, I hope you don't mind my staying for dinner.'

Peter looked back at his daughter; a surprised expression painted across his features.

'Well, it's refreshing to meet such a polite young man, Xander. I'm sure you'll be great company,' he said, gesturing for him to sit down at the table.

Meanwhile, Rose winked at her daughter.

'Nice walk?' she smirked, staring pointedly at Elara's blushed cheeks as she handed her two glasses of water and turned back to the stove.

Elara cleared her throat awkwardly, placing one of the glasses down in front of Xander with an apologetic smile.

'Now whilst we wait for my wife's delicious meal, how about we look at some of Elara's baby photos?' her dad said with a grin, bringing out a large photo-album as if from thin air.

Elara rolled her eyes, 'Dad we really don't have to, Xander isn't interested in that.'

'Oh, you're wrong Elara. I am in fact, very interested in that,' he said with a devilish grin, scooting his chair closer to Elara's dad.

Peter stroked the cover, wiping away a speck of dust.

'Our Elara Hazel,' he murmured.

'Hazel?' Xander asked, 'I didn't know that was your middle name, it's pretty.'

Elara scoffed, nibbling at a bread roll from the centre of the table.

Her dad started flipping through the photos, pointing out things he found funny here and there. Rose chiming in from the kitchen with little stories and memories.

'You know,' Rose called with her head buried in the fridge, 'that photo where she's got red mush all over her face? It was taken five minutes after we'd found her grandmother's antique golden bowl smashed to pieces in the kitchen. My mother would use that bowl when special guests came round, she would serve strawberries dusted in sugar as a treat. El swore it was her cousin who broke the bowl, though that cheeky face tells a different story.'

'Very cute,' Xander chuckled, glancing up at Elara with a twinkle in his eye. 'Where are the photos of you as a baby though? You're a toddler in all of these.'

Elara's parents looked surprised. 'Oh well, we didn't get her until she was just turned two, and her birth parents didn't leave any new-born photos.'

Elara shifted uncomfortably in her seat.

'Birth parents?' Xander asked, looking between the family.

'Yeah, didn't she tell you?' Peter replied, 'Elara's adopted, we met her when she was only little. The best decision of our lives,' Peter said, smiling at his daughter.

'We couldn't have children of our own,' Rose said, placing the spaghetti down in the centre of the table, 'It was almost like Elara fell out of the sky and into our family. She made us whole,' she said, kissing her daughter's forehead.

Elara glanced over at Xander; she hadn't really wanted anyone to know this piece of information. She often found it made people look at her differently. Take pity on her. She didn't want their pity; she loved her family and was glad that she knew nothing about her birth parents. But as she looked over at Xander, he was just smiling at her. There was no sadness there, he wasn't looking down on her.

'I'm sure she did,' he murmured with a smile, reaching out under the table, and taking her hand. He gave her a quick wink and turned back to her parents.

'Any more stories to tell?'

'So,' Xander said, sitting down on the step outside of Elara's house.

'So,' she replied, closing the door behind her, and sitting down next to him.

'We should do this again sometime, it's been fun,' he smirked, resting a tentative hand on her knee. Elara took his hand in hers, willing some of her usual confidence back into her shaky movements.

'You don't feel sorry for me then, being a poor little adoptee?' she joked, as she looked up at the stars in the clear night sky.

'Why should I feel sorry for you? Feel sorry that you have a family who loves you, who literally handpicked you to be theirs? Don't expect my pity Anderson, cos you're not gonna get it.'

Elara laughed, 'good I definitely did not want it. Hey, look, you see up there, straight ahead?' she used hers and Xander's linked hands to point up at the sky, 'that's Orion's Belt, my favourite constellation. My mum taught me to see that one when I was four. Anywhere I go in the world, that's the one I look for. It reminds me of home,' she smiled up at it for a moment longer before turning to face Xander, to find he wasn't even looking at it, he was looking at her.

Just as Elara went to ask why he was staring, he silenced her with a soft hand on her jaw, his thumb stroking her chin. So calm and gentle and in an instant, he was kissing her. His hand ran along her jawline and up into her hair, pulling at the roots. She cupped his face in her hands and leaned against his chest. The warmth from his skin seeping through his shirt and heating up her whole body felt like the most natural thing in the world. So much so that Elara could hardly believe they hadn't been doing this the whole time. He wrapped his arms around her waist and pulled her closer, she could feel the muscles flexing in his arms as he held her tightly, so tightly he felt almost like an extension of her own body. He smelled like summer nights and the ocean in a way that Elara couldn't explain. The scent enveloped her and held her senses captive. Xander released his grip on her only slightly and Elara smiled against his lips and pulled away, resting her forehead against his so only their noses were touching. He squeezed his eyes shut for a moment before focussing them on Elara's, sighing quietly.

'What did I do to deserve that?' he asked with a smile.

'What do you mean?' she laughed.

'Are you kidding?' he asked, pulling away from her and looking around him as though he had an audience. 'Look at you, girls like you, do not go for guys like me,' he laughed, tucking a strand of hair behind her ear, 'six short months ago I had train tracks for teeth, Elara. Train tracks! And now I'm sat here, kissing possibly the most beautiful girl in the world under the stars. I think I might just faint,' he swooned, but a second later his eyes were focussed on her lips again, a hunger burning in the blue that turned his expression serious.

'Well Alexander, you've certainly outgrown the train tracks. I'm sure there are plenty of girls who would give you the time of day now. Only that didn't come from me, so pretend you never heard it,' she grinned as she pushed his chest lightly, but a moment later forced her hands back into her lap, when they'd stayed splayed across the front of his t-shirt.

'I don't think you understand how beautiful you are. I swear any guy in a five-mile radius would drop dead for you and you don't even know it,' he shook his head.

Elara scrunched her nose at him, standing up and offering him her hand, 'you're very theatrical, Xander, but I'll take your word for it. If I ever need someone to die for me, I'll make sure I give you a call. Though if you're unavailable, you best give me the numbers of some of your friends too. Can't keep me waiting,' she smirked as he stood up, dusting off his joggers.

Now stood in front of her, he was almost a head taller than her. Elara wasn't short, she'd stopped growing at around five foot six, but Xander must be at least six feet tall, and as he cupped her face in his hands, she pushed up onto her tiptoes and gripped the front of his T-shirt to kiss him back. Already it was comfortable, easy. Then he wrapped his arms around her waist, holding her in a tight hug that melted Elara to her core. Her arms tightened around his neck as she wove her fingers into his hair. He kissed her on the forehead before setting her back down.

'I'll call you tomorrow. Enjoy the rest of your evening,' he said with a warm smile, turning down her drive to walk away.

As he disappeared around the corner, Elara smiled to herself, brushing her finger along her lips, and letting the feelings from the whole evening flood over her, but a quiet rustle to her right snapped her back to reality. She glanced sharply to the side, just in time to see the same silver-haired figure from earlier skulking away into the bushes. Elara marched over to the bush, 'I don't know who you are, but I will call the police,' she hissed, before storming confidently back to her house. Hiding her shaking hands in front of her and trying to ignore the insistent feeling that she knew exactly who the silver-haired man was but couldn't for the life of her pinpoint why.

As soon as she got back up to her room, Elara stood in front of her floor length mirror, studying her reflection. Elara had always been told she was lucky when it came to her looks, but she'd always felt so different to the rest of her family, that feeling as though she stuck out like a sore thumb had chipped away at any self-confidence she might've had. Her hair was long and light blonde, almost white at the tips, standing out against her tanned skin. She had light, honey coloured eyes rimmed with green, that her mother insisted were her namesake. Her limbs were long and willowy, athletic despite the fact she'd never played any sports. Her parents on the other hand, both had dark, chocolatey brown hair, though her mother's was saturated with beachy highlights, and deep, soulful eyes. Her mother loved to dance to 'Brown Eyed Girl' by Van Morrison on her birthday, and Elara had always wished she could join in.
Elara frowned and her reflection frowned back at her, wondering if anyone else saw her the way Xander did. She wasn't sure she wanted that attention, at least certainly not from strangers.

That Sunday as planned; Elara turned up Jenna's as early as she could to escape her mother's obsessive study sessions. At least Jenna broke up the work with snacks and gossip, plus Elara would love to have one proper friend at college. Jenna greeted her at the door with a warm smile, stepping back to let her into the house. Jenna was half Indian and her home paid tribute to that. The walls were deep reds and oranges, beautiful tapestries hung from hooks, and statues and figurines littered the shelves. Elara loved coming here because it always smelt like Jenna's mum's home cooking and the incense they liked to burn. Jenna also had three younger siblings, surprisingly Elara liked the noise and craziness. It was a stark difference to her own quiet home.

'Would you like a drink? Or something to eat?'

'Coffee would be great, thank you. Is Alfie joining us today?' Elara asked, following Jenna into the kitchen. She smiled at Jenna's youngest sister Anika who was refusing some orange looking mush in her highchair.

'No, not today, I think he has hockey practice. Umm, Nat did say she might pop round later though,' Jenna said sheepishly, the collection of bangles on her wrist jangling as she handed the steaming hot cup of coffee to her.

'Sorry, I know you two don't exactly see eye to eye.'

Elara stared down at her coffee. 'No, but maybe this is a good chance for us to start over, away from college.'

'Yeah, exactly. I know she can be pretty cold at first but trust me you'll love her once you get to know each other,' Jenna replied, as she started up the stairs towards her room.

Elara sighed, tossing her backpack onto her shoulder, and following Jenna.

They'd barely been studying for half an hour when the doorbell rang again. Jenna glanced at Elara, smiling sympathetically before hurrying down the stairs to greet Natalia.

Elara took the opportunity to send a quick message to Xander. They'd decided not to mention to anyone about Friday night, it'd cause too much tension and Elara was still trying to find her place in the group. Though she was sure he'd find it hilarious that Natalia was joining in on the study-session fun.

Elara heard Natalia before she could see her. The lilting Scottish accent weaving through the house as she shouted a greeting to each of Jenna's family members.

They eventually emerged at the top of the stairs, and Natalia was clutching at a collection of dresses that looked barely more than lingerie and what seemed like dozens of bags and accessories strewn along her arms, with Jenna emerging behind her carrying at least four shoeboxes.

'Don't worry, you can keep studying. Jen and I are just gonna pick out my outfit for next weekend. I don't think I'll want your opinion,' Natalia said with a deceivingly sweet smile.

'Next weekend?' Elara asked, peering round at Jenna.

'Yes. I'm having a party. Half the year group is coming,' Natalia replied, already perched at Jenna's dressing table, rifling through her lipsticks, her long nails clacking against the plastic.

'Oh, sounds like you'll have fun,' Elara smiled, raising her eyebrows at Jenna who was still looking slightly worried, her brown eyes wide.

'Oh, you wanted to come?' Natalia asked with a very fake surprised look on her face, 'that's too bad, Xan said you wouldn't be interested,' she said, looking pitifully down at Elara, as Elara rolled her eyes, turning back to her politics worksheet.

'So, Elara, what is the deal with you and Xander? It's sweet how he's being so nice to you. Probably just because you're new though, it'll wear off soon,' Natalia said, plopping down on the bed next to her, thumbing through a textbook, one perfectly-shaped eyebrow raised.

'Probably,' Elara purred, 'is that what he did to you? That might explain why you're so bitter,' Elara smiled sweetly, offering an enraged Natalia a chocolate biscuit.

'You just don't know who you're dealing with Elara. I'd watch your tone if I were you,' Natalia hissed, grabbing some of her clothing and flouncing out of the room.

Jenna sighed, perching on the end of the bed.

'Well maybe by the time we finish college, you'll like each other.'

'You just keep dreaming, Jenna,' Elara replied, handing her the biscuits.

CHAPTER FOUR

Elara

That week at school, Natalia barely even glanced at Elara. The tension between them at the table at lunch was so strong you could almost taste it, but the others seemed to be talking even more to make up for it. Elara was enjoying getting to know Alfie and Jenna more. Matt rarely joined them as he often had theatre group at lunch. He was doing a play at the end of term that he'd invited everyone to, along with Elara. Alfie was often busy after school and at weekends, he played hockey, football, and rugby, and was intending on going to Loughborough University on a sports scholarship. From the few games Elara had seen him in, she had no doubt that he'd get there easily. Jenna also clearly had a thing for him. Elara often saw them flirt across the table, and Jenna always thought of something to ask him about, whether it was sports or his family. It was sweet. However, that left Natalia with all the free time in the world to chat to Xander. Of course, blatantly ignoring Elara. Though, where he could, Xander would try his best to include her.

She and Xander had walked together every evening after school. Often, they ended up back at the cliffside, but he also showed her new places around the village and Elara loved his guided tours. They went to the old-fashioned sweet shop that he had visited as a child for sherbet lemons and strawberry bon-bons, the field where he learnt to ride a quadbike that was littered with wild-flowers, and Elara's personal favourite, the rocky beach on the outskirts of the village where they could look endlessly for interesting rocks and pebbles.

Elara was also glad that almost a week had gone by without her seeing the strange silver-haired man, and without her having any more nightmares. She was enjoying settling into her new life and her parents into theirs. Some of her family were already planning on coming up to see them at Christmas, she couldn't wait for her little house to be bustling with people and Christmas spirit.

Her mum had also become slightly obsessed with Xander. She was very strict on him coming in the house after college, as she insisted Elara had to study, but every time he dropped her off, she always appeared magically at the door with a homemade snack, and questions about his day. It was cute really, though Elara wished her mum would calm down slightly, it wasn't as though she'd never dated anyone before, and it made her feel marginally like a child.

By the time Friday rolled around, Elara had almost forgotten about the mention of Natalia's party, until Xander brought it up as they sat down on the beach, steaming hot takeaway coffees in hand.

'So, Nat's having a party tomorrow night, I don't know if you've heard?'

Elara snorted, gazing out at the view.

'Oh, I heard about it. Straight from the devil's mouth.'

Xander grinned, rolling his eyes at her.

'Well, I'm going, so are Jenna, Matt and Alfie. I thought you might wanna come with?' he asked, taking a sip of his drink.

Elara scrunched her nose. 'I highly doubt Natalia would want me there, she'd probably bite my head off the second I walked through the door.'

Xander smirked, 'well you can come with me and we're picking up Alfie on the way. I'm sure we can protect you against her wrath. Jenna and Matt will already be there helping her set up. She'll be distracted anyway; I doubt she'll even notice.'

Elara threw a look at Xander.

'Okay, okay she'll notice. But I want you there, she'll just have to cope,' he grinned.

'My knight in shining armour,' Elara pretended to swoon, before resting her head on Xander's shoulder. 'I'm glad that you want me there though. Now I just have to find something to wear.'

'You'll look beautiful in whatever you choose,' Xander replied, 'I can't wait to see what you pick out.' He smiled, lifting her chin, and kissing her softly. She could taste the sweet coffee on his lips as she pulled him in closer. His hand came up to her face, he stroked her cheek lightly and ran his fingertips along her jaw, making her spine tingle. After a moment, he pulled away and planted a quick kiss on the end of her nose, before smiling and taking another sip of his coffee.

'You want me to find you a gift?' Elara asked as she unfurled her long limbs from underneath her, wincing at the cracks of her knees as she stood.

Xander snorted, shielding his eyes against the sun to look up at her.

'Do I have a choice?'

Elara shook her head, already hunting amongst the pebbles.

She found a light blue polished piece of sea-glass sticking out from underneath a rock. As she pulled it out it glinted in the late September sunlight and she could see it was engraved with something, though she couldn't exactly see what.

'Merry Christmas,' she said, holding it out to Xander.

'My little kleptomaniac magpie,' he replied, holding it up against the watery sun's rays. 'Come on, we best get you home before Rose calls the police for a crime against lack of studying,' he joked, pocketing the glass, and holding out a hand to Elara who took it gladly.

'Hey, mum, Xander's invited me to a party with him tomorrow night at Natalia's house. Can I go? Jenna, Alfie and Matt will be there too.'

Her mother frowned, folding and refolding a tea-towel in her hands.

'I thought Natalia was the girl you didn't like?' she asked, suspiciously.

'We don't exactly get on, but my other friends are gonna be there, plus it'll be a good chance for me to meet other people in my year group outside of college,' Elara smiled, a hopeful look on her face.

'Come on Rose, she's been working hard this term and needs to get to know her peers. Loosen up on her a bit,' her dad chimed in from the sofa, thumbing through a newspaper.

'Hmmm,' Rose considered, folding the tea-towel one last time, 'fine, but I want the address of this girl, Alexander's mobile number, no drinking, and back by 12:30 on the dot. I'll wait up for you.'

'Mum you really don't need to wait up, Xander will be picking me up and dropping me back off, he'll look after me.'

'I don't think so El. I don't want him thinking he can stay the night either, you know how I feel about that,' Rose said, a frown on her face.

'Mum he won't be staying over, he'll just drop me at the front door to make sure I get back okay, I swear. Please don't wait up, it's embarrassing,' she pleaded, looking to her dad for support.

'She's right Rose, we'll probably hear the front door when it goes anyway, she's 16 and very responsible. We can trust you, can't we Elara?' her dad asked, raising an eyebrow at her mother with a smile on his face.

'Of course you can. 12:30 on the dot, I'll be walking through that door,' Elara said with a sweet smile, going to kiss her mother on the cheek.

'You two are a nightmare, you know that?' she said reluctantly. 'Right, sit Elara. I'm sure you have homework to be getting on with.'

Elara spent much of that Saturday texting with Jenna. It was the most normal she'd felt in weeks. Planning their outfits, gossiping about who was going to be there, deciding which drinks they were going to smuggle in. By the time 7pm rolled around, Elara had already been waiting for an hour. Sat tapping her foot impatiently on the kitchen floor as she checked her phone for a message from Xander.

'Wow, you look great Elara! I know a certain mother, however, who will not be happy at all with this choice of outfit,' her dad said jokingly from where he was plopped down in front of the TV.

Elara rolled her eyes, 'if mum had it her way, I'd already be getting back from the party and I'd be wearing a pantsuit and heels. I don't feel like getting bullied out of my first college party.'

Her dad grinned, standing up to kiss her forehead and click the kettle on.

'You're not wrong, dear daughter. In fact, there's a plastic bag out in the porch with some drinks that you might find more to your taste. Just for crying out loud don't tell your mother, and if you do come back drunk, I'll kick you out of the house myself,' he said with a wink, just as Elara's mother emerged into the kitchen.

Elara could see her immediately try and smooth out the look of surprise on her face as soon as she caught a glimpse of Elara's outfit and instead force a smile.

'Well, I'm so glad to see you expressing your sense of creativity, Els. Remember, 12:30, no drinks, no drugs, no sleeping out. I looked up where this girl lives, and you know I won't hesitate to come and get you,' she said with a stern look on her face, as Elara exchanged bemused glances with her father.

'Yes, mother. All duly noted and well understood.'

Elara's outfit probably wouldn't even be considered risky by the rest of her generation, but in her mother's eyes, she was practically playing dress up as a stripper. In place of a blouse and knee length skirt, was a simple black dress. It cut off on the shorter side of mid-thigh, with a deep neckline, spaghetti straps and almost completely backless, except from a few thin ribbons that wove corset-style across her skin. Her eye-makeup was a little darker than she'd usually go for, but Jenna had assured her it would complement her outfit, plus Elara liked that it made her feel a little edgy. Her long hair was loose over her shoulders and wavy, soft and warm on her back. Her tattered black Converse and some silver jewellery finished off the look.

Just when Elara thought her mother was going to change her mind on the whole thing, and keep her locked away in the house, the doorbell went. A loud shrill that startled everyone. As Elara went to grab her jacket, her mum raced to the door. Swinging it open to a surprised Xander, who had barely had time to finish ringing the doorbell.

Rose looked Xander up and down, taking in his tapered blue jeans, slouchy green t-shirt, and a very nice black corduroy shirt draped over his arm that Elara already knew she wanted to steal.

Rose glanced back at Elara, 'you two look like you're going to very different parties,' she said with a raised eyebrow. Elara rolled her eyes.

'What did you expect him to be wearing mum, a suit? This isn't prom.'

Xander choked back a laugh before peering around the door at Elara.

'Wow, El. You do look amazing though, perhaps I should've dressed up more for you. Next time I'll come to you for fashion advice Mrs Anderson.'

Elara blushed, as her dad nodded with approval.

'Come on, let's get going and leave these two to their thrilling night of reality TV,' Elara grinned at her parents, leaning in for a kiss on the cheek from her dad.

Her mum still looked incredibly apprehensive, but Elara raced out of the door before she could say another word, closing it quickly behind her.

Elara was already half-way down the drive when she realised Xander wasn't walking next to her. She stopped and turned to find him still at the front door watching her from a distance.

'What are you doing?' she laughed nervously, walking back up the drive to him.

A smile grew slowly on his face as he continued to stare at her.

'Quit staring,' she laughed, giving him a gentle shove, 'it's freaking me out.'

Xander shook his head, smiling down at the ground. 'Seriously, which planet did your parents adopt you from? Because I swear you can't be human to be allowed to look like that,' he grinned, planting a kiss on her cheek.

'100% the daughter of Aphrodite. She was the Goddess of Beauty, right?'

Elara frowned at him, 'you know you should really be studying theatre, if you're inclined to be this dramatic.'

Xander laughed up at the sky, his smile wide in the last dregs of sunlight that rippled through his hair and lit up his eyes.

'Come on, trouble. We're going to be late,' he said, throwing an arm around her shoulders and starting towards Alfie's house.

Alfie lived pretty near Natalia, in the nicest part of town. The houses were a soft grey brick and a minimum of three stories high. As they waited outside for him to come out, Elara could see the edge of a swimming pool peeking out from behind the house, and as he opened the front door, she caught a glimpse of a large chandelier glinting in the hall.

'So, he's rich rich,' Elara smirked to Xander, draping her jacket over her shoulders as a cool breeze picked up.

Alfie had dressed up too. It was weird to see him in something other than joggers or sports uniforms. He had on loose fitting blue jeans, a black oversized jumper, and a dark green checked shirt over the top. He'd turned up the bottom of his jeans and had some chunky, retro looking trainers on. He'd even painted his nails a green that matched his shirt with cute smiley faces on his pinkies.

'Whoah, is that Alfie Graham, the sports star? Can I get your autograph? You look so stylish,' Elara joked, holding her phone up to take pictures.

'Yeah, who are you and what have you done with Alfie? This guy looks cool!' Xander laughed, walking towards him and pulling him in for a hug.

'You two are real jokesters,' Alfie rolled his eyes, but grinned nonetheless. He looked over at Elara.

'Oh! Elara, wow. You look, erm, great. Really great,' he said, sounding surprisingly shy. Elara blushed awkwardly as Xander laughed jogging back over to her.

'Is that a bit of drool I see, Alf? Sorry buddy but you're a few weeks too late,' he smiled, putting his arm back around her shoulders and kissing the top of her head.

Alfie closed the gate behind him as they began walking down the road. 'Doesn't surprise me. You two look great together though. Maybe just steer clear of Natalia for a while, or she'll probably skin you both alive,' Alfie joked, tapping away a message on his phone.

'Yeah, what actually is Natalia's problem? No-one's ever said exactly why she hates me so much. Or why it would be such a problem for me to spend time with Xander,' Elara asked, looking around at Alfie.

'Could be the fact that Nat's been in love with Xander for the past two years, but no matter what she's done she's never been able to win him over, but you come in and within an hour he's smitten,' Alfie said, laughing.

Elara's jaw dropped. 'She's in love with you?' she asked, stopping dead in her tracks. 'I could tell she didn't like me, but I thought it was just because I said what I said on the first day. How could you not tell me?'

'I didn't think you really needed to know, Els. Nothing ever really happened between us. Plus, it's Nat's problem, not mine or yours,' Xander explained, looking slightly sheepish.

'Nothing ever really happened. Alfie is that true?' Elara asked, looking sternly at him.

'Umm- well... I mean,' Alfie stuttered, so Elara turned her attention back to Xander.

'Look El, we were best friends for like two years, we spoke all the time, spent a lot of time together, but she clearly thought more of it than me. Then during summer, we did kiss once. She initiated it and I told her that I didn't want to go there with her. That I just liked being friends. She took it badly at first, but I thought she would've gotten over it by now. I'm sorry, I really didn't think it was important,' he said, walking back over to where Elara had stopped. He looked worried as he reached out to her, tucking a strand of hair behind her ear as he always did. His furrowed brow and tense jaw immediately softened Elara. She sighed, looking up at him.

'It's not important, as long as you're happy with your best friend hating me forever,' she said with a soft smile.

His face instantly relaxed into a grin, pulling her in for a hug.

'So that's how long you think we'll be together?' he asked, a confident tone colouring his voice.

'Let's not push it.'

They could hear the music from Natalia's house before they could see it. People were spilling out onto the road; coloured lights were dancing in the windows and Elara could barely see the front door for how many people were trying to fight their way inside.

Xander raised his eyebrows at her as he took her hand and the three of them began weaving their way through the crowd.

As soon as they fought their way into the kitchen, Elara could see Jenna and Matt dancing madly in the middle of a large group. She pointed them out to Alfie and Xander and started making her way over to the group as Xander took the bag of drinks over to a counter overflowing with bottles and cups. Jenna met Elara with a squeal, holding her at arms-length to take in her outfit.

'Wow, Elara. You look like a model! No wonder you've got Xander looking at you like that,' she said with a wink. Elara turned to see Xander stood with two cups in hand, watching her and Jenna speak. Elara smiled to herself as she turned back round to her friend.

'You know,' she whispered, leaning in close so Jenna could hear her, 'I'm not the only one who's got an admirer,' she grinned, gesturing with her head over to where Alfie was stood. He had some girl talking to him, but he kept glancing back at Jenna, a smitten look on his face. Jenna's cheeks instantly coloured as she looked back to Elara.

'Do you think I should go over there?' she asked, fluffing her hair nervously.

'Are you kidding?' Matt laughed, reaching around to hand Jenna her drink, 'he's practically begging for you to go and speak to him. Go now before that girl drags him away!' he said, as Elara untwisted the strap on Jenna's dark blue, bodycon dress.

'You look stunning,' she smiled, 'go show him what he's missing!'

Jenna nodded and took a quick gulp of her drink. As she made her way through the crowded kitchen towards Alfie, Elara saw his face instantly light up.

Elara turned back towards Matt with a smile, 'this party is insane; how many invitations did Natalia send out?'

Matt shook his head and knocked back the last of his drink, before tossing the empty cup over a crowd of people's heads in the direction of the sink.

'She said to her parents it would be 15 at most. Her dads are gonna flip when they find out she got into their whiskey cabinet.' Elara giggled, when suddenly Matt's eyes widened, his gaze focussing over her left shoulder.

'Incoming,' he winked, 'God he looks gorgeous, you're a lucky girl.'

Elara turned to see Xander walking towards them.

'Alright Matty?' He handed Elara one of the drinks to pull Matt in for a hug, kissing his cheek as Matt pretended to swoon.

'How was your rugby match today? Win for Oakbridge?'

Matt shook his head, snatching a drink out of the hand of a random girl as she passed, and downing it before she could complain.

'Nah, we lost to Lochside Creek. Got my show on Wednesday though, so I'm trying to focus on that instead. Are you guys still coming?'

'Wouldn't miss it for the world, Matty boy, we can't wait to see you up on stage like the star you are,' Xander grinned, as Matt smiled and allowed himself to be dragged away by a very handsome basketball player from the year above.

'Double Malibu and Coke, courtesy of Mr Peter Anderson for you, and apple juice courtesy of Nat's fridge for me,' Xander nodded at the drinks, turning back towards Elara as he clinked their plastic cups together and took a mouthful. Elara followed suit.

'You don't drink?' she asked over the thumping music. Xander shook his head.

'My dad's an alcoholic, I don't like the lack of control it gives him, and I don't want the same for myself,' he replied with a shrug.

'That seems reasonable,' Elara said, smiling up at him. Her respect levels were just going up and up for this boy.

After a while of chatting, Elara and Xander dragged Jenna and Alfie into the living room where the music was coming from to dance. They still hadn't seen Natalia, not that Elara was complaining. She'd seen a couple of people from her other classes and to her surprise they greeted her with hugs and conversation. Even though she'd known these people for almost 2 months now, she didn't think they'd want to associate with her outside of college. Though maybe the added alcohol factor helped. Elara was having the best time dancing and singing madly with Jenna whilst the boys stood around, acting cool. Though she was surprised at the number of girls that made their way over to Xander. Clearly flirting, twiddling their hair and leaning in close to talk in his ear. Elara wanted to say something each time, but every time another girl came around, she had to remind herself that she and Xander were hardly even official, and it wasn't her place to but in. Luckily for her, he waved them away every time, turning his attention back to her with a smile.

An hour passed by quickly in the increasingly crowded room. Elara was starting to get tired from all the dancing, so the group made their way over to the corner of the room to perch on the edge of Natalia's sofa. As Elara sat down on the arm of the chair, she almost fell backwards into a couple who were making out very aggressively, but Xander caught her at the last second with a wink. She widened her eyes and gestured to the suckerfishes behind her with a laugh. Just as Elara was hoping she might get through the whole evening without seeing Natalia, she saw Xander's expression change. She turned around to see that familiar bright red hair standing out from the crowd. Natalia. She was of course drawing attention to herself as she stumbled through the room, clutching at the top of her dress with one hand, and holding a very blue looking drink with the other. She grinned at Xander, almost tripping over her own feet as she neared the group. She threw her arms around Xander's neck, falling into him. Completely oblivious to everyone else standing around.

'Xan, I'm so glad you came! Hey, do you like my dress?' she shouted, stepping back to do a slightly wobbly spin.

Xander forced a grin, 'yeah, Natalia. It's nice. This is a great party,' he said, nodding to the rest of the room and crossing his arms across his chest.

'Isn't it!' she exclaimed. She threw her arms up in the air and Elara managed to dodge out of the way just in time for the majority of the blue liquid to fall on the sucker-couple rather than on her. They jumped up screaming and ran out of the room in a blur.

'Nat, don't you think you've had enough to drink?' Xander asked, frowning at her as Alfie stood up, holding her arm to steady her.

'Awww, are my boys worried about me? That's so sweet,' Natalia cooed, pulling them both in for a sloppy hug. Meanwhile, Elara shared a despairing look with Jenna, who was trying to refrain from laughing.

Finally, Natalia turned to face Jenna and Elara. 'Jen! My God, bubs, you look amazing. Alfie's lucky that it's him you wanted to dress up for!' she smiled as Jenna's cheeks flared red.

'Natalia!' Jenna whispered as she glanced back at Alfie who was looking embarrassed.

'Ooops! Did I say too much? I told you you should've just gone for it, Jenna. You were made for each other!'

Jenna rolled her eyes at Natalia and pushed past her out of the room, Alfie following closely behind.

Natalia pulled an annoyed face, 'God, she's touchy tonight. Someone needs to let their hair down for once,' she sighed, taking a long sip of her drink. This was when she finally noticed Elara, sitting quietly on the arm of the sofa.

'Who invited you?' Natalia spat. Elara cleared her throat awkwardly, wondering if it was possible for her to suddenly master the skill of teleportation. She should probably go to Mexico, or maybe Brazil. Somewhere far away, where Natalia couldn't boot her off the planet all together.

'I did,' Xander responded, taking Elara's hand and pulling her up next to him. He wove an arm around her waist and squeezed her gently, instantly relaxing her.

Natalia looked Elara up and down. An expression of disgust clouding her pretty features.

'I told you I didn't want her here, Xander. You had no right bringing her.'

Her words were starting to slur.

'Well I did, Natalia. So, if you want her out, I'm going with her. And no doubt Jenna and Alfie would come with us too. I'm sick of you being like this with her Nat, she's done nothing wrong.'

Elara could feel Xander's heart pumping in his chest and could see the muscles tightening angrily in his jaw. She leaned into him slightly, feeling his body heat wash over her. She watched as his jaw softened and smiled as his heartbeat slowed down.

Natalia looked Elara up and down one more time, before mumbling something under her breath and stumbling away.

'Wow,' Elara breathed a sigh of relief, 'I didn't expect you to stand up to her like that. Thank you,' she said, looking up at him as he shook his head.

'Neither did I. I don't know what happened,' he grinned, 'guess you just bring it out of me.' He looked down at Elara, meeting her gaze. She instantly felt his energy change, as he leaned down and kissed her. He tasted sweet from the apple juice, and his hands were gentle on her face. He moved them down, under her hair, and she shivered slightly from the feel of his warm skin skimming over the ribbon that laced across her back. She brought a hand up to his face, pulling him in closer as she drifted into the kiss. A warm, bubbly feeling working its way down her chest and into her stomach.

Suddenly, a memory flashed into her mind. Something similar had happened before. As Xander traced his fingertips over a piece of ribbon close to the base of her spine, the memory filled her mind like a movie. So powerful and real she almost couldn't focus on Xander at all. In her memory, she was wearing a white corset, her hair flowing long and free in an autumn breeze. There was someone holding her, they were tracing their fingers over the lace that synched the corset in. Their other hand came up to her face and brushed along her lips. So soft it almost tickled. They smelled like bonfires and the sea, and it was the most beautiful memory.

Only it wasn't Elara's to remember.

Xander pulled away. 'What's up? Are you okay?' he asked, looking concerned.

Elara snapped back to attention, forcing the scene out of her mind, and smiling at Xander.

'Sorry, just zoned out for a second,' Elara said shakily, taking another sip of her drink.

Xander still looked slightly confused but returned her smile anyway.

'Come on trouble, looks like Jenna's dancing alone and we can't have that, can we?' he pointed to a figure in the middle of the room.

'I'm gonna go get us another drink and try and find Alfie. I'll be back in 10 minutes. If I'm not back by then, send out a search party as Nat's probably murdered me,' he said with a sinister look on his face, before kissing Elara quickly and disappearing off into the crowd.

10 minutes of dancing later, and Xander still hadn't re-emerged. He was probably still looking for Alfie, Elara thought to herself. She wouldn't be surprised if it took him an hour in this crowded house.

'Elara don't look too quickly, but there's a guy over there completely eyeing you up,' Jenna suddenly whispered excitedly, glancing over to a group of boys by the door. Elara looked in the reflection from the window, and sure enough, a very tall looking guy was staring straight at her.

'Oh my God, he's coming over. He can't be in our year; he looks about 30!'

Elara cleared her throat, taking another sip of her drink and pretended not to notice the guy making his way over.

Elara felt a tap on her shoulder and braced herself momentarily before turning around. This guy was even taller than Xander and Jenna was right, he did look much older.

'Hey,' he said, leaning in slightly too close for Elara's liking. 'I'm Cameron, what's your name? I don't think I've seen you round here before; I think I'd remember a body like that,' he slurred, his thick Scottish accent blurring his words together even more. He smelled so strongly of alcohol that Elara had to take a step back.

'Hey, where do you think you're going?' he snapped, grabbing her arm, 'I wasn't done speaking to you.'

Elara shrugged his hand off. 'I'm Elara and I'm not taking that as a compliment,' she said bitterly, looking him up and down.

'Elara,' he repeated, rolling her name around in his mouth, 'a pretty name, for a pretty girl. Why don't we go somewhere less crowded? Get to know each other better if you know what I mean,' he leered, as his friends crowded around her too. All taking gulps from beer cans and smirking down at her. They licked their lips in such a way that Elara wouldn't be surprised if they all suddenly dropped down on all fours and started circling her like a pack of hyenas, allowing themselves the joy of the kill.

'You're all way too old to be at this party, I'm 16,' Elara looked back for Jenna, but she was no-where to be seen.

'Age is just a number, princess. I bet that feistiness comes in handy in the bedroom. Why don't you show me?' he asked, cupping her face in his large hand. A gesture that should be so gentle, but instead his hand was rough against her cheek and his grin was menacing. Elara smacked his hand away trying to make her way towards the door, but some of his ogre friends blocked her in.

'Don't walk away from me again, princess. You don't want to embarrass yourself in front of all your friends, do you?' he hissed, bringing his face so close to hers, his hair tickled her forehead, and she felt his hand clamp around her wrist. His grip was so forceful, she couldn't move her arm an inch.

Elara could feel his intentions crawling along her skin. She felt as though his every emotion, frustration, anger and desperation, were creeping their way down her spine. Rough on the edges and scraping her bones.

She felt her own anger stabbing in her chest. Her skin started to prickle with heat as she felt his clammy hand stroke down her back. She gritted her teeth and tried to focus on calming down, all she needed to do was work her way out of this situation. But the anger was growing. It was in her throat now and running down her arms, through her hands and into her fingertips. Elara couldn't tell if it was her, or the Earth shaking, but now she was too angry to notice.

Cameron moved his hand round to the front of her dress and slowly began stroking down her chest, his mouth close to her ear.

'Get your hands off me!' she screamed and shoved him away. In an instant, the whole house went black and silent as the floor began to tremor. Screams erupted every room in the house, as the darkness descended. Elara could hear objects falling to the floor. Glasses smashing and books thudding as rippling shakes rocked the house. Bulbs started to blow and shatter, bringing bright sparks of light and fire before dulling completely. In the distance Elara could hear Natalia screaming.

'The kitchen's flooding, someone turn on a light!' She heard similar shouts from other rooms in the house.

Elara stood looking around in horror at what was happening. She heard her name being called from the doorway, but she couldn't respond out of pure shock. She also still didn't want to take her eyes off Cameron who was glaring down at her, his face a picture of rage. His cheeks had turned a bright, unattractive red and he was holding his beer can so tightly, the brown sticky liquid was beginning to bubble out of the top and the metal began to crumple.

Evidently not a happy drunk.

She felt Xander's presence before she saw him, she could sense his worry and confusion. He followed her gaze up to Cameron and instantly his manner changed. Xander stepped in between them and turned to look at Elara.

'El? Are you okay? What did he do, did he hurt you?' he asked insistently, holding her face in his hands.

'Your skin, it's burning hot! What did he do?'

'He wouldn't let me go,' Elara murmured, not taking her eyes off Cameron. Xander was still searching her face, running his hands down her arms until he saw the red rim around her wrist that was slowly turning an ugly blue colour.

The clear fingerprint shaped bruises imprinted on her skin. Xander's face instantly hardened. His jaw set and Elara knew exactly what he was going to do.

Xander spun round and punched Cameron straight in the nose. Knocking him so off balance he fell to the floor as the room gasped. Cameron's friends immediately scattered as the rest of the people in the room began shining their phone's lights to see what was happening.

Jenna ran over to Elara, putting an arm around her waist starting to lead her away, but Xander wasn't done.

He stood over Cameron who was sprawled out on the floor, clutching his nose. His whimpers loud now in the silence and Elara saw the bright red blood begin to trickle down over his lips and drip onto his white shirt. Xander crouched down and held Cameron's face, so he had no choice but to look him in the eye.

'If you ever touch her again, I'll break your fucking arm. Do you understand?' Xander spat at him, pressing so hard against Cameron's skin that it began to turn a mottled purple.

'You're a vile human being, you don't even deserve to walk away from this,' he hissed, shoving Cameron's face away so hard, Elara heard his teeth knock together. Xander stood up and took Elara's hand, leading her and Jenna away from the gawking group in silence as they burst out into the cold, fresh air.

She could hear Xander breathing heavily, and she looked down at his hand and saw it was a bright red from where he'd hit Cameron. This skin split slightly across his knuckles.

'Xan? Xander slow down. It's okay,' Elara said, grabbing onto his arm with her other hand to pull him to a stop. He turned, his chest heaving with anger and Elara could see Jenna looking nervous next to her.

'Jenna, go grab Alfie. We should probably all go,' Elara whispered with a tight smile.

Jenna nodded gladly and rushed back into the dark house.

'Hey, hey. It's okay,' Elara whispered to Xander. Pushing up on her tiptoes so she could lean her forehead against his. 'We're all good.'

He wrapped his arms around her in an instant, pulling her so close it felt as though they became one person for a moment as their bodies melted together. Immediately, Elara felt his emotions soften and his shoulders release the tension that was holding him. He pulled away quickly and took her hand, examining the bruise on her wrist. It had already darkened enough to see the grooves of each finger that had held her. Elara tugged her hand away, holding it behind her back.

'It's okay, I'll be fine. Nothing permanent,' she soothed, smiling sincerely in the hope it would calm Xander down, who looked like he was ready to storm back in there for round two. He took a deep breath, and began pacing in the cool air, running a hand nervously through his hair.

After a few minutes, Jenna emerged from the house with a confused looking Alfie.

'Do you guys know what happened in there? Everything was chaos,' he said, tossing on his jacket.

'It's not important,' Elara replied, glancing over at Xander who was still looking slightly shaken up, 'it's too early for us to go home, does anyone have somewhere we could go?'

'Yeah, I do,' said Xander, standing up from where he was perched near Natalia's gate, 'I have a shed behind my house where I always used to hang out, you remember Alf? We can go back there, just chat for a while?'

'Sounds good,' Elara smiled, taking Xander's hand, 'lead the way.'

As soon as they started walking in the direction of Xander's house, they heard the sirens in the distance, getting louder and louder. Then they saw the blue flashing lights around the corner onto the street.

'We should probably get going,' Alfie whispered, as the group immediately broke into a run laughing and stumbling, trying to hold each other up.

Xander's shed was much nicer than Elara was expecting. Hidden from direct view of his house by bushes and trees, it was laden with beanbags, posters and cozy throws. There was an ancient looking speaker in the corner, and a tiny little wood burner against the back wall. A lightbulb that swung from the ceiling gently lit the room.

The group piled into the shed, plopping down on the squishy beanbags, but Elara stood for a minute, looking around all the different posters. It reminded her of her own room with her artwork on the walls. There were dozens of different bands, singers and musicians featured, some posters were even signed.

'My grandad kitted all of this out for me for my 10th birthday. Best gift I ever got,' Xander said, with a sad smile on his face as he reached into a mini fridge covered in stickers, pulling out four cans of diet coke.

They all settled into the comfy chairs, wrapped in blankets as Xander lit the little fire, and clicked on a set of hidden fairy lights that made the shed feel magical. Elara smiled quietly to herself as Alfie made a joke and they all laughed comfortably together. She knew this was one of those nights she would remember for a long time.

It was just past 11 by the time Alfie stood up, stretching out his long limbs after sitting on the beanbags for so long.

'Okay, I think I best get going now, I have football practise in the morning. It's been really great hanging out with you guys though, and Elara, it's nice to get to know you more, you're pretty cool,' he grinned.

Elara laughed, 'wow, a compliment from the biggest sports star in Oakbridge? I feel honoured.'

'Yeah, I should get going too. My mum won't want me out too late,' Jenna said, standing up and dusting off her dress.

'Oh, I'll walk you back then. It's pretty much the same direction anyway.'

Xander and Elara shared a knowing smile as Alfie blushed and Jenna's cheeks turned pink.

Elara stood up too, giving Jenna a quick hug.

'Message me when you get back,' she said with a wink, that turned Jenna's cheeks even redder.

As they left, Elara sat down, comfortable in the silence. Xander reached over and stroked her cheek with his thumb.

'What a night, eh?' he asked, looking tired.

'A night to remember, that's for sure,' Elara joked, leaning her head into his hand.

'I don't know what came over me earlier,' he said, looking off into the distance, that worried look flushing over his features.

'You were just looking out for me Xander, that guy was a creep! You did me a favour,' Elara said, scooting closer to him and resting a hand on his knee. 'You don't need to feel guilty, he deserved what he got.'

'No, I know he did. It was just like I couldn't help myself. Like something took over my body and acted for me. I swear, Elara, in that moment I would've killed him to protect you. But that's not like me at all, I hate confrontation. I don't know what happened.'

Without a word, Elara got up and sat down next to him. Tucking herself under his arm and wrapping the blanket around them both. He rested his cheek against her forehead, stroking her arm softly.

'Well, whatever it was, I'm grateful I had you to look out for me. It felt nice, someone wanting to protect me,' Elara said. As she reached up to kiss his cheek, he met her half-way and planted a gentle kiss on her lips. Elara smiled, leaning her head back down on his chest as he played with her hair.

That next week at college, all anyone could talk about was Natalia's party. No one had seen her or knew exactly what had happened after the police kicked everyone out, but a million rumours seemed to be flying round. Some said Natalia had been sent to boarding school by her dads to learn some discipline, others said she'd gone to jail for underage drinking. No one had any theories about the random earthquake yet, but Elara wished they'd think of some. She could really do with an explanation.

As September faded to October and Autumn began to take hold, Elara felt more and more at home by the day. She'd gotten into a routine now. Each day at college would be busy, jumping between classes and different friend groups. Then in the afternoons she and Xander would walk together, chatting and laughing and sneaking playful kisses in the watery sunshine. In the evenings, Elara would study religiously with her mother, as she always had.

Natalia had finally turned up again at college after almost a week. She of course had fantastical stories about police raids, nights in jail and attractive police officers. Not that anyone was sure what was true. She still avoided Elara like the plague, but, if possible, her attention turned even more towards Xander, flirting with him at every given opportunity as the rest of the table looked on.

CHAPTER FIVE

Elara

'I'm absolutely frozen,' Jenna whined as they perched on the bleachers at yet another of Alfie's football games, her foot tapping repeatedly.

'Well, what did you expect Jenna. It's almost November and your outfit is more suitable for a foam party in Magaluf,' Matt joked, looking pointedly at her short skirt and strappy top. Jenna rolled her eyes as Matt dramatically examined his gloved hands and dusted off the sleeves of his winter coat with a wink.

Elara snorted, pulling her thin jacket tighter around her shoulders. 'It is cold though, is the game nearly over? I'm ready for a hot chocolate.'

'About five minutes left,' Xander said, glancing up at the clock as he rubbed his hands together, his breath pooling in the cold air. No one had scored a goal yet, and although Elara wasn't the biggest fan of football, she knew that this wasn't great. Especially as there were scouts here today to watch the players.

As the game started to narrow down to the last minute, Elara began to feel an uncomfortable prickle work its way up her spine and onto her neck, making her hairs stand on end.

She shivered, trying to shake the feeling away but it wouldn't go. She felt as though she was being watched and the goosebumps on her skin had nothing to do with the time of year. She slowly glanced around the pitch, looking for anyone out of place, her heartbeat racing. Suddenly she caught a glimpse of a shock of silver hair. That wiry figure and the dark clothing. She could see his face clearly now. Sharp cheekbones stuck out against pale, white skin. His eyes dark and piercing, almost bug-like in comparison with his petite features. He blatantly stood out from the crowd, with his proud posture and intimidating presence. Elara wanted to look away the second she met his gaze but forced herself to stare back. A knot twisting in her stomach and butterflies flocking up her throat. Just as she thought she might burst from the intensity, a roar from the crowd shocked her back to attention. Elara turned to face the pitch just in time to see the ball fly into the back of the net and the rest of his teammates crowd Alfie in joy. Elara jumped up with the rest of her friends, screaming and clapping as the whistle for the end of the match sounded, but still she kept the silver-haired man in the corner of her gaze.

The local café was flooded with football supporters, cheering and chanting, singing Alfie's praises as at least a dozen people offered to buy him a hot-drink or snack. Elara was overjoyed for Alfie. One of the scouts had even approached him with a business card and personal phone number. But through all the celebrations, Elara couldn't shake the feeling that was sitting heavily on her chest. She recognised that silver-haired man. He was familiar she was sure of it. But why on Earth would he be stalking her? Or where in fact would she know him from? She wanted to confront him, ask him exactly who he was. She knew better though, he could be dangerous, plus Xander would hate it. After the incident at the party, he'd become much more protective of her. Rarely leaving her side and shooting stern glances at anyone who looked her way for too long.

He seemed to sense that Elara was feeling on edge. He kept turning to her with a worried look on his face, the furrowed brow and tense jaw that Elara knew all too well. She kept smiling back at him, but she knew the second they left the café, he'd be quizzing her on what was wrong.

As Alfie chatted to what seemed like everybody in the café, Xander, Elara, Jenna and Matt slid into a cosy booth by a window overlooking the main street. All cradling hot drinks to try and thaw from the icy 90 minutes. As the group chatted easily, Elara found her attention drifting. She watched the busy people hurry by, bundled up in warm clothing and pointing up at the fairy-lights that had made their way around the town-square. An early Christmas decoration.

Then she saw him again. He was closer this time. He was watching her so intently she felt as though he could see into her brain and sense her every thought. He was holding something in his hand. Could it be a knife? Her pulse quickened. No. It was too thin to be a knife and there was no glint of metal. It looked more like wood, but why would a grown man be carrying around a stick? His stance wasn't menacing, but it didn't look friendly either and the longer Elara looked at him, the harder it seemed it would be to look away. Almost as though he was pulling her in, tightening his grip on her in such a way that she would do anything he asked.

He rolled the wooden stick around over his fingers, a quick flash of motion, yet clearly well practised, and in an instant, Elara felt herself falling into a memory.

She was stood in front of a man. He reminded her somewhat of a tree-trunk, his shoulders broad and he towered above her. His brown hair was long and curly, and tied back loosely from a kind face, but there was a glint in his eye that set her on edge. It took her a while to notice the crown bestowed upon his head. It was a delicate gold wreath, made up of leaves and vibrant green jewel stones that reflected the sunlight, casting tiny rainbows around the room. He was speaking to her, but she couldn't hear what he was saying. It felt as though she'd lost her hearing and she tried her best to read his lips, but to no avail. Suddenly a woman walked into the room. She looked like a magical warrior, and as soon as she neared, Elara felt a warm joy spread through her entire body. The anxiety that she'd felt only seconds ago, melted away in the woman's presence. She met her gaze with a gentle nod, a flutter of serenity staking its claim in her chest as the woman smiled at her. Slowly, the man's words became crystal clear.

'Tempest, I ask politely that you leave us be. Nerida and I were in the middle of a rather important conversation.'

Elara gathered that the man was referring to her as Nerida. For some reason, she felt no need to correct him and turned instead to the woman, Tempest.

'No, please do stay. We were just finishing up here,' Elara replied, smiling at Tempest. Tempest's tough expression softened as she smiled back at Elara. Her jet-black hair was pulled tightly away from her face, fastened into a ponytail that ruffled in the breeze from the open windows. Every inch of her arms that wasn't encased in black armour was covered in beautiful pictures, writing and symbols. Bright colours and dark lines that stood out against her pale skin. Her hands were laden with heavy silver jewellery, beautiful gemstones and ornate settings, each ring different from the next. She was tall and slim, though Elara knew that within this woman was incredible power and strength, that no doubt deceived even the brightest minds.

Elara turned back to the man in front of her, 'was there anything more, sir? Or may I be leaving.'

The man looked confused, an angry expression flashing across his features for a brief second before he collected himself once more.

'Nerida, I just told you that I am in love with you. I just asked you to marry me. Do I not deserve a response of some kind? I wish for you to rule by my side. Be my Queen. Felicia will be ours, as we serve as equals.'

Elara took a step back, suddenly unsteady on her feet and she felt Tempest rush to her side, placing a hand on her arm to steady her.

'You wish to marry me?' Elara asked, uncertainly. Her voice quivering slightly.

'I thought I had made my intentions clear, Nerida. Now that the community is thriving and Felicia is running smoothly, we can be together. We can start a family and be the rulers that our world needs.' He was reaching out to her now. The look on his face was earnest, but Elara knew better. There were many unanswered questions running through her mind, but one thing was certain. She did not love this man stood before her; she wasn't sure she even trusted him. No. She loved the woman standing by her side, with every ounce of her being.

'Your Majesty,' she started shakily, 'I am afraid I must decline your offer. For I do not love you, nor do I wish to rule. I love her,' she said, turning to look at Tempest as the King's face dropped.

Tempest looked scared. An emotion Elara was sure the warrior didn't often experience. She moved her hand from Elara's arm as quickly as though it was burning hot and she took a step away, dropping her eyes to the floor. The many people who had been bustling around the room, suddenly came to a stop, gawking at Elara as she felt her cheeks blaze red.

'You love her?' the King spat, looking Tempest up and down. 'You want to be with her?'

Elara gritted her teeth, 'yes, your Majesty.'

'You are refusing the title of Queen, to run around in the forests playing with pixies and nymphs, and neglect your responsibilities?' His face was turning an angry purple as Elara felt the ground begin to shake.

'I will not allow it! You are more than this Nerida; I can give you more! I told you I love you, what else could you want? I am the King!' His voice was more of a growl now as the skies began to darken, the staff surrounding them slowly began to scatter. Elara sensed Tempest take another step back.

'You will be my Queen, and there will be no choice in the matter. Do you hear me?' he shouted, storming towards her and clasping a huge hand tightly around her neck.

'No!' Tempest screamed, immediately pulling a sword out from her belt, and pointing it at the King.

He simply waved a hand, and a branch from a tree flew in through the open window and knocked the sword out from Tempest's grip and it clattered uselessly to the marble floor.

'Do not disrespect me!' he roared as with another flick of his fingers, the tree branch began to wrap itself around Tempest, slamming her back into the wall behind them so hard, Elara heard cracks splinter in the plaster. She whimpered slightly, trying to strain against his tight grip to turn and see if Tempest was okay, but he was too strong.

'Say you'll marry me, Nerida. Say it.'

Elara bit her lip, trying to keep the tears that threatened to spill down her cheeks at bay.

'Say it!' he screamed, shaking her as she heard Tempest's breathing begin to grow ragged behind her.

'No,' she whispered, 'I will not marry you.'

In an instant, the King dropped her to the ground, and she landed with a thump on the hard floor.

Elara watched in horror as the King reached down into the ground, forcing his hands through the marble tiles and into the soil and dirt beneath the foundations. He grabbed at a huge root and pulled it up out of the ground as easily as you might pull a splinter from your finger, and with a deafening crack, snapped the root in half. Leaving him with a huge, sharp weapon, a hundred tiny daggers jutting out from the wood.

'Fine,' the King smiled sweetly, 'have it your way then.'

He charged at Tempest who was still pinned up against the wall, and Elara didn't even have time to move before the King plunged the wood straight through Tempest's stomach with a sickening crunch.

Elara couldn't breathe. The air was trapped in her lungs, and she wasn't sure it would ever make its way out. Tempest's beautiful face became the picture of pure shock as she looked down at the huge root sticking out from her abdomen. The sticky red blood beginning to ooze its way down her body and dripping onto the tiles in a disgustingly rhythmic pattern.

She looked over at Elara, a single tear dripping down her porcelain cheek, as Elara felt her entire heart and soul be ripped from her body by the devil himself. Her throat ached from unshed tears, and she was entirely sure that she was paralysed and would now have to live out her sorrow crouched on this floor.

'I love you,' Tempest whispered to her, her eyes filled with tears as her lips turned blue and a trail of glistening blood dripped down from the corner of her mouth. Her gaze held Elara's until finally her head went limp and slumped down against her chest.

'No!' Elara screeched, the pain carving away at her throat and cutting her mouth like glass. Her head filled with noise as her vision blurred and darkened, her tears like acid melting away her eyes.

'Elara? Elara what's going on?' Xander was shaking her, the rest of the table staring at her in shock. The café had gone silent and every single person had turned to look at her. Elara could feel her cheeks were wet with tears, her hands shaking.

'What happened?' she whispered, dragging her sleeves across her face and tucking her hair behind her ears.

'You were screaming, El. What were you screaming at?'

'Are you hurt? Did someone do something?' Jenna asked across the table, looking concerned as she reached out to take Elara's hand.

'No, um, it was just dejavú, a memory, I'm sorry,' Elara whispered as the rest of the café finally began to turn back to their conversations.

'El, memories don't make you scream. Dejavú doesn't make you cry. Are you sure that was it?'

'I don't know, I'm sorry. I think I should go home now, maybe I just need some sleep.'

'Are you sure? Do you want me to come with you?' Xander asked, standing up from the table.

'No really it's okay, I just need some time to myself. I'm sorry I scared you, I'll see you tomorrow,' Elara smiled quickly, before turning and hurrying away from the table.

She left the café in a blur; she could still hear Xander shouting after her, but she didn't bother to turn back. A cold chill had descended on the evening. The crisp autumn afternoon had morphed into a heavy darkness that weighed down on Elara's soul. Every shadow she passed, she stared at for a second, half expecting someone to jump out at her, wielding their own curiously formed weapon.

Elara burst through her front door with a final glance behind her, startling both her parents who were sat at the kitchen table.

'What are you doing back so early, El? Is everything okay?' her mum asked, cupping a large mug of tea in her hands.

'Yeah, no, it's all good. Sorry, I didn't mean to scare you, it was just cold out there. The game finished early, I was tired, so I decided to come back,' Elara smiled, hoping it was convincing.

'Well would you like some dinner? Your father and I have just eaten, but I can make you something if you'd like?'

her mum persisted, standing up to busy herself with clearing the plates.

'No, that's okay, I'm not really hungry. Just gonna go straight to bed I think, maybe then I'll wake up early and get some studying in.' The lie fooled her mother, and Rose nodded approvingly at her daughter.

'I've taught you well, Elara. Sleep well then sweetheart. Remember to take your medicine.' Her mum smiled, kissing the top of her head.

Elara hurried off to her room, skipping up the ladder two rungs at a time and flinging herself face down onto her bed. A sigh of relief escaping her lungs.

As she got ready for bed, she tried to push the memories to the back of her mind. When she was little, she'd had to see a therapist for her nightmares and occasionally these strange memories that they'd just call dejavú. As a child they were very rare, and no-where near as graphic as what her brain was coming up with nowadays, but they'd traumatised her all the same. The therapist had taught her how to forget the nasty images. To imagine squeezing them down into a box. Closing the lid and locking them tight away, before pushing them deep down into the depths of her mind, helping her to heal.

Elara stood at her bedroom window and went through this process, as she looked out into the forest. At each step, she felt her anxiety melt away, a calmness washing over her in the quiet room. Suddenly a face was staring back at her from the treeline. The silver hair. The piercing eyes. Elara felt herself stumble backwards as her breath caught in her throat. She fell onto the floor with a thump and as she struggled to calm her breathing, the bulb in her bedside lamp blew, plunging her into darkness. Elara felt her shoulders start to shake and sweat drip down her spine, as she suddenly got the feeling that she wasn't alone in the dark.

She slammed herself back against the wall, the cold from the concrete seeping into her bones. The heaviness of the night seemed to weigh down on Elara's shoulders, pressing on her chest as she heaved in slow, deep breaths and stared intently at the dark shape by the window. As she watched, the figure emerged silently from the shadows. The silver-haired man was stood in her room. Elara could feel his energy buzzing around her in waves, the vibrations tingling against her skin. The moonlight was catching on his features, the sharp contours of his nose and cheekbones and the soft wrinkles that fell around his eyes. Elara focussed on his eyes for a second, they were an unusual light violet colour that Elara couldn't help but stare at. He stared back down at her, his face unmoving.

'Get up,' he said softly, his arms crossed against his chest.

Elara stayed pressed against the wall, her hands shaking.

'Get up,' he said again, his tone more demanding now and Elara slowly rose to her feet, her gaze never dropping from his violet eyes.

'Turn on the light.' He glanced back at the lamp on her bedside table.

'The bulb blew,' Elara replied, her voice quivered with confusion as mentally she searched around her room for anything that could defend her.

'Come now Miss Anderson, you and I both know you can fix that yourself. Go ahead. Turn on the light,' he said, a smirk pulling at his thin lips with a peculiar look on his face.

Elara slowly stepped to the side towards the lamp, still staring at the man before her.

'Please you can take anything you want; I won't say a word I swear,' she murmured, grasping at the wall behind her, trying to stay upright.

The man looked confused for a moment, before a surprised chuckle escaped his lips.

'Trust me, I'm certainly not here to steal from you. Now come on, you know what to do, just touch the glass and focus on the energy.'

Elara frowned, she couldn't tell if he was messing her around, trying to throw her off. But he was watching intently, it didn't seem as though he was joking.

Reluctantly, Elara reached her fingertips over to the bulb. It was still warm and immediately she could feel the streams of energy pulsing below the surface of the glass. She focussed on the vibrations, making them spark and splutter until suddenly the bulb flashed to life once more, bathing the room in a soft, golden light.

Elara shook her head, as if waking from a trance.

'Well, of course. As I suspected,' the man said with a knowing smile. Now that his face was finally fully visible, he looked much kinder than Elara had anticipated. There was something enticing about him, that for some reason made Elara trust him, yet still she was wary.

'How did you even get in here? And why have you been following me around for weeks? Do I know you? What's your name?' Elara asked, more and more questions springing to mind. The man suddenly looked exhausted, shutting his eyes against her flurry of words.

'All of that will become clear to you Elara, on your 17th birthday. It is not my place to tell you now, I'm simply here to keep an eye on you. Your gifts are manifesting when they really shouldn't be. They're much stronger than I would've expected, so it seems you need a baby-sitter,' he said with a smirk.

'Gifts? What on Earth are you talking about? Did my parents hire you to make sure I study?' she asked in disbelief, her brain so overwhelmed with what she was hearing, all of her fear seemed to have melted away.

'This is a need-to-know basis, Miss. And all you need to know right now, is that if anything goes wrong, like at your little party the other night, I'm the one who must clean up after you. So please be careful, I'm getting too old for stunts like this. I should've retired years ago like they told me to,' he said with a sigh.

Elara's face conveyed her every emotion as she sank down onto her bed, trying and failing to make sense of his words. Her brain was so full of confusion, she was sure the buzzing of her thoughts was audible in the quiet room.

'What do you mean about the party? Do you mean Xander punching that guy? That wasn't my fault. Or the police coming either.' A headache was beginning to cloud at the base of her skull.

The man frowned down at her.

'Xander? Police? I have no idea what they have to do with anything Miss Anderson. No, I'm talking about when you blew every electrical supply in the neighbourhood, flooded the house full of humans, and caused a minor earthquake, all within the space of a minute. That's the kind of thing I have to clean up after,' he laughed, the most emotion Elara had seen him portray.

'Wait, you mean I did all of that? How? Why?'

'I have no idea. That's something we'll figure out when you come of age. In the meantime, I just make people forget. Clean up after you. You see?'

Elara didn't see in the slightest, but she nodded absently as she bit relentlessly on her lip, even the metallic tang of blood on her tongue did little to quieten her whirring mind.

'So, if you can't tell me anything that's going on, why on Earth did you come here to see me? Are you just trying to scare me? Or have I finally gone completely mad, and this is just another dream?' Elara asked, staring at the man with a cold expression on her face.

'No. In fact, the council will probably have my hat for coming to see you. But you know you can trust me; you know you recognise me even if you can't remember why. Plus, I could tell it was starting to scare you, seeing me around all the time. I wanted to show you I mean no harm, I am simply here to make sure you make it to your 17th birthday, undetected.'

His eyes softened, and Elara instantly felt guilty for snapping at him.

'What's so special about my 17th birthday anyway? And should I remember you?'

'You'll see soon enough Miss Anderson, have some patience. And no, if you don't remember me, we did our job excellently. But, for your own peace of mind, my name is Osmond. We will become much more acquainted soon, I'm sure of it,' he said with a smile, before disappearing completely in front of her eyes.

Elara spent the entire night led silently on top of her covers as her hand trailed along the crystals lined up neatly on her bedside table. Watching as the shadows flickered around her room in the moonlight and listening to the rustle of the leaves from the forest. A million questions assaulted her brain, knocking around her skull as she forced herself to ignore them. Though her fears of the silver-haired man had somehow miraculously been resolved, a million others took its place. Jostling for room in her already full brain. The questions were endless, they flew through her veins more fluidly than her blood ever had and Elara's ears rang from the insistence of it all. The incessant buzzing of her phone didn't help either. Every few minutes another chime as no doubt Xander was going out of his mind with worry, maybe a quick check up from Jenna or Alfie every few hours or so.

Elara desperately wanted to ring Xander, beg him to come over so she had someone to talk to. But what on Earth would she tell him? He would laugh in her face and walk straight back out of the front door at even the first sentence, convinced she was crazy for believing an infinitely old man with purple eyes had manifested into her room, with a fantastical story of how Elara magically had the ability to manipulate electricity and flood houses. She'd be sent to a psych-ward before the sun had time to rise.

So instead, Elara stayed there. Drowning in her own thoughts.

Elara must have slipped into a restless sleep at some point, as she was brought back to her senses by the harsh light of dawn, flooding in through the open window. She slipped quietly out of bed, glancing for a second in her floor length mirror. Her hair was tousled and the dark circles around her eyes greeted her wordlessly. A testament to the night before. It was too fantastical for Elara to have dreamt anyway.
Elara didn't bother changing from the clothes she had slept in, instead grabbing a thin sweatshirt off the floor, and tossing it over her tank top. She tied the drawstring from her joggers tightly around her waist, and soundlessly grabbed her guitar from where it was resting against a stack of books. She slipped her phone into her pocket as a last-minute thought, no doubt her mum would wake soon, and wonder where she was.

The morning was cold and fresh. The air seemed to hum with tranquillity as the birds began to sing and insects buzzed in the trees. The dew in the grass was icy against Elara's bare feet, but she didn't mind and instead wriggled her toes into the soft ground. She couldn't imagine doing this in London. If there had even been the privilege of greenery within walking distance of her flat, she would have been harassed by the early workers and those out from the night before. Pointing out and cat-calling her, as they laughed at her choice of clothes. Elara turned like a sunflower into the early morning light, letting the sun's warm rays wash over her skin. She smiled as rainbows danced along her eyelashes, and the breeze tickled the base of her neck. Elara tied her hair up loosely, pulling it away from her face in a well-rehearsed gesture and slowly she began to spin. With her guitar behind her back, the warm weight pressed against her on a hand-woven strap. She could hear the breeze whistling through the strings as she spun faster and faster, laughing, and flinging out her arms as a child would. The wind whipped at her ponytail and the cool breeze pricked her skin, but Elara didn't care. She wondered briefly if Osmond was watching her from his quiet reserve in the treeline, but quickly enough, the thought left her mind. Flying away towards the horizon and leaving her head clear and free.

 Elara began to walk to the spot at the top of the cliff, where Xander had brought her all those weeks before. The image of him, his smile, his eyes, his touch, filled her mind as she skipped over the rocks and danced over the fallen trees as she had so many times before. Each time she emerged onto the cliffside was just as breath-taking as the last. The crescent shaped forest on either side of the ravine fading from vibrant reds and yellows to warm browns and oranges as October began to make way for November. The steep drop at the edge of the cliff where the water crashed and echoed, and the endless horizon, which at this time in the morning could rival the most beautiful watercolour painting. Lemon and peach clouds danced lazily above the trees, whilst the powder-blue sky staked its claim against the darkness of the night.

 Elara perched carefully on the rock closest to the cliffs edge. It was her favourite, as daisies always sprouted up around its base and tickled at her ankles. It meant that she could just about see over the edge and down into the water below, without feeling as though she could tumble down at any moment. The whole forest seemed to silence as Elara began to strum the chords to her favourite song. Her hands were nimble on the strings, her long fingers stretching easily between the chords of the song she knew so well. The melody of Amy McDonald's 'Spark' was simple and enchanting. The lyrics washed over Elara, and she felt as though all the birds had quietened to listen, so she let her voice soar over the treetops, smiling at the renewed sense of freedom.

Elara carried on playing and humming to herself for some time, lost in the chords and mesmerised by the way nature so easily enveloped her. The worries of last night were brushed aside as though they'd never happened and today was a fresh start. After a while, she heard a rustle behind her and before she had the time to turn around, she heard a familiar pattern of footsteps. She turned to see Xander stood behind her, a bemused look on his face.

'So, you run out of a café crying over ten hours ago, I call and text you all night with no response, and at half past 8 the next morning find you by the side of a cliff, playing guitar to a forest?' he asked, his eyebrows raised with his arms folded sternly across his chest.

Elara cleared her throat nervously, shifting her guitar off her lap and laying it down on the rock next to her. Busying herself with smoothing out the strap so she wouldn't have to look Xander in the eye.

'You wanna tell me what happened? I was worried, El.'

Xander crouched down in front her, his expression anxious as he took her hand in his.

'I didn't mean to worry you, I swear. I just didn't feel like talking, Xander. I'm sorry if I panicked you.'

'Elara, I was this close to coming round and breaking down your front door to make sure you were okay. You couldn't have at least messaged me back? You literally screamed down an entire café for no reason, then fled without an explanation. What happened?'

Elara could see Xander grit his teeth, the muscles flexing in his jaw until she reached out and stroked his cheek and he instantly softened.

'Trust me, it's just going to sound even crazier if I tell you. It doesn't matter, I'm okay today. I am really sorry though,' she said, brushing her thumb gently across his bottom lip.

She could almost see the thoughts churning inside his brain. Weighing up whether he should push it and keep asking, but Elara stopped his thoughts in their tracks. He met her kiss with a softness at first, gentle and slightly reluctant. Then instantly his emotions changed, and his hands were on her face, in her hair. He stood up from his crouched position, pulling her with him as she stood up on her tiptoes to reach. His face was almost burning hot against hers and she could taste the minty-ness of his toothpaste. His hand was firm on her jaw, pulling her closer as his other stroked the bare skin of her back where her sweatshirt had come up slightly. Her arms wove around his neck, her cold fingertips twisting into his hair, returning his insistency. Time seemed to pass differently, she couldn't tell if it was minutes or hours that they stayed that way, but Elara didn't care. Xander didn't seem to notice much either.

Eventually, Elara broke away. Her mind swimming as though she'd been in a trance, and she felt a little unsteady on her feet. But Xander's arms were still around her, holding her close. He smiled down at her as she took a deep breath, he tucked a stray hair from her ponytail behind her ear.

'We're not done with this conversation by the way, Elara Hazel. However, you might've made me forget it, just for a little while.' Elara grinned up at him, reaching to give him one last sweet kiss.

'Whatever you say Alexander. Though we both know this is on my terms,' she said with a laugh, reaching down to pick up her guitar.

She stood up and noticed a peculiar expression had clouded Xander's handsome features, an unspoken question lingering in his blue eyes.

Elara took a deep lungful of air before asking, 'what is it?'

Xander glanced down at the ground, then back up to Elara's face, and down at the floor once more.

'…Where the hell are your shoes?'

An unexpected laugh erupted from Elara's chest, her hair falling forward as she doubled over in fits of giggles.

'I'm honestly not sure how to answer that,' she said, finally catching her breath as Xander's bemused expression returned once more. 'You want to come back to mine for some breakfast?' she asked as he rolled his eyes at her. He took her hand and planted a quick kiss on her cheek.

'I thought you'd never ask.'

CHAPTER SIX

Elara

Surprisingly back at the house, neither of Elara's parents were awake yet. Xander immediately made himself at home at the kitchen table. Elara watched him in the reflection of the kitchen window as she busied herself with coffee, smiling at he gently stroked the leaves of the roses stood as a proud centrepiece in the middle of the table. As she placed a selection of jams, spreads and fruit down in front of Xander, he looked up at her with a smile.

'So, a little birdy tells me that you have a birthday coming up,' he said quietly with a glint in his eye.

Elara sat down at the table opposite him, spreading Nutella thickly on her slice of homemade bread, her stomach already growling with a ravenous appetite.

'May I ask who that little birdy was?' Elara replied, as she raised her eyebrows expectantly.

'Your parent's family diary,' he laughed, gesturing to the thick book strewn across the table, littered with post-it notes, slips of paper and in the middle of it all, a piece of orange card, with 'pick up El's birthday cake' written in bright purple pen across the centre.

'Yeah, that would do it,' Elara sighed, taking a large bite out of her toast.

'Why didn't you tell me? When is it?' Xander asked, shoving her shoulder gently with a grin.

'November 5th, and you didn't tell me about yours… I was just repaying the favour!' Elara laughed, leaning over to wipe a smear of homemade blueberry jam from Xander's cheek.

'November 5th? That's so soon! Are we celebrating?'

Elara laughed, 'hah! We? Who said I was spending the day with you?' she teased.

'Come on now, Els. Who else would you rather spend your time with, when you know I'll treat you like a princess?' he winked, holding out a plump strawberry for Elara to take a bite. The sharp ripeness of the fruit exploded over her tongue, and she scrunched up her nose in response.

'Oh really? Now who says I don't have a queue of people lined up, ready to treat me like a Queen?' she joked, leaning over to rest her hands on his knees so that their faces were inches apart.

Xander shook his head at her. 'I'm certain you do, however I'm clearly first in line. So, I'll be taking on responsibility for this year. I know, you're welcome,' he sighed tiredly, holding his hands up in the air with a tortured smile.

Elara snorted, leaning back against her own chair to take a sip of her coffee. 'You're ridiculous, you know that?'

Xander grinned back at her, lifting her hand to plant a quick kiss on her knuckles with a wink.

'All for your entertainment, Your Highness.'

As Elara cleared away the plates from breakfast, Xander stood up behind her, wrapping his arms around her waist as he kissed the top of her head.

'So, did you have any plans for today? Or can you spare some of your precious time for a peasant like me?'

Elara grinned; glad he couldn't see the blush colouring her cheeks.

'You know, I could shift around a few things in my incredibly busy schedule. Give you a couple of hours to entertain me?'

'Mmmm, that sounds like a deal to me,' he said, suddenly grabbing the material of her sweatshirt and spinning her round to face him, as Elara felt herself pushed back against the counter, the warmth of him flooding her skin. He kissed her gently, his hands soft on her waist as she relaxed into his arms. Suddenly, she heard a creak from upstairs, and she pulled away.

'Hey, you wanna go upstairs?' she asked, her voice hushed.

'Elara Anderson! How forward of you!' Xander murmured against her lips.

She pushed him away with a smile, biting her lip to refrain from laughing.

'Xander! I just don't fancy my parents coming down for a quiet cup of tea, to find us making out on the counter. That would most certainly not be my mum's idea of a perfect morning.'

Xander scrunched his nose at her, 'well then, I guess your bed will do, if you insist!'

Elara gasped at him, a theatrical look on her face, 'Alexander! I would never suggest such a scandal. Now hurry up and get your ass in my room before Rose kicks you out of the house altogether,' she grinned, grabbing her guitar from the sofa, and hurrying quietly up the stairs, Xander in tow.

Now the sun had risen fully over the trees, Elara's room had turned into a sauna. The yellow sunlight bathed her room in glowing warmth. Elara opened her skylight, and instantly the cool breeze began to weave its way through the windchimes and dreamcatchers embedded with crystals that were taped to her ceiling. The soft clink of glass and wood filling the room with a gentle melody.

As Elara quickly tidied her messy floor, Xander sat down on her bed, watching her work. She could see him gazing around at the hundreds of books that were stacked up against the already full bookshelves. His gaze stopped briefly over each of her glinting crystals as he worked his way over to the half a dozen potted plants that were neatly lined up by the window. A smile growing on his face.

After tidying around the room, Elara started to get warm despite the breeze drifting through the window. She slipped the thin sweatshirt over her head and as she went to drop it on the bed behind Xander, he grabbed her wrist, almost making her lose her balance, but instead he steadied her with a hand on her waist. He tipped his head up towards her, and she met his gaze with a smile, immediately leaning down to kiss him. Xander wrapped his other arm around her waist, as he pulled her swiftly down onto his lap. Elara weaved her legs around him as his arms tightened across her back. He kept one hand firm against the back of her neck, his grip sure and gentle. Elara ran her fingertips along his jaw, skimming over the sharp angles and gripping his chin as his breath caught in his throat, the sound made a warm heat begin to flood through Elara's stomach.

He carefully threaded his hand up into her hair, pulling at the roots slowly as he began to kiss along her jawline and down her neck, stopping at the bare skin of her collarbone, planting soft kisses that made Elara's heart race. She stroked his cheek, her breaths short and shallow as she tried and failed to control her heart rate. As he kissed the skin where her shoulder met the base of her neck, he grazed the tender skin gently with his teeth. Elara gasped as her fingernails dug into his skin, smiling as she felt him shiver.

Her stomach fizzed with nerves and a tingle shot up her spine as she felt his fingertips carefully slip below the waistline of her joggers. She pulled back and met his gaze, resting her nose against his as she traced the very tip of her nail around his lips. His eyes were heavy with intent, his jaw rigid when instantly his energy changed and she couldn't help but match it with the same velocity, a raging fire burning in her chest. Elara reached down and tugged at the hem of his T-shirt, pulling the soft material up and over his head. Xander held her close to him as he shifted their position, laying her down gently on the quilt as he leaned in to kiss her. His actions were hungrier now, and she could feel his want for her bubbling along his skin. The room buzzed with warmth and Elara could almost see the ruby glow of tantalizing chemistry seeping into the air. His skin felt alive under her fingertips, his muscles flexing below the rippling waves of his golden skin. He dropped kisses along the length of her neck, his lips tentative, questioning. All Elara could manage in response was the arch of her back, revelling in the weight of his body against hers.

    Elara had had experience with relationships before. Amateur flings with boys on holiday, sending a few flirty messages back and forth with guys her friends told her had a crush on her. But never had she gotten to this level with anyone. This was different. It felt as though she needed Xander, as though she couldn't get close enough to him. That if she could only melt into his skin, she'd feel everything as strongly as he did. He made her feel alive. She sensed he felt the same way too. It was as though they fed off one another's emotions. Sparks of heat darting around them just waiting to catch fire. It was the most beautifully enticing thing Elara had ever felt.
    Xander was still kissing her, she returned from her venture into their emotions with a crash and kissed him back with such intensity it felt as though she could explode. Her hands were deep in his hair, pulling her body as close as she could to his, her heart skipping a beat every time their bare

skin touched. Elara's breath caught in her chest, as his hand slipped up under her tank-top and his fingertips gripped her side, his thumb stroking gently along the ridges of her ribs.

Elara suddenly heard a creak underneath her floorboards, no doubt her parents getting ready for the day. She suddenly became very aware of how she would have next to no excuse if her mum suddenly appeared at the hatch to her room, and how quickly this was moving.
Xander seemed to sense Elara's uncertainty. He pulled back away from her, smiling down at her.
'You're right, that got a little intense. Maybe we should slow down a bit,' he murmured, his voice shaky.
'Maybe,' Elara smiled back, 'I'm sorry.'
'Don't you dare be sorry, Elara Hazel. You're completely right. I however… am just gonna need a minute,' he said with a grin, as he planted a quick kiss on her nose, and sat up on the edge of the bed.
Elara smiled to herself, dragging herself up as she re-tied her hair into a bun. She sat cross-legged behind him, kissing lightly along his shoulder blades and tracing little love hearts at the base of his spine.
Xander laughed.
'El you're not helping,' he groaned, resting his elbows on his knees, and dropping his head down into his hands.
Elara giggled to herself as she leant back on her pillows and sighed, covering her face as they both laughed.

CHAPTER SEVEN

Elara

The day before Elara's birthday held mixed emotions. She'd always loved celebrating, spending time with her family, but this year would be different. Her grandparents, aunts and uncles were down in London, and she was still very unsure about what Osmond meant when he'd said that she'd understand everything on her 17th birthday. She'd tried to convince herself that the whole evening had been a crazy fever dream, and a part of her almost did. But a larger part remembered it way too clearly for it to ever have been a figment of her imagination. Instead, she'd tried to push it to the back of her mind, to stop it from consuming her completely.

'Morning sweetheart! Happy birthday eve!' her mum sang as Elara made her way into the kitchen. It was only half eight in the morning, yet already there was a giant stack of pancakes in the centre of the kitchen table. Colourful jugs of every juice imaginable, and a rainbow array of fruit. It was tradition in the Anderson household. However, this morning, for the first time in 15 years, there was someone new at the table.

'Morning, sunshine!' Xander grinned, a cheeky look on his face.

'Hey! What are you doing here?' Elara asked as she slipped into the chair next to him.

'I invited him!' Rose called from the kitchen; Elara could hear the smile in her voice.

Xander winked at her, slipping his hand over onto her leg under the tablecloth.

'So, this is quite a spread you've got going on here,' Xander grinned. 'Are you feeding the five thousand?'

Elara rolled her eyes. 'It's family tradition, Mr Griffin. You're gonna have to get used to it.'

'Oh, am I now?' he murmured, leaning into her slightly, before Peter suddenly came clomping down the stairs into the kitchen, and Rose emerged from the cupboard with a tray of syrups.

'Morning, family,' Elara's dad smiled; he was unusually perky for this time in the morning, a slight skip in his step.

'Oh, and there's my beautiful daughter, soon to be 17. How does it feel, Els?' he asked, leaning down to kiss her cheek.

'Same as every other year, Dad,' Elara laughed, starting to pile pancakes onto her plate.

'Well, I don't know about that,' Pete replied, 'I'm sure this year I can see a few grey hairs starting to poke through. And are those some wrinkles I see?' he joked, popping a shiny grape into his mouth with a wink.

'A classic Peter Anderson line, everybody,' Elara drawled as she rolled her eyes at her father.

'Well, anyway. Alexander, great to see you again kid. What've you been up to lately?' Pete asked, turning his attention away from his daughter.

Xander smiled easily as he held a firm hand out to Elara's father. Pete looked surprised for a moment at the gesture but took it gladly as Elara smiled to herself. She could see her mother looking impressed out of the corner of her eye.

'Just been busy with college work recently, sir. I've got exams coming up in December, so I've been studying hard for them.'

Elara knew this wasn't entirely true. Most of Xander's free time was spent either with her or helping his mum out at the pharmacy. It was a good line to impress her parents though.

'Well, Xander, I'm glad to see you taking your studies seriously. Maybe you'll be a good influence on Elara,' her mum said, raising an eyebrow at her daughter.

'From what I've heard, Elara would more likely be the good influence on me,' Xander replied, 'she seems to spend almost too much time worrying about work and exams. Needs to spend more time out in the wide world if you ask me,' he squeezed her leg gently under the table.

Peter laughed. 'You tell her son! They both need to lighten up on the workload in my opinion.'

He widened his eyes and gestured with his head over to his wife, who was shaking her head in despair as Elara tried to hold back a laugh.

'Alright, enough out of you two,' Rose sighed, 'let's eat!'

After a hearty breakfast that left Elara so full, she felt as though she might explode, Rose opened the doors to the conservatory, and together they all sat for a while in the sunshine, chatting and laughing easily.

'Right, well I better go off and make myself busy,' Peter said after a while, standing up and ducking to avoid clunking his head on the low ceiling. 'I'll see you kids later,' he grinned, and as he left, winking meaningfully at Rose.

Elara frowned after him.

'Okay… So… well,' Rose started as she fidgeted nervously in her chair.

'Oh God, what?' Elara sighed. No doubt she wasn't going to like what was in store.

'No, I just needed to chat to you both about something,' Elara's mother said, refusing to meet Elara's gaze as Xander started to shift uncomfortably next to her.

'Mum, if you're about to give us the sex talk, please don't bother. My primary school teacher beat you to it years ago.'

'Oh, God no. Nothing like that, really,' Rose said hurriedly, beginning to pick at her nails,

'I just wanted to chat to you about tonight. You'll be staying over at Xander's if that's okay,' she said with a tight smile.

Elara and Xander shared a confused look.

'Well, you're both old enough to take care of yourselves, and we need you out of the way ready for tomorrow. I originally rang Jenna's mum to see if you could go there, but they're all away for the weekend and it's just Jenna and her sister there, so I didn't feel comfortable with that, so you know, Pete suggested…' she rambled, still fidgeting in her chair.

'Why do you need me out of the way?' Elara interrupted, frowning at her mother.

'That's for me to know, and you to find out, Els. Anyway, I cleared it with Xander's mother, there's a spare room for you to sleep in, then you'll be back here tomorrow. Does that sound okay?'

Elara cleared her throat, trying to stop the blush from spreading along her cheeks. She could see Xander out of the corner of her eye also looking a little shocked. Rose was the most uptight woman they knew, even this lapse in authority was vastly surprising.

'Yeah, mum that's fine. Of course. Did dad force you to talk to us about this, instead of him?' Elara smirked as her mum looked sheepish.

'How did you guess?' Rose replied with a tight smile, 'anyway, no funny business, and you sleep in separate rooms. Alexander's mother will be checking, okay?'

She sounded remarkably like a teacher telling off her students, but Elara smiled at her mother anyway.

'Whatever you say, boss,' she grinned.

Rose smiled wistfully at her daughter for a moment, before leaving the conservatory, straightening out her blouse as she went.

'Well damn, El. Your mum's finally gone insane!' Xander said with a sigh as he leant back on the sofa, his hands behind his head.

Elara laughed, 'come on now, maybe she's actually starting to treat me like an adult!'

Xander grinned, 'I guess that means I have to tidy my room then, if I've got a girl coming over.'

Elara scrunched her nose at him, laughing as he raised his eyebrows with a wink.

'Come on you muppet, come help me pack. Also, give me some tips for meeting your mum, I've never met a boyfriend's family before.'

Xander stopped in his tracks, a smile growing on his face as Elara realised what she'd said and tried to regain her composure.

'Sorry, sorry, I must have misheard,' he said, trying to keep his face serious, but Elara could see the smirk tugging at his lips, 'go ahead, repeat what you just said. A little louder.'

Elara bit her lip, shaking her head as Xander's face broke into a grin.

'I said, I've never met a boyfriend's family before,' she said defiantly, crossing her arms over her chest.

Xander stopped and stared at her for a second, before flinging himself back against the sofa cushions, his arms wide.

'The crowd goes wild!' Xander gushed, his voice breathy, 'Alexander Griffin ties down Elara Anderson, it's official!'

Elara groaned, her hands over her face to hide her grin. 'Alright, alright Xander. I get it.'

He laughed, reaching over to pull her hands away from her face. 'I'm messing with you, El. I'm the luckiest guy alive though, seriously.' His smile was sincere now, a softness to his face that Elara rarely saw.

'Come here.' He dragged her up and off the fluffy stool next to him, pulling her in for a tight hug.

'You're sweet, you know,' he murmured into her ear.

'Shhhh,' Elara replied, a finger on his lips, 'that'll be our secret,' she said with a wink.

'Now, as I said. Come help me pack.'

She grabbed his hand to pull him up from the sofa, smiling as she felt the warm contentedness flush across his skin.

Elara had only been in Xander's house once before, and she'd never been further than the kitchen. It was a tiny little house, despite the amount of people that lived there, and very well kept. All the walls were a harsh white, the wood flooring so well polished, Elara had to keep a tight grip on Xander's hand to keep from slipping over. In Elara's house, pictures of her littered the walls. Magazines, half read books, cozy blankets and coffee mugs warmed up the space, but there was none of that here. No personal items, no pictures of Xander and his family. It felt a little unwelcoming.

Xander led her into the kitchen, one of his brothers was sat at the table, running a little toy truck up and down the centre of the placemats.

'Hey, Jamie. You alright kid?' Xander asked as he walked over to the fridge, emerging a second later with two cans of Diet Coke.

Jamie mumbled something in response, staring quietly at Elara as she smiled uncomfortably back.

'Where's mum? Is she here?' Xander asked as he grabbed a couple of apples on his way past the fruit bowl.

'Mmm no. She's gone to get Callum,' Jamie replied, still not shifting his gaze away from Elara.

'Ahh right, we're going upstairs, okay bud?'

Jamie stayed silent, nodding his head slightly as Xander turned around, widening his eyes at Elara with a smirk.

'So, Callum is?' Elara asked, plopping down on Xander's bed.

'My eldest brother,' Xander replied as he chucked her the apple.

'Right, so there's you, Jamie is younger, Callum is older, and then there's one more?' Elara asked with a frown, twisting the stem on her apple.

'Yeah, then there's Evan, in between me and Jamie.'

'I don't know how you remember all those names,' Elara said with a laugh.

'Half the time I don't honestly. It's chaotic.'

'So, your mum left Jamie here alone whilst she went to pick up your other brother? Isn't he a bit young to be left alone?' Elara asked with a frown.

'She'll only have been gone a few minutes. Plus, my dad should be around here somewhere, not that he's much help. Steer clear of him whilst you're here, trust me, he'll just harass you,' Xander sighed, a sad look washing over his features.

Elara's heart ached for a moment, wanting to tell Xander it was okay, that he didn't need his father. But she knew that wasn't what he needed to hear right now.

'So, did you have anything planned for this evening?' Elara asked, scooching closer to Xander, swinging her legs over his. He leant back on the wall with a smile, stroking her ankle.

'Well, I'm sure what I had in mind wouldn't be Rose Anderson approved,' he said with a wink, 'so how about your favourite movie, we'll order in some greasy burgers, and I'll promise not to complain about whatever film you pick. Sound okay?'

Elara smiled happily, 'like a dream come true.'

CHAPTER EIGHT

Elara

The view was foggy. Elara tried to focus on the shapes before her, but her eyes drifted over bright colours and blurry objects, and she felt as though she was watching from far away on a small movie screen. She could hear people talking in lilting accents, some of the words sounded familiar, but they were muffled as though her head was filled with cotton wool. Elara could just make out someone with their arms stretched out towards a small, blonde child. They beckoned her in for a hug whilst a slight, young looking woman held her fiercely from behind. Someone was crying but Elara couldn't figure out where it was coming from. The person crouched before the child sighed disappointedly and tugged on her tiny hand, pulling her from the warm embrace.

'Let her go, Mrs Sylvaine, we want to keep her safe.' Elara made out. 'She'll have a better life with us. You of all people should know that,' murmured the voice.

The crying grew louder as the child was lifted from the ground and thrust towards an unfriendly looking figure, who's face turned to disgust as the blonde bundle was dropped into his arms.

'Esmé, Gabe, you are aware of the consequences if this agreement becomes common knowledge, yes? Keep your mouths shut, and we will not fate your daughter to exile with you. She will stay here fulfilling her destiny as a respected Ardent witch, without the weight of your actions. Do you understand?' the voice snapped as the tortured cries quietened, and Elara's vision went black.

Elara's 17th birthday went by in a chaotic blur. In the morning, she'd been greeted by a bunch of beautiful pink roses on her pillow, and a sweet card from Xander, then a coffee and a cupcake from his mum. She was very quiet and watched Elara with an intense gaze, but it was nice of her all the same. Back at her house, she could hear a group of people singing 'Happy Birthday' as she'd rounded the corner and on her drive, stood Jenna, Alfie and Matt and Elara's parents, holding a beautiful birthday cake. Her grandparents had also been sat inside on the sofa waiting for her, their faces beaming with pride as they welcomed her gladly. Their warm embrace bringing a tear to Elara's eye, they'd travelled a long way to get there, and Elara couldn't have been more grateful.

The whole of the downstairs space had been decorated in classic Rose Anderson fashion. Colour coordinated streamers and balloons hung from the ceiling, a huge banner draped across the conservatory doors, and the table was laden with every party food you could imagine. As Elara gazed around in wonder, she felt Jenna rush to her side.

'I helped!' she whispered excitedly, 'your mum is so cool, she let me ice the cupcakes!'

Elara laughed as she turned to tightly hug her friend. As she did, she caught sight of Xander over Jenna's shoulder. He was watching the exchange with a smile, completely ignoring whatever Alfie was murmuring in his ear.

Almost immediately, Rose disappeared off into the kitchen and emerged a moment later as the lights went dark.

She was holding a beautiful sage green coloured birthday cake dusted with gold glitter and 17 candles precariously balanced on the top. Rose loved the tradition and could hardly ever wait more than five minutes into a party to bring one out.

A chorus of out of tune 'Happy Birthday' started up and the glow from the candles warmed Elara's cheeks as they neared. As she went to blow out the flames, she looked up at Xander, the candlelight reflecting in his light eyes. He smiled at her expression, whipping out his phone to capture the moment, as the flames perished to smoke.

After an hour or so of easy conversation, with soft music humming warmly in the background, there was a sharp knock at the door. Immediately, Elara felt a tingle down her spine as she quickly leapt up from the sofa, startling her grandparents who were in the middle of telling Xander about the wonders of modern trains.

'I'll get that,' Rose smiled, suddenly appearing gracefully from the kitchen.

'No!' Elara said a little too loudly, earning surprised glances from everyone in the room.

'I'm expecting a friend, I'll get it. They said they had a surprise for me.'

Elara wondered how far this was from the truth as she slid out into the porch to answer the door hidden from view. Who knew who would be waiting for her?

'Now,' Osmond murmured the second Elara stepped out onto the driveway, and instantly, a tall figure in a hooded cloak revealed a small glass bottle from somewhere beneath their robes. It shattered soundlessly at Elara's feet, emitting a yellow vapour that flooded into the air. Creeping like vines up each of Elara's legs, along her torso and around her arms until finally it crawled up her neck. Elara couldn't even muster the energy to hold her breath as the familiar scent enveloped her. The warm sweetness washing away her doubt and anxiety, in return leaving a calm sense of serenity that planted a smile on her face.

Elara caught glimpses of a dark forest around her. She could feel the watery sunlight filtering through the dying canopy and heard the crunch of leaves below someone heavy-footed. However, Elara felt weightless. She could've been trotting through the forest on all fours with hooves and a tail for all she knew, her brain felt muddy. Even simple thoughts lost deep below the surface.

She could hear some odd sounds that didn't sound familiar. Chants and gasps, sing-song accents, and unfamiliar phrases. Elara just laughed along, hearing a chuckle alongside her in response.

Even the sudden feeling of being flipped upside down and squeezed through a gap that would scarcely fit a mouse didn't faze Elara. The smile remained tattooed on her face as she took all these strange occurrences in her stride.

Even with her eyes squeezed tightly shut, Elara could feel the weight of unexplained curiosity bearing down on her. Where earlier, she had comfortably been transported through darkness, she was suddenly faced with such bright light that it forced her eyelids open. She sat and blinked for a while as salty tears stung the corners of her eyes, begging to be left back in the darkness. Eventually she composed herself. Elara was perched on what felt like a small metal stool. Sitting up straighter, she reached up to shield her eyes from the light, but the slight addition of shade hardly even made a difference.

'Turn those bastard lights down, would you? Stakes alight, you'll burn out her retinas,' Osmond exclaimed from somewhere off to her right.

Elara stifled a giggle as finally the white orbs diminished slightly, and her eyes adjusted.

However, ignorance was bliss, and Elara briefly wished she was still blind, as sat in a packed semi-circle around her, was a hoard of gawking faces. Each one staring at her as though she were some sort of circus act who had just fallen from her trapeze. Some held spiral-bound notepads and delicate quills, others were holding sticks similar to the one Osmond carried. Many were dressed in garish, ornate robes, though a few were dressed similarly to Osmond, in practical black clothing. Non-descript and marginally scary.

Suddenly she felt a nudge as Osmond appeared as if from no-where at her side.

'Go on then, introduce yourself,' he growled.

Elara cleared her throat nervously, twisting her hands together in her lap.

'Um, hi. My name's Elara Anderson and I'm erm, 16, no, 17 years old. Yeah… H-Hey.'

Her voice was clear and rang melodically in the space, but clearly her vocabulary and people skills had all but deserted her.

But suddenly, the whole audience erupted into clapping and laughter. Standing up from their seats and shouting to each other and to Elara.

'We did it! We bloody did it!'

'A true miracle, even Hecate would be impressed.'

Elara couldn't catch much as suddenly the noise in the previously quiet space was completely overwhelming, and Elara felt herself shrinking back a little, pulling her legs underneath the stool and twisting her hands together even tighter.

Osmond stepped out from beside her and put himself in between her and the crowd as though he sensed her discomfort, providing a welcome shield for Elara. He seemed strangely protective over her, despite his intimidating disposition. It was sweet.

'Alright, alright that's enough,' called out another voice, 'settle down, we have plenty of time to discuss and to ask questions of Miss Anderson. Firstly, I think we owe her an explanation.'

Elara was escorted quickly out of the bright busy room by Osmond. They walked a short distance through a very dark corridor lit only by candles, and she fired questions at him as they went.
'Where are we?'
'Won't my parents be wondering where I am?'
'Should I call them and tell them I'm alright?'
'Who were all those people, why were they clapping me?'
Elara hurried to keep up with Osmond's quick strides, and he batted each question away with a simple shake of his head, until finally they arrived at a tall dark wood door that was entwined with delicate carvings and embellished with ornate gold handles.
'I'll be right out here,' Osmond whispered, 'holler if you need anything.'
He smiled at her almost sadly, before quickly knocking a practised phrase on the old door. The echo sounded down the corridor, making Elara jump. The door swung open silently, revealing a huge, dimly lit room. The ceilings towered so high, Elara was sure she couldn't see the roof, though she was unsure of how such a tall room would fit into such a small space. The floor was made up of a beautiful cherry wood, littered with countless burgundy rugs. A roaring fire took up the entirety of one wall, and surrounding it were deep, plush sofas and chairs. They were so black they were almost difficult to see, like shadows. Lanterns and candles were scattered across every surface, and the shelves of books were so high on the opposite side of the room, Elara guessed you would need a ladder to reach the third shelf.
Before she'd had a chance to move an inch, the door had shut soundlessly behind her, and Elara was stood in the huge room all alone. Or so she thought.

As soon as she stepped a foot forward, the wooden floor creaked and a man and woman stood up quickly from one of the dark sofas. They turned around with huge smiles on their faces, almost as though they'd rehearsed it and rushed towards Elara before having said a word.

'My darling,' the woman cooed, stretching her arms out and clasping Elara tightly, overwhelming her with a strong, lavender scent that stuck in Elara's throat and made her eyes water. 'Oh sweetheart, you're crying! Oh, I'm sure it must be just as emotional for you as it is for us, to be reunited after all of this time,' the lady murmured in a soothing voice, as the man stood back and watched, tears glinting in his dark eyes.

'Come into the light, let me look at you properly,' the woman purred, grasping Elara's arm tightly and pulling her over to a slim window. The man rushed over beside her, tugging the heavy curtain back and tying it behind a hook, letting warm sunlight filter in through the glass.

'My, my, my! So beautiful! I mean you were such a gorgeous baby, it's hardly a surprise, but my goodness! All of the boys in Felicia will be laying down their wands for a girl like you!' the lady sighed wistfully, stroking a long finger down Elara's cheek with a smile.

'I'm so sorry,' Elara started, her voice catching in her throat, 'I don't mean to be rude, but I have no idea what's going on. Who are you?' she asked, trying to sound as polite as possible. But the couple simply smiled.

'Of course, we knew you wouldn't remember darling, Dear Erinyes we've thought about it every day for 15 years. We should've introduced ourselves straightaway, poor girl. We must have overwhelmed you! I was just so excited to see you, I got carried away,' the woman rambled; her hand draped artfully across her chest as though she was afraid of being overcome with emotion. Elara remained standing there awkwardly, a forced smile painted across her face.

The woman took Elara's hands in her own. Elara noticed they were beautifully manicured, with long, red, pointy nails, and stunning silver jewellery that looked fit for royalty.

'My name is Darya, and this is my husband Dritan. We're your parents, Elara.'

'Osmond. I want Osmond in here,' Elara whispered as she all but fell back into one of the sofas. She gripped the cushions so tightly her knuckles pressed white against her tanned skin.

'Who?'

'Osmond! He's right outside that door, I want him now,' Elara said through gritted teeth, trying and failing to meet Darya's eyes.

'Oh Elara, dear, this is a family matter, I'm sure we don't need your Guardian imposing,' Dritan said hurriedly in hushed tones, crouching down in front of Elara with a sincere smile on his face.

Elara's jaw hardened as a frown clouded her features.

'Please, get Osmond. I need to speak to him.'

Elara expected her voice to shake, but it was strong and steady, a touch of anger colouring the edges as the room suddenly darkened.

An irritated look passed briefly across Darya's face, but she caught it quickly and turned it into a glowing smile.

'Of course, Elara. Anything you wish, is yours.' She threw a stern glance at her husband who instantly rushed to the door and welcomed in a confused Osmond.

'Mr Levett, Elara requested your presence for our conversation. Please, do sit.'

Her Guardian reclined his head slightly as he passed, dropping his eyes respectfully to the floor.

Elara immediately felt calmer as Osmond neared, she looked up at him as he sat down across from her, he looked almost guilty as he saw her confused expression.

'We understand that this is a lot for you to take in, Elara, and anything that will make this easier will of course be granted to you. We want you to feel comfortable and at home here, and we would really like to get to know you better,' Darya continued with a hopeful smile.

'There is so much for you to learn about your homeland, your history, and who you are. We need you to understand why we did what we did, so that you can come to terms with it.'

Elara's brain was beginning to fill with white noise again. An insistent ringing in her ears as she tried to focus on Darya's words.

The group was looking at her expectantly, waiting to hear what she had to say. Elara was surprised she was still breathing and couldn't even comprehend stringing together a sentence right now.

Darya's face was beginning twist a little into that irritated expression Elara had noticed before. She watched intently as Dritan also saw this and took his wife's hand firmly. Instantly her expression softened again, and she reached her spare hand out to Elara.

'I'm sorry sweetheart, we don't mean to upset you, we've just been dreaming of this day for 15 years, there's so much we don't know about you! Also, we are in a bit of a rush today you see. There is a very important meeting later, that you are expected to be at. By our side of course. Mr Levett can come too if you wish,' she carried on with a small glance to Osmond who was looking as shell-shocked as Elara felt.

'Um, it truly is lovely to meet you both. But I have parents, and a home. I have friends and family. I'd love to get to know you both better, but my home is in Oakbridge with them,' Elara said quietly, trying to muster a smile.

'Those people are NOT your true family, Elara. You will come to learn that. It is time for you to be here with us. Your flesh and blood,' Darya hissed, her cheeks turning a garish red colour as she gripped Elara's hand tightly.

Elara recoiled slightly at the outburst, she could see an angry look begin to weigh on Osmond's face as he moved to the edge of the sofa, clearly ready to leave this conversation. Elara hoped that if he did, he took her with him.

'I'm sorry, Elara,' Dritan soothed, his expression neutral and his manner relaxed, 'my wife- your mother, she's struggled greatly all of these years without you. Of course, we understand that you have your... other family, who must love you very much after all this time. Maybe one day we'll get to meet them too. We're just desperate to explain everything to you now... if you'll let us,' he said calmly, smiling warmly at Elara.

She couldn't help but smile back at his kind face, she relaxed slightly, resting back against the cushions. Osmond still had an odd look on his face, but she chose to ignore it and instead focussed on Dritan, who was watching her carefully.

'Perfect,' he smiled, glancing at his wife, 'Darya? Would you like to tell her?'

Darya leaned forward, dabbing gently at the corner of her eyes with a lace handkerchief that at some point had materialised into her hands.

'You were about to turn 2 years old,' she started, a wistful look in her eyes as Elara felt herself slipping into the story and sinking deep down into the sofa cushions.

'You were born, right here, in the Northern Quarter Medical Wing of the Magicis Concilio, more commonly referred to as the Council. Because Elara... you're a witch,' Darya said quietly. Elara sat upright from her slouched position.

'A what?' she asked, her voice breathy.

'A witch,' Darya repeated, her voice prouder now.

Elara almost surprised herself as a wave of laughter erupted out into the quiet room. Her eyes streaming as Darya and Dritan exchanged confused looks.

Immediately Elara quietened, looking between the three adults for a hint that she was either dreaming, or this was all some kind of twisted joke.

'Oh wait, you're serious?' Elara asked, sitting up even straighter, 'like brewing potions, black cats, flying around on a broom... witch?' her mind spinning with disbelief. Surely they were pulling some crazy kind of practical joke.

'Well, most of that has gone out of fashion now of course. Or was based off folklore to begin with. I mean very few warlocks have black cats, and we never flew around on brooms, that's simply ridiculous,' Darya rambled on before a raised eyebrow from Dritan quietened her, 'but anyway, aside from those things, yes, you're a witch.'

'So, you mean I can brew potions to make people turn into frogs, or like curse people and stuff?' Elara asked, her eyes wide.

'Alchemy is practised by a specific sector of warlock families; we just use the potions they create. There are many different types of magic that families specialise in, most won't ever brew a single potion in their lives and instead practise defensive spells, manipulate electricity, or tend to plants. Each family has gifts in a specific area, it's in their blood which type of magic they will succeed in. Families marry together with another family that is rooted in the same or complimentary gifts, that way each generation will be more powerful than the last. It's a simple system really,' Darya said matter-of-factly as Elara reeled at the information that she was being presented with, when suddenly a thought flashed across her mind.

'Wait, so I have real-life magic? What kind of magic?'

Elara thought back to when Osmond had encouraged her to light the bulb with her bare hands and told her she'd burned out the electricity in a whole neighbourhood and flooded an entire house. Up until this second, she still hadn't completely believed that he was telling the truth. She felt a little guilty for doubting him now.

'We're not too sure just yet' Dritan admitted, his brow creasing as he seemed deep in thought, 'it's highly likely you'll have the same stream as us, though only a Wand Ceremony will truly tell,' he said with a small smile.

'What do you mean? What magic do you have?' Elara asked, leaning forward as curiosity bubbled in her brain, accented with a touch of understanding, as though all the odd occurrences in her entire life were beginning to fall into place.

'We're both what they call 'Ardent Witches'. It comes from the Latin 'to burn' but in terms of magic, it encompasses everything to do with emotions. There are two types of Ardents; those who can sense emotions, and those who can alter others' emotions to their will, with varying degrees of capability. In our stream of magic, we can shift people's emotions, sometimes with great effect. With training and the help of a wand, we have developed our gifts over the years, and we'll help you do the same. Everything about us inclines outsiders to feel the way we want them to. After all these years it's almost second nature. It's a powerful gift, and not one to be taken lightly. It is also very rare, there are only twelve remaining families who possess Ardent magic. All but one are guarded carefully in society, as we can come in very handy in the right setting. Which is why we live here, in the Magicis Concilio and work here too. The other families are all the same, living and serving in the other quarters.'

'What about that one family that doesn't live here, where are they?'

Darya sighed, 'they were exiled many years ago. They used their gifts for chaos and strife, rather than good.

They're not discussed here though, Elara,' Darya said with a stern look, and Elara sat back against the sofa, regretting that she'd asked.

'You can use your gifts on other witches?' Elara asked, desperate to divert the conversation.

'To some extent, we can't help our magic influencing others, it's the nature of our gift, however, it will have only a very minor effect on others unless we use a wand to channel it. We only use certain aspects of Ardent magic within our jobs. For example, if we need to know if a criminal is telling the truth, with the help of a spell, they will share their every thought, even those that are buried deep within their subconscious. It certainly keeps the crime rates down, but our magic is monitored very carefully. If we were to use it on the public to the same extent, we'd be exiled for treason. Though as I said, our magic is somewhat innate, to perform those more complex spells we need a wand. They channel our energy and magic stream to allow for much more power. Our wands are bound to us as tightly as if they were an extension of our bodies, yet they can betray us at a moment's notice. Warlocks who specialise in wand making and reading can determine exactly what type of magic, and which spells have been used in a person's lifetime. Almost as though traces are etched into the wood, that other witches can't see. It's fascinating really.'

Elara ran a hand through her hair. She couldn't believe what she was hearing, there was so much to learn and understand, yet all of it still seemed so farfetched. She wasn't entirely sure she wasn't still daydreaming.

'Anyway, that's enough about us, back to your story,' Dritan smiled as Darya began to pour herself a glass of water from a crystal pitcher that at some point had been placed on the low table next to Elara.

'So, you were born right here, in the medical wing, and you lived here in this house with us for almost two beautifully happy years. But just before you were born, there was an uprising beginning in the Magicis Concilio. You see, once upon a time, witches and humans lived in harmony on Earth, but one day humans began to turn on us. Our gifts were no longer gifts to them, and they decided our ancestors were being controlled by the devil. We tried to establish peace, but in turn they burned us at the stake.'

Dritan said this calmly, as though he was simply deciding what to have for tea, but Elara thought back to the years of nightmares depicting that exact scene. A strip of sweat broke out along her hairline, she felt her pulse quicken and her palms were clammy. She slowed her breathing in an attempt to calm down as Dritan carried on.

'There was a strong divide in Felicia, those who wished to remain here, where we knew we were safe, in the land we created for ourselves… the land that was forged by some of the most powerful witches that ever lived, and those who wanted to return to Earth, our original homeland and live in harmony with humans. We're running out of space and time here in Felicia. In the city, people are living in crippling poverty, with not enough food or jobs to go around. However, making Felicia sustainable would be incredibly difficult, there isn't a single witch talented enough to solve all of our problems.'

'Those of us within the Council who were passionate about the movement decided to take matters into our own hands, and begin trials on Earth, to assess whether we would ever be able to reintegrate into society. We needed to see if humanity had changed and would accept us peacefully. However, witches had scarcely set foot on Earth since our ancestors were burnt, aside from the few brave warlocks who specialised in human studies that had visited Earth for brief expeditions. But we found the trials to be too short, and a waste of time. We could never learn enough whilst we were there. So we decided on a stronger, more well thought out plan that we prayed would give us the hope we so desperately needed. We chose someone who was willing to live with the humans and learn everything about their culture. How they raised their children, where they lived, what they did in their spare time. All of those mundane things that an outsider could never fully understand.'

Realisation was beginning to dawn on Elara.

'We sent a woman named Luciana. She had worked for the Council for over 70 years, she was well-trusted, her gifts were in Herbology, a simple form of magic that is easy to conceal, but she was incredibly skilled in Human Studies, and she supported the expedition to better understand humanity, and whether we could ever have a future on Earth. We decided she would live for a year on Earth, and that would give her time to learn everything she needed to know. Unfortunately, Luciana spent 3 months living in Ireland before deciding there was no way we could ever return to Earth. She stated that humans were still hateful, spiteful creatures who knew no sense of humanity and would never accept us for who we were. She spoke with such distaste of those she had lived alongside, that much of the Council was convinced and the movement all but ended, deciding it was time to work on Felicia. However, a small group of us still believed in the cause. Even if we had to modify our expectations and couldn't live in freedom on Earth, we still wanted to fully explore the possibility to return to our native homeland and not cheat ourselves out of a safer and happier future. Some could choose to stay in Felicia if they wished, but those who were happy to live without their gifts or suppressing them to some extent, could return to Earth. Then maybe one day, humans would learn to accept and rejoice in all the things we could provide for them.'

Darya was smiling proudly at her husband as he spoke with a twinkle in his dark eyes. Elara looked to Osmond, but he refused to meet her gaze. Instead, he looked down at what Elara now knew was his wand, and he twisted it artfully between his fingers.

'The second you were born; we knew what we had to do. It was our duty to Felicia to explore all possible options for the sake of our evolution. We kept you with us for a couple of years, to spend time with our only daughter, but then we sent you out with a Guardian to be initiated into the human world, to be brought back the day you turned 17. It would be a long process, and of course we would face many challenges, but it seemed the only true way to explore all of our options. We knew the people of Felicia may feel differently, which is why only a select few have been trusted with the information. You could tell us your findings about the humans, tell us everything you've ever learnt, all of your experiences, and in turn we would teach you about your true self. That way, everybody gets what they want, and you my dear, could have forged the future for all of Felicia.'

Within her speech, Darya had risen from her chair, holding her hands up as she looked proudly down on Elara. Her eyes bright with inspiration and passion.

Elara felt no such way. Anger bubbled deep in her chest. Her throat ached with contempt as she dug her fingernails deep into the palms of her hands, not even wincing as she drew blood.

In front of her, Darya and Dritan clearly sensed her change in demeanour, and Dritan stood too, positioning himself slightly in front of his wife. She dropped her hands as he raised his defensively.

'Now, Elara, I can tell you're upset, but you must understand, we made this hugely difficult decision for the future of Felicia! It was our duty... yours too!'

Elara stood up slowly and took a step back away from her 'parents.' Her blood felt as though it was boiling beneath the surface of her skin as she tensed and untensed her jaw. Osmond immediately rushed to her side, placing a cool hand on her forearm. His face searched hers, imploring her to sit back down, hear out the traitors, but Elara was already too angry.

'Oh, I see. It was so difficult for you, was it? Whilst you sat in your cushty little house, after giving up your only daughter, in order to use her as a pawn in some kind of social experiment, when your only job as parents is to love and care for a child. Clearly you have a very funny way of showing love, as instead of raising me you sent me to a foreign world to be cared for by strangers before I could even understand why I had to go through the trauma of abandonment. What the hell is wrong with you people? Do you know how many years I spent feeling unwanted? Like I wasn't good enough? I was just a tiny baby, not part of your ridiculous experiment! Did you even think of all the things that could've gone wrong? Or how I might have felt about it? Did you stop and think for a second about anyone other than YOURSELVES?'

Elara hadn't even realised she was shouting until she stopped, and her throat ached with the effort. As she looked around, she realised every single lantern and candle had been blown out, and now little tendrils of smoke were weaving through the sunlight, each book had been thrown from the shelves and their open pages ruffled in a slight breeze.

Elara's chest heaved with painful breaths as Darya and Dritan stared at her in complete horror. As she glanced over at Osmond, she was surprised to see him looking somewhat proud, though he was doing a good job of hiding the expression.

Suddenly a quiet knock on the door startled everyone in the room.

'Come in!' called Darya, her voice a little shaky and her face still flushed.

A girl who looked similar to Elara's age popped around from behind the door. Her hair was raven black and cut choppily down to her shoulders. Her face was strong and angular, she looked a scary but incredibly beautiful. Her eyes were kind, a soft violet that looked familiar. Elara couldn't place why, but as she turned to Osmond for an explanation, those same eyes shone proudly back at the girl.

'Ah, Ivara. Yes, thank you for joining us on such short notice. Please come in,' Darya gushed, she fanned her hand in front of her face for a second, before regaining composure, and sitting back down on the sofa, arranging her dress artfully around her.

'Just Ivy is fine, Mrs Headley.'

Ivy looked embarrassed to have entered at what clearly wasn't a good time, however, she bowed her head graciously, and stepped out from behind the door. She was wearing a similar outfit to Osmond. A black jumpsuit hugged her wiry frame, though she was slim, Elara could see strong muscles in her shoulders and legs. They added to the scary factor, just a little. The jumpsuit was short sleeved and scattered across her forearms were lots of little patchwork tattoos. Elara glimpsed a small black cat, drawn to seemingly be chasing a ball of wool. She smiled at it for a second when suddenly it turned to look at her. Elara blinked a couple of times to make sure she was seeing right, and as she did, it turned back to its wool and began pawing at it.

Ivy smirked at her confusion. 'It's enchanted. It's like they're living little lives of their own on my skin,' she explained, twisting her arm to look at some of the other drawings, 'what, you've never seen an Enchanter's work before?' she asked, sounding surprised.

'Ivy, this is Elara Anderson; she was brought up in the human world,' Osmond butted in, smiling purposefully at his daughter.

'Stakes alight, of course! I'm so sorry, Elara. It's lovely to meet you. I've heard so much about you, just never a face to put to the name,' Ivy corrected herself, standing a little taller and offering an outstretched hand, which Elara shook gladly. Ivy had the same soft Scottish accent as Xander. The reminder of reality almost brought Elara to tears as her heart suddenly ached for home.

'So, Ivara, I'm sure someone in the Council has informed you of your duty for the next few hours. Show Elara around a little, I'm sure she has plenty of questions. Don't go introducing her to too many people, if you would, there's a time and a place for this to come out, and it's certainly not today. Keep her within the Northern Quarter please.'

Ivy nodded dutifully, lowering her eyes down to the floor as Darya spoke.

'I'm sure we could all do with a break, maybe get her something to eat, Ivy,' Osmond joined in, smiling at both girls sincerely.

'Indeed. Off you go you two, Mr Levett, please stay here. There is much to discuss.'

Dark undertones coloured Dritan's words and for a second Elara hesitated, reluctant to leave the Guardian who seemed to genuinely care for her. But Darya gave Ivy a stern look, and instantly Ivy took Elara's hand, and pulled her back into the corridor.

'So,' Ivy started, turning to face an overwhelmed looking Elara, 'where do you wanna start first? The refec might be a good idea, you look like you could use a coffee or something,' she said with a kind smile.

'Refec?' Elara had never heard the term before, maybe it was like Starbucks if it served coffee.

'Like refectory? It's a cafeteria where they serve food. Wow human life must be weird if you don't even know what that is.' Ivy laughed easily; it was a warm laugh that brought a smile to Elara's face.

'Oh, I get it. Yeah, honestly coffee would be great.'

The refectory was the complete opposite to any other part of the building Elara had seen. Where the corridors were dark and lit by candles, this room was huge and bright white. The floor to ceiling windows let warm sunlight flood through and pool onto the marble floors. Plants and greenery littered the walls, the whole room smelled fresh like a forest after rain. It wasn't busy in here either. Elara had expected hordes of prying eyes, or fellow witches draped in long cloaks whispering spells and enchantments as she passed, maybe trying to read her mind or stop her heart, something weird anyway. Instead, there were just a few people dotted around on quiet tables, scarcely even looking up as Elara sat down, and Ivy headed towards an elderly looking woman at the drinks table, in search of two strong, steaming hot coffees.

Elara must have been lost in thought, as when Ivy placed the coffee down on the table, Elara jumped, almost knocking the full cup straight back over.

'Well, somebody's got a guilty conscience,' Ivy joked, raising a perfectly arched eyebrow.

'Is that your gift? You can tell that?' Elara asked in a worried whisper.

Ivy laughed, sitting down opposite Elara, and cradling the polystyrene cup in her hands.

'No, I wish! People are just often jumpier when something's making them feel anxious. So go on, what is it?'

Something about the look on Ivy's face encouraged Elara to spill all her worldly secrets. She took a sip of the coffee and rested her chin on her hand, suddenly exhausted.

'I literally just met my birth parents for the first time in my life, after assuming they were like, dead or something for the last 15 years, and I screamed in their faces.'

Elara sighed, a frown pulling at her face.

'Plus, it's my birthday and I abandoned my adoptive parents' party because I got gassed with a yellow mist that smelled really good, and they're probably super worried and Xander's going to be so upset because he doesn't know where I am, and no one will even let me call them. And my grandparents were there, I've really missed them,' Elara rambled as a tear trickled down her cheek. All the confusion, guilt, and new-found abandonment was a little too much to take, especially on her birthday.

'Hey, hey! Don't cry, it's okay,' Ivy soothed, reaching out to cover Elara's jittery hands with her own. 'Obviously I can't even begin to understand what you're going through; this all must be so overwhelming for you. However, I can maybe take one thing off your mind. In school they taught us a little about Earth, and one thing that always stuck with me, is that time passes differently there. The days in Felicia are longer, time isn't really a solid construct. So even if you've been here for what feels like an hour, in the human world, you may have only been gone a few minutes. Easy to explain away.'

Elara felt a little of the weight drop off her shoulders. They were still heavy, but it was bearable.

She roughly tugged the back of her hand across her cheeks, drying her tears as she took another sip of the coffee. She now realised it smelled strongly of some sort of plant, and she eyed the dark liquid carefully.

'Are you trying to drug me or something?' Elara asked, looking up at a bemused Ivy.

'It's rosemary, makes the coffee less bitter. Plus, it has calming properties. You really think I would drug you on your first day here? That's at least a third or fourth day type of thing,' she said with a twinkle in her eye that reminded Elara of Osmond.

'Anyway, come on you must have tons of questions about this place. What do you want to know?'

Elara pondered on the question for a moment. There was so much she didn't know that it was difficult finding a place to start, or even a simple question to lead with.

'Do you have a wand?' she asked limply, feeling a little silly that those words had even come out of her mouth.

Ivy looked at her with a peculiar look on her face.

'Of course, everybody over the age of 15 has one. I'm guessing by that question that you don't?'

Elara shook her head, wondering whether that was something to be embarrassed about.

'Don't worry, I'm sure you'll get assigned one soon. They usually do it as a ceremony for each age group, a Reader will judge your magic stream, aura, and essence and assign you a wand accordingly. Each unique wand will access types of magic differently, allowing you to be more successful in spells related to your gifts. It becomes like an extension of your body, as it has a similar magical make-up to you. I'm guessing since your age category already has wands, they'll do yours privately.'

Ivy looked deep in thought for a moment before Elara interrupted.

'Aura and essence? I can't even act like I know what they are.' Ivy's eyes widened in shock.

'Dear Erinyes, you truly don't know anything about witches and magic?' she gasped. Elara shook her head once more.

'Wow, there's a lot for you to catch up on then. Good job you've got me,' Ivy laughed, crossing her legs on the wooden bench, and resting her elbows on the table.

'Now, where to start.'

Elara and Ivy talked easily for what seemed like hours, but the sun's position in the sky had hardly changed, so she guessed not. Elara's brain was filling up rapidly with all the witchcraft basics that Ivy could think of, each one more obscure than the last. Every now and then, she needed to pinch her arm to remind herself that this was real, and she wasn't dreaming.

'So, you all go to school? Like normal kids?' Elara asked as she drained the last of her coffee.

'Of course! We learn the basics like English and maths, science is more focused towards plants and animals, and history only includes witch history, but other than that, we go to school just like you do. We can also take a module elective to learn about Human Studies, but then we have Saturday school to learn specifically about our own stream and meet others with similar gifts,' Ivy smiled.

Elara could tell she was enjoying telling her stories and culture to an outsider.

'Okay, so which gift is the rarest and which is the most common?' Elara asked, leaning forward on her elbows, interested in where the conversation would go next.

Ivy raised her eyebrows, tilting her head as she suddenly looked deep in thought. 'Well, you see that's a complicated question. There are the four main streams of magic, of course they subdivide into specific categories, but essentially everyone in Felicia falls under Practical Magic, Alchemy, Inchoate Magic, or Ardent Magic. That's the most to least common order too, to answer your question. There are sectors of each stream that are more uncommon, but formally, you would be classed as part of that group.'

Elara started chewing on her nail, willing her brain to keep up with the overload of information.

'For example, my family all possess Inchoate magic, my mother and I are what we call 'Origins' as we can manipulate the elements, my dad is a Trixter who can manipulate electricity, and my brother is what they call a 'Fender'. He's incredible at defensive spells and works to protect Felicia. He was the top of his class in school,' Ivy said proudly, losing her focus for a second.

'Anyway,' she continued, shaking her head to make her hair fall messily around her shoulders, 'Origins, like me, are the most uncommon within the Inchoate magic stream, but it's still Inchoate magic, if you get me,' she said with a grin as Elara raked her hands through her hair, pulling on the tips a little in despair. How was she ever going to keep up with all of this?

'What about the other witches in here? Can any of them read my mind?' Elara asked worriedly, pulling her jacket tighter around her shoulders.

Ivy chuckled and shook her head, letting her jet black hair fall to frame her face.

'No of course not! Out of anyone in here, you'd be best equipped to do that,' Elara's face dropped, 'maybe after some training,' Ivy added hurriedly.

'During the day it's mostly Broomies and Greenies in here on their breaks. They're Practical witches who do the mundane jobs around the Council. Broomie witches do the cleaning because they're good at enchanting the supplies, and Greenies do the cooking and stuff like that because of their hyper-sensitivity to ingredients.'

'So, my birth parents, they're Ardent witches?' Elara asked, a little proud that she'd finally thought of a question that sounded somewhat like she understood all this craziness.

'Yes, they're Shifters. Don't call them that though, they're a little traditional and I'm not sure they'd like it,' Ivy whispered with a mischievous grin.

'You call them Shifters because they can manipulate people's emotions?'

'Exactly! See, you catch on quick.'

'So, everyone falls under those four categories, there's no exceptions?'

Ivy looked shifty for a second. 'Well, there is one other type of witch, though I probably shouldn't be telling you about them.'

Elara's intrigue spiked, internally she begged Ivy to cave and tell her.

'No one really talks about them you see, they're incredibly rare. If ever one appeared in society, they'd immediately be Heir to the Throne of Felicia, as it means they're a direct descendant of the Original Witches. That also makes them the most powerful warlock alive, but they can be deadly. There's only been a few confirmed in the history of Felicia, and they had to be exiled for using what we call 'Shade Magic', the dark enchantments and spells that are used for power and destruction.'

Elara was itching to know more, but the second it seemed as though Ivy was about to tell her, her eyes suddenly flitted up to look over Elara's shoulder, where Osmond had appeared, giving his daughter a stern look.

'Come, Miss Anderson. Your meeting is now, Mr and Mrs Headley expect you to join them.'

Elara met Ivy's eyes; Ivy looked almost sad that their conversation had ended.

'Miss,' Osmond said sharply. He looked anxious, his gaze darting rapidly over to the open doors, as he finally grabbed Elara's arm, pulling her away from the table and back to the oppressive corridor.

'Ow. Osmond, Jesus Christ. Can you calm down? I can walk alone!'

Osmond immediately dropped her arm, as though it were burning hot.

'I'm sorry, Miss Anderson. But we really must hurry.'

'Elara is fine, no 'Miss Anderson' stuff, I'm not a teacher.'

Osmond slowed long enough to turn and smile at her, his face finally relaxing a little. 'Of course, Elara.'

The large room seemed to appear as if from thin air in a strangely familiar fashion. Rows of seats towered up from the floor, and a large podium stood proudly beneath a glistening chandelier in the centre of the room. The plush seats were filling up noisily as Osmond ushered Elara into the room, she gazed around in wonder as a dozen pairs of eyes turned to stare back at her. An uneasy feeling settled promptly in her chest as Osmond guided her towards the podium with a steady hand on her shoulder. Darya and Dritan were already stood on the raised platform, they waited for Elara to join them proudly with an air of distinguished class. Despite Elara's previous outburst, her birthparents greeted her with warm smiles, Darya planting a kiss on each of Elara's cheeks as she neared. Dritan gestured towards a large leather seat, he watched carefully as Elara walked over to it, then waited until she had sat comfortably before taking his own seat. It was a strange interaction, Elara thought to herself, before noticing that Osmond was stood awkwardly off to the side of the platform. Shifting from foot to foot.

'Oh, Osmond, you wanna sit down?' Elara asked, standing up from her seat and stepping out of the way so that he could take her place.

The crowd gasped audibly as Osmond's face immediately reddened and Darya shot Elara a stern glance.

'No, no Miss Anderson. I'm happy to stand, though thank you for your human manners,' Osmond murmured quietly.

Elara sensed that he had tactfully diverted her from a disgrace, though she couldn't figure out quite what she had done that had been so terrible. Regardless, she silently sat down and forced a smile back onto her face.

Suddenly, dark doors at the back of the room swung open, and in walked a very tall man. He was swathed in ruby coloured robes that swept the floor as he walked. He wore black boots with a little heel that clicked on the polished floor, and satin gloves that rippled in the light and disappeared beneath his billowing sleeves. He had long dark hair that was greying at the roots, twisted back into an intricate plait that trailed almost down to the ground, Elara wondered briefly if they were extensions and had to hold back a giggle at how ridiculous the thought seemed in the circumstances. She suddenly realised that everyone in the room had stood in the man's presence, holding their hands reverently behind their backs.

'Stand,' growled Osmond as Elara quickly scrambled to her feet, her chair scraping loudly in the silence. She winced at the glare this erected from Darya.

Behind the man, a line of men and women marched in unison, each wearing what looked like an army uniform, proudly carrying silver swords and spears. A yell from someone walking at the back of the line suddenly brought the group to a halt, and in a clearly practised motion, they formed a semi-circle around the man, switching their weapons over to their left hands and chanting something in a foreign language. Elara watched the whole display in awe, yet no one else in the room seemed to share her excitement for the impressive demonstration.

The man began making his way toward the podium. He nodded his head slightly at both Darya and Dritan who returned the gesture, and his eyes briefly hovered over Osmond before moving straight to Elara. He stopped in his tracks, staring intensely at her as she shifted uncomfortably, hoping the smile on her face looked sincere.

His gaze was weighted as he looked Elara up and down. Taking in her hair, face, and clothes in a prying way, judging her solely on her appearance.

He ascended the steps to the podium, holding out a gloved hand to Elara. She took it reluctantly, and to her surprise, he dropped before her into a deep bow, planting a kiss on her knuckles. As he stood slowly, he reached out to touch her face, his fingertips barely scraping her cheek before he thought better of it and dropped his hand back to his side.

Darya and Dritan were gazing proudly, Darya's hands clasped at her chest as Dritan's eyes began to glisten with unshed tears.

Elara ignored them and instead looked to Osmond for reassurance, but he looked as uncertain as she felt.

'May I pronounce, Elara Hazel Anderson,' the man boomed, turning swiftly to face the watching audience. 'The witch who has provided Felicia with unimaginable knowledge, service and sacrifice, in the form of her life. Today we commend her, and welcome her back into our loving community, on this her 17th birthday.' He turned back to Elara, taking her hand once more and holding it close to his chest. 'Elara, we are forever indebted to you and hope we may in some way return the favour, by reuniting you with your family,' her birthparents beamed out at the crowd, 'by supporting you in your life and education to allow you to grow into the witch we always knew you would be, and by using your first-hand knowledge to develop, educate and evolve our community.'

Immediately the crowd erupted into cheers, as the man held his and Elara's linked hands high in the air, his face glowing with excitement.

Elara began to pull her hand away from the man, overwhelmed by the wall of noise that echoed around the room, but that only made him hang on tighter, as suddenly tendrils of water began to weave through the feet of the small army he had brought with him. The crowd cheered louder and louder as the water began to shoot up into the vast space of the room, the jets exploding before they hit the ceiling and bursting into fireworks that rained down into the air, boiling off into mist before anyone could feel a drip.

The tendrils of water were rushing down the walls now, shimmering blue puddles pooling like a lake around the podium.

In a dramatic crescendo, the water shot up from the ground, forming a jagged wall between the audience and the platform. All Elara could focus on was their cries of joy and the cool spray fanning out into the air. Her birthparents watched with straight faces, but it was clear they were equally as impressed or as terrified as the rest of the room, just much better at hiding it.

The water vanished as quickly as it had appeared, the man held a proud look on his face. Elara found herself scanning the room, looking for drops of water on the floor, or stains running down the walls, but it was as though nothing had ever happened as everyone settled quietly back into their seats.

'Well, Elara, now that my dramatics are out of the way,' the man smiled, settling into an elaborately designed wooden chair, 'I do believe we should get to know one another better. Of course, many of my consorts feel they know you well, having watched you since you were an infant. However, I would like to know more than just the logistics. But first, my name is Forneus, and my position within the Magicis Concilio is to lead Felicia. I was chosen as a skilled Inchoate Warlock to rule over the land, of course with the help of the rest of the council. I have ruled for almost two decades now, in fact, one of my first accomplishments as Ruler, was deciding to go ahead with this experiment. It had been my father's dream before mine, so for him I made it happen.'

Forneus looked deep in thought for a second as the room appeared to collectively sigh, seemingly remembering a fallen hero from times gone by, as Elara shifted in her seat, trying to focus on the story.

'I feel very close to you Elara. Our journeys started almost in accordance with one another, both sacrificing our personal lives to serve Felicia. I suspect we have a lot in common, we'll get on well,' he said with a twinkle in his eye.

Elara felt a flicker of what should have been anger in her chest. She didn't sacrifice her personal life for Felicia, she hardly even knew what Felicia was, let alone what she had done for it. She led a happy life, filled with family and love, plus she was still thinking back to something he'd said previously, 'my consorts feel they know you well, having watched you since you were an infant'. Ordinarily, this statement alone would have sent Elara into a state of fury, the thought of strangers watching her every move without her even knowing felt like a disgusting violation of her privacy, yet her brain felt a little fuzzy, as though she couldn't quite muster up the energy to be angry, or even focus on what Forneus was saying at all.

Elara briefly wondered if the rosemary coffee from earlier was having some sort of adverse effect on her. As the thought flitted through her mind, Dritan reached out and covered Elara's hand with his own. Elara realised that Forneus was still speaking, Darya, Dritan, Osmond and the rest of the audience nodding along empathetically, smiling sadly down on Elara.

She suddenly felt a rush of clarity down her spine, like a stream of cold water chilling her core. The feeling stretched along her arm and out into her hand, the one being held by her birthfather. The feeling was uncomfortable; edgy and raw. Elara lowered her head, hoping her peers would mistake it for tiredness and looked up at Dritan through lowered eyelids. Although he was nodding along to Forneus's dull speech along with the rest of the congregation, he had a vacant look in his eyes, seemingly focussed on something in the back of his mind. Glancing over, Elara noticed Darya looked similarly dazed and the tip of her wand was just barely poking out under one of her voluminous sleeves.

Elara felt an unfamiliar prickle working its way down her neck, clawing at her throat. She tugged at the feeling and envisioned throwing it away, rolling it into a tight, spiky little ball and letting it barrel through the air and out of the building. The second she did, Dritan snapped away his hand, a surprised look on his face as Darya also came clattering back down to Earth, her head recoiling to the side slightly as she turned to face Elara, her jaw set into a harsh line and her eyes turned to disgust. Elara smiled innocently, hoping her sweetness would mask the fact that now her feelings were crystal clear, and she was angrier than ever.

CHAPTER NINE

Elara

As soon as the so-called 'meeting' had finished, Osmond escorted Elara quickly off the stage to a round of applause and out into the corridor, shutting the door firmly behind them. He was looking at her with a wary expression, standing with his hands held out slightly in front of him, as though he were surrendering.

'I can tell you're angry. Please understand, this was never anything personal Miss Anderson. You happened to be born at the right time, to the right set of parents. You were fulfilling your duty to Felicia.'

Osmond's voice was soothing, but not quite soothing enough.

'My duty?' Elara laughed, the laugh was too high-pitched, too raw and Osmond winced at the sound. 'I was a baby, Osmond. I didn't even know my left from right, yet the council decided it was fair to send me to a whole other world, to be raised by a random family! They could've been anyone! What if they had found out? Or if I'd accidentally cast a spell on them? You saw the damage I did at Natalia's house, that could have happened anywhere!' Elara hissed, her hands starting to tingle with anger.

'Please, Elara, keep your voice down! I understand how you're feeling, but you don't yet understand everything. Why this was necessary. There was a building amount of pressure within the Council and Felicia to do something… anything. Whether that be return to our rightful homeland and live in harmony with humans or declare that world dead to us and work on making Felicia sustainable. We made sure your family was safe as soon as they decided to adopt you, you never went a day unwatched.'

Elara rolled her eyes, 'don't even get me started on that, Osmond. Do you know what kind of violation that is of my privacy?'

'We always left you space in your life, you had privacy. But our job was to keep you safe, and if that meant watching you break your grandmother's antique, gold-plated bowl and blame it on your cousin? Then so be it,' he said firmly, folding his arms across his chest.

Elara had to stifle a giggle at the memory, it might be funny, but she was still so angry.

'You know what, Osmond? The council might have done what was best for Felicia. I might have provided you with invaluable information, but you stole my entire life from me. They say I'm a witch, yet I don't know a single spell, or anything about my ancestors. I don't even have a wand which this morning would have sounded stupid to say out loud, but I'm gathering that it's a big deal! I may have been raised in the human world, but I was born into this one. This is where I should've stayed.'

Elara felt her anger subsiding, but in its place was left a cold, hollow feeling of emptiness. A mourning for the life she should've had and the person she could've been. The corridor seemed to darken in her sadness, and the air cooled casting a chill down her spine. Elara could see the hurt she felt mirrored in Osmond's eyes, he was clearly trying to think of what to say next as the door behind them opened.

Out stepped a young man dressed in the dark uniform of those in the demonstration. His hair was wavy and jet black, but his eyes were a startling midnight blue that glittered in the candlelight. He was very tall, maybe even a little taller than Xander as Elara had to tilt her head to look up at him. The heavy black jacket from his uniform was gone now, exposing sleeves of tattoos running up and down his arms. Elara watched as some of them moved, as Ivy's had, but where hers had been sweet black cats and bubbling potions, his were dark stormy skies that wept inky rain onto his skin and bows and arrows that fired angrily across his forearms. Elara blushed as he noticed her staring, she smiled at him hoping to appear less creepy, but he continued to glare, his eyes ice cold as Elara's smile faded.

'Forneus would like Miss Headley returned to her home as promptly as possible. He fears she has been away for too long. He recommends the use of the Vail Elixir on the family; they are suspicious, and he would like them to remain as docile as possible,' the man said sternly, he turned to face Osmond, but kept a watchful eye trained to Elara.

'An elixir? What are you going to do to them?' she asked worriedly.

'Stakes alight,' the man murmured under his breath, looking tired of the conversation already.

Osmond shot a cold look at him before turning to Elara with a warm smile. 'Don't worry, Miss. It causes them no harm; we've been using the same elixir on them for years. Whenever they started to get suspicious about something, or we needed to take you away for a while to check you over and assess your memory, we used the elixir on them. It simply calms them, makes them less aware of their surroundings, and blurs their memory a little of the last few hours. It's similar to one we used on you earlier to bring you here. Less effective on you mind, especially as you've gotten older.'

Elara's mind reeled at his words. The thought of her parents being subject to witchy potions for the last 15 years made her uncomfortable. They truly didn't know what they were signing up for when they adopted her.

'Alright that's enough of the fairy-tales. Come on Miss Headley, we should go,' the man said, clasping Elara's arm tightly and beginning to drag her away.

'Son, she can walk alone. You don't need to be so rough with her, she'll come happily,' Osmond said shortly, 'and she prefers Miss Anderson, that is the name she was raised with after all.'

Elara smiled at Osmond, she felt warm inside at his obvious attempt to respect her.

The man dropped her arm, his gaze never leaving hers. 'Of course, Miss Anderson, I apologise for the confusion.' His voice sounded mocking as he emphasised her name. Elara clenched her jaw and stared back up at him, hoping her confidence masked her fear.

As he turned and began to march away, Osmond followed a few steps behind, 'I apologise for my son, Archer; he takes his job very seriously and sometimes it marks on his manners. He doesn't intend on being rude.'

'He's your son?' The surprise was evident in Elara's voice. 'Ivy's brother?'

Osmond nodded, 'and whilst you're in Felicia, your primary Fender. You've become quite the family project,' Osmond joked before suddenly his face fell.

'Not that you're a project, Miss Anderson, or something that needs fixing. No! not something- someone,' Osmond stammered, his cheeks turning an alarming shade of red before he saw the look on Elara's face as she started laughing. It was nice for someone to talk to her as a normal human being, and not some kind of charity case or hero. His shoulders dropped in relief as he began to chuckle too. She liked seeing him smile, he usually looked so anxious.

Walking out of the Council's gates felt surreal. Although she'd been able to see bright sunlight and fields of green grass through the windows of the refectory, part of her had expected a hellish world of lava and cackling green witches, full of demons and monsters and dark stormy skies. But the Felicia that unfolded before her was breathtakingly beautiful. Behind her, the soaring stone buildings of the Magicis Concilio rose high into the clouds, the tips of the towers barely visible from the ground. Heather grey stones were dusted with streams of ivy that clawed at windows and balconies. Witches of all ages buzzed around, chatting, and laughing in groups, reading under trees, watering plants and above all, barely sparing Elara a glance. It seemed eerily ordinary, which was the last thing she was expecting.

'The four towers are the four quarters of the Council: North, South, East and West. Each has its own cafeteria, medical wing, common areas, and of course space for the workers to live. In the centre of the whole building is a small school, and the room we were in today,' Osmond said proudly, pointing to each section with his wand.

Elara gazed up at the building in wonder, trying to ignore Osmond's son tapping his foot impatiently on the gravel path.

'So, all of the witches in Felicia live here?' she asked, turning to face Osmond.

'Stakes alight no! The only witches that live here are Ardent witches, and some Inchoate families, like us,' he said, smiling proudly at his son. 'Ardent witches are required by law to live within the Council, so that their gifts can be monitored and put to good use. Inchoate witches however are welcome to live here if they have a job within the Council, or if their families are here. Altogether, there's around a two hundred people who currently live behind these walls. Though there's room for many more.'

'So how many witches are there altogether, that just live in Felicia?' Elara asked, beginning to follow Osmond down the path.

'I'd say, close to ten thousand?' Archer nodded in agreement from a few strides ahead.

'Ten thousand witches? In Felicia?' Elara gasped; she had expected a few hundred at most. 'Where do the rest of them live?'

Osmond smiled as they reached a turn in the path. 'Right here.'

The path overlooked a huge valley that was like the one Xander had brought her to all those months before. Surrounded by mountains and forests was what looked like a city centre. A thin river ran directly through the middle of it all, and on its banks were buildings, shops, houses, and people. So many people. It didn't look like the crazy underworld in Elara's imagination, nor did it look like Scotland or London for that matter. It was its very own version of picturesque. A busy little paradise nestled amongst the mountains.

'Wow,' Elara breathed, gazing down at the city. 'It's incredible. Can we go down and look?'

A flash of sadness skimmed across Osmond's eyes for a second, before it was replaced with hopeful optimism.

'Maybe another time, we need to get you back now. The elixir isn't strong enough to account for this amount of time, we'll have to come up with something to explain anyway and we don't want your family and friends getting worried. Come now. There's plenty of time for you to explore your home.'

He smiled sincerely, placing a hand on Elara's shoulder, and guiding her away from the city. She watched it get smaller and craned her neck until it faded out of view.

As they arrived at a derelict looking stone building, there was a small semicircle of people waiting to greet them, all dressed in the same uniform as Osmond. They looked at Elara expectantly.

'Elara, these are a few of Forneus's consorts. Each person here has spent many years watching you grow and keeping you safe.' He smiled proudly as they shifted around awkwardly, bowing their heads a little in her presence.

'Oh, well erm, thank you. I appreciate it,' Elara said uncertainly, hoping her smile made up for how displeased she sounded.

'Archer will escort you back home Elara, I'm sure he's thought of some kind of story to tell your parents.'

Osmond pushed her towards the door of the building, and it swung open silently.

'Aren't you coming too?' Elara glanced back at the crowd of uniformed guards, where Osmond had always been very striking before, he now blended in perfectly with the group and it took her a second to find him.

'I'm afraid not Miss, there is much I have to attend to here. You'll be perfectly safe with Archer; he was the top Fender in his class you know,' he cooed, a distant look in his eyes as Archer appeared from the dark room looking smug. Elara rolled her eyes.

'So I've heard,' she replied, stepping over the threshold and through the door.

As her eyes readjusted to the dark room, she looked around for Archer who was suddenly nowhere to be seen.

'Hey, Archer? How are we getting back?' she asked nervously as suddenly with a loud bang, a huge wooden door began to creak open on its rusty hinges. Elara jumped at the sound, almost tripping back into the wall behind her. Archer caught her wrist just before she could hit the concrete.

'Someone scares easy,' he smirked, raising an eyebrow, 'we're just using the back door. It's a little old.'

Elara cleared her throat and dusted off her jacket. 'Yeah, well you'd think in a land of witches and warlocks they'd know how to use a little oil,' she mumbled under her breath

as she ducked under Archer's arm and back out into the forest. Archer let out a short laugh.
'You would think.'

The walk back to her house was quiet. Archer didn't speak much but he appeared to be taking everything in. At some point he had changed out of his army uniform and was now wearing a surprisingly normal outfit, jeans and a hoody.
Elara cleared her throat awkwardly and Archer turned to face her with an expectant look on his face.
'So, um, have you ever been in the human world before?' she asked, hoping this was a normal question to ask.
Archer looked bemused.
'Well seeing as you were assigned as one of my Protectants, and you live in the human world, yes, I've been a few times. My dad obviously was your main Guardian, but if ever he couldn't be here, I was assigned instead.'
Elara nodded thoughtfully.
'How often was Osmond here? Looking after me I mean.'
Archer frowned for a moment, pushing the sleeves of his hoody up for a second before remembering his tattoos and thinking better of it.
'Day in, day out. Every day since the moment you were adopted. The council tried to persuade him to take less shifts, let some of the other Guardians step up more, but he wouldn't let them. I don't think he really trusted anyone else with your safety. Of course, there was always another person around with him, but they rotated more. My father, he was always here.'
Elara felt the undertones of jealousy and sadness in Archer's words. It burnt at the back of her brain.
'So, he wasn't around as much for you then, you resent him a little for that?' she asked, looking up at Archer as surprise registered on his face.

'There's no need for us to speak, you know. We're not friends, I am simply doing my job,' he hissed harshly, before stopping for a second, 'wait, what's your gift again?'

Elara shrugged, a laugh bubbling in her chest, 'no one seems to have figured it out yet.'

Archer looked irritated for a second. 'Well, it would seem very clear to me that you're an Ardent witch. Maybe not the same stream as your parents, but certainly Ardent. Why would there be any confusion about that?'

He'd stopped walking now and was watching Elara suspiciously. She felt her cheeks colour as she came to a stop a few steps behind him.

'I flooded a house and blew an entire neighbourhoods electricity supply when I was angry,' she said quietly as what she recognised as fear instilled itself in Archer's chest.

'Hemlock's Curse. I feel like you shouldn't have told me that,' he whispered, his brow creasing, 'You certainly shouldn't tell anyone else either. I presume my father cleared up the mess for you?' Elara nodded silently. 'You must keep this quiet, Miss Anderson. Don't mention what you did to another soul.'

'What does it mean, I don't understand, do I have two gifts? Or is my gift just different to everyone else's?'

Archer had started walking again and it was difficult to keep up with his long strides.

'Please explain, I'm just confused.'

Archer stopped sharply in his tracks and Elara almost ran straight into his back.

'You wouldn't understand, Miss Anderson, so I won't waste my time explaining. If you could just refrain from causing a scene in the future, it would be greatly appreciated. Right now I just need to get you home, so that I can return to Felicia and speak with my father.'

He turned on his heel and began striding ahead, leaving Elara in his wake.

'You've been gone for ages, sweetheart! Was your surprise nice though?' Rose asked the second Elara walked through the door with Archer in tow.

She glanced at the clock, she'd been gone almost three hours and her heart sank a little. She tried to mask the look on her face as Archer immediately stepped forward, holding out a hand to Rose.

'I'm so sorry to have kept her for so long Mrs Anderson. My house is across town, and we'd blown up balloons and stuff for her. Banners and all, right Elara?' His eyes glistened, from the look on his face, Elara could tell she had no choice but to go along with his intricate lies.

She nodded absently with a forced smile. Jenna and Matt were gazing up at Archer, drool practically dripping from their chins as a peculiar look settled on Xander's face.

'Show us the present then! We've been waiting to see it,' Rose gushed, holding her palm out expectantly.

A trickle of sweat dripped down Elara's back. It was clear someone had fed them all a story along with the elixir, she just wished she'd been given the props to bring it to life.

As if sensing her sudden anxiety, Archer slipped a small wooden box to Elara, so swiftly she almost dropped it. An intricate 'E' was carved into the centre of the lid, vines trailed around the edges of the letter. She stared at it for a moment, tracing her fingertips over the ornate engravement before she noticed everyone crowding round to see what was inside, looking as intently as her. She opened the lid, and the inside of the box was lined with plush burgundy fabric with a foreign inscription in gold calligraphy. Sitting delicately on top of the cushion was a silver chain connected to a tiny locket with a planet etched into the centre. Jupiter.

'Oh of course,' her mother breathed, dramatically placing a hand on her chest, 'Elara is one of the moons of Jupiter, oh Archer. It's simply beautiful.'

Elara could see the glisten of unshed tears in her eyes, her dad looked equally moved.

Xander suddenly cleared his throat loudly, startling the group, and Elara noticed he was looking unusually uncomfortable.

'Hey, man it's nice to meet you. I'm Xander,' he said shortly, as he stepped forward out of the group.

Archer smiled easily and shook his outstretched hand. 'Of course, Elara has told me all about you, it's great to finally meet you, Xander.'

Elara struggled to fight back a giggle. A couple of hours ago she'd never even met this guy, yet here he was in her living room shaking hands with her boyfriend, who apparently, he knew all about.

'So, you two were in the same adoption agency, right?' Jenna piped up, still not taking her eyes off Archer, 'how did you figure that one out?'

Her family looked at her expectantly.

'Erm, well... I–'

'My family own the bookstore on the edge of town, I was there helping my mum when Elara came in for a textbook that had been left by the college for her, and when she gave her name for collection my dad came running in from the back. He'd loved Elara as a baby. When they were in the process of adopting me, sometimes they would bring her gifts or she'd join us for day trips, they were so sad to leave her behind, but they knew the perfect family was just out there waiting.'

He threw a winning smile at Rose who sighed audibly.

He had completely captured everyone in the room's attention. They were all gazing at him like he was some sort of storytelling God as Elara rolled her eyes.

'You must truly have a special bond then,' Rose butted in, still stroking the wooden jewellery box, 'to remember one another from so long ago and with having such a similar start in life. And I must meet your family, Archer. To thank them for caring so much about our daughter,' she sighed happily, reaching behind her for her husband's hand.

'Hmm,' Elara nodded in agreement, 'anyway, whilst this has been delightful, Archer, I should see you out,' she said pointedly, tugging on his sleeve to drag him away from her adoring family.

'Please, do come again Archer. You're welcome anytime,' Pete chimed in from behind his wife, waving enthusiastically.

Elara shut the front door quickly behind them, ushering her bemused Guardian out onto the drive.

'Exactly what story did you tell them? How did they already know your name? How were we gone for three whole hours, I thought time passed differently in Felicia?'

Archer stood silently, watching as Elara collapsed down on the front step of her house, and raked her hands through her hair in exhaustion and for just a moment, he felt sorry for her. It must be a lot to take in. The momentary lapse in his cool façade was gone in an instant however, and he laughed, turning to walk back down the drive.

'I'm sure it was my sister who told you about time passing differently. She's always had a particular interest in that, yet her memory is a little twisted. Time passes the same, but in Felicia the sun moves differently. It rises in the morning, as yours does, then stays at midday until nightfall. Moving only as you look at it from opposing angles. The witches who created Felicia were fiercely talented, but not quite enough to control every movement of their forged sun. I do apologise for the time you lost here, however. We will try not to keep you for so long in the future, I could tell your boyfriend wasn't too convinced and that's the last thing we need. The rest of your answers on the other hand, are for me to know, and you to not find out. I doubt you'd have the right level of clearance anyway,' he said with a snide glint in his eye.

'And the necklace?' Elara asked, exhausted with Archer's quips.

'A gift from your parents I presume. Or perhaps sent by Forneus to sweeten you up. I must remind them that it is not in my job description to be a delivery boy,' he pondered thoughtfully, 'anyway, I should go. I've spent far too much time here for my liking,' he said, slight disgust colouring his tone.

Elara nodded silently, standing up from the step to turn back inside.

'Why thank-you for dropping me off home safe, Archer. It is so greatly appreciated,' he mocked in a high voice. Elara glared at him.

'I can't tell if you're simply rude or vibrantly sarcastic,' she said with a sharp laugh.

He bowed his head, usually a mark of respect but Elara guessed otherwise.

'Then my job here is done.' He turned on his heel and walked away quickly into the night.

CHAPTER TEN

Elara

Jenna stayed the night at Elara's house. They'd been banished to the living room onto the sofa bed, so that her grandparents could take her parent's room. Curled up in a tiny ball, Jenna scarcely took up space enough for a mouse as Elara tossed and turned for the entire night, watching the window as the stars moved slowly across the frame. The peaceful indigo sky gave way to brighter tones, and Elara finally gave up with trying to sleep. The sheer number of agonising questions in her mind were way too much to handle.

She quietly crept up the stairs, wincing at every creek and groan the old house made, in search of a jacket. She stopped at the door to her parent's bedroom to watch her grandparents resting peacefully for a second. They were cuddled quietly together, and Elara smiled wistfully, she hadn't realised how much she'd missed them until they were back in her hectic life.

Elara was forced to bite back a scream as she closed her front door and turned to find Xander stood silently on her drive, looking as surprised as she felt.

'We really need to stop meeting like this Xander, I'm sure I age about ten years every time you spook me,' Elara joked, raking a hand through her hair.

Xander cracked a small smile, but remained standing silently, his hands in his pockets.

'What are you doing up so early anyway, and why are you lurking outside my house?'

Xander blinked at her for a second. She waited, before taking a breath to repeat the question.

'Xander? Did you hear –'

'Yeah, sorry. I was actually coming to see you. Last night all seemed to go by in a blur and I wanted to ask you about the rest of your birthday.'

'Tell me about it,' Elara mumbled under her breath as she slipped her arm through Xander's. He pulled a packet of half-eaten sour Skittles out of his pocket and offered a purple one to her. It was her favourite flavour, so she took it gratefully, sucking on the hard shell for a moment before asking, 'how did you know I'd be up this early?'

She shielded her eyes against the bright clouds to look up at him.

Xander shrugged. 'No idea, guess it was intuition,' he smiled, though he still looked a little unsure. Something was off about him today, though Elara couldn't quite put her finger on what.

'So that guy... Archie was it? He seems nice.' Xander cleared his throat.

Elara hid a smile, there it was.

'Archer? He has his quirks.'

'Well, he must like you a lot to get you such a thoughtful present.'

Elara frowned; she'd barely given the necklace a second thought since yesterday, but clearly it had been playing on Xander's mind.

'Oh that? It was mainly from his parents. Think they feel sorry for me or something, you know being adopted and all that. They must know what it's like seeing as Archer had a similar experience.'

Elara hoped she sounded nonchalant enough, though a hot, guilty stake burnt through her chest at how easily she'd just lied to Xander. They'd been together officially a day and already she was withholding the truth from him. Not the ideal start to a relationship, though nothing that had happened yesterday had been ideal.

'You know, I don't even remember you mentioning meeting him at all,' Xander said, coming to a stop just before the forest clearing. He turned to look at Elara, jealousy and anxiety weighing down heavily on his face and immediately her smile dropped.

'Everyone else knew who he was or had at least heard about him. He felt like he should seem familiar, but I couldn't put my finger on why.'

A crease appeared in his brow as he looked past Elara, not meeting her gaze.

'I'm sure I mentioned him at some point Xander, if I didn't, I'm sorry, it wasn't intentional, we've both just been so busy, you know?'

She reached out to stroke his arm, a painful pang making its way down her throat at yet another silky lie. In the back of her mind, a million questions were battering around, desperate to know why Xander was so unsure about Archer and why everyone else had welcomed him with open arms. Why hadn't the elixir worked properly on him?

Regardless, she moved her hand up to his face, stroking her thumb down his jaw and along the bow of his lips. He shivered slightly, relaxing into her touch as she reached up onto her tiptoes to kiss him. A soft, gentle kiss with the harmonious melodies of the forest behind them.
Immediately, she felt his worries melt away and sink into the ground. The soil welcomed them soundlessly, almost as though they were helping Elara to keep her secret for another day.

The week of half term seemed to fly by. Elara filled every waking moment to distract herself. She studied for hours on end with her mother, took her grandparents on walks around the village she now called home, and spent happy, lazy mornings with Xander. They sat for hours, chatting easily or simply enjoying one another's company. Yet throughout all the distractions, Elara felt like she was playing a part. Biding her time until someone came to whisk her away. She'd grown accustomed to seeing the darting shadows of her watchful Guardians wherever she went, though she could never tell if they were familiar or a stranger. Late at night, she snuck to the cliffside, hoping Osmond or Archer would appear with instructions on what to do next, but they never did.

As weeks of exams and Christmas preparations took up Elara's time, she began to convince herself that it had all been some crazy dream. Even the necklace sat proudly on her bedside table couldn't tether the events of her birthday to reality. Each night she stared at it, turning it back and forth again and again, willing Osmond to appear in her room as he had so many weeks before. She hadn't figured out the locket mechanism yet, though she had tried just about everything she could think of, the metal clasp wouldn't budge.

Even Archer's short temper and snide sarcasm would be welcomed gratefully, just for proof that she wasn't going insane. The prickly feeling of being watched by her silent Guardians became few and far between, no matter how hard she stared at the wispy shadows. Xander seemed to sense that she wasn't feeling quite herself, he organised date nights and special treats, brought her vanilla coffee every morning and picked daisies from the woods, but nothing could shake the distant iciness that weighed down on her, until she felt as though another ounce of pressure would crush her entirely.

CHAPTER ELEVEN

Archer

Back through the old door, Archer was met with a worried looking guard, pacing back and forth across the gravel path that led up to the back entrance of the Council.

'What's going on? You look as though you've seen a ghost,' he smirked as he grabbed his uniform out of the warlock's arms, shouldered his spear, and kicked off his strange human trainers in favour of sturdy black boots.

'Word's gotten out about the girl. All around the Council rumours are flying faster than a witches' broom, and they're angry, and scared.'

Archer stopped dead in his tracks, an instant iciness flooding his veins as he looked up at the guard. 'What do you mean word's gotten out? How?! Everyone swore an oath of secrecy!' he hissed, quickly slipping out of the casual hoody and into a Council approved combat jacket, pocketing a small golden dagger.

'No idea, sir. But we need some damage control, or your father is as good as ash, you know they'll put it on him.'

Archer threw down the rest of his clothes in frustration, dropping his head into his hands.

'We've kept this bastard experiment secret for fifteen years, all that's in it for the person who told is a one-way ticket to Helabasus. I'll see to it myself.'

He turned on his heel, beginning to storm back up the hill towards the Council.

'Inform Elara's Guardians that she must not, under any circumstances, return to Felicia before I or my father ensure it is safe. And stakes alight, make sure she doesn't ask any questions. No doubt her human curiosity is at an all-time high, let alone if there is a full-scale civil war on our hands,' he shouted over his shoulder, before breaking into a run without a backward glance.

Archer could hear the noise from the Council even before the large gates had opened to welcome him. He nodded soberly to the Watchpersons of the Gate, their gifts as Fenders had come in handy, enchanting the grounds of the Council to ensure no one could enter or leave without their permission. A spell Archer had performed many times. Ivy met him at the door that led to the Northern Quarter, her hands shook as she bolted the locks behind them and held open the curtain that led to the underground tunnels that wove beneath the entire building, that were usually reserved for the Practical witches, ensuring they could move from room to room unseen.

'Forneus has closed off all other entrances to the Northern Quarter. No one is permitted to enter or leave, except for you. He's requested your presence specifically,' Ivy whispered, Archer could tell she was holding back tears, but he didn't have time for her dramatics right now.

'And father? Where is he?' he asked sharply, turning a corner and narrowly missing walking headfirst into a worried looking Broomie witch, who failed to notice Archer and Ivy, and instead flicked her wand slightly, encouraging the feather duster levitating behind her to snatch a cobweb from the ceiling.

'In the commons, being interrogated by Forneus probably. Every single quarter has heard about Elara, stories are spiralling about Forneus being a corrupted leader, sending a tiny baby to live with the people who murdered her ancestors. Some are praying she'll be used to reclaim our homeland, to finish what Forneus' father started and save us from starvation. Those who always intended to stay in Felicia are convinced Forneus is testing fate, and Elara will be the downfall of our species.'

Ivy's hushed tones added to the suspense as a drip of sweat trickled down Archer's chest.

'Okay, that's enough Ivy. They'll get the Shifters in to fix this mess. That is their duty, after all. They cannot refuse.'

Ivy looked pointedly at her brother. 'They can, and they are. It may be their duty, but no one can force them into it. We'll have to think of something else.'

'Hemlock's curse,' Archer swore as pushed through the last door into the Northern Quarter, where they were met by a wall of noise and chaos.

Witches with eyes brighter than the full moon whispered excitedly of an outlawed warlock with powerful gifts who was destined to be the face of the revolution. Others looked stricken with fear as they sobbed for their sacrificed ancestors and the lies of their supposed leader as they huddled together on the marble floors.

Archer held his head up high and readjusted his jacket, hoisting his spear higher onto his shoulder. He pulled his wand out from a hidden pocket and drew a square in the air, muttering an enchantment under his breath.

A translucent box formed around himself and Ivy, rendering them invisible to their fellow witches. It allowed them to walk through the crowd untouched, and unnoticed, which was a priceless blessing, given the fact that Archer's main job in life was to protect the witch that had caused this chaos.

The moment they neared the door to Forneus' chamber, the protective box dissipated into the air, and Archer nodded at his sister, who took the opportunity to slip down another hidden corridor and out of sight. The door opened from the inside, revealing a room filled with anxious witches, who turned to look at Archer as he entered. Some looked grateful for his presence, others glared at him as though they were ready to tie him to a stake themselves.

He spotted his mother and father sat quietly in the centre of the semicircle. Their expressions were guarded, and his father gripped his mother's hand so tightly, her fingertips had turned white.

Mr and Mrs Headley were stood in the corner of the room. He'd only met them a handful of times, although he was entrusted with the protection of their daughter, they'd never made much of an effort with him, yet the second Darya Headley looked up from crying into her handkerchief, she gasped theatrically and ran over to Archer, her arms outstretched to envelop him in a desperate hug.

'Is she home safely? Did you get her out in time?' she cried, burying her face into his shoulder.

Archer cleared his throat uncomfortably, patting Darya's back before stepping back purposefully.

'Yes, Ma'am. She's fine, with a team of Guardians ensuring her safety. She won't return to Felicia until myself or my father deem it safe to do so. You have nothing to worry about.'

Darya flung herself dramatically onto the nearby sofa, almost flattening the members of the council who were already sat there.

'Oh, what I would do to have her back safe in my arms, my poor baby! She doesn't deserve any of this!'

Dritan made his way over to his wife and patted her on the arm somewhat reluctantly.

'Elara has no idea there's anything going on over here, Mrs Headley. She is back with her adoptive family now.'

Darya shot Archer a stern look and immediately he quietened, straightened his jacket, and stood up tall.

The room suddenly fell silent as Forneus appeared as if from nowhere behind Archer. He gazed around the room, capturing everyone's attention as they bowed their heads reverently. Archer stepped out of his way, feeling his heart rate quicken as a chill descended on the room.

'We clearly have a difficult situation on our hands,' Forneus boomed, his voice echoing from the corners of the ceiling. 'Nobody outside of this room, should know about our experiment with Miss Anderson, yet somehow…' he paused for dramatic effect, 'the entire population of the Council is screaming it at the top of their lungs, at this very second.'

He glared around the room, Archer didn't need to be an Ardent witch to sense the seething anger that could erupt from Forneus at any second, no doubt causing a catastrophic amount of damage.

'A full-scale investigation will be conducted into which warlock took it upon themselves to involve the general public, however, my current concern is getting this situation back under wraps. I don't care how you do it, I don't care who does it, I need this sorted, or every single person in this room will be sent to Helabasus for the destruction of the Kingdom of Felicia. The people of Felicia will not understand why this decision was made until it is explicitly clear, and until then, they will deem me untrustworthy. No doubt they will be unnecessarily angry for Miss Anderson as well, unfairly using her as a channel for their anger… a source of hope for their feverish ideas, if you will. You all know as well as I do, that if this gets out, we will have a nation-wide riot on our hands. I believe none of you would want that, am I correct in assuming this?'

The room nodded collectively in silence. Out of the corner of his eye, Archer could see his mother shaking. He wanted desperately to go to her but knew it would be in his best interest to not move a muscle until Forneus had calmed from his simmering rage.

'Archer and Osmond Levett, I wish to speak to you regarding Elara's safety. Mr and Mrs Headley, you are welcome to join us too, of course.'

Archer saw his father's face drop, but he remained his cool composure and stood up swiftly, nodding to Forneus.

They were ushered quickly into a small study just off the main room. The second the door closed behind them, the noise and nervous chatter faded away, leaving an eerily silent room.

Forneus sat behind the mahogany desk, he laid his wand down and Archer eyed it carefully, knowing of its power and strength.

'Now of course, you are two of my most trusted warlocks,' Forneus began, looking the two men up and down as though he didn't mean a word he said, 'so, I am very sorry to have to do this, but unfortunately as you have both worked so closely with Miss Anderson and know the most about her case, I am left with no choice.'

Archer almost laughed at the insincerity in his leader's voice. This was a man he had served for almost five years, and his father much longer. Clearly that meant nothing anymore.

Forneus nodded to the young woman who had been stood quietly watching the interaction.

She was his personal Guardian, never left his side and possessed strong Ardent gifts. She had the ability to both read and manipulate emotions, a rare talent even within the powerful strain of magic. Most could only do one. She rarely spoke, and held everyone at a cold distance, probably as instructed by Forneus. Archer had often tried to chat with her, he wasn't ashamed to admit that she was breathtakingly beautiful, and he would've prided himself in using his charm on her, yet he'd never gotten more than a word back. No one ever did.

'Ianira, proceed,' Forneus said softly.

Ianira stepped forward, a waft of her peach scented perfume flooded through the air as her eyes focussed on Archer. As soon as he met her gaze, he felt weightless, as though every one of his worries had been relieved and replaced with a happy, giddy feeling. He tried for a moment to fight it off, but it was pointless, there was nothing he could do but embrace the warmth. Ianira smiled effortlessly, Archer fancied it was the first time she had ever displayed the expression, and he had the honour of being at the receiving end. If possible, her beauty was even more apparent now. Her skin glowed as though it had been blessed with Zeus' summer rain, and her dark hair glistened almost as though a halo were bestowed upon her head. Her eyes shone a brighter green than Archer had ever seen before, and the temptation to reach out and touch her was unmatched.

'Archer Levett, do you agree with the following statement: you are Elara Anderson's primary Defender, and are therefore entrusted with her safekeeping?'

Ianira's voice was so melodic, Archer swayed slightly, desperately fighting to keep his eyes in focus.

'Yes, that is correct.' His voice was breathy, it shook in a way that it never had before.

'You returned her safely to her home on the other side of the wall at around 6pm this evening, November 5th, having left the Council grounds with your father?'

'I arrived first at the gate and informed the guards. I changed out of my uniform and walked her home. Spoke to her family myself.'

'The other guards can account for this? They can provide me with accurate time stamps for the events of this evening?'

'Of course,' Archer smiled, 'I'm sure they'd chew off their right arms if you asked them to,' he giggled to himself.

'Did you speak to anyone within the Council before you left, perhaps accidentally slipping into conversation information about your position with Miss Anderson? Indicating a witch in the human world?'

'No. I would never,' he said as firmly as he could manage.

'Just to be clear, you spoke to absolutely no one, other than those who are authorised, about Elara Hazel Anderson and our business with her?'

'I would sooner die, than risk Elara's safety. That is the oath I agreed to and that is the oath I stand by. Forneus has made it very clear the part she plays in Felicia. The extent of her research is unparalleled and no matter the outcome, she is the future of our nation.'

Ianira smiled one last time, before snapping back to her position next to Forneus, her expression neutral once more. The world suddenly felt a little duller, as the warmth within his chest faded slowly away.

He watched in awe as his father gave similar answers to Ianira's questions. The tingle of their emotions being played with lingered in the room even when directed elsewhere, though Archer found it marginally easier to ignore now.

Finally, Ianira stepped back and settled into her place next to her leader, seemingly content with the answers forced out of Archer and his father. A slight nod in the direction of the Fenders guarding the doors was indication enough for them to be ushered back out into the chamber. Archer recognised the witch on the right to be a Fender he once studied with. They'd been friendly all those years ago, now only coldness was left as his eyes swam past them, barely registering their presence at all.

CHAPTER TWELVE

Elara

With the end of the year, came a new sense of clarity for Elara. It had been months since she'd seen Archer, Osmond or even a hint of magic. At first, she'd been angry, they'd left her with so many questions and not a single answer. Instead she'd convinced herself it had all been a kind of crazy prank, a very well executed one, but a prank none the less. Now she just felt silly for believing it in the first place.

Things were going great in her life anyway; she didn't need anything that Osmond had promised. She'd spent the Christmas holidays with her family, they'd travelled up from London to stay in the village and Elara's cousins had loved the Scottish countryside as much as she did, taking to Xander in an instant. It made her heart flutter at how easily he chatted with them, his bright smile and polite demeanour winning over even the hardest to please members of her family.

She'd spent plenty of cosy nights tucked up on the sofa with Jenna and Matt, Christmas decorations twinkling in the dark as they watched film after film, the cheesier the better. She's the Man was a particular favourite with the group.

Sometimes Alfie and Xander joined them, but they joked and chattered throughout, so were often banned.

Rose loved having people over at Christmas. In London, they'd always been so busy and not had time for the proper festivities. This year, the entire house had been glitzed up from top to bottom by mid-November, and every day, the kitchen would smell of freshly baked cookies, homemade hot chocolate, and the pile under the Christmas tree had grown astronomical.

Elara loved seeing her family so relaxed, it was a long time since they'd all spent this much time together. Her father had spent pretty much every day on the sofa in matching pyjamas that Rose had picked out for him. Perfectly content with a constant brew next to him, and a delightful assortment of home-baked goodies.

Elara was sure this was as picture-perfect as Christmas could get. The kind of holiday she'd always wished for in the hectic craziness that was her London life.

'I wanna take you on a date to the city,' Xander said one afternoon, as they were huddled up in a million blankets on the freezing cold beach, sipping hot chocolate.

'Oh really?' Elara asked playfully, her teeth chattering a little.

The whole beach was empty except for a few squawking seagulls, but that was the way she liked it. She felt as though there was no one else in the world besides them.

'You've lived here almost five months now, Elara Hazel, and yet you've never been anywhere other than the fields of Oakbridge. There's the whole of Scotland out there for you to explore,' he smiled, gazing out over the grey sea.

'I came from the city Xander, surely they can't be that different. I don't feel like I'm missing out on anything.'

'See that, is where you're wrong, Elara. Edinburgh isn't like any other city in the world. Once you've visited, you'll never want to leave.'

Elara pondered for a moment, watching as her breath clouded in the air.

'Say I agree, what type of date did you have in mind?'

'There's a firework festival happening on New Years Eve. I used to go with my brothers and Grandad. It's incredible Elara honestly, there's fireworks, music, hot food, bonfires, anything you can imagine.'

'The Loch Ness Monster?' Elara grinned as Xander rolled his eyes.

'I'm serious, El! You'd love it, I promise. Anyway, I've booked the tickets so you can't say no.'

He looked up at her shyly, as Elara's heart pounded, and she begged her cheeks not to blush.

'I don't think I could say no if I wanted to,' she whispered.

He held her gaze for a heart stopping moment longer before a cheeky smile returned to his face and he kissed her softly.

'I'm sure it's the cold air that's making your cheeks pink, but I'll kid myself into thinking it's me,' he said, laughing as Elara cleared her throat and turned away, shaking her head at the sea.

CHAPTER THIRTEEN

Archer

The semicircle of guards around both entrances to the Council was now six people deep. It was a scary sight if you weren't expecting it, dozens of Fenders clad in black uniform, sharp silver spears pointed skyward and some of the most powerful witches in Felicia hidden in the treeline, ready for attack.

Though news about Elara somehow hadn't breached the walls of the Council, every witch that worked for Forneus was on full alert, fearful of the wrath they would face if matters got worse.

Ianira had been working on overdrive, desperate to find the source of the leak before her leader spontaneously combusted from the simmering rage he had been harbouring. Everyone in the Council could feel his anger, it rippled through the air like a brewing storm, darkening the hallways and leaving each room he entered cold and damp.

There were two clear groups forming within the residents of the Council. Those who supported the experiment wholeheartedly, and were desperate to return to their previous land, even if that was by force… and those who despised Forneus, furious at his decision to take a baby from her rightful home and leave her in a world where the people had once slaughtered her ancestors and risk the premature exposure of her species. No doubt the sides forming within the Council would be a hundred times more vicious in Felicia, where the people already despised the culture and richness of Forneus' consorts. Whilst they starved and worked themselves to the bone to provide for their families, Forneus threw balls and celebrations, taking no liberties with his title.

Archer wasn't sure which side he belonged on; he mostly spent the days worrying about his father.

Osmond had been banned from travelling to Scotland to guard Elara until the mess had been sorted. He became more withdrawn each day with the inability to fulfil his duties, and not that he would admit it, but he missed Elara. He'd watched over her almost every day for fifteen years. The hours seemed longer without her cheeky quips, sweet nature, and dramatic flair, even if he had only experienced it from a distance. In recent years, he'd loved monitoring her witchy tendencies. The way she was drawn to crystals and plants, her love of the moon and early mornings, though of course it became slightly less endearing to watch when she was flooding houses and manipulating people to her will without even realising.

'So, what's the plan?' Ivy asked one night, a strict curfew had been put in place by Forneus, so they were all sat around the dining table as the sun dipped rapidly below the horizon. Osmond looked at her wearily, rubbing his hands together as Archer swirled the water in his glass.

'I wish I had one for you, Ivy.' Their father's voice was tired, in a way they hadn't heard it before as they shared a worried glance.

'Well, Forneus has got to get it under control, surely.'

Osmond rubbed his temples. 'There aren't nearly enough witches in his court to control the whole council. His best shot is involving Alchemists from the outside, and it would have to be a lot at that to produce enough memory elixirs for the whole council, and even then, the witches who produced the potions would still know something was going on, as you know their creations won't work on themselves.'

Ivy frowned. 'What about the Ardents? Can't they like erase people's memory or something?'

Archer rolled his eyes, 'did you even go to school Ivy? Don't be ridiculous.'

'It's a valid question,' Ivy argued, 'how am I supposed to know exactly what they can do?'

'The limit of their ability is that they can only alter people's emotions, maybe mess with their minds a little. Ianira is the most skilled, she might be able to encourage people to forget about Elara, but who knows if it would work. If it didn't, it would expose Forneus, make him seem less powerful, then people would doubt his leadership even more. He's stuck really. Needs something creative.'

'What about the Fenders?' Ivy asked, turning to face her brother, 'isn't there anything they can do?'

'Yes, and they're already doing it. They've stopped communication and limited the ability to enter or leave the Council. We're not the most helpful in this situation,' Archer replied, before draining the last of his water.

Ivy bit her lip, considering for a moment. 'Well surely people in the city are going to start getting suspicious soon, with no one going in or out of the Council. Forneus will have to think of something.'

'Wow,' Archer said dryly, 'you deserve an award, Ivy.' He rolled his eyes at his sister before standing up from the table. His mother winced as the wooden legs of the chair scraped loudly against the stone floor. 'I'm going to bed,' he said shortly, mustering a faint smile.

'I'll follow you,' his father said standing up, planting a kiss on his wife's cheek. 'Maybe I'll dream up a solution.'

Months that felt like years trawled by. Still no solution was dreamt up, and tensions grew by the day. People became angrier and angrier at their inability to leave the stone walls of the Council. Finally, just when Archer thought a magical riot was about to break out, Forneus called an emergency meeting. A few dozen witches gathered promptly in the main chamber, the heavy weight of nerves hung in the air as Archer joined his fellow Fenders at the front of the room, stood in dark solidarity waiting for Forneus' speech.

'An oppressive shadow has been hanging over this council for many months now,' Forneus boomed from the doorway, taking everyone by surprise.
'I understand the torment and worry that our business with Miss Anderson has caused. It has cost many of you jobs, ignited arguments within families, and worst of all, my people no longer see me as being a trustworthy leader. I of course want to fix this. I am truly sorry it has taken so long for my court and I to come to a suitable conclusion.'
He gazed around the room as he spoke, Ianira was stood a step behind him, staring at each witch in turn. Archer glanced over to Mr and Mrs Headley, who were also stood with Forneus. They seemed to have the same intense expression on their face, their eyes glazed over. However, as quickly as the scepticism entered his mind, it abruptly left, as Ianira threw a smile in his direction, her green eyes twinkling. A small sigh escaped his chest, and he returned the smile eagerly.
'You'll all be glad to know, my closest consort, Ianira, tracked down the offending witch who released this private information.'
The whole room gasped as Ianira looked proud, a toying smile pulling at her ruby lips.

'Defenders, you may have noticed someone missing amongst your ranks.'

Archer's eyes flitted around as he looked for an empty spot.

'Acacius Gerald was questioned this morning. He did not plead innocence, had no alibi for his whereabouts on the evening in question, November 5th, and knew a great deal about Elara's case. He was sentenced to a lifetime in Helabasus just a few hours ago and will live out his remaining years in solitude. I feel this is an appropriate punishment for risking the safety of Elara and being the sole cause of an uprising within the Council.'

Ianira and Elara's parents nodded in agreement. Archer felt his heart sink a little, a splinter of memory from his time in Forneus' chamber being questioned by Ianira flashed before his eyes. Acacius stood on the right-hand side of the door, ushering him and his father out coldly. The talented Fender he'd once studied with as friends. It was a waste, that's for sure.

'Whilst of course it is comforting that we have now tidied up the source of the leak, we now unfortunately have to deal with the leak itself.'

Archer felt a sharp stab of annoyance at how much of an inconvenience this sounded to his leader. As though it were merely irritating that he had to pull his weight to help guard an innocent young witch. As though he were above it and would much rather leave the mess to somebody else.

'I have spent countless nights discussing possibilities with both my consorts and Elara's parents, however, as of yet we have no reasonable plan. Except for one.'

Archer felt a flash of hope rocket through his chest. He saw his father's head suddenly snap up from where it had been drooped down towards the ground.

'We have decided that it is safest to bring Elara back to Felicia as soon as possible, exhaust every drop of information from her about her human life, get her some basic training and set up with a wand, and show the rest of the Council that she is, in no means, a threat or a traumatised child abandoned by her people... but in fact a healthy young witch, willing to learn and educate, with the support of her family around her. By the time anyone knows she's here, she shall be functioning as a witch, somewhat undereducated, but a witch none the less. We will hold a conference in which Elara will explain exactly what she was instructed to do in the human world and convince our fellow members that she was not intended to cause harm, but instead, be a societal experiment, crucial to the evolution of Felicia. It will be so much more sincere coming from her, and of course she will have the support of her parents and myself in coaching her for this important task, that we know she is capable of. I know you have all been feeling cooped up here in the Council, some of you away from your families. I want to try and get you home and back to your normal lives as quickly as possible, and I hope this is the way to do that.'

The whole room seemed to be nodding in agreement, smiles growing on their faces at the new hope for the project they had spent years working on, yet Archer couldn't share in their excitement. He could see from the looks on his parents' faces that they felt the exact same way.

'We shall hold a ball, which we broadcast along with the conference to every corner of Felicia. The people will grow to love her as much as we do, she'll be a fresh face to root for, a 'Darling' of the Council... if you will. Their anger will cease, and she will bring them new-found hope, no matter the outcome of her experiment.'

His father's cheeks drained of colour, and Archer suddenly caught on to exactly what he was thinking. Initiating Elara into the world of warlocks, would mean testing her gifts, assigning her a wand based on whereabouts she fell and then projecting her into every home in the city. The public would be terrified by the thought of her possessing more than one gift. Who knew how many she even had? In the original plan for Elara's rehabilitation, she would've been kept very private, her identity kept secret, slowly integrating into society as though she'd always been there... not catapulted to centre stage without an ounce of knowledge.

Even worse than that, what would Forneus do? If Elara's gifts meant what Archer thought they did, it would immediately place her as the most powerful witch in Felicia, therefore the rightful leader or a cause of great destruction. A drip of sweat ran down Archer's temple at the thought. This was completely uncharted territory.

The room had begun dispersing, though Archer had stayed planted solidly at the front of the room, forcing the other Fenders to dodge around him. Suddenly, his father jumped up from his chair and began storming towards Forneus. Archer darted forwards in front of him, his hand creeping towards the wand in his pocket.

'What were you thinking, Forneus? I should have been included or at least considered in this decision. It's a death sentence! The people of Felicia will use her to fight their battles and will lose every ounce of trust in you. They'll never understand that you thought you were doing what was best,' Osmond hissed, he stood so close to his powerful leader that their noses almost touched, and Archer was sure he saw a flicker of fear in Forneus' eyes.

Ianira stepped forward clenching her fists, Archer was almost sure he saw bursts of lightening splay across her palms, though it must have been a trick of the light as two other Fenders flanked her on either side, their wands pointed at Archer's father.

'Now now, Osmond. Please don't get yourself so upset. I appreciate your concern for me, and I am well aware of your close bond with Miss Anderson, you have guarded her with such care and dedication, and we are all so grateful for that. However, this is not of your concern.' Forneus kept a light smile on his face, but his tone was harsh. The room instantly cooled by a few degrees, a dampness lingering in the air.

'If Elara's parents hadn't agreed, of course we wouldn't have gone ahead with this plan. But it was their call, and they support it wholeheartedly. Therefore, so should you. Your duty is to keep Elara out of harm's way until she returns to Felicia. Nothing more, nothing less. Know your place.'

Archer winced at the degrading tone of Forneus' words and couldn't bring himself to see the look on his father's face. It was the cruellest thing that he could've been told, and no doubt it stung.

'Now, Archer. I need your assistance if you will,' Forneus said, his tone suddenly bright again, 'I want Elara back here by midnight, safely with her family. She will need some belongings, enough to stay for a few weeks so get practising your folding.'

He smiled smugly at the surprised Fender stood in front of him.

'What do you propose I tell her family, sir. Her adoptive parents? She still has school to attend in the human world.'

'I'm sure you'll think of something creative, Mr Levett. No need for that silly human school when she will soon be fulfilling her true destiny. Stop dithering now, you have a lot to prepare. Perhaps ask that sister of yours to assist Mr and Mrs Headley in setting up a room, Elara will need somewhere to stay of course.'

'Of course,' Archer echoed quietly, as Forneus flounced out of the room with a swish of his cape as Ianira finally relaxed from her tense stance and smiled a final time, gone with a flick of her dark hair.

'Stakes alight, this is a broom-crash waiting to happen,' Archer breathed, the look on his father's face displaying precisely how Archer felt inside as he ran his hands through his hair and followed his leader out into the hall.

CHAPTER FOURTEEN

Elara

'You know, escalators have really taken the rest of the world by storm. I'm sure Edinburgh would greatly appreciate their benefits,' Elara puffed as she climbed yet another set of stairs in search of Edinburgh Castle.

'The only way to truly experience this wonderous city, is to spend the entire time completely out of breath from the hills. It's the way the locals do it,' Xander said with a twinkle in his eye, grabbing Elara's wrist to drag her along as she threw her head back dramatically in exhaustion.

'Well, I hope you feel guilty when it kills me,' she grumbled, grabbing on to the railings beside her as if her life depended on it.

'Hey, did you know that Edinburgh Castle was built on top of a volcano?' Xander asked, gazing up at the towering turrets.

'Nope, nope and nope.'

Elara turned quickly and began trotting back down the steps. 'No way are you taking me to a place where the ground might erupt at any second with burning hot lava. Not today, Alexander, not ever.'

Xander laughed, grabbing her sleeve before she could escape down too many steps.

'Can you calm down? It last erupted millions of years ago now. Why would they build a castle on an active volcano?'

Elara looked up at him sceptically, 'because if the stairs didn't kill intruders off, they needed a Plan B?'

He rolled his eyes, taking her hand once more, 'come on, I promise it's worth it at the top.'

Elara hated to admit when Xander was right, but this might just have been one of those occasions. The view was immense. Twinkling lights from the city blurred before her eyes as the distant busy sounds faded away. Hundreds of people were crowded in front of the castle, watching a light display take up the sky. Music streamed from a pair of speakers to their right, haunting melodies in a sing-song language that people danced to, swaying in time with the rhythm.

Elara could see Xander watching her carefully out of the corner of her eye.

'So? What do you think?' His voice was hopeful.

'It's stunning. Nothing like London, you were right,' she replied with a smile, tearing her eyes momentarily away from the view.

A beaming grin broke out across Xander's face. Elara was sure he'd never looked more beautiful than in that moment. The city lights made his eyes twinkle like the inside of a treasure chest. The moonlight reflected off strands of golden-brown hair strewn lazily across his forehead and his smile was bright. The little dimple in his cheek creased in perfect imperfection as Elara felt herself smiling back.

He held her gaze for a moment longer, Elara was sure she was about to implode, but finally he dragged his eyes away with a small smile and nodded towards a line of vans and market stalls.

'The fireworks are going to start soon. Let's go check out their hot chocolate range.'

Elara beamed, grabbing his hand as he began to run towards the stalls. They dodged around people, weaving in between hundreds of strangers gawking at the sky. Elara looked up with them, trusting Xander to lead her. She laughed as the stars followed them, the moon chasing quickly behind. She let out a squeal as Xander suddenly dragged her around a sharp corner into a street filled with fairy lights, banners, and balloons. The smell of freshly cooked food wafted out onto the street, and tables with lines of gleaming jewellery and accessories reflected the light.

Xander saw her staring at one of the jewellery stands, he smiled as he thought back to the crystal collections in her room, and the hundreds of pieces of sea-glass she had given him from the beach.

'So, what will it be, my little magpie. A shimmering hair piece? A delicate bracelet? An ornate ring or two? Anything you like,' he said with a flourish of his arms.

'You don't need to get me anything! You brought me all the way here, that's enough,' Elara replied.

'No really, I want to get you something. Consider it a late birthday gift. Or a token from our first proper date.' There was a mischievous glint in his eye that Elara couldn't refuse.

'Well, Alexander. If you insist, you know I'd never turn down jewellery.'

He threw her a quick wink before placing a steady hand on her waist and guiding her towards the biggest stand on the street. It was almost difficult to look at it was that bright, but Elara was immediately drawn to it, hovering her hand over the pieces to see which one called out to her.

She lingered over a small silver circlet; intricate vines wove around the main band with shimmering leaves planted delicately amongst the winding patterns. She picked it up slowly, holding it to the light.

'We call that the Crown of Hazel,' said the lady behind the table. She held her hands out for the jewellery and left it hanging between her fingertips.

'It sits like a crown; one you might see in fairy tales on elves or nymphs. The leaves are tiny replicas of those you would find on a hazel tree. All handmade.'

'A hazel tree?' Elara whispered, unable to pry her eyes away from the sparkling metal.

'Sounds like it was meant to be,' Xander smiled, reaching for his wallet, 'we'll take it.'

The lady bowed her head in gratitude and turned to wrap the crown.

'Oh, don't worry about packaging it up, Elara why don't you try it on now?'

Elara nodded and bent down so that the lady could place the circlet perfectly amongst her hair.

'What a pretty picture,' the lady smiled, clasping her hands together in front of her chin. 'There's a mirror there, dear, if you'd like to make sure you're happy with the purchase.'

Elara made her way over to a tiny circle mirror hanging by a piece of ribbon from the ceiling of the gazebo. She tilted her head slowly, careful not to dislodge her new belonging, and met her eyes in the mirror. She let out a little gasp as a girl she hardly recognised looked back at her. Something about the crown lit up her features, sat perfectly among her blonde waves as though it had always been there. The girl in the mirror smiled confidently at Elara, her face glowing and bright as the music in the background built to a dramatic crescendo, before the world fell into eerie silence.

'You look beautiful Elara. A tiara for my very own princess,' Xander murmured under his breath. At some point he'd arrived at her side, his eyes interlocked with her own in the mirror and she rested back against him, smiling as she felt the warm weight of his hand on her back.

'If you would do me the greatest honour of accompanying me to the firework display, I would so greatly appreciate it,' Xander grinned, stepping back into a low bow as he held out a hand to Elara.

'Well, sir, as you ask so nicely, it would be my pleasure,' she replied, taking his hand as he spun her away from the stall in a blur of lights and colours.

The crowd of people in front of the castle had grown so large they had to jostle for space, crammed together like sardines in a can. Not that Elara minded being so close to Xander. He held her close, his arm wrapped around her waist to keep her safely by his side and warm.

She looked up at him, a smile on her face.

'It's almost midnight, are you going to make a wish for the New Year?' she asked, tapping her feet to warm up her toes.

'You're supposed to make a resolution, not a wish.'

'Not in my family, you make a list of wishes that you want to come true by the end of the year, then you can tick them all off.'

'Well, that does sound enticing. I think I only have one wish for this year.'

Elara stared at him for a moment, waiting for him to continue.

'Well? What's your wish?' she asked impatiently.

He scrunched his nose at her, holding back a laugh at her curiosity. 'I can't tell you, or it won't come true!'

'Just a little hint then?'

She looked up at him, waiting for his answer, but he simply stared back, the slightest smile on his face. Without a word he leaned down and kissed her. Elara put her hands on his chest, pulling him closer as she felt a strong wave of emotion buzz across his skin. She couldn't put her finger on exactly what it was, but she was desperate to be a part of it. He felt almost like a source of pure energy beneath her fingertips as she pushed closer to him, addicted to the warm and powerful feeling.

Around them, the crowd began counting down from ten, yelling louder and louder as they drew closer to the new year. Elara just stayed with her arms around Xander, her forehead pressed against his. The whole world could have been exploding around them and she wouldn't have even felt a shake in the ground matched with the force of the energy that was radiating in waves from Xander.

'Elara?' he whispered as the crowd counted down from five, four, three, two, one.

'I love you.'

CHAPTER FIFTEEN

Elara

'That's enough of that, come on now, time to stop playing house. You have a job to do.'

A hand clamped over Elara's mouth, and something was whispered quickly behind her. She could see Xander looking frantically around, his face the picture of pure shock wondering where she'd gone. Elara fought against her attacker, kicking her legs out from under her and flailing them around to loosen their grip, she winced as the heel of her foot made contact with something very solid, and her knee gave way in response. Biting down as hard as possible on the hand across her mouth only earned a small grunt in reply as suddenly her legs were bound together with what felt like rope.

'Why didn't you do that in the first place, Isa? Stakes alight, she almost took out Denzel.'

There was an annoyed sounding grunt from somewhere in front of her.

'I'm okay, I'm okay.'

'Good lad Denzel. Now Hemlock's Curse, Isa, get her under control, I can't perform the enchantments if I'm holding onto her, and she's bloody feisty. Pretty sure you bit a hole in my glove sweetheart, you owe me a new one.'

Elara continued to struggle against the ties that bound her, trying to shout out beyond the scratchy glove pressed across her mouth to Xander who was still gazing dumbfounded around the crowd, before suddenly a shadowy figure emerged behind him and tapped his shoulder. As soon as Xander turned, a sparkling green powder flew into his face, immediately knocking him back as he stumbled a few feet. The shadowy figure grabbed his arm to stop him from tripping and whispered something in his ear. Xander nodded in agreement to whatever was being said, and without a backward glance began walking towards the steps that would lead him back to Edinburgh's cobbled streets. Hot tears burned at her eyes as he disappeared out of view, her limbs growing achy and tired from the resistance they were constantly met with.

'Okay, you can calm down now. He's going home and you're coming with us,' a hushed voice whispered into her ear.

She flung her head back with all her strength to headbutt the attacker, but a firm hand wove around her throat, holding her still and struggling for breath. Suddenly the shadow figure appeared in front of them, barely inches from Elara's face. They looked slightly distorted as though they were reflected in a cracked mirror, but even still she wouldn't mistake those violet eyes anywhere. A pale hand rose to lift away the hooded cloak, revealing a tell-tale shock of silver hair and pointed features. He smiled mischievously, twirling the wooden stick between his fingers as he had done so many times before, and finally Elara became still.

'Hello again, Miss Anderson,' he grinned.

'Osmond.'

'Miss Anderson, please stop trying to kick me, we bound you for your own safety. Plus, it hurts.'

'That's the point, get off me Archer,' Elara gasped, shaking her head as he kept his hand clamped firmly around her windpipe.

'Fine, fine! But do stop attacking us, you're acting like a spoilt brat. This is a protective enchantment box; you can't get out until we remove it. It is simply so we can escort you back to Felicia without causing a scene. No humans can see inside or hear us, we're invisible to them. There is no point in screaming, and your hands and ankles will remain enchanted. Okay?'

She pondered for a moment, her shoulders shaking, but it was becoming more and more difficult to breath by the second, so she nodded silently and slowly; Archer removed his hands placing them instead on her shoulders to spin her around.

'See that wasn't so bad, was it? Blighted burner,' he hissed at her, his eyes flaring. 'Refuses to go down without a fight. Sorry we couldn't escort you out in a pretty pink helicopter, sweetheart. Though next time, could you not injure my team? In fact, you could exercise some of those human manners I've heard so much about!'

He let confidence drip from his tone, nodding at two other witches behind him who laughed snarkily. Elara felt smaller than a mouse as they looked her up and down, her bedraggled hair, the metal crown askew on her head, her cardigan had dropped from her shoulder with her wrists still bound behind her back. Dark makeup pooled in salty tears beneath her eyes, as the fireworks in the background began to fizzle away, and the cries of the crowd died down.

As Archer turned back to face her, the look on his face made her want to drop into a ball and cry until they all went away. Instead, she almost smiled before leaning backwards and spitting sharply in his face, grinning at the horrified look it warranted from every witch around them. Her heart began to race as Archer's features darkened and his breathing quickened.

Suddenly, he thrust his hand forward and grabbed her jaw so harshly, her head snapped back with the force, her neck emitting a concerningly loud crack.

'You bitch-' he growled; his face close to hers.

'Archer, man chill out. She's just throwing a tantrum, come on Forneus is waiting.'

Archer hesitated a moment longer, his fingertips digging into her skin as she smirked. Elara wondered for a moment if he would spit back at her, she wouldn't have put it past him, but instead with his audience watching carefully, he stepped away, a smile on his face that told Elara everything she needed to know. He dragged his sleeve roughly across his cheek without dropping her gaze.

'Isa? Denzel? Let's go. She has important business to attend to.'

As the group began walking in formation away from the castle, he guided her with a sharp finger between her shoulder blades, her cheeks reddened at the tiny shuffling steps she had to take due to her bound ankles.

'What did you do to Xander?' she whispered.

'Compliancy powder. He went home because he believed your little date was over and that he won't be seeing you for a few weeks because you're on a college trip.'

'Are you kidding? I'm going home right now; you can't force me to go anywhere,' she hissed.

'Oh yeah? How do you plan of getting out of those magic binds, and this magic box for that matter?'

Elara huffed, writhing her wrists inside the invisible ropes to no avail, much to Archer's entertainment.

'You know, you just showed up out of the blue after months of leaving me abandoned and alone, questioning my sanity, only to ruin perhaps the most perfect life of my night. Your timing is horrific, I deserve an apology,' she grumbled angrily over her shoulder.

'I'm so sorry we messed up your teenage love story, sweetheart, but we're close to having a full-blown civil war on our hands in Felicia, and you're the only one who can fix it. I think our problem slightly outweighs yours.'

'A civil war? What do you mean I can fix it?'

Archer remained silent, the only sound inside the box the stamping of the Fender's feet and the shuffle of Elara's.

'Archer?'

She turned around, she expected annoyance, boredom, some kind of sick joke. Instead, his grim expression matched hers, and she was sure she saw a glint of nervousness in his eyes as he spun her back around.

'Just keep walking, Elara. Please.'

CHAPTER SIXTEEN

Elara

Preparing to re-enter the walls of the Council felt more surreal than Elara could have imagined.

Archer had ushered Elara somewhat clumsily into the back of a very expensive looking car. The paintwork was a sleek matte black and the seats a plush tan leather.

'Where on Earth did you learn to drive?' Elara asked as the engine roared to life.

Archer eyed her up in the mirror momentarily. 'I didn't. But I don't see you getting behind the wheel. So shut it.'

Osmond had finally convinced his nightmare-born son to cast the enchantment that would unbind Elara's wrists and ankles and had then spent most of the journey apologising profusely for the past few months. He also tried to explain what had been going on in Felicia, but the information was overwhelming, and Elara still wasn't sure where her job came in.

Elara had expected she would be going home to pack some belongings and say goodbye to her parents, but apparently there was no time, and nobody in the group wanted to face Forneus' wrath. Elara inwardly prayed there would be signal in Felicia for her to call her mum, she'd never been away from her for more than a week before.

'So, we'll get you settled in with your parents first of all.'

'Darya and Dritan.'

'Of course... get you settled in with Darya and Dritan,' Osmond shifted awkwardly in his seat, 'then it'll be straight to learning, I'm afraid.'

Elara fiddled with a strand of her hair, struggling to process the last hour of her life, and how all these seemingly ridiculous logistics were going to work.

'Ivy will help you unpack, introduce you to the members of the Council who are involved in your case, just the basics really.'

Osmond dusted his wand with the hem of his cloak as he spoke, looking remarkably like a crazy scientist preparing for lab work.

'Will I get to visit Felicia?' Elara asked hopefully.

'Don't be stupid,' Archer butted in from the front seat of the car. 'You'll start a riot if anyone figures out what you are. You can't even be left alone in the Council, let alone the city.'

Elara stared at him in the reflection of the mirror, feeling every bit like she wanted to yell at him, kick, and scream at being treated like a child, but that would probably only reiterate his point.

'So, wait, I can't walk around in the Council at all?'

'The Northern Quarter is fine, but that is all I'm afraid. After the three-week training programme is up and you've been reintroduced into society, we can truly get you reacquainted with your home.' Osmond beamed excitedly, but something in the pit of Elara's stomach didn't feel right. She saw the hint of anxiety pulling at his smile, the new creases of worry etched into his forehead. She returned his smile but felt fear begin to bubble under her skin, along her arms and into the tips of her fingers. She tucked her hands tightly between her legs as sparks of electricity began to splutter across her palms, desperately praying no one else had seen.

Instead of the peculiar entrance of her last visit, Elara was ushered in through what looked like servants' quarters. Weaving through underground corridors lit by candles, hearing the echoes of noise from above.
'Oh, sweet girl! We missed you so much!' Darya gushed, running to her daughter the second she stepped through the door.
'I- we, can't believe you're finally going to be living with us! Like a true family!' Darya grasped at her husband's hand, pulling him forwards as he held an arm out to Elara, inviting her in somewhat forcefully for a tight hug that was dominated by the scent of Darya's lavender perfume.
'There's so much for you to see and learn, you must be so excited! How was your journey, did your Guardians take good care of you?'
Darya eyed up Archer carefully, Elara waited to see if his icy demeanour would falter at all, but he held her gaze, confident as ever.
Dritan cleared his throat meaningfully and everyone snapped back to attention, the moment of uncertainty abruptly ended.
'Ivy, if you wouldn't mind showing Elara to her room? I'm sure she'd like to get settled before her classes begin.'
Elara hadn't even noticed Ivy in the room, she'd been stood quietly behind her brother, watching the interaction intently, her rich violet eyes not missing a second.
'Of course, sir. This way Elara.'

Elara was glad to see Ivy's familiar face, though she couldn't help but notice the unease that clouded around her usually commanding features. The jitteriness in her hands and the uncertainty that wove like a snake up her spine.

'How have you been, Ivy? It's been a while,' Elara joked, expecting a witty response, but she was met only with a tight smile.

'This is your room, your parents said they left it as it looked when you left. They hoped it might feel familiar.'

Ivy had led Elara down a small corridor with only one door. It was painted a bright white in stark contrast with everything else in the house. It opened soundlessly on its hinges to reveal a vast room flooded with natural light.

The walls were a muted violet, hand painted murals took up the empty space. A detailed sun on one wall, a glowing moon on the opposite. Elara watched in wonder as slowly but surely, each painting swam gracefully across the room, clouds moving across the sun and stars sparkling behind the moon as though time was passing only in this room. Her eyes drifted up towards the ceiling and a gasp escaped her lungs as the entire night sky unfolded before her. Shooting stars and every constellation nestled amongst inky darkness, perhaps one of the most beautiful paintings Elara had ever seen.

There was a four-poster bed by the window. The sheets were crisp and white, and the opaque canopy rustled in the breeze.

'Of course, there was a cot in here before, but they updated the bed. They added the balcony too so you would have some outdoor space,' Ivy said from the doorway, her arms folded across her chest.

'They added a balcony?' Elara asked, not even attempting to mask the surprise in her voice.

'Well, not them personally. They probably got a Broomie to do it for them, but essentially, yes they added a balcony.'

Elara laughed incredulously, gazing around the room. Suddenly a thought flashed across her mind.

'If this was my room from when I was little, where's all my stuff?' she asked, turning back to face Ivy. 'Like books, toys, clothes, stuff like that?'

Ivy shrugged, tucking her hands into the pockets of her jumpsuit. 'No idea, they didn't mention anything like that. There's a few books on that desk over there, maybe they were yours?'

Elara walked towards the large white desk. It was undoubtedly beautiful, with swirling wooden vines creeping up the wall behind it, glittering diamonds as handles for the drawers and a pointed shard of amethyst acting as a lamp, but Elara couldn't help but notice that it was an interesting choice for a toddler. She would've expected a tiny desk, worn with age. A floor littered with toys and games, messy pictures on the walls. The room was stunning, but she didn't feel an ounce of familiarity with the space.

'All of these books are brand new,' Elara murmured, flipping through the stiff pages. They were certainly books for a child, but as she opened them, the spines creaked as though they'd never been read before.

'Ivy, these books are new. They can't have been mine.'

Ivy sighed wearily, 'look, I don't know Elara. I just came in to make the bed and drop off a bag with the things you'll need for your classes. Your parents sorted the rest, I'm sorry I don't know more.'

She held out a leather satchel that was bursting at the seams with books and files.

'Your tutor will be here within the hour, someone else should be here before then with your human belongings. Try not to worry about it all, it'll seem strange at first, but you'll get used to it.'

Elara nodded silently, surprised at Ivy's cold tone, she sounded almost annoyed.

'Your timetable is in this bag, you'll have eight hours of learning a day, four will be independent study. You'll have half an hour for lunch, and your evenings are free to get to know others within the Northern Quarter. Your classes will rotate between Social Studies and Etiquette, the History of Felicia, Ancestry, and Magical Gifts. You will be tested on each topic weekly. The weekends will be spent preparing you for your introduction to the people of Felicia, and Forneus has requested you create a report filled with details of your human life, after all, that is the main aim of this experiment. At the end of the three weeks, you will need to successfully answer any question about your human and witch life and prove that you are no threat to our kind, and that the social experiment was a success. Does that all make sense?'

Elara couldn't even find the effort to nod as the information Ivy had presented her with echoed through her mind, the weight of what Elara had to achieve was beginning to press down on her. The absurdity of the situation was unfathomable, and she was already feeling a little homesick.

'What about my parents and my friends? They'll be wondering where I am.'

Ivy shook her head. 'They believe you're on a three-week excursion for your art class, a creative workshop in Wales. We'll send a letter to your parents on your behalf in a week or so, detailing your experience and letting them know you're okay,' Ivy said bluntly, as though she were reading from a manual.

'Can't I send them a letter? I won't say anything about where I really am, I promise.'

'You'll be too busy with your studies, Elara. It's only three weeks, I'm sure you'll cope.'

Elara sank down into the chair at her desk with tears threatening to fall, she dragged a shaky hand through her hair that was still knotted from the Edinburgh wind.

'What about you? Will I see you again soon?'

Ivy pondered silently for a moment, as though she didn't know what her answer should be. Her face softened after a moment; Elara was sure she almost saw a smile pull at her lips.

'Sure, if that's what you want. We can hang out in the evenings when you have free time.' Elara felt a little weight lift off her shoulders. She had a feeling she was desperately going to need a friend or two in the next few weeks.

'In the meantime, if you need anything, my father should be checking on you regularly to make sure you're okay, and you'll be detailed a Defender who will pretty much follow you round wherever you go, so you'll do well to be nice to them,' Ivy said with a twinkle in her eye.

Elara rolled her eyes, leaning back against the desk.

'Better not be your brother then.'

'Famous last words,' Elara mumbled as she opened her door to none other than Archer Levett lounged against the opposite wall.

'Tell me about it.'

He whistled to two other witches at the end of the corridor, 'come on, bring those bags.'

He pushed past Elara into the room and looked around for a moment. He didn't look very impressed.

Three binbags filled with Elara's belongings were dropped at her feet. Clothes that she hadn't seen in months spilling out onto the floor. The two witches who had brought them began muttering under their breath, twisting their wands, and encouraging the clothes into the floor to ceiling wardrobe by the door.

'Oh, you don't have to do that, I'll sort it.' Elara began pulling things out of the bags and folding them neatly.

'Just let them do their jobs, Miss Anderson. You're not here to fold, you're here to learn.'

Archer had sat down on the bed, lounging comfortably as garments, books and accessories flew around him.

A threadbare green Christmas jumper floated past Elara on its way to the wardrobe, she reached out and caught it in mid-air.

'Who packed this stuff?' she asked, looking the jumper up and down as it tried to pull away.

'I did,' Archer replied, a twinge of annoyance in his voice, 'just be glad I packed you anything at all, trust me, it isn't in my job description.'

Elara raised her eyebrows silently before releasing the jumper, watching as it dashed over to a waiting hanger and nestled itself comfortably on the rail.

'So, why are you here? I'm certain it's not for the pleasure of your company,' Elara sighed, sitting back down at the desk.

'Well, I'm sure you'll be thrilled to know, that my station whilst you're in Felicia is right outside that door,' Archer grimaced, 'anywhere you go, I go too. Anything you need, unfortunately I must see to. So please, if it's not too much trouble, stay silently in your room for the next three weeks, and you'll make both of our lives a tad happier,' he said with a sarcastic smile.

'But right now, your tutor is on their way to drop off some light reading for you, and then this evening is your… wand ceremony.'

'That's where they assign me a wand based on my gifts?' Elara asked, her voice shaking a little.

'That's right.' Surprisingly, Archer sounded equally nervous.

'Oh.'

'Exactly,' he said abruptly, standing up from the bed and straightening out his uniform. 'My father has unfortunately volunteered myself to escort you, as your parents are in a very important meeting,' he said pointedly, walking over to the door. 'In the meantime, get your things ready for the tutor. They're very strict, and don't appreciate tardiness, messiness, or laziness. Comprende?'

Elara nodded absently and reached for the pencil case that had been placed neatly on the desk.

'Does she know anything about my gifts?' Elara asked, just before Archer could close the door.

'Does who know?'

'My tutor. Did you tell her about me? Surely if she'll be spending everyday teaching me about magic, she'll figure something out.'

Archer stepped back into the room, there was a disappointed look on his face and Elara immediately regretted asking.

'Your tutor is non-binary. It's very common around here and incredibly impolite to misgender them. Make sure you take the time to learn. And no, of course I didn't tell them anything about you. I quite like my head being attached to my body.'

Archer's voice was so cold Elara could almost feel the snow beginning to fall from the ceiling.

'I'm sorry, I didn't know,' she whispered, looking down at the pencil case.

Archer rolled his eyes before slamming the door behind him with a jolting bang.

CHAPTER SEVENTEEN

Elara

Valen was nice, a little strict and rather blunt, but nice all the same. They had taken Elara by surprise in their fancy robes that draped to the ground and ability to hold her attention whether she liked it or not. Very different from her teachers back in Scotland.

Out of everyone she'd met in her small time within the Council, Valen was undoubtedly the most witch-like. Their hair was incredibly long and perfectly ringleted, so fine and silvery it looked almost like thread against their russet reddish-brown skin. Terrifyingly ruby-coloured eyes heavily lined with dark makeup shone out at Elara, and immediately her skin tingled with waves of intelligence that radiated from her new tutor.

Elara was intimidated by how clearly Valen expected greatness from her, and just how far from that expectation she was. There were endless books to read, theories and traditions to learn, and that barely even scraped the surface. This was going to be a long three weeks.

Valen opened the door to Archer sat against the wall opposite Elara's bedroom. Elara had heard his fingers drumming anxiously against his knee throughout the entirety of her class, and it stopped abruptly as Valen stood tall in the doorway. She smirked as he scrambled to his feet, and then the expression dropped as he unexpectedly bowed his head respectfully to the tutor.

'She's a… spirited character.'

They shook their head, glancing quickly back to Elara who was sat hidden out of sight at her desk, silver curls waving around them like a halo.

'She certainly is, you'll have your hands full I'm afraid…'

'Valen. Valen is fine.'

'Valen.'

Elara scowled at Archer from her hidden viewpoint, absent-mindedly doodling a flower on her worksheet as she strained to hear Valen's hushed tones.

'I believe her wand ceremony is tonight? She'll clearly follow in her parents lead. She read me like a book.' Valen cleared their throat, before readjusting the collar on their suede coat.

'I'm afraid she has a habit of doing that, it can be rather disconcerting at first.'

Valen laughed shortly. 'I was surprised at quite how skilled she was, considering she's had no training or guidance. Many Ardent witches take years of honing their gift to become quite so successful in reading emotions.'

Elara's ears perked up. She hadn't realised she had been reading Valen. Maybe she was better at this witchy stuff than she had expected. She peered through the crack in the door to see the interaction, expecting Archer to look impressed. Instead, he cleared his throat, his hand jittering nervously at his side. He flexed his shoulders as Valen looked him up and down suspiciously. A cool atmosphere hung over the interaction, each party clearly withholding something from the other. Finally, Archer broke the silence.

'She does have incredibly powerful witches for parents. Perhaps they passed down their aptitude for Ardent magic.'

Valen still seemed unconvinced, but nonetheless smiled a goodbye and began walking down the hall, their long burgundy coat dragging along the floor.

'Stakes alight,' Archer jumped, turning back towards the room where Elara was now stood, arms folded across her chest.

'Hey babysitter,' she grinned, leaning against her doorframe.

He rolled his eyes. 'I am not, in any sense of the word, your babysitter. I am your assigned Guardian by the order of the Magicis Concilio,' he said proudly as she looked sceptically back at him.

'You're a babysitter. Don't lie to yourself,' she said with a laugh, stepping back into the room to hover in front of her open wardrobe.

'So anyway, what am I supposed to wear to this 'Wand Ceremony'? Like, is this okay?' she asked, gesturing down to the T-shirt and leggings she'd changed into. As she glanced down, she noticed a questionable stain across the front of the shirt. She scowled, wondering how long it had been there.

He raised an eyebrow at her. 'No,' he replied bluntly, disdain dripping from his tone, 'you're supposed to dress nice for the ceremony.'

'What do you mean, nice? Like jeans and a nice top? Or a prom dress kind of style?'

He stared blankly at her. She doubted he even knew what a prom dress was.

'Ugh, could you get Ivy please? She might be able to help.'

Elara waited a moment as Archer stayed still, his expression hard as shadows began to darken the whites of his eyes.

'You know my family isn't at your beck and call, why don't you figure it out for yourself?' he snapped, a red glow beginning to seep from his skin.

'I'm stressed enough about this stupid ceremony as it is. Please get your sister so she can at least give me some help on what I'm supposed to wear to the magical stick ritual, where no doubt they'll tell me I'm a freak of nature who needs to be banished.'

There was a moment of silence where they stared each other down. Elara wondered if he was going to laugh in her face, turn and leave her alone.

'Alright, alright. Keep your hat on, I'll go find Ivy.'

CHAPTER EIGHTEEN

Elara

Elara was a little embarrassed at the state she was in when Ivy walked into the room. Clothes were littered across every available surface, shoes hanging from the corners of the bed, accessories, belts, and bags dropped in every empty space.

Ivy stood in the doorway, looking around the room as she tried her hardest to mask the surprise on her face at the sheer chaos Elara had managed to cause.

'Umm...' Ivy started, startling Elara with her presence.

Elara scrambled up from where she was sat cross-legged on the floor, almost slipping on a sparkly purple T-shirt that was tucked into her lap.

'Looks like you've been being productive,' Ivy smirked, eyeing up the floor, trying to figure out her best route across the room.

'Oh my God, Ivy, I'm so glad you're here,' Elara said breathlessly, running over to her friend to envelop her in a tight hug. 'I am in desperate need of your help, Archer packed me the most dreadful clothes and I have no clue what I'm supposed to wear in the first place,' she whined, gesturing at the room behind her despairingly.

'You definitely need my help, that's for sure.' Ivy raised her eyebrows before picking up the article of clothing nearest to her, a grey jumper with a glossy picture of a cartoon dog on it. She looked at Elara, biting back a laugh as Elara flopped onto her bed, groaning in despair.

'Okay, okay. I'll find you something, don't worry. You just get going on your hair and makeup.'

Elara dragged herself over to her desk, her vast makeup collection from home had dwindled drastically to just a few random tubes and pallets. She sighed, exasperated as she watched Ivy in the mirror begin to pick up items of clothing on the end of her wand before throwing them back to the floor.

A few minutes later, Ivy turned around with a frown on her face.

'You don't have a single thing here that you can wear, I've got something at home that might work. You wanna try that?' she asked, folding her arms across her chest.

Elara smiled gratefully. 'That would be amazing, thank you.'

As she waited, Elara dusted some dark eyeshadow across her eyelids, the same way she'd done for Natalia's party all those months ago. The motion sparked a pang in her chest for her friends at home. She'd only been here a day, how on Earth would she get through almost a month in this crazy wonderland?

She jumped as Ivy came back into the room, she saw briefly through the open door Archer leaning against the doorframe, tapping his foot impatiently.

'Okay, this is the dress I wore for my Wand Ceremony, I think it should fit fine.'

Ivy held out a long black dress, the material glistened in the light. Elara reached out a hand to touch it and it was soft and silky under her fingertips.

'It's beautiful,' Elara breathed.

'It is, but my mum picked it out. I'd wanted to wear a suit, but apparently that wasn't 'ladylike,'' Ivy said with a roll of her eyes and very overdramatic air quotes.

'You should've just worn one anyway.'

Elara began teasing her hair out from the crown that she'd forgotten was on her head, the hazel leaves woven deep into her knotty hair.

'Here,' Ivy said quietly, dropping the dress to the bed as she nudged Elara's hands out of the way, working gently to pull the crown free.

Elara sat and watched Ivy work in the mirror. For the first time all day, she felt genuinely peaceful. No one was snapping at her, complaining at her, or expected anything from her. She felt calm.

Ivy met her gaze in the mirror. The sun had dropped quickly below the horizon now, gone in an instant instead of the gradual sunset at home. The darkness was soothing, just the faint light from the lamp lit up Ivy's face. Ivy held her gaze for a moment longer before handing the circlet round to her, a faint smile on her face.

Elara returned the smile before reaching for the one bottle of perfume on the desk, luckily it was her favourite one, so she spritzed it generously, watching the cloud of orange blossom and vanilla dissipate into the air around her. She smoothed her hair down with her hands, teasing out the knots with her fingers. She considered finding her straighteners in the mess but decided the natural waves from the damp Edinburgh air were acceptable.

Ivy left the room politely so that Elara could change. The dress slipped on like a second skin, the cool silk leaving goosebumps along her arms. The dress was undoubtedly stunning, a high slit cut right up to the top of her thigh, the neckline a deep plunge all the way down to a thick waistband, preserving some of her decency with delicate black lace. Elara admired the silhouette of the dress for a moment before as a last-minute thought, placing her hazel crown back amongst her blonde waves.

She opened her bedroom door to Ivy and Archer stood talking quietly, though they both silenced in her presence.

'Ivy, could you fasten me up?' Elara asked, turning around, and holding up her hair so that Ivy could reach the zip. She waited for a second, nobody moved.

'Ivy?' she asked again, turning back to her friend to find both siblings stood silently watching her.

'Yeah, sorry.' Ivy cleared her throat, wiping her palms on the rough material of her jumpsuit before reaching out to zip up the dress. Her cool fingertips brushed lightly against Elara's back, making her shiver as the dress pulled tight across her skin.

'So, is this okay then?' Elara asked, turning back around to face them. 'I'm not overdressed or anything?'

Ivy smiled reassuringly at her. 'No, you look great, amazing in fact.'

Elara was sure she saw a slight blush colour Ivy's cheeks.

'Okay, if you're sure,' she said, returning the smile nervously back.

She turned towards Archer who was now looking up and down the corridor, when he suddenly seemed to remember something and reached into his pocket, pulling out a slip of yellowed paper.

'My dad sent this for you. He said you'd understand.'

Elara took the note and unravelled it carefully. Osmond's handwriting was loopy and intricate, so she held it up to the light to see better. It read:

'Miss Anderson, I'm sorry I cannot be there tonight to support you. There is nothing to worry about, your Ardent gifts are clear to all, if you truly believe in yourself and trust in your innate talent, no Wand Reader will question your magic. Trust Archer to keep you safe from outside the room, he's a beggar for interfering.

Osmond'

Elara read the note a few times, taking in Osmond's message. She didn't feel skilled enough to be faced with this task, but it looked like she didn't have a choice.

'Come, Elara. We need to get going.'

Archer began walking quickly down the corridor, Elara followed but Ivy stayed stood still.

'You aren't coming?' Elara asked, turning back to face her. Ivy looked to her brother.

'No. Ivy will stay here. You can see her tomorrow, Elara.'

Elara scowled at Archer before running back down the corridor and flinging her arms around Ivy's neck.

'Wish me luck,' she whispered with a tight smile, before following Archer out into the Northern Quarter without a backward glance.

CHAPTER NINETEEN

Elara

They walked quickly to a room in the Council that Elara had never visited before. Archer's long strides carried him far ahead, and Elara struggled to keep up in her heels. Ivy had mentioned to her months ago that Wand Ceremonies were usually done in groups, however due to Elara's situation she'd be facing it alone. She wasn't sure if this was better or worse.

An uncomfortable energy radiated off Archer. When he turned to glance back at her she could see the beads of sweat glistening across his forehead. His back was rigid and his jaw tight. She struggled to keep her breathing steady in the close-fitting dress, so instead settled for short shallow breaths and a touch of light-headedness.

Archer reached the arched doorway before she did. He turned to look at her, but she avoided his gaze, focussing instead on the hem of her dress sweeping along the floor and the warmth of her hair around her shoulders. The crown on her head felt heavier than before, but the rainbows it cast across the walls in the candlelight brought a smile to her face.

As she neared the door, Archer reached out for the handle, his suit jacket pulling open just wide enough for Elara to see the handle of his wand tucked neatly out of sight, but within easy reach. He seemed jittery, his stomach turning with nerves. It didn't take Elara long to figure out why, he'd been radiating the same energy all day. The same as when she'd originally told him about her uncontrollable bursts of magic. She sucked in a deep breath through her teeth, squeezing her eyes shut for a second before reaching out quickly and putting a hand on his forearm, stopping him from opening the door.

To her surprise, he didn't shake her off.

'What happens to me if they tell me I'm not Ardent? Has this happened before?' she asked quietly, her voice shaking.

She could almost see the thoughts churning in his brain, wondering what he was and wasn't allowed to tell her.

'Yes, this has happened before.'

She felt relief for a moment, but the fear clouded her mind once more as she saw the uncertainty in his eyes.

'I'm not exactly sure what Forneus will do to you, I only know my orders for today and that is to get you through this Wand Ceremony, no matter what it takes,' he whispered.

She bit her lip, pulling at her waistband that seemed to be sucking tighter against her lungs by the second. 'What would it take?'

He stared at her for a moment, silent.

'Anything.'

CHAPTER TWENTY

Archer

The wait by the door for Elara to re-emerge felt like the longest hour of Archer's life. He had assumed he would be joining her in the room, but she requested specifically for him to wait outside. He'd protested a little, but it turned out she could be quite stubborn when she wanted to be. He paced back and forth, checking his watch every six steps. The fear of what his father would do to him if Elara didn't make it out of her ceremony safe was ten times worse than anything he could imagine them doing to Elara if her secret was found out. He strained his ears to listen through the heavy wooden door, but someone must have enchanted it, as it was completely soundproof. He wondered briefly how much trouble he would get into for knocking the door off its hinges but decided it would probably be more than it was worth, so finally he slipped down the opposite wall onto the floor, his head in his hands, the wrath of Forneus, his father and probably Ivy weighing down on his shoulders. Every scenario possible was racing through his brain as the minutes ticked by, the fear of his punishment if his oath to Elara's safety was broken overpowered them all. His thoughts so loud he was sure the buzz of his brain could be heard in the quiet corridor.

    Finally, just as Archer was sure Elara had been whisked away through some underground tunnels by Forneus's consorts, the hinges creaked and the door swung open, flooding light into the dark hallway. Archer practically jumped to his feet, straining his eyes against the brightness as he searched the room. A slender figure emerged out from behind the door, their presence blocking the light enough for Archer's eyes to readjust. The smile on Elara's face outshone even the witch-made sun, as she held out her hand, a beautifully intricate wooden wand nestled into her small palm.
    'I did it,' she grinned.

CHAPTER TWENTY-ONE

Elara

The wand was so much more beautiful than Elara had been expecting. From what she'd seen of Ivy and Archer's, they were usually rather plain. Simply crafted with a small inscription. Hers, however, was stunning. It was long and slender, a light ivory wood with detailed vines raised up the along the length of the sides. Small flowers littered the base of the wand, covered by her hand when she held it properly, but they became few and far between towards the tip. She ran her fingertips along the wood, searching for the inscription that revealed the stream of magic she had been sorted into. She smiled to herself as instead of finding the characteristic 'A' of Ardent witches, a simple circle lay in its place. Hidden carefully between the vines so that you could only see it if you knew where to look.

She dragged her eyes away from the wand for a moment to find a very confused looking Archer. A deep crease between his eyebrows as he held his hand out for the wand. He turned it over in his palm, held it up to the light and rattled it a couple of times next to his ear.

'Can I help you?' Elara asked, bemused.

He handed it back to her, shaking his head. 'It's real?' he asked.

'Of course. I believe it is treason to wield an unlawful wand?' she smirked.

'Well... yes. But how? How did you do it?'

Elara enjoyed basking in his confusion, so she left him hanging. Turning on her heel to begin walking back down the corridor, twirling the wand between her fingers.

'Elara?'

She heard the shuffle of his shoes as he began hurrying after her.

'Hey!' he snapped, grabbing her shoulder to spin her around. 'How did you do it?' His face was hard now, his jaw tense. She stopped, smiling sweetly.

'I did exactly what your father told me to do. You really shouldn't underestimate me, Archer. Plus, I saw the look on your face, and funnily enough, I didn't fancy being the cause of somebody's death today,' she hissed quietly, reaching a quick hand into the inside pocket of his jacket, and pulling out the golden dagger that had been nestled safely in there all day next to his own wand.

Archer quickly snatched it back, stuffing it into his jacket.

'What the hell is wrong with you?' Elara whispered, 'you were going to kill an innocent witch for doing their job? It wouldn't have been his fault that I'm a freak!'

The stress of the day was heavy in her voice, all she wanted to do was go home, nestle herself comfortably in Xander's arms and tell him everything. It killed her to know he wouldn't even be questioning her absence thanks to Osmond's compliancy powder.

Elara snapped back from her Xander daydream and was shocked to see Archer looking almost upset. But the flash of emotion was quickly replaced by that cold glare she'd come to know well.

'You think I would've enjoyed killing an innocent warlock just to keep your secret safe? You think I had a choice?' he growled; his face close to hers.

'Trust me, there are a thousand things I would rather do than commit treason for you. Or run around after you, or even babysit you at all for that matter. But this is my job, and I don't have the luxury of a choice. I took a binding oath to protect you no matter the cost, to betray the oath is to betray Felicia, and that would've meant a one way ticket to exile for me, and no doubt for my family too.'

His breathing was heavy as Elara reclined a little.

'You know it was easier for me when you lived in the human world? All I had to do was keep track of where you were, and who was guarding you. I could live my life as normal, and you were just a small inconvenience that interrupted me protecting my city. Yet now, here you are constantly. I'm physically bound to be within a few metres of you at all times. My whole family obsesses over making sure you're okay, whilst you get to swan around whining, telling me how to do my job, and acting like you're better than us just because you were raised by burners. I'm sick of it, Elara. I'm sick of you,' he spat, his face red with emotion.

Elara stumbled back, leaning on the wall behind her for support as she felt Archer's every emotion rumble through the air like shock waves. A piercing headache clouded her skull as her spine ached with contempt, she'd never felt such hatred and anger from one person, and she was sure she would faint from the exhaustion of it. Heaving breaths grasped at her chest, the dress suddenly felt as tight as a writhing snake squeezing the air out of her lungs as the silk slipped beneath her fingertips.

She looked up at Archer, tears pooling in her eyes as she shook, struggling to stand upright and regain some composure.

'You think I asked for any of this?' she whispered, gesturing around the corridor with one hand as the other held onto the wall for support.

He held her gaze silently, she bit her lip to keep from melting into a complete sobbing mess and held her head high.

'I'll walk myself home. You should take the evening away from me. You clearly need it.' She said, her voice stronger than she expected as she whirled back around and began walking in the direction she assumed would take her home.

CHAPTER TWENTY-TWO

Ivy

The house was eerily silent as Ivy crept through the lavish rooms. She gazed around in wonder, it was so different to her family home where the small rooms were plain and cramped. It took all her willpower not to snoop in the bookshelves and cabinets that filled every empty space.

'Oh my God, Ivy! You scared me,' Elara jumped, dropping her shoes to the floor with a bang as she opened the door to her room to find her sat silently at the desk.

'Wait, did you tidy up in here?' Elara asked, as she looked around the room which earlier had been a bombsite of clothes, but instead the floor was spotless. Not a thing out of place.

Ivy smiled. 'I thought you'd appreciate it.' She stood up to greet her friend, but her smile dropped quickly as she saw the look on Elara's face. She rushed forward as Elara seemed to lose her grip on the last bit of sanity that had been holding her together, and her chin began to tremble, heavy tears streaming down her face. Elara dropped to the floor in front of her; the black dress pooling like an inky lake that could envelop her at any moment.

Ivy crouched down in front of her, unsure as to what exactly she was supposed to do. Elara looked up at her from beneath wet eyelashes, black mascara tears trailing down her pink cheeks. Ivy felt a wave of anger and protectiveness for her new friend, who looked so small in amongst the waves of silky black fabric.

She reached a hand out, wiping a tear from Elara's cheek and leaving a black smudge across her thumb. She pursed her lips together as Elara noticed the makeup, and dragged her own hand across her face, resulting in even more of a mess. Elara stared at her hand for a moment, Ivy was worried it would set her off crying again, but instead a small smile pulled at Elara's lips. Ivy returned the smile as Elara began to giggle, groaning as she pushed her long hair away from her face, knocking her crown off as she did.

'God, I must look an absolute state,' she laughed shakily.

Ivy scrunched her nose in response, proud as this earned another laugh from Elara.

'Come on. You can come back to mine and I'll make you a hot drink. Maybe find you a damp cloth,' Ivy teased, standing up and holding out a slender hand to Elara who took it gratefully.

'Will your brother be back any time soon?' she asked, staring hard at the floor.

'I doubt it. I'm guessing he has something to do with all this?' Ivy asked, searching Elara's face.

Elara cleared her throat, finally meeting Ivy's gaze.

'Can I have a cup of tea?'

Ivy softened, ignoring the clear avoidance technique.

'Of course you can, come on.'

As she turned, she realised she was still grasping tightly onto Elara's hand. Elara noticed too, looking down at their linked fingers.

'Um-' she started, beginning to pull away, but before she could say another word, Ivy dropped her hand as though it was burning hot, smiling quickly as she turned to hide the blush spreading rapidly across her cheeks.

'You'll have to tell me how to make a cup of tea, though,' she joked. Elara laughed quietly behind her.

'Of course.'

CHAPTER TWENTY-THREE

Elara

By the end of her first week, Elara was beginning to get into a routine. Breakfast with Darya and Dritan early in the morning consisted of complete silence and herbal coffee, then Social Studies and History for a couple of tedious hours, lunch alone in her room, then Ancestry and Magical Gifts in the afternoon. Each day, Valen would turn up with an armful of books filled with countless highlighted passages that reminded Elara of her mother. There was a lot to take in, but Elara couldn't help but admit how fascinating her studies were. Learning entirely about a new culture was eye opening, and she loved all the magnificent stories in her history class. She wasn't the biggest fan of Social Studies and Etiquette, so Valen made the classes as airbrushed as possible. Leaving most information on a need-to-know basis as Elara pulled faces at the warlock's outdated hierarchy, and in particular the marriage laws surrounding gifts. However, no matter how hectic her days were, Elara always had each evening to look forward to, her free time with Ivy.

    Wherever possible, Elara avoided Archer like the plague, having barely said two words to him since their fight. Of course, he was still required to be within shouting distance of her 24/7, but that was the extent of their relationship. Ivy tried to talk Elara round, insisting her brother would grow on her with time, but every conversation surrounding Archer Levett was ended quickly with a stern glare.

'I just don't understand why anyone finds it acceptable to be forced to marry a certain type of witch,' Elara whined for the third time that day, books, papers and pens littered around her on the bed.

Ivy rolled her eyes. 'It's not as if you're being sent to Helabasus for marrying out of your gift, it is simply suggested that you marry within your sector to produce the most gifted children. Technically, you can marry whoever you like, but then if you have kids, they'll be looked down upon for the rest of their life. They don't have pure magic anymore.'

Elara pulled a disgusted face, closing her most recent textbook sharply.

'That's ridiculous, Ivy. Who a child's parents are should never be a reason to treat them any differently. Surely diversity should be encouraged.'

Ivy shook her head. 'It has nothing to do with diversity. It is simply to do with keeping each stream of magic clean and powerful. Plus, the sense of community you get from being surrounded by similarly gifted witches is unmatched. It isn't a bad thing.'

Elara sighed, clearly, they wouldn't see eye to eye on this particular topic.

'What about this crazy hierarchy of gifts. That seems completely uncalled for.' Elara threw Ivy a pointed look, running her wand through her fingers as she tapped her foot, waiting for a response.

Ivy thought for a second, precariously rocking back on two legs of Elara's desk chair. 'It isn't so much a hierarchy… more a natural gradient of how rare a gift is.'

Elara groaned, falling back against her headboard. Her brain ached with the sheer willpower of trying to understand rules she didn't even agree with.

'For example, Shifters are far less common than say... Broomies. Sure, it might not make the magic any more important, but there's so few of them around in comparison to the hundreds of Practical witches. Therefore, they're regarded higher in society because of their sought-after gift,' Ivy sighed, leaning her elbows on her knees, tapping her black fingernails together.

'I know you don't want to hear it, but it's just the way it is Elara.'

The blonde-haired witch began packing her books and papers away into her satchel, not meeting Ivy's gaze.

'Look,' Ivy started, standing up from the chair and walking over to the stack of books that had been growing beside the window. She pulled out a large hard-back book labelled 'Human Studies'. Elara had asked for it specifically, she hadn't gotten round to reading it yet, but was interested in how the species she associated with was being portrayed. Ivy flipped through the pages until she found the chapter she wanted, then quickly skimmed down the lines.

'See, you can't look down on us because we regard certain witches more highly, you do it too!' she exclaimed, holding out a book and pointing to a picture of the Queen. Elara giggled at the sight, then shook her head.

'That's different Ivy. She's in charge of like, loads of countries. She quite literally owns all the Dolphins in the UK. I really wouldn't put Ardent witches on the same pedestal as the Queen of England.'

Ivy rolled her eyes, dropping the book back onto the growing pile. 'Okay, maybe that's a bit extreme. But what about doctors, lawyers, politicians... surely they're higher up in society because of their skill in a certain area?'

Elara stayed quiet for a moment. 'I mean... I guess. But they trained for years for that, I was just born.'

Ivy shrugged. 'Doesn't matter, that's just the way it is. Everyone accepts the system, and it keeps things running smoothly.'

'Fine. But I still don't like how the witches who come in to clean my room bow to me. I'm about half their age, they don't need to do that.'

'It's a requirement. You could ask them to stop, but I'm not sure if they'd listen. Anyone with Practical magic status must bow to an Ardent witch, whether in or out of the Council. It's a respect thing,' Ivy explained, seemingly not noticing the angry flush spreading up Elara's neck.

'So, in Felicia, if I was being served in a shop by a witch with Practical magic, they'd have to bow to me?'

Ivy glanced up, surprised by the tight restraint in Elara's voice.

'Not like a full curtsey down to the ground, more like a discreet bow, as a mark of politeness.'

Elara's breathing was getting gradually heavier, the flush now colouring her cheeks.

'What about the other witches, Alchemy, Inchoate… would you have to bow to me if we were in public?'

Ivy shifted awkwardly from foot to foot. 'A slight recline of the head would be sufficient. I would be expected to open doors for you, walk a few steps behind you, that kind of thing.'

'What if I bowed to you if it is simply 'out of respect'?'

'You just wouldn't do that Elara, people would think you were strange, and I would get funny looks, not to mention an awful reputation for thinking I'm above my gift. It's just the way of our world, how it's always been.'

'How would anyone even know what my stream of magic is?' Elara asked through her teeth. She could feel that familiar tingling working along her arms, the sharp needles of anger that were reaching out to grasp at her fingertips. She twisted her hands together tightly, trying to keep the feeling at bay.

'Your clothes would be… different,' Ivy said softly, 'in our homes, we can wear whatever we like, but in public or whilst working, our clothes indicate which stream of magic we belong to. Surely you've noticed my black jumpsuits, or Archer's uniform. Or the way your parents wear such lavish gowns and suits. You can easily tell a witch by their clothes, you would wear dresses and cloaks, blouses, and jewellery out in public, never the dark jumpsuit of an Origin, or the plain garments of a Broomie.'

Elara was struggling at this point to heave out a breath at all. Her ribs laced together with anger and confusion. All this time, she'd been studying so hard, relentlessly figuring out how she was going to fit in unnoticed with this crazy world, only to be told she would pretty much be regarded as royalty by the entire population. Wearing outfits and jewellery fit for a princess, whilst others, her friends included, bowed and served her. She'd never felt less like she belonged.

'Um, Elara… What's that?' Ivy's voice suddenly snapped her back to attention, her emotions fighting to stay level as the aching in her chest grew worse.
As she looked up, Elara saw the traces of electricity fizzing along the creases in her palms. The room had gone dark, the warm light from the lamp uttering a few useless embers as the soft curtains surrounding the bed blew in the breeze from the now open doors.
The electricity in her palms grew brighter and brighter as Elara watched. Usually it would've subsided by now, fizzled out into nothing, but instead it spread up her arms, the heat warm against her cold skin.
Elara tried to settle her anger, to draw back the tingles in her fingertips, but the more she tried to push it aside, the more the sparks grew.
'Elara?'

Ivy's voice sounded timid against the roar in Elara's ears. She noticed out of the corner of her eye, the fresh bunch of flowers that had been placed on her desk by a delightful Greenie witch were turning brown, their heads drooping below the rim of the vase as the once bright petals fell to the ground. The air felt cold and damp, the cool breeze from the open doors turning instantly to a freezing wind the second it entered the room.

'Elara?'

Ivy's voice was scared now, Elara tried to focus on her breathing, hoping it would ground her, but the wind was getting louder. It enveloped the room so fast, every book clattered to the floor, sheets of paper whirled up to the ceiling and the wardrobe doors flew open with a bang.

'Elara! What's happening?' Ivy yelled, holding onto one of the posters of the bed, as close to her friend as she dared to go.

'I don't know!' Elara cried, her voice shaking with fear as she saw her expression mirrored in Ivy's face, when suddenly, the sparks from her hands shot up into the air, a beautiful but terrifying crescendo of burning light. It struck the glistening chandelier in the centre of the night sky painting with a deafening bang, engulfing the crystals in flames before time seemed to stand still. Almost in slow motion, the chandelier came crashing down to the floor, exploding with fire and smoke. Elara dived for her friend, knocking her down beside the bed as shards of flaming shrapnel burst out into the room.

Ivy's screams were barely audible over the sound of shattering glass. Elara wrapped her arms tightly around her friend, hunching her shoulders over to act as a shield. The shards of chandelier dug their way through her thin T-shirt into any bit of skin they could find. Burning hot and burying deep into her flesh, searing pain radiated down her spine, as the tiny needles peppered every inch of her body, expelling a gasp of pain from her lungs.

The wind and chaos subsided as quickly as it had arrived. Ivy looked up at her as slowly the wind changed back to a gentle breeze, her violet eyes dark and weighted with fear. Elara tried to steady her breathing, not wanting Ivy to know how much pain she was in, as she carefully uncurled her arms. The movement caused the shards of glass to shift slightly, she was sure Ivy saw her wince as hot, sticky blood began to seep down her back.

Ivy stood up and gazed around the room, her features contorted in confusion. Now in complete silence, the desk lamp flickered reluctantly back on, bathing the room in a cozy glow that only enhanced the level of destruction Elara had caused.

Without a word, Ivy stepped gingerly over the remnants of the chandelier and hurried towards the door, almost falling in her haste.

Elara didn't bother to try and stop her as the door slammed shut, and the room fell quiet once more. She waited for the tell-tale scurrying of Darya and Dritan's feet, the screaming and shouting for the daughter they'd wanted compared to the daughter they'd received, but it never came. It was only then when she let the tears fall. They dripped to the wooden floor with a satisfying 'plop' and formed into a little puddle around her knees.

As she made her way to her feet, the glass crunched in a sickening harmony, cutting through the thin material of her socks with ease. Straightening her back brought new waves of pain that radiated all the way up to the base of her skull and strained whimpers escaped her pursed lips. As she turned to look in the mirror, the sight almost made her retch. Her shirt was stained almost completely with blood, daggers of glass poking out in neat lines, almost as though they'd been deliberately placed.

Groaning, Elara made her way over to the door. Her movements jerky and robotic from the pain. She fought to keep the darkness attempting to descend on her vision at bay but she couldn't ignore the swaying that dragged her from side to side.

As quietly as she could manage, Elara peeped her head out of her door frame. Looking down the hall for either her magical parents, or Archer, sporting an irritated look for the chaos she'd caused. However, confusingly, she found neither. The whole house was in fact eerily silent, an empty chill descending on the rooms.

Making her way down the corridor, the only sound was the greasy shuffle of Elara's socks on the wooden floor. Leaving a faint trail of blood in her wake. Not a single witch hurried past her, no quiet murmurings or wands swishing. It felt as though the Northern Quarter had suddenly become abandoned.

Elara made her way to the refectory. She hoped there would be a first aid kit there, though of course this was unlikely, as usually the help of a Fender or Alchemist would cure any ailment in seconds. The huge room was dark, the only light seeping into the space was from the glow of the moon filtering through the floor to ceiling windows.

Elara stopped dead in her tracks as she noticed a tall figure hunched over one of the tables, their shadow severe in the moonlight. As she held her breath, they lifted their head, and she wasn't sure whether to be relieved or shuffle for the hills as she recognised Archer's strong profile.

He seemed to sense her presence and whipped his head around. His expression was colder than Elara had been expecting, perhaps it shouldn't have been a surprise considering the last few days. She briefly considered shrinking back into the shadows, the only thing that stopped her was the burning pain that bubbled the second she tried to move.

'What the hell are you doing out here Elara? I thought you were with Ivy. She knows as well as you do that you shouldn't be wandering the halls alone. I didn't think you were that stupid.' His tone was harsh, Elara felt fresh tears build in her eyes.

'I… I didn't know where else to go,' her voice cracked, the air catching in her throat.

Archer turned his whole body round to face her, peering at her more intently as he tried to decipher her expression. She saw his face change as he noticed the faint dripping of blood onto the floor around Elara's feet. The sticky trails leading up to where she was standing, and her tear-stained cheeks.

He was stood in front of her before she could register him moving. His hands reaching out to catch her before she even felt her knees buckle.

He searched her face, waiting for an explanation, but Elara was worried that if she opened her mouth she would throw up, so she stayed silent, pushing her lips painfully together.

More carefully than she'd expected, he turned her sideways, wincing along with her as he took in the sight before him.

'What in Helabasus did you do?' he whispered.

His soft tone shocked Elara more than any event that had ensued that night. A shaky smile tugged at her lips.

'I had a fight with a chandelier,' she murmured, her voice barely louder than a whisper.

She couldn't tell if his expression was surprised or disappointed when suddenly he cracked a smile right back. The first time she'd seen him smile since she'd been in Felicia.

'You were right. I absolutely should not have underestimated you,' he joked back; an expression Elara didn't recognise still faintly creased between his eyebrows.

Elara tried to laugh, but the motion sent a jerk of pain across her skin, so it turned into a gasp instead. Immediately his smile dropped, replaced by his usual frown. Elara could almost see the thoughts and questions whirring through his brain.

'I can't take you to my father, he's in a meeting along with the rest of the council. I'll have to sort this,' he said, his voice so low Elara struggled to hear him. She wasn't certain he was even talking to her, rather running through his own thoughts out loud.

'We need to go somewhere more private. Can you walk further?'

He didn't wait for her response before beginning to lead the way out of the door. Elara could almost guarantee that this wasn't going to be a sympathetic experience.

The room he chose was filled with cleaning supplies. The irony of two witches stuffed into a broom cupboard didn't go unnoticed in Elara's slightly hazy brain. She giggled to herself, only adding to the deep lines in Archer's forehead.

The only light was a swinging bulb, hanging low from the ceiling. Archer had to duck to avoid getting smacked in the face.

'You know this really wasn't in my job description,' he said through gritted teeth, dropping his uniform jacket to the floor to reveal a plain black T-shirt and even more tattoos etched up his arms than the last time she'd seen him.

'You say that about a lot of things.'

Archer rolled his eyes, clearly as delightful as ever.

'Could you just turn around so I can get a better look?'

Elara turned obediently and stood still. The blood on her shirt had dried a little, and she could feel the crunchiness of it caked to her back.

'Is there any way you can make this bulb brighter?' he asked suddenly, tapping the glass orb above them.

'Are you joking? My hyper-connectivity to electricity is what got me in this mess.'

'Yes, I know,' he sounded exasperated, 'but I can barely see a thing in here,' he grumbled, shifting in the small space and accidentally kicking a bucket with his steel-capped boot.

Elara sighed, at least the bulb wasn't too high, so she wouldn't have to rip her skin apart to reach it.

Gingerly, she bent her elbow to force her fingertips upwards. There was a slight numbness in her hand which she was sure indicated nerve damage, but she tried to ignore it. The very tips of her fingers could just about brush against the glass curve of the light. She focussed on the streams of energy below the surface. Catching them and willing them to fizz and splutter. Even Archer looked surprised as the bulb now shone a bright white, and Elara silently thanked Osmond for his lesson in her room many months ago.

Archer was quiet for a moment, before sucking in a deep breath through his teeth.

'You're going to need to take this off.' He plucked at the shoulder of her shirt.

Elara glanced at him in the peripherals of her vision.

'There are a million reasons why I think you're joking right now,' she grimaced, her face reddening with the sheer thought of it.

'Well unluckily for the both of us, I'm not. There's so much blood here, I can hardly see where the shards go into your skin. Plus, your T-shirt has dried around them, I need to pry it away to dig them out.'

Elara shuddered at the image this conjured in her brain.

'Archer, I can't even lift my arms up to take it off in the first place. Not to mention the fact that it is literally being held to my body with glass.'

Archer sighed, 'well, I'll have to cut it then.'

Elara noticed she could see his reflection in a small mirror attached to a bathroom-style cabinet. The shadows cast across his face made him look scarier than usual. His dark hair was longer than the first time she'd met him, now it hung in loose waves around his jaw and resulted in the shadows cutting across his cheeks like a tiger's stripes.

'I like this shirt though,' she whined at the reflection.

He looked baffled. 'Elara, there's already about a million holes in it. Plus, I quite literally cannot see the shirt anymore, for how much blood is on it. Stop being a brat and let me cut it.'

He suddenly brandished a gleaming pair of scissors, seemingly out of thin air, and before Elara could protest any more, sliced cleanly up the back of the T-shirt. Neatly dodging each shard of glass.

Elara held her breath as he began to peel the shirt away from the nape of her neck, wincing at the slight tugging it caused on the splinters sticking out of her shoulders.

'Hemlock's Curse,' he swore under his breath.

Elara could feel the pure horror radiating off him as she struggled to keep her heartrate in check.

'You must have Fender Magic. This should've killed you, Elara.'

Elara looked once more in the mirror.

'What do you mean?'

'Fenders have a higher injury and pain tolerance. We still get hurt, but we heal much quicker. We use this type of magic to help others too.'

'Why aren't I healing already then?'

'Because the obstruction is still in your-'

Suddenly he stopped pulling the material away from her skin. His breathing quickened.

'Crown of Hades,' he whispered, staring at something near the base of her spine.

'What? What is it?'

Elara tried to crane her neck back to see what he was looking at, but she felt a sharp dagger at the base of her skull worm a little deeper with each movement.

He pulled the shirt along one arm, almost apologetically, he dropped the material from her torso. She followed his gaze down to just underneath the last ridge of her ribs, on the left hand side of her body, where a glistening gold metal spike was protruding at least an inch out from her skin.

'What the hell is that?' she whispered, a bead of sweat trickling down the side of her face, as a roll of nausea cursed through her stomach, turning her deathly pale.

'That's the metal hook that attaches… ed, your chandelier to your ceiling,' he murmured, tilting his head to get a better look.

'And it's gone all the way through my body?'

'Clearly.'

'I think I'm gonna be sick,' she whimpered, steadying herself with a hand against the cracked plaster to her right, closing her eyes as the world began to spin.

'Fuck this,' Archer breathed, dropping down onto the balls of his feet, his elbows rested on his knees.

Now in front of her, Elara could see the drops of sweat that mimicked her own pooling across his forehead.

'How could you let this happen, Elara? What is wrong with you?' he asked so quietly under his breath Elara could barely hear him.

Heat flooded her cheeks, her increasingly guilty heart dropping to the pit of her stomach.

'What do you mean? What is wrong with me? You really think I did this on purpose?'

Archer shot up to his full height, domineering the space. Darkness pulsated around the corners of his eyes, a deep chamber of emptiness and hatred bore down on his pupils, almost sucking Elara in.

'I don't know what to think, burner. For all I know, you did this deliberately… maybe you wanted attention, maybe you wanted to make my life a living hell,' he spat, the darkness enveloping the whites of his eyes.

Elara took an involuntary step back, her breathing shallow. 'Fine, Archer. If that's how you feel, then go. I'll find someone else to help me,' she hissed through gritted teeth. Elara turned slowly and pulled on the door handle. The door stayed shut. She tugged once more, before noticing the whispering coming from behind her.

Archer's gaze was focussed on the door, his wand pointed towards the handle as a blackened sheen began to engulf his tanned skin, snaking out from his tattoos.

'You'll do no such thing. Ten more steps down that hallway, and you die from your injuries. I have enough blood on my hands as it is, I don't need to be sent to Helabasus for your stupidity.'

Elara turned, but almost couldn't bear to look at Archer. Gone were the handsome features, the taunting smirk, and in their place was a monster straight out of a nightmare. His skin charred with hatred, his eyes black pools of anger, his gravelly voice a roar of anguish.

'Fine,' Elara whispered, tears stinging her eyes as finally Archer morphed back to himself and she settled with her back to him, though she kept a watchful eye on his reflection. Finally the crease in his eyebrows diminished, but every time his fingertips brushed Elara's skin, ice pierced through her veins.

CHAPTER TWENTY-FOUR

Elara

For a few minutes Archer worked in silence. This was the most time they'd spent together since her wand ceremony. Elara hadn't even noticed she was holding her breath against the waves of nausea that were beginning to cramp in her stomach until light-headedness cornered her mind, and she had to lean shakily against the sink in front of her, her arms threatening to buckle under her weight.
 The splinters took longer to get out than Elara had expected, she stood silently for the duration, her only nod to the pain a slight wince whenever one of the ragged glass edges got stuck under her skin and he had to dig it in further in order to release it. He certainly wasn't gentle, but he didn't seem to take as much satisfaction from the activity as she might've expected.
 'Archer?' she asked timidly as he pulled a particularly large shard from just below her shoulder. For all she knew, she was going to die in here. If she did, she might as well ask the question that had been burning on her tongue since the day she'd met her vicious Fender.
 There was silence for a moment, but he met her gaze in the muddied glass of the mirror, waiting for her to go on.

'Why do you hate me so much?'

Her voice was soft in a way she hadn't expected. Perhaps the blood loss was truly going to her head. He sighed and stepped away from her, she stifled a smile as he narrowly avoided tripping over a mop.

He raked a bloody hand through his hair, leaving streaks across his forehead. He looked for the most part like a complete psycho, but his eyes were surprisingly calm and devoid of darkness, his expression even.

'I don't hate you, Miss Anderson.'

Her laugh erupted almost manically, igniting a dangerous fire in her chest.

'Archer, I can sense every single one of your emotions. I can feel the anger and contempt burning at the base of your spine, the constant battle between fight and flight in your throat, the tiredness that is making your brain ache. So please don't insult me by trying to lie. The nervous butterflies in your stomach are knocking me sick.'

She met his eyes in the reflection of the mirror, she smiled to herself as she felt the wave of vulnerability flutter across his chest. She gathered it wasn't a common emotion for him.

'You can feel all of that?'

'It's intense.'

'How do you separate your own emotions from everyone else's?' he asked, dodging her original question so easily she guessed it came naturally to him.

Her reflection frowned at him in the mirror as he plucked out yet another shard of glass.

'I'm not sure, really. Half the time I don't think I do. It's stronger here than it was back home, or maybe I just never really noticed it before. Perhaps it's all the magic swimming around in the air, it's sending me insane.'

He smirked for a moment before recollecting his usual bored expression.

They were quiet again, the only sound in the tiny broom cupboard, the rhythmic clinking of glass dropping to the floor.

'I truly don't hate you, Elara,' Archer murmured finally, breaking the silence.

Elara hesitated before she replied with another snarky comment, sensing he wasn't finished.

'I hate that my life has been taken over by somebody I've only met a handful of times. I hate how much my father cares about you, nothing I did, or Ivy did could ever live up to you. As a kid, I worked so hard to be the top of my class. I spent every minute of every day studying, perfecting my gift, so that even before I was assigned a wand, I had a respected job within the Council so that I might work alongside my father so that finally he would be more impressed with me than he was with you. But nothing could split his focus.'

Elara didn't bother to interrupt, his eyes were turning dark, and she knew that if she stopped him, he'd never speak about it again.

'You know, my mother decided to leave when I was thirteen. She said my dad never made time for her anymore, cared about blighted burners more than his own blood. So, he came back for a couple of days, courted and wooed her to win her affections once more, then off he went and we didn't see him for almost a year. He missed my Wand Ceremony, countless birthdays, and every time his excuse was 'Elara needs someone too'. You'll never be able to understand how intently he doted on you… brainwashed himself into believing you were our future. He couldn't have cared less about how he left Ivy and I, what he left me to deal with. Selfish prick.' Archer laughed sharply, but Elara knew it wasn't out of humour.

She was shocked at the true resentment in Archer's tone. Whilst Elara's life over the past few months had been less than ideal, the one constant, was Osmond. Kind and caring Osmond who spoke of his children with such pride.

'You shouldn't say stuff like that, he's still your dad. He was just passionate about his job, it didn't make him love you any less,' Elara said, turning around so they were face to face.

Archer laughed, shaking his head, 'you don't understand, Elara. For fifteen years, all he talked about was you. We all wanted to support him because we were so proud of him for being assigned such a prestigious job, but he was obsessed. Talked about you as though you were his own kid and forgot about me and Ivy.'

An envious fire was beginning to burn in his chest, Elara squirmed uncomfortably at the feeling of it.

'Look, I'm really sorry that you feel that way, and that it seemed unfair, but I didn't even know he was there; you can't take your anger for him out on me.'

'I'm not taking anything out on you, Elara. You asked me a question and I answered it, it's not my fault if you don't like what I have to say. Just because you had a perfect little life with a wonderful, supportive family, doesn't mean I did. You do not get to tell me what I can and can't feel. Look, I don't know you well enough to be anything other than professional, so forget I said anything.'

She could hear the defensiveness in his voice, clearly, he could too as he began to frown.

'You know you're perfectly welcome to get to know me, in fact I would love to know more about your life. All you have to do is ask me a few questions and not yell at me the second we start talking. You've obviously got all this pent-up resentment and you blame your dad's absence on me, and that's why you're so angry all the time. You've just never had anyone to take it out on before, constantly holding people at arm's length, but I won't let you do that so I'm getting the full treatment.'

'You don't know what you're talking about, Elara. STOP intruding on my emotions and turn back around.'

He tried to turn her forwards, but she resisted, despite the burning sensation it sent across her back as the skin twisted and contorted around the glass and metal. She knew she shouldn't push him, should just be grateful that he was helping her at all. But the fire that was rising in her throat was uncontrollable, her clenched fists shaking at her sides.

'I don't know what I'm talking about. Are you kidding me?' she laughed incredulously, and she felt her pulse quicken. She knew another storm was brewing and they were right at the eye.

'You think I don't understand what it's like to feel abandoned… or to hate somebody you don't even know? I spent my entire LIFE thinking that my parents gave me up because they didn't want me, because I wasn't good enough for them. Sound familiar? I didn't have anyone who could understand me, and I love my parents so much, but I've never been truly theirs, there's always been this- this… thing that made me different. And just when I thought I might be settling in, a new house, new friends, and a boyfriend who actually makes me feel seen, I get catapulted into this upside-down world, where nobody likes me, everyone wants something from me, and my only friend happens to be the sister of the person who blames every second of his childhood trauma on ME!'

'Get OUT of my head, burner. You don't know a THING about me, or my family. Don't even try and act like you care about anyone other than yourself.'

They were shouting now, Elara was half worried someone would burst in, wondering what all the yelling was.

'This is ridiculous, Archer. Just get this metal thing out of me so I can go and check on Ivy, who probably also isn't my biggest fan right now seeing as I just nearly killed her and have been lying about my magic for over a week.

Knowing my luck, she'll have gone and told somebody, and now the whole Council is out looking to lock me away for good.'

'My sister would never say a word against you. Turn around, let me get this done quickly for the both of us.'

An angry red rash was seeping up Elara's neck, above where she was holding the torn, stained T-shirt across her chest.

She attempted to steady her breathing as Archer studied the metal hook for a moment, there was absolutely no easy way to take it out and who knew what damage actually removing it would do. But the edges of her skin around the metal were beginning to turn a grim purple, with black snaking lines edging further out across her back.

After another couple of minute in painful silence, she sighed, shifting from foot to foot.

'What is taking so long, Archer? I'm tired, I wanna go home.'

She tried to ignore how slurred her speech was. Clearly Archer noticed it too and gave a quick, experimental tug on the metal.

'Ow.'

'Quit whining.'

'Well just yank it, one quick, painless motion.'

'Elara it's a solid piece of metal, not a flimsy human plaster.'

'Ugh, you're a wimp. I'll do it myself.'

She swayed slightly as she stood in front of the mirror, turning so that she could see her back.

'No, Miss Anderson, just leave it to me please.'

'No, I got this, I did a first aid training course you know,' she smiled wearily; her eyes beginning to lose focus.

'I doubt that's going to help you here, Elara. Stop playing the hero and just let me do it.'

She smiled at him in the reflection one last time, before linking her index and middle finger around the hook. She took a deep breath and squeezed her eyes shut before tugging with all her might on the metal.

She gasped as it squelched free, Archer felt his heart drop to his feet as he lunged forward a second too late, barely catching her as she crumpled to the ground, blood pouring out of the open wound.

CHAPTER TWENTY-FIVE

Elara

The swinging bulb felt brighter than the sun as Elara finally opened her eyes. The corners of her vision were still an inky black, and her head felt like it had been hit with a ton of bricks.

As she finally came to a little, she went to prop herself up on her elbows.

'Don't sit up... not just yet,' said a quiet voice to her left.

It was Archer sat cross-legged on the floor beside her, his head resting in his hands.

Her eyes adjusted to the light, and she saw that he was absolutely covered in blood. His hands, his arms, his chest... his chest? Where was his shirt? Oh. It had been draped artfully over her torso. The T-shirt that she had been wearing was balled up by her feet in a bloody mess, looking more like evidence from a crime scene than an item of clothing. His skin was shrouded in darkness, cloaked with an opaque shadow.

'What happened?'

Archer smirked; he'd left smears of blood across his jaw from his head resting on his hands.

'Of course you don't remember. You just almost killed yourself and I, unsurprisingly, had to pick up the pieces.'

Elara lifted the T-shirt to look down at what she expected to be a gaping hole. Instead, her skin was already beginning to fuse back together, a jagged red line the only reminder something had ever happened.

'How long was I out?'

'A couple of hours? You woke up a few of times, but then blacked out again straight away. Not surprising really.'

'Hours?! Oh God. Darya and Dritan are gonna be so worried.'

Archer snorted, 'the blood trail leading down the hall probably won't help either.'

Elara groaned, pulling herself up into a sitting position, with a surprisingly little amount of pain.

'Why was there so much blood? You literally look like you've been in a warzone.'

Archer looked down at his hands, turning them over a couple of times to review the damage.

'I had to keep the entry and exit points of the hook open until I could make sure your lung and rib had healed up. I didn't want to risk your skin closing if your lung was still punctured. Luckily for you, you seemed to miss any other vital organs, especially your spine, I'm not sure that would've healed right at all.'

He said it so matter-of-factly, whilst Elara was trying her best not to puke.

'I punctured my lung?'

'And broke a rib. Nothing too serious though.'

She glared up at him, but there was a slight smile pulling at his lips. Perhaps humour was his coping mechanism.

'I need to go and find Ivy, hopefully if I apologise now, she'll actually speak to me again before I leave.'

She glanced down at Archer's T-shirt.

'Um, can I take this?'

He looked pained for a moment, his lip curling a little.

'I guess if you have to.'

Elara laughed, pushing up from the cold ground.

'Well, it doesn't look like I have much choice, does it?'

She turned to quickly slip on the soft cotton shirt. It could almost have been a dress on her, but at least it was semi-clean.

She glanced around for something to tie up her knotted hair. The blonde waves threaded with murky blood. Nothing suitable jumped out at her, so instead she twisted her hair up on top of her head, pulling the ends through a loop to make a knot. She pulled out a couple of baby hairs to frame her face, then glanced in the mirror. Wiping black smudges of mascara from under her eyes and pinching her cheeks to add some colour. She was looking disturbingly grey.

She turned around to see a surprised looking Archer, still in the process of getting up off the ground.

'You just...' He gestured a hand around at her appearance, a confused frown pulling at his eyebrows.

She shrugged. 'It's a girl thing.'

Elara had forgotten how tall Archer was, as when he stood up, he seemed to completely dominate the small space. She found herself level with his chest, her dried blood still smeared across it.

She looked up and met his eyes, the lightbulb swinging over them cast moving shadows across his face. They reminded her of the enchanted tattoos that swam along his skin.

His gaze held hers for a moment longer than she'd expected, she felt a blush burning across her cheeks, so she dropped her gaze back down to his chest, and then quickly to the ground where his uniform jacket was strewn carelessly across the floor.

She passed it to him before skirting around to stand in front of the door.

'Um, thank you. For not letting me die.' Elara plucked at her T-shirt as she waited for Archer to turn back around.

'Just doing my job, Miss Anderson.'

'You said this wasn't in your job description.'

He almost smiled as he ran a hand over his chin.
'Okay, you get an exception. Just this once.'

Finding Ivy was surprisingly easy now that Elara knew where to look. Ivy had shown her this particular spot a couple of days ago, trying to combat Elara's cabin fever having not left the walls of the Council since she'd arrived.

It was a wide window ledge right at the end of the corridor that Ivy's family lived on, as far North in the Northern Quarter as you could get. Covered by two heavy velvet curtains and with a stunning view out over the grounds, Ivy had added cushions and fairy lights over the years, making an incredibly cosy little hideaway.

'Hey.'

'Hi.'

Elara slipped onto the ledge across from Ivy, letting the curtain swing closed behind her.

'You're not an Ardent witch, are you?'

Elara shook her head silently.

'Then…what are you?'

'I'm not sure.'

'Okay.'

Ivy was silent for a moment.

'You exploded a chandelier.'

It was a statement, not a question.

'Yeah.'

'We both could've died.'

'But we didn't.'

Ivy rose an eyebrow at her.

'Okay, we could have, and I'm sorry. It was a complete accident, I swear. I just need to figure out what's going on in my head… do a little damage control.'

'Ha! You don't say.'

Elara smiled apologetically, following her friend's gaze out of the window.

'If it makes you feel any better, I just spent the last three hours of my life with your brother having glass pulled out of my back.'

Ivy's gaze shot round to look at her, the defensive, annoyed expression gone, and replaced with true concern, then her eyes drifted down to the cotton T-shirt Elara was wearing.

'Is that Archer's?'

Was that a flash of irritation Elara felt course through Ivy's stomach? It was gone as quickly as it had arrived, exhausted confusion taking its place.

'Yeah, mine got absolutely shredded, plus it was covered in blood. Needed something to walk back home in, just so I wasn't wandering about in a bra.' Elara laughed, but the sound trailed away as Ivy stayed silent, not meeting her gaze.

'You were injured?'

Elara shifted awkwardly, suddenly feeling very exhausted.

'Yeah. Pretty badly.'

She held up the hem of the shirt to show Ivy the scar that had already faded to a gentle pink, compared to the angry red from twenty minutes ago.

'How did it heal so quickly? That's just like Archer does,' Ivy said, reaching out to touch Elara's ribs before thinking better of it and snatching her hand away.

'He says I've got Fender magic. That's the only way I didn't die.'

She dropped the shirt back over her stomach, leaning back against the cold frame of the window.

'So, what, you're some kind of Inchoate witch?' Ivy asked, her tone coloured with suspicion. 'How is that possible when your parents are Ardent?'

Elara shook her head. 'I'm Ardent too. Archer said there's probably other streams in my blood as well, we haven't really had the time to test it out,' she said dryly.

It all sounded even more ridiculous now that Elara was hearing it out loud. Clearly Ivy wasn't overly impressed either, a disbelieving frown deeply creased between her brows.

'But... how are you? That would mean- surely not.'

'You gonna finish any of those sentences?'

'Don't you know what that means, Elara?' Ivy asked, pushing her dark hair off her face as she leant forward.

'No, Ivy. Do I look like I know what you mean?' She crossed her legs and dropped her elbows onto her knees, her face a few centimetres from Ivy's.

'If you truly have more than one type of magic, from different streams I mean- remember, months ago, when you first visited, I started telling you about a rare kind of witch, they thought they managed to eradicate them all. We aren't supposed to speak about them, we always got taught that they were dangerous and unpredictable. They possess all types of magic, and are direct descendants from the Original Witches themselves, meaning they're heir to the throne of Felicia, as long as they can prove they aren't volatile and have true control over their gifts. Stakes alight, Elara, you really are royalty,' Ivy breathed; her cheeks flushed a dark pink that glowed against her pale skin.

Elara's breath caught in her throat, her chest tight as though all the air had been knocked from her lungs.

'Heir?'

Ivy nodded excitedly. 'Elara, Felicia is yours. You must be descended from the big four, and inherited their gifts, meaning you are the most powerful witch in existence. We weren't supposed to learn about people like you in school, but we had this really cool teacher who got us books from the restricted section...' Ivy rambled, getting more and more excited by the second, 'anyway, we can teach you how to control your gifts, Elara. Then you'll be able to rule!'

Elara could feel sweat trickling down her back, she suddenly felt incredibly claustrophobic in the small space.

The neck of the cotton T-shirt seemed to be rising to greet her throat, pulling tighter and tighter against her skin, crushing her windpipe slowly but surely. She tugged at the soft material, but it didn't give, her skin prickled with the insistency of it.

'I need some air,' she gasped, tumbling off the window ledge and barely avoiding getting wrapped up in the velvet curtains.

'Oh, I was just going to check you'd actually gone home, but clearly... Miss Anderson?'

Her breath was coming in ragged gulps, the air felt hot and sticky, and Archer was barely a blur as she pushed past him, desperate to be outside.

'Elara, where are you going? You need to go home!'

She could hear Ivy shouting after her from somewhere in the distance, but that seemed unimportant. All she could focus on was the heavy wooden doors at the other end of the hallway, that she knew would take her to the grounds of the Council.

The second she pushed through them, there were thumping footsteps pounding down the corridor behind her. She didn't bother turning around, she knew whose they were.

Elara made a run for the large weeping willow tree in the centre of the grounds. She'd seen it every day from her custom-made balcony and couldn't imagine anything better right now than being under its branches, hearing the breeze rustle through the leaves, and feeling the bark against her back.

She slipped through the cascade of vines and dropped down to the ground before she could even process what she was doing. Digging her fingernails underneath the soil and feeling the gentle streams of energy rippling along the surface.

Instantly her head felt a little lighter, the cool January air coursed through her veins, and the twinkling of the stars above blinking between the canopy of leaves provided a welcome distraction.

She sucked in deep breaths through her teeth, shivering at the sensitivity it caused.

Muffled footsteps grew gradually louder as a shadowy figure emerged out of the darkness. Elara braced herself for the flurry of anger that no doubt was about to be showered upon her from Archer, his breathing heavy as he batted away the vines, making his own way into the private den. But no anger came. No shouting. No blaming. Nothing.

Elara turned to find her Defender looking surprisingly starstruck, his jaw hanging uncharacteristically open as he gazed around in wonder.

Elara began to ask him what was wrong, but he silenced her with a pointed finger, gesturing to something just out of view, over her left shoulder.

She turned to see tiny orbs of light swimming through the air. Glowing warm white and emitting a gentle heat that burnt against Elara's cold cheeks. Thousands of them drifted so gracefully, they looked like tiny jellyfish soundlessly being dragged along inky black waves.

The light cast winding shadows of the vines along the grass, where suddenly, tall flowers had elegantly sprung from the ground in a perfect circle around where Elara was crouched. The centre of each petal was a delicate dusty pink, that faded to a rich burgundy at the tips. They seemed to turn and face Elara as she looked around them in awe, almost like sunflowers turning towards the sun.

She looked back at Archer; he was staring at her in disbelief.

'How did you do that?' he whispered.

Elara looked down at her hands that were still pushed deep down into the Earth, her fingertips clutched at the soil.

It was then that Ivy, with Osmond in tow, broke through the wall of vines, her expression instantly matching her brother's as she was met with the unusual sight.

'Wow,' she breathed, her face lit up as her dad pushed past her, his eyes trained only on Elara.

'I think we need to refocus your training,' he murmured, grabbing the top of her arm, and pulling her up from the ground.

The second her hands left the soil, the lights dulled. The beautiful flowers wilted instantly, their petals turning an ugly brown as they dropped to the greying grass below.

CHAPTER TWENTY-SIX

Elara

'Elara, could you at least try and concentrate? We've been working on this spell for the last hour, and it's one of the simplest in the book.'

She turned to glare at him, irritated.

'Maybe it's easy for you, Archer, but I have no clue what I'm doing.'

It was Elara's last week of training. Her days had been so ridiculously full of activities, she was always dropping off during tea with Darya and Dritan.

During the day, she practised her official studies with Valen, then at every given chance, she was whisked out of the Council by Osmond with the help of Archer's protective enchantments, and she was to learn as many spells as possible to control her erratic magic. Though so far, she hadn't mastered a single one

'Elara, if you know the spells, your magic won't get as out of hand. You need to focus.'

Elara swished her wand wearily, muttering the Greenie enchantment under her breath, attempting to encourage the young daisies to sprout past their usual height, and soar to eye level. A simple spell that far undertook many of the things Elara had accomplished with much less effort.

Archer rolled his eyes, standing up from his watchful position on the hillside around the corner from any unwanted attention.

'You literally set fire to a chandelier with just your mind, how can you not grow a daisy with a wand?'

She watched him stifle a laugh as he took note of her grumpy expression.

'I don't know, Archer. You tell me,' she whined, flicking her wand again then jumping as the daisy suddenly flew into the sky, way above both their heads.

She pursed her lips together, staring tearfully at the wand.

'Hey, alright don't cry. Look, I think you're just flourishing your wand too much. Come here.'

He came and stood beside her, holding her wrist gently to guide the movement. She almost flinched at his touch, expecting some kind of catastrophic explosion. But instead his skin was surprisingly soft against hers, his movements cautious.

'Like a gentle swirl, then a line. Gentle swirl, line.'

Elara's arm flopped in his grasp.

'I'm sick of this Archer, it's clearly not working.'

She groaned, turning to face him as he stepped away.

'Just because you're reading what I'm supposed to do in a book, doesn't mean that will actually work,' she sighed, pointing with her wand over to the thick hardbacked book that he had been pouring over for the last few days.

'I just don't understand how you could do such complicated magic before, but now you can't even get a simple spell.'

She scowled angrily at him. 'Way to knock a girl when she's down.'

His eyebrows furrowed, suddenly deep in thought.

'No, I mean there's something missing. Your magic is unusual enough as it is, maybe you access it in a different way too.'

She stared blankly at him, exhaustion fogging her mind.

He walked around in circles for a few moments, the repetitive motion set Elara's teeth on edge.

'I don't really think you need a wand.'

'…Right.'

'I think a wand will only be necessary to make you look the part. Every witch needs a wand, except you I'm guessing.'

She rolled her eyes as he gave her a pointed look.

'Okay, so how am I doing the magic stuff then? I thought I was only supposed to be able to do the spell stuff through the wand?'

'I think your emotions are what fuel your gift. Whenever you get angry, or overwhelmed or even upset, catastrophic things happen. They're stronger than the average witches, you've shown that plenty of times, and maybe that means your magic can flourish without any other help, you just need to learn some emotional control.'

Elara felt her heart drop a little. Sure, it sounded cool that she might be innately magic, but she'd risked hers and Archer's lives for that wand, only for her to not need it at all.

'So not one single thing about me is normal.'

He shrugged.

'Guess not.'

She was about to start protesting when he plucked the wand from her hand, slipping it into his pocket.

'Just forget about the wand right now. It's not important, okay? Focus on an emotion, any emotion.'

She looked sceptical; her brow creased.

'Would you just trust me for two seconds? Focus on an emotion Elara.'

His sharp tone surprised her, it seemed easier for him to be stern rather than gentle with her.

'Fine,' she huffed, closing her eyes.

They both stood in silence for a moment, nothing happened.

She squinted one eye open at him, there was an expectant look on his face.

'Okay, I have the emotion… you haven't told me what I'm supposed to do next.'

'Stakes alight, it's like explaining hat etiquette to a toddler.' He paused, considering his words, 'channel that emotion into the spell, I don't think you even need to bother saying it out loud. Just picture in your head exactly what you want from the daisy. Whether you want it to grow, change colour or burst into flames. Anything.'

She held his gaze for a moment longer, her palms beginning to sweat, before closing her eyes.

A moment of silent stillness descended upon the hillside; Elara could almost feel the storm brewing on the hillside, with warm waves radiating off her.

Then, all in a rush, a bright glow began to seep from her skin, surrounding her like a protective shield. It threaded its way gracefully towards the patch of daisies, reaching out gentle fingers to cup each plant individually and lift it high up out of the ground.

'You know, I wasn't sure that would actually work,' Archer breathed, as she opened her eyes; surprised delight registering on her face.

'Definitely a change of pace compared to your usual ferocious spells. What changed?'

Elara smiled to herself, ducking her head to hide her expression.

'I wasn't angry or upset or stressed. I was just calm, thinking about something else.'

Thoughts of Xander had flooded her brain. The way her skin hummed with serenity whenever he was near, the way her cheeks blushed when he smiled, the look in his eyes when he was about to kiss her. It had filled her with such warmth it had felt like she might explode.

Archer cleared his throat, snapping her back from her daydream.

'Right, so your emotional state determines how your magic presents itself. Fascinating.'

She grinned at him, and she was almost sure he gave her a little smile back. Since her near-death experience, she was certain he'd been more tolerating of her. Though she couldn't quite figure out why.

'I think we've been looking at your training wrong. You don't need to be learning the spells, you just need to figure out how to control your emotions. That way your magic will stay in check. I must tell my father; he'll be most interested to hear our progress.'

Elara turned her attention back to the daisies, wondering what else she could do.

'Come on, Miss Anderson. You can have the rest of the evening off. I think my sister mentioned having some time free later.'

Archer formed the enchantment box around them as he had so many times over the past few days, and they walked in comfortable silence back towards the Northern Quarter.

As they stepped into the dark hallway, the invisible walls dissipated around them, Elara looked in the direction of the refectory, searching for Ivy's tell-tale choppy black hair.

Just as she was about to walk away, she glanced back for a moment and looked up to meet Archer's gaze.

'My wand?'

Archer slipped it out of his pocket, flipping it quickly in his hand to present her with the embellished handle.

She let it balance in her palm, holding his dark gaze.

'Thank you, Archer. Not just for tonight. For giving me a second chance. I really do appreciate the time you've given me.'

He opened his mouth to say something in response, but before he had the chance, she turned on her heel and started walking quickly down the corridor, hearing a moment later as Archer did the same.

CHAPTER TWENTY-SEVEN

Elara

The refectory was as quiet as ever. Warm sunlight spilled in through the windows and melancholy music sung over the speakers. Elara only ever saw a couple of other witches in the large room, and they hardly ever paid her any attention. It was why she spent so much time there.

The old lady from her first ever day in Felicia greeted her with a bright smile and a well-rehearsed curtsey. She worked most days, always seeming happy to do so and due to her exceptional Greenie talents, she made incredible herbal teas and coffees.

Elara sat on her favourite bench by the windows in the corner of the room, where she could see out onto the grounds. It was almost time for the sun to set, so plenty of witches were making their way across the gardens, leaving their jobs and socialising to meet the curfew Forneus had put in place.

Elara enjoyed seeing new witches each day. She had been afraid that she'd be kept isolated, not seeing another soul for three weeks during her training. Luckily for her, nobody seemed that bothered by her whereabouts. Forneus had all but left her alone, getting any information out of her through Valen, despite Ivy's previous claims, and even Archer had taken to leaving her to her own devices, other than when they were training.

Elara found it slightly harder that she hadn't seen Osmond much. She'd been counting on him checking up on her, almost like a tether to her home life, yet she hadn't seen him in over a week, ever since the chandelier incident.

She'd taken instead to writing in a diary. At home she would've painted the onslaught of thoughts and images in her head. Swiping at the paper with anger and tenderness. However, she didn't have that luxury here, and there was no one for her to truly talk to who would have the first clue about the chaos inside her head. Darya and Dritan seemed more and more like strangers by the day. She hardly spoke with them, and the more they tried to make her feel at home, the less comfortable she felt. She chose instead to stay in her room, eating, sleeping and living alone in the four walls, dreaming of her family back in Oakbridge.

Her only proof that everything she experienced was real, were the words written in her diary. Already dozens of entries, sometimes five a day, whenever Elara experienced or learnt something she didn't want to forget.

She wrote as though she was talking to Xander. The sharp pain of missing him had subsided slightly, the ache in her stomach diminished each day as it became her normality, and Elara convinced herself more each day that he wouldn't be missing her at all. Luckily her days were so packed full that she hardly had time to think about him, or her family.

'Evening, love.'

The elderly woman set down a steaming hot cup of tea in front of Elara, tendrils of fruity steam made their way towards her, notes of elderflower and apple filling the air.

'Elderberry and green apple tea. I think you'll really like this one.'

The witch dropped into a low curtsey, holding her long grey skirt out politely.

Elara cleared her throat awkwardly, and the witch snapped back up, standing straight with a sheepish look on her face.

'Sorry, love. Old habits.'

Elara smiled, reaching out to wrap her chilled hands around the cup.

'That's alright, Olive. This one smells incredible.'

Olive beamed.

'New recipe! You're the first to try it.'

Olive slipped onto the bench across from Elara, spreading her skirt out around her.

Her curly grey hair was frizzy from a long day of work, plaited tightly back into a bun.

It was unusual to see grey hair around here, many witches aged differently thanks to serums and elixirs that slowed down the aging of their cells, but Olive had decided to 'go grey gracefully'. At almost 82, she was one of the oldest 'natural' witches in the whole of Felicia, yet still, thanks to the peaceful lifestyle, she hardly looked a day over 50.

The thick liquid was sticky and sweet, with a sharp ripeness that took Elara by surprise.

'This is incredible, Olive. I think it's my new favourite.'

The old witch's cheeks glowed.

'I'm so glad you like it. You looked like you needed a pick-me-up. Anything you want to share? I'm all ears.'

Olive had such a kind expression, it made Elara want to spill all her secrets. Her rich brown eyes were quietly inviting, and she smelled like citrus, vanilla and Christmas. In fact, she looked like she could almost be Mrs Claus.

'No, that's okay. It's just been a crazy week, lots of work to be done.'

Olive's expression turned pitying.

'I'm sure Forneus is keeping you very busy, love. And Osmond's son is a kind boy, but he does seem to run a tight ship. He's particularly hard on you from what I've seen.'

Elara looked up at Olive somewhat suspiciously.

'You aren't really supposed to know about that kind of thing, Olive. In fact, I'm not really supposed to talk to you at all.'

Olive smiled knowingly. 'Your secrets are safe with me, Miss. News travels fast in the Council, lots of gossips you see.'

She winked mischievously, standing up from the bench.

'I'll leave you to your tea. Let me know if you need anything.'

Elara watched as Olive swished away, almost sad to see her friendly face go.

Within the short span of their conversation, the sun had completely disappeared behind the horizon. In its place was the glowing, white moon, dark clouds and glittering stars. The nights were so much clearer here than at home, thanks to the minimal light pollution.

With the darkness came a light chill in the January air. Elara pulled the hood of her hoody up over her hair, creating a shield between her and the outside world, as she slipped her diary out of her pocket to write about her evening.

Hey, Xander.

I can't get you off my mind today, there's so much I want to tell you.

Archer finally figured out why my spells aren't working. Apparently, I don't need a wand… just some emotional control. Easier said than done, right?

Thank God my time here is almost up, but Forneus says I need to be a fully-functioning witch before they introduce me to the public. They don't want me to be a threat, but Ivy says people outside the Council are terrified and angry, and everything will turn ugly if they don't trust in Forneus. I can tell there are things they aren't telling me; the story goes way beyond anything I'm involved in... I just know it.

I'm desperate to hear your voice, we could talk about NORMAL things. I want to hear about how your driving lessons are going, whether Jenna and Alfie have finally found the courage to discuss their feelings, if that seagull on the beach is recovered from its leg injury. Dumb stuff, I know.

Knowing that I can't tell you about everything that's happened recently is awful, I need someone to confide in.

I miss you more than ever,
Elara x

Elara closed the book quickly as someone dropped onto the bench across from her, making the table shake. Elara glanced up to find Ivy dressed head to toe in black, including her dark nail varnish. Her smile was wide, but that didn't distract Elara from the flurry of motion over her shoulder as someone with long, dark hair disappeared quickly out of the refectory with a final glance back over their shoulder, bright green eyes trained on Elara's face.

'What are you writing?' Ivy grinned playfully, her black hair brushing over her shoulders.

Elara snapped to attention and smiled back; it was always nice to see Ivy's cheerful face. A stark contrast to her brother's moody expression.

'Nothing really. Just keeping track of my crazy life.' She slipped the book off the table and onto her lap, hoping to divert Ivy's attention.

'Is this another Olive creation?' she asked, gesturing to the tea.

'Elderberry and green apple.' Elara pushed the cup towards her friend.

Ivy took a tentative sip, before her features lit up.

'Stakes alight! I think this is my new favourite!' She took another swig.

Elara laughed. 'That's exactly what I said.'

Olive waved at them from across the room, and as Ivy threw an enthusiastic thumbs up back, they could hear the old witch laugh as she disappeared back off into the kitchens.

'So, I saw Archer,' Ivy whispered, dragging a hand across her mouth.

'Oh yeah?' Elara pulled the hood further in front of her face, leaning her elbows on the hard table.

'He said you've figured out the magic problem. You're an Empath!'

Elara looked up at Ivy quizzically.

'Archer didn't use that word.'

'He didn't know it, most people don't. Another finding from the restricted section,' Ivy said with a wink. 'It means you access your magic using your emotions, not a wand. The way you feel corresponds with how your magic will present itself. For example, if you're angry or stressed, it'll be a lot of destructive, violent magic, like with the chandelier. Being an Empath often comes hand in hand with having all types of magic. It's what gives people like you a bad name because they never learn to control their emotions and then become dangerous. Good job you have us, eh?'

Elara rolled her eyes. 'I guess. How do you know about all this stuff? No one else seems to.'

Ivy looked around suspiciously, leaning closer to Elara over the table.

'We're never taught this stuff in school, in fact it's pretty taboo. Some witches don't even believe it in the first place, they think people like you are old folktales, used to scare little kids at night. Only because your magic is so powerful, and anyone in the past who claimed to have multiple gifts was dangerous and vengeful, quickly exiled by society for being different. It's very closely linked with Shade Magic, the dark spells and enchantments that we aren't allowed to use. But in Felicia's main library, there's a tiny area in the restricted section that talks about all of this. I was always fascinated by it, used to get told off for it in school. But now I feel like it finally makes sense.'

Elara dropped her head into her hands, sighing deeply.

'So basically, I'm always going to have to mask as an Ardent witch, just so I don't get exiled to Helabasus?'

Ivy pondered for a moment, a thoughtful crease between her eyebrows.

'I don't know. Maybe, or maybe you'll be the change in Felicia, and a whole generation of people like you will pop out of the ground.'

Elara groaned, pushing her hood back out of her face.

'I don't want to be the change, Ivy. I've only been a witch for three weeks; I don't have a clue what I'm doing.'

Ivy frowned at her, and the enchanted black kitten inked onto her arm stopped playing with its ball of wool for a second, turning to give Elara an equally disappointed look.

'You have always been a witch, Elara. You were born with these gifts, this purpose in life. I think it's your duty to yourself to see it through. To make a difference! Felicia has completely misjudged people like you, who knows what kind of power you actually have. You just have to go about it in the right way.'

Ivy's tone was hushed, but her excitement was clear. She wasn't going to give up on this one easily.

Elara was hoping to sneak silently back to her room, avoiding Darya and Dritan and their curiosity and work through the questions in her own head. However, she had no such luck.

'Elara honey? Is that you?' Darya called the second Elara slipped into the house.

All the lights flooded on in an instant to reveal Darya sat by one of the floor to ceiling windows, a stunning aubergine cloak draped around her shoulders.

'Excellent, we've been waiting up. We have a surprise!'

Darya beamed ecstatically as shivers worked their way down Elara's arms. Who knew what kind of surprise Darya would have in mind.

Dritan suddenly appeared from a doorway to Elara's right, making her jump. He closed the door quickly behind him and locked it in a flash before standing next to his wife. She stared at the door for a moment longer. She'd hardly ever noticed it being there before, now she was suddenly desperate to know what was inside.

When she turned back to face her strange witchy-parents, they were stood only a few inches from her, close enough for Elara to smell Darya's lavender perfume.

'We know you have been missing your adoptive family dreadfully,' Darya started, looking irritatingly tearful as she so often did, 'and whilst we simply adore having you back with us, where you belong, we don't want you to be unhappy. So, we got you a gift.'

Darya suddenly brandished a metallic looking brick from her billowing sleeves, holding it in her slender hand out towards Elara.

'We of course have no clue how it works, but we sent Archer, and he said that you would know how to use it.'

She flipped the slab over in her hand to reveal Elara's scratched phone, that lit up instantly as it recognised her face.

Elara gasped, grabbing it from Darya's hand and turned it over a few times, squealing as it revealed her lock-screen picture again and again, a happy snap of her and her family beside the Christmas tree.

She looked up at Darya and Dritan, behind their smiles was a true sadness Elara hadn't seen before. Not their usual performative dramatics, but a genuine ache for lost time and experiences. Elara noticed the crease between Darya's eyebrows, the way she was ringing her hands together under her sleeves. Dritan's jaw set slightly too harshly and the tense way he stood. She suddenly felt an overwhelming amount of guilt for how selfish she'd been. All this time, she had been thinking about how hard this had been on her, she hadn't spent a moment of time considering how they must be feeling. For them to get their daughter back after fifteen years, and her not say more than two words to them a day.

She bit her cheek harshly to stop herself from crying. The sudden collision of her two worlds and the feelings that came with them were too much to handle right now.

To her surprise, it was Elara that reached out to envelop them both in a tight hug. Darya grasped her back as though her life depended on it, and Dritan's cheek felt wet against hers. Elara felt as though they were holding her together, stopping her from crumbling into a million pieces. She pressed her face into Darya's shoulder, the fabric of her cloak was soft against her skin, so she rubbed her cheek against it.

As she pulled away, she dragged her sleeve across her face, trying and failing to keep her emotions in check. Darya reached out with a handkerchief that had appeared from nowhere, and lightly dusted Elara's cheeks. The tickle of the fabric made Elara laugh and the smile this generated from Darya almost made her start balling again.

'Go and make your calls. We trust you to spare the unnecessary details,' Dritan said with a knowing wink.

Elara turned to head back out into the corridor, before turning with a last minute thought.

'Thank you, both. I really appreciate this.'

She turned again to walk out of the door.

'Maybe we could watch a moving picture tomorrow if you have the time? I hear they're all the rage on Earth,' Darya blurted out just before Elara could open the door.

She turned; the hopeful looks on both her parent's faces were enough to make her decision for her.

'Of course. I would love that. Maybe ask Archer if he can figure out how to set up Netflix though, I'm not sure you'll have that here.'

Dritan rushed to grab a notebook off one of the end tables. 'Ask Archer about Nettle Flix. Got it.'

Elara stifled a laugh before finally slipping back out of the door.

'Xander? Xander, can you hear me? It's Elara.'

The connection was crackly as Elara cupped her hand around the bottom of the phone, straining to hear anything in response.

'Elara? Hey! I can hear you.' Xander's voice was muffled and scratchy, but the familiarity of it almost brought Elara to tears.

'Hi,' she sobbed into the speaker. 'I missed you.'

He chuckled down the line. Elara could almost imagine he was tucked away behind the curtain in Ivy's hiding spot with her. His arm around her waist and cheek pressed to her forehead.

'I missed you too. I've been waiting to hear from you, how's the art retreat? My little Van Gogh.'

Elara's mind went blank for a moment, she'd forgotten about her cover story. A three week art retreat in Wales, spending time studying and creating drawings and paintings amongst team building and inspiring exercises.

'Oh, umm... It's great. Really eye-opening.'

'Good. You can show me some of your masterpieces when you get home. How much longer are you away for? It feels like you left so suddenly.'

Elara's heart ached; she bit her cheek so hard she tasted blood.

'Not long, I hope. I'm desperate to see you. The signal's been so bad here, it's been so hard not speaking to you.'

Xander was quiet for a moment.

'Yeah, your parents said you mentioned the signal in your letter. I was wondering where my postcard was.' He laughed, but Elara could hear the tension in his voice.

'I know, I'm sorry. I couldn't even buy a stamp, I had to borrow one from Mr Costello. I kept sending you texts, but they just bounced back. Honestly, we were so far out in the country-side all I saw for a week was sheep. But we're back in one of the towns now, so hopefully we can speak more.'

Her stomach dropped at the lie that slipped so silkily off her tongue.

'Yeah, I would like that.'

She was silent for a moment, suddenly struck with nerves as though Xander was a stranger, and she was an actress desperately clinging to her role.

'How's Mr Bobs?' she asked finally, her heartrate pounding.

Xander chuckled down the line, and the sound sent a warm flush across her cheeks.

'He's doing good. I took him a chip butty yesterday and his leg seems to be healing up. He misses you though.'

Elara grinned, sinking down into the cushions. 'I miss him too.'

When the call had ended, Elara leant back against the cold wall of the windowsill. It rarely rained in Felicia, but tonight dark black clouds obscured the moon, and rain heavy enough to rival that of even Scotland pelted against the glass. Seemed a pretty accurate rendition of Elara's mood. She was about to leave the comfort of the windowsill, when she heard footsteps approaching, making their way towards Ivy's front door.

'We need to figure out something to tell them. They're starting to notice how often she's gone.'

The voice was hushed, but Elara recognised instantly that it was Osmond's.

'If anyone finds out about her, all hell will break loose,' he hissed. Elara's heart began to race painfully in her chest.

'Get better at lying then.' Another male voice, it took a second for it to register, but Elara knew that voice. 'You're her Guardian. If you can't protect her one secret, then what can you do?'

Elara was surprised at the growl of anger in Archer's voice. She could see their shadows underneath the curtain elongated on the floor, Archer towering above his father, his posture domineering.

'It's not just her that I have to protect, Archer. If this got out, we'd all be as good as ash. You, me, Ivy, your mother. You know it isn't as simple as it sounds, there's so much corruption under Forneus's reign, we wouldn't even be sent to Helabasus if the truth came out. You're a smart boy Archer. Figure it out.'

Elara's ears were ringing so badly she could hardly hear what Osmond was saying, her own thoughts an incessant buzz knocking around in her skull.

'Why must you be so cryptic? What isn't simple about it?' Archer's voice rumbled down the hallway and Elara shivered as she sensed his anger turn to fear.

Both men fell silent. From her hiding place at the end of the corridor, it felt every bit like a Russian standoff, who would fire first? When suddenly the front door opened letting a cool draft into the hallway.

Elara could sense Ivy's presence, she was calm and collected, a stark contrast to her brother, as usual.

'She's not theirs.'

CHAPTER TWENTY-EIGHT

Elara

'So, Archer sorted Netflix?'

Elara flopped down on one of the giant sofas which was now pointed at a large flatscreen TV that hadn't been there yesterday.

Darya frowned at the screen. 'Well, I would presume so, but I can't see anything. Can you?'

Elara stifled a laugh as Dritan brought his nose so close to it that the glass fogged up, then jumped back in surprise as it lit up in front of him.

'You have to use a remote.'

She waggled it in the air, before clicking the button to take them straight to the Netflix homepage.

'Fascinating,' Darya exclaimed, smoothing her skirt around her.

Elara, as usual, felt incredibly underdressed in her sweatshirt and leggings, compared to the formal attire of her witchy-parents.

'You know, people often wear comfy clothes to watch movies in. Like pjs.'

Darya looked down at her silk blouse. 'But this is comfortable.'

Elara snorted, reaching for her takeaway cup of tea from Olive. Today it was mandarin and honey.

'Do you two like popcorn?' Elara was met with blank stares as though she had just asked them if they cut off their toes every night before bed.

'Like corn that's been cooked, then flavoured?'

Clearly by their expressions they thought she was going insane.

'This place is so weird,' Elara chuckled, wrapping her blanket around her.

'Well, I would love to try popcorn,' Dritan piped up, though the slight curl of his lip indicated differently.

Darya reluctantly reached over to the bell placed on the end table beside her, giving it a quick shrill ring.

The Greenie witch who had brought Elara flowers in her first week entered immediately, her head bowed in respect.

Elara beamed at her, throwing a small wave in her direction. The witch smiled politely back and dipped into a low curtsy.

'Good evening, Mr, Mrs and Miss Headley. How may I be of assistance?'

Darya and Dritan turned to look at Elara expectantly.

'Oh! Good evening, how are you?'

The witch looked confused, glancing back at the door she'd come from as though she wanted nothing more than to go back out of it.

'Oh no, Elara sweetie. You don't have to make conversation with them, you just tell them what you want.'

Elara stared in disbelief at Darya for a second, but Darya's expression remained unchanging, her eyebrow slightly raised.

'Right. Um, please may we have some salted popcorn? With a couple of bowls to put it in if that's okay.'

The Greenie witch nodded, her expression relieved.

'Oh, wait! I'm sorry I don't know your name.'

This time both Darya and Dritan turned to glare at her, but Elara kept her gaze focussed on the witch, her smile unfaltering.

'Erm, it's Fleur,' she said quietly, not meeting Elara's gaze.

'Fleur! Thank you, I'm Elara, it's lovely to officially meet you.'

Fleur dashed out of the door as quickly as she could, whilst Darya and Dritan's gaze remained firmly on Elara.

'Sweetheart, we know you haven't become accustomed to life here just yet, but it isn't correct practise to make friends with the help. They are simply here to do a job, not waste our and their time standing about chatting. It is your right as an Ardent witch to tell them exactly what you want and when you want it.'

Elara stared at her birth-mother. 'Where I come from, it is rude if you are not polite to someone who is doing you a service. Manners are a simple courtesy.'

Elara settled back onto the sofa as Darya and Dritan finally turned their attention back to the TV.

'Anyone ever seen Mean Girls?'

By the end of the film, Darya had kicked off her shoes and tucked her feet under her long skirt. She'd been through four bowls of popcorn and let her light hair down from its usual tight top-knot. Dritan had loosened his tie, and his blazer jacket was strewn carelessly on the floor.

'I can't believe that is what normal humans are like! Their schools, their clothes, everything!' Darya exclaimed as the end credits rolled, leaning back on the sofa, more relaxed than Elara had ever seen her.

'You would have saved a lot of time with this experiment if you had just watched some ordinary human films,' Elara laughed.

'It's just unbelievable, the way they talk and interact with one another. I thought I knew a decent deal about

Human Studies, but they never acted like this in the old archives!'

'That's the modern day for you. You can't base your experience of humans off scrolls from the 17th century. Times have changed drastically.'

'Clearly,' Darya breathed.

'Well, I'm exhausted from just watching that. I think it's time for me to go to bed!' Dritan exclaimed, offering his hand out to his wife as he stood up. She unfolded herself carefully from where she'd been curled up all evening, taking his hand graciously. It was strange to see them be so normal with one another.

Darya paused for a moment, before turning and bending to kiss Elara's forehead. 'Goodnight sweetheart. We had a lovely evening.'

Elara's cheeks burned red as they made their way into their bedroom, before wiping the lipstick smudge from her forehead, suddenly feeling as though she had been holding her breath for the entire evening.

As soon as she heard their door lock with the characteristic click, she darted over to the room that Dritan had exited yesterday. The room that she'd hardly ever noticed before, but Dritan seemed so keen to keep prying eyes away from.

As she'd predicted, the door was locked, and the handle creaked loudly the second she tried to move it. Clearly picking the lock was not the way to go. She dropped down silently to the ground, balancing on the balls of her feet. Peering underneath the door she could see a light still on, a little lamp atop a desk laden with paper and files. It only made her even more interested to see what Dritan kept so secretive.

She stood back up and peered at the lock for a moment. She knew Archer would be the perfect person to call on right now, of course he would know how to get into a locked room, however, she didn't feel like that was too smart of an idea.

Suddenly, a thought popped into her head. Both Archer and Ivy had said that her magic worked differently, and that she had all types of magic. Surely one stream had the ability to unlock doors, though she wasn't sure which one. All she needed to do was focus on an emotion, but not one that made her angry or stressed, and then will the door to open. Surely it couldn't be too hard?

Half an hour later she was still stood staring intently at the lock. Nothing had changed, yet she had been thinking about Xander the whole time. Maybe Ivy and Archer were wrong. She sighed in frustration, tiredness winning the battle against her closing eyes, when suddenly the door clicked and swung open on its hinges. She stared at it in disbelief as the soft warm glow crept out into the living room, a smile making its way onto her face. She glanced over her shoulder, making sure Darya and Dritan weren't stood watching her every move, before slipping into the tiny room and closing the door behind her.

The room was unbelievably full in comparison to the relative emptiness of the rest of the house. Papers, photographs and news articles littered every wall and surface. Files and books were piled high on the floor and the desk, looking ready to topple over at the slightest breeze. It was almost overwhelming enough to make Elara turn around and walk back out of the door, but she needed to know exactly what Ivy meant.

So instead, she got to work rifling through the desk. Old newspaper cuttings flew out at her, pictures dropped to the floor, and pages and pages of notes swam before her eyes. It was her life, on paper. Everything she'd ever done, everywhere she'd been, the people she'd spoken to, written down in front of her. Pictures of her all the way from being a toddler, walking down the pavement holding her mum's hand, her first day at primary school, her family holiday to the Isle of Man, all taken from the perspective of an innocent bystander, though of course she knew that it must be Osmond's handiwork. Elara's cheeks flushed a deep crimson as she stumbled across her first kiss with Xander, her heart beating rapidly.

She couldn't handle any more photos, so she turned instead to the file on the corner of the desk that was bursting at the seams. On the front page was a solemn looking photo of Darya and Dritan, a few years younger holding a blonde toddler. No one in the photo was smiling, and baby Elara was reaching out to someone or something beyond the frame. Elara flicked through a couple more pages, each had a similar photo. Elara being held by her birth-parents. Each one was captioned the same thing, 'Darya and Dritan Headley with their daughter, Elara (aged 1)'. It was surreal to see, and Elara could hardly connect herself to the little blonde girl in the picture, despite her own familiar eyes looking out at her. As she looked a little harder, she couldn't help but notice the tense way they held her, as if it was the first time they had been near a child, and how uncomfortable she looked in their arms.

She flipped somewhere towards the middle of file and found a copy of her adoption certificate. When she was younger, her parents had had it displayed proudly above the fireplace, meaning Elara could look at it whenever she wished. Their openness about her adoption was one of the many reasons she loved them so much, but just as she was about to flick past the page, she noticed something that looked unusual. On her parent's copy, there had never been a 'birthparents' section, with it being a closed adoption, but as she scanned over the document there were two clear names listed:

Esmé Sylvaine (Mother)
Gabriel Sylvaine (Father)

Suddenly, Elara heard a creak from the direction of Darya and Dritan's bedroom. She scrambled to close the file and put it back where she'd found it, in the process knocking off a stack of photographs. She dropped to the ground, trying desperately to pick them up in the right order, but her clammy hands slipped over the laminated paper. A sweat broke out along her brow as she weighed up her options. She had about ten seconds before her fate would be sealed. Ten seconds until her world came crumbling down.

With a steadying breath, she abandoned the desk and darted out of the room closing the door as silently as she could behind her and desperately hoping whatever trick she'd used to unlock the door would do its magic once more. Just as she dived back onto the sofa, Dritan popped his head out of the bedroom door, a flash of his burgundy dressing gown poking out from behind the doorframe.

'Go to bed soon please, Elara. You have classes tomorrow.'

Elara nodded, hoping that her smile was genuine and that he didn't notice her heavy breathing, and the adoption certificate hastily tucked beneath the blanket.

He threw her a final tight smile, before disappearing back into the room. Elara let her head drop back onto the sofa cushions, her chest heaving up and down with deep breaths. It was all she could do to keep the tears that threatened to fall down her cheeks at bay.

CHAPTER TWENTY-NINE

Elara

'I can't believe I finally get to see you next week,' Xander sighed down the phone.

Their phone calls had become a nightly ritual, and the only thing that was keeping Elara sane. Whilst she usually spent this time with Ivy, she'd been keeping her distance trying to process what had become abundantly clear to her. That somehow or another, Darya and Dritan also weren't her birth-parents, despite their claims. Not only that, but Ivy and Osmond had figured this out, and not thought it of any importance to let Elara in on their little secret. Just when she thought she might have been making some progress with her witchy heritage, yet again her world had been turned on its head. Now she was longing more than ever to be back with her real family, in her sleepy village, with Xander by her side.

'I know, it's felt like forever,' Elara whispered, holding back tears.

'I'm never going to let you forget how much you've missed me these past few weeks,' Xander joked.

Elara giggled back, curling up tighter under her duvet. She liked to keep the balcony doors open so that she could see out into the night. The stars twinkling down at her, and the cool breeze dusting her cheeks.

'Don't get me wrong, I'm excited to hear about your trip, but I'm more excited to kiss you and touch you and hold you,' he murmured.

Elara felt her cheeks flush red and her heart pick up the pace.

'I'm excited for that too. I could really do with a hug.'

'Ouch, friend-zoned to the max,' Xander laughed.

Elara smiled to herself, relaxing comfortably in the silence.

'You ready to get back to the college life?' he asked.

Elara considered for a moment. She had plenty of assignments and due dates coming up, plus the joy of seeing Natalia, but that didn't outweigh her desire for normality.

'Yes. Definitely. I need some time just living my life, it's felt crazy recently.'

'I can't wait to live our lives together.'

Elara felt a warm happiness creep into her stomach, and she was glad Xander wasn't here to see her cheesy grin and rosy cheeks.

'I can almost feel you smiling right now,' he laughed.

'Shh, you feel nothing,' Elara joked back, hiding behind her hand.

'Oh, I feel something,' he murmured, his voice growing sleepy, 'and I'm pretty sure you feel it too, I'm just waiting for you to get home so you can say it back.'

Elara was silent for a moment her heart pounding, when suddenly her call was interrupted by a sharp knock on her door.

'Elara? You have visitors.'

She wished the call didn't have to end so soon, but she knew Darya wouldn't wait around for her to hang up before bursting in through the door.

'Okay, hold on,' she shouted back.

'Hey, Xander? I have to go, there's a workshop on that I'm missing,' she fibbed, her voice sincere, 'I'll text you though.'

'Okay no worries. I love hearing your voice though.'

'I miss you.'

'I miss you most. Hey, Elara? Don't say it back, but... I love you.'

Elara's breath hitched in her throat; she was never going to get tired of hearing that.

'Your reintroduction event is this Friday, Elara.'

Darya was perched expectantly on the sofa, Dritan next to her, and Ivy and Osmond opposite.

'You've worked so hard, and there's absolutely nothing to worry about, you're completely ready. You've got the knowledge and the skills, though your manners may still need a little bit of work.'

Elara rolled her eyes, which earned a pointed look from Dritan.

'In the first hour, there will be a time for questions from select members of the press, we'll be by your side to aid with any answers you aren't sure on, but Forneus has already pre-approved what may be asked of you.'

Elara frowned. 'That doesn't sound very genuine, sounds like he'll only be telling people what they want to hear.'

'That's exactly what he's doing, sweetheart. The only reason this event is being held is to stop misinformation spreading like wildfire, and the people of Felicia losing their trust in their ruler. It would cause riots across the nation, people using you as a scapegoat for their own qualms. Many of them won't understand why we did what we did, or that it was for the good of the nation. Forneus needs you to convince them that you were unharmed and lived a happy life which can now expand to include your warlock heritage. It began before you arrived, even here in the Council, though Forneus bravely stepped up and found the source of the problem, eliminated it and therefore reinstated his authority.

That was easily done within the walls, in Felicia people are different. They seek their own gain, have strong opinions, and like to challenge those in power. It is the way it's always been, and something of this scale, so controversial, would cause the downfall of Felicia. You don't want that, do you Elara?'

Elara shook her head silently. She really wasn't too happy about how much pressure there was on her to get something right that she never signed up for.

'Anyway, questions first, then there will be a reading of the report you have been working on with Valen.'

Elara thought back with despair to the dreaded report. Every day for the last week she had spent at least two hours working on it, writing up as many memories, experiences, feelings, interactions and stories as she could think of which Osmond had then been filing away with evidence and pictures that he'd collected over the years. Elara had written about her family, her friends, the way she felt like she'd never entirely fit in in London, but how Scotland had immediately felt like home, as soon as she met Xander. She blushed at the detail she'd gone into about her time spent with him, how much clarity and hope he seemed to have given her life. She desperately hoped they would leave much of that out of the reading. There was something about Valen that had made her spill all her worldly secrets, all the repressed memories and deepest feelings. No doubt it had something to do with their being an Ardent witch.

'Forneus will then make a speech,' Darya snapped her back to attention with a sharp clap of her hands, 'describing the success of the experiment. Ideally, we would already have the next plan in motion, however, we had to work so quickly that it simply wasn't possible.'

Ivy was starting to wriggle impatiently in her seat. She caught Elara's eye, throwing her a quick wink before turning back to stare at Darya intently. Elara stifled a giggle.

'Then, what we have all been looking forward to, the ball itself.' Darya clasped her hands in front of her, looking out into the far off distance. 'Everybody important will be at that ball, all of the most powerful witches, all of the Ardent families, people you would have attended school with. It'll be an excellent chance for you to win people over, make connections, and set up your place in society,' Darya cooed, seemingly not noticing the peculiar look on Elara's face. Dritan caught it though.

'I think you mean make friends, darling, you don't need connections Elara, simply to meet those who you were always destined to know.'

He smiled kindly at her, but Elara still felt uneasy. This was not her cup of tea at all.

'Will you be there?' she asked, turning to look at Osmond and Ivy.

'Of course, we wouldn't miss it for the world.'

Elara wanted nothing more than to hug Osmond in that moment, she'd missed him.

'So! Now all the logistics are out of the way, we get to focus on the fun part!' Darya exclaimed, jumping up from the sofa. Perhaps the most animated Elara had ever seen her.

'I always dreamt of the day when I would get to dress my daughter up for her Wand Ceremony, then that dream was taken away, but that's why this is even more special.'

As usual, there were tears in her eyes and Dritan was gripping her hand for dear life. However, Osmond and Ivy looked as sceptical as she felt. She was desperate to ask them about what she'd heard in the corridor that night, to tell them about what she'd found in Dritan's study, but it seemed as though Darya was going to be holding her hostage for the next couple of days in a hair and outfit frenzy.

'Now, Ivara, I believe you brought a selection of dresses gifted by your mother for Elara to try on?'

Ivy's eyebrows shot up at the mention of her full name, she despised being called Ivara.

'Umm yeah. My mum bought a ton for my Wand Ceremony, but obviously I only wore the one, so these are all spare. She said she has a good Broomie who can do any adjustments by Friday as well.'

'Excellent,' Darya breathed, reaching out for the boxes.

'Matching shoes? Accessories?'

'All in the boxes.'

Darya's face lit up like it was Christmas day as Elara groaned inwardly.

'We can try them all on, have a little fashion show even! Doesn't that sound fun sweetheart?'

Elara forced a smile, she wondered how genuine it looked.

Darya started rifling through one of the boxes, Elara's eyes widened at the rolls of hot pink chiffon that erupted over the sides, Ivy unsuccessfully turned a laugh into a cough and immediately started choking, earning a despaired look from Osmond.

'Now, Elara honey. Who taught you how to dance?'

CHAPTER THIRTY

Elara

'You best be joking.'
She was stood opposite Archer in the middle of the living room, all the furniture had been pushed to the edges of the room, with chairs balanced precariously on top of tables.
'I most certainly am not,' Darya huffed, hitching her skirt up around her ankles to kick off her heeled boots.
'It seems no-one thought it appropriate to teach you how to dance properly, and I absolutely will not have my daughter make a fool of herself at her first ever ball. Now Archer is a little tall, I must admit, however he is our best option short of making you dance with a broom.'
Elara rolled her eyes at Archer's bemused expression.
'Plus, he has nothing better to do, so he'll suffice.'
Elara was the one smiling now as Archer looked offended.
'You'll be expected to open the ball with a traditional ballroom dance, Elara. Ordinarily at a ball, you would have the opportunity to seek out the most suitable dance partner, however obviously we don't have that luxury, so it is best that you learn with Archer now, so he can fill the place at the ball itself.'

Archer stared at Darya, his expression unimpressed.

'I'll be stationed with the other Defenders, at Forneus's aid. I cannot abandon my post for a- a... performance.'

'You can, and you will,' Darya glared back at him, 'Forneus himself requested it.'

Archer raised an eyebrow at Elara, his eyes lazily trailing up and down her frame, his expression bored as though there were ten million things he'd rather be doing with his time. Elara squirmed uncomfortably, trying and failing to keep her face blank.

'Alright, Archer hand at her waist, Elara, your hand goes on his shoulder.'

'This wasn't my idea you know,' Elara hissed.

'Hah! Like you don't love the way they dress you up like a doll to show you off. Isn't that a human girl's dream? Burner,' he whispered back as piano music began to play from a hidden speaker.

'Would you quit calling me that? And no that is certainly not my dream, thank you very much. Why would I want showing off?'

Elara sensed his emotions shift from irritated to confused. He thought she was naïve.

'You don't truly think they're having this ball to get the information out there, do you?' Elara's mind remained blank.

'Informing people of the purpose of the experiment won't make a shred of difference, in Felicia they're probably too starved to even listen. But showing off the next darling of Felicia, a fresh face of hope dressed like a princess, now that will calm the riots. Forneus knows that you'll play his part exactly as he intended... his little robot burner girl with pretty blonde hair and trained by his own court. What could possibly go wrong?'

Elara looked up at him, but he didn't meet her gaze, instead with one hand he held hers, and the other he dropped lightly to her waist.

'Follow my lead,' he murmured.

Darya ran a tight ship, not to Elara's surprise. They skipped and galloped to all corners of the room, there were spins and jumps, and Elara was more out of shape than she cared to admit. In one intense turn sequence, she spun so fast that she all but fell out of the routine, narrowly missing crashing into a large floor lamp and instead dropping down onto the sofa in a fit of dizzy giggles.

'Okay, okay I'm done. If I take another step, I think I'll die,' she laughed as the room rushed around her.

Archer flopped down on the sofa opposite her, instead of his usual brooding darkness, she was surprised to find a bright grin on his face.

'Alright you two. But if you could practise in your own time, I think the routine will really come together,' Darya declared.

Elara wondered whether the mysterious Ardent witch had been a prima ballerina in a past life, as she'd never met someone more obsessed with leg placement and neck extension.

'You surprised me there,' Elara said turning towards Archer, her voice breathy from the exertion of the dance.

Archer frowned at her as he sat up straight on the sofa, regaining his composure and smoothing out the creases in his relaxed linen shirt. It was strange to see him out of his usual uniform.

'I don't know what you mean.'

Elara snorted. 'Well, you can certainly dance better than I can, and from the look on your face you enjoyed it just as much. Don't try and fib, you know it won't work.'

Archer cleared his throat uncomfortably before standing up from the sofa.

'I was simply doing my duty, Miss Anderson. I was ordered to dance, so that is what I did. Goodnight.'

'You know there's no shame in letting your guard down, Archer. Having talent isn't something to be embarrassed about.'

She darted in front of him, blocking his path to the exit.

He stopped in his tracks and stared at her; a peculiar expression painted across his features. The candles that had been lit artfully around the room cast harsh shadows across his face. Elara felt her heartrate quicken as he flexed his jaw, no doubt he was about to unleash some torrent of suppressed anger on her. But to her surprise, his face softened, and he smiled.

'I never said I was embarrassed, Miss Anderson. My mother taught me to dance and I'm very proud of that. Just usually, I don't get the time, or my peers find it amusing. I'm glad you were impressed, however.'

He took another step towards her, and Elara's heartrate sped up even faster, so much so she was sure he could hear it through the thin material of her t-shirt. He leant towards her, that half-smirk on his face as her breath caught in her throat.

A moment of stillness passed between them, a match in energy as the look on Archer's face changed, before suddenly he reached around her, plucking his wand from the ebony end-table and slipping it into his shirt pocket in the blink of an eye. He held her gaze for a moment longer, the flickering candle in the corner of the room seemed to all of a sudden be emitting so much heat that Elara was sure she would faint.

'Goodnight, Elara,' he murmured, before silently making his way out of the door. Elara stayed stood in the middle of the room as rain began to clatter against the windows and the wind howled through the willow tree.

That evening, Elara had tried to call Xander as planned, but before the first ring could sound the call dropped, no doubt thanks to the horrific weather that had plagued Felicia for the last couple of days.

After her thirteenth attempt, she finally gave in with a sigh, dropping her phone onto the bed beside her.

There was still a ton of reading for her to do that Valen had left, but the thought of making notes on yet another chapter filled her with dread, so instead she flopped back against her pillows, staring as the stars twinkled at her from her night sky, winking and giggling at her as she frowned, certain they were mocking her sullen mood.

Having time to herself was so few and far between these days, but despite being perfectly happy in her own company at home, in her Council confinement she'd found she needed constant entertainment. Anything to keep her emotions at bay, especially when they had become so temperamental.

Elara glanced at clock on her bedside table, almost midnight. Perhaps a midnight snack would be a good distraction. Her stomach growled in agreement, all of that dancing had worked up an appetite.

Elara padded out of her room; her fluffy socks quiet on the wooden floor. She hoped Darya and Dritan had gone to bed, she didn't fancy making awkward small talk.

As she emerged around the corner into the kitchen, she had to bite off a scream, pressing her hand against her mouth as goosebumps erupted along her arms.

The kitchen was pitch black aside from two thin streams of moonlight dancing in through the open windows. A hulking figure with glowing eyes was leaning against the kitchen countertop, his stance protective, anticipative. In her presence, the figure turned towards the doorway where Elara was frozen to the spot, her eyes wide.

'Oh. I didn't think you'd still be awake.' The glowing eyes diminished, and Elara finally got her bearings enough to note the wavy black hair and sharp features that allowed her to recognise Archer… who seemed to be making a sandwich.

'What the hell are you doing in here? You scared me half to death!' Elara sighed, flicking on the light switch to her left to bathe the room in a soft glow.

Archer seemed disgruntled at the sudden onset of light, a frown clouding his brow.

'What does it look like I'm doing?' he asked, waving the knife around.

'Why don't you make a sandwich in your own house?' Elara leant against the door frame; her eyebrows raised.

'Your parents are with Forneus. I thought I might as well make use out of your house rather than sit outside all night.'

He looked proudly at his sandwich before taking a large bite, and finally turning to face Elara, wiping a crumb from his lip.

'What are they doing with Forneus?' Elara asked, trying to sound uninterested.

Archer shrugged, taking another bite. 'Not got a clue. Complaining about you no doubt.'

Elara scowled at him before pushing off the doorframe and stepping into the kitchen.

'Why are you up anyway? You're not normally around this late.'

'I'm bored, so I wanted a snack.'

Archer laughed incredulously. 'You're bored? You're living in a land of witches and magic, how in Helabasus are you bored?'

Elara grabbed an apple from the fruit bowl before hopping up onto the counter, letting her legs dangle. She'd much prefer a packet of crisps, but her favourite human snacks were few and far between in Darya and Dritan's health-crazy home. Not that they ever needed to worry about things like diabetes, no doubt there was a potion for that.

'I'm not allowed to leave the Northern Quarter, my phone isn't working, and Ivy's asleep. I'm bored.'

Archer shook his head, leaning back against the sofa. 'Blighted burners. So high maintenance.'

'I hate when you call me that. I have a name you know.'

Archer chuckled gruffly. 'Do you even know what it means?'

Elara pondered for a moment. She'd never actually heard anyone use the word aside from Archer. She shook her head.

'It's a slang term for humans. Because they burned us at the stake.'

Elara's cheeks flushed crimson. 'I'm not even human,' she said hotly, unsure why guilt was creeping along her spine.

Archer snorted, looking her up and down as that uncomfortable darkness began to blanket his skin. 'As good as,' he retorted, his eyes flashing.

Elara slid off the counter and leant back against it, hoping to appear nonchalant. 'If you hate humans so much, why did you agree to become my Fender? You knew I was raised with humans.'

Archer was silent for a moment as he polished off his sandwich. 'I don't hate humans, I just don't particularly like them,' he said, his mouth still full, 'I think humans and witches should keep to themselves, the way nature intended. And I already told you, I agreed to be your Fender to be closer to my father. I couldn't help where you'd been stationed, and at the time I wasn't aware of how intense my job was to be. I assumed even in Felicia; my father would keep you as his ward. It didn't occur to me that you would need a different type of magic to protect you. Stupid I guess, though I was only sixteen when I agreed.'

Elara couldn't help the shock that registered on her face. 'You've been watching me since you were sixteen?'

A slight smile pulled at Archer's lips. 'Don't flatter yourself,' his voice was silky, seducing. 'I've simply been your Fender since I was sixteen. But most of the time, I hardly knew where you were or what you were doing. My father took on that responsibility.'

Elara nodded, her thoughts quietly whirring. There were so many questions she wanted to ask Archer, but who knew which would descend him into fury, his blue eyes glowing as his skin turned as dark as the night.

'What do you fill your time with at home when you're bored? Or do you just find someone to annoy?' he asked, one eyebrow slightly raised.

'I go and see Xander, or study. Sometimes I paint or go for coffee with my friends.'

'Well you could study, I'm certain Valen left enough reading for you to do for the next decade.'

Elara snorted; he wasn't wrong. There were so many books now in her room that the bookcase had all but collapsed, and piles of thick hardbacks were erupting from the floor. It wasn't that Elara didn't like to read, in fact it was one of her favourite hobbies, but two dozen textbooks on poisonous plants weren't exactly her cup of tea.

'Yeah, that's a no from me. How about you do my reading for me, and I just make the notes?'

Archer gave her an amused glance, stuffing his hands into his pockets. 'And what would I get out of that particular deal?'

Elara considered, chewing on her lip. 'I'd keep you company?' she said finally with a bright grin, her eyes sparkling daringly.

Archer bit on his bottom lip with a shake of his head. 'Yeah, I don't think that will quite cut it for me. But fine, if you don't want to study, why not paint?'

Elara crossed her arms over her chest. 'You didn't pack any of my painting supplies.'

He frowned, picking up a polaroid camera from the table beside him, another human 'trinket' that her parents had requested for her. He pointed it at Elara and pressed the button before she could protest, the flash almost blinding her as the picture immediately began to emerge out of the top.

'Fascinating,' Archer murmured as he plucked the image from the top, observing it as it came to life. Then he frowned, 'you don't photograph well,' he said with a grimace.

'Give me that,' Elara huffed, darting forwards to snatch it from his grasp. He held it high above his head, dangling it between his fingertips with a smile dancing on his lips.

'I want my own deal. How about I go and fetch your painting supplies for no reason other than to give you a distraction from annoying me... and I get to keep the photo.'

Elara stopped, a peculiar expression settling on her serious features. 'Why on Earth would you want it?'

Archer smiled slyly, his midnight blue eyes giving nothing away. 'A memento of our precious time together. Or to throw darts at... you decide.'

'Fine,' Elara sighed, taking a small step away from Archer, 'but will you actually get my painting stuff?' She could hear the doubt in her tone, evidently, he could too as he pocketed the picture with a stern expression.

'I never break a promise.'

They stood in silence for a moment. He seemed uncharacteristically relaxed compared to usual, enough so that a tingle of confidence flourished in the pit of Elara's stomach.

'Does Ivy hate your father too?' The words shot out before she could help it. Ever since she'd realised that Archer's hatred for her extended from his feeling towards his father, she'd wondered if Ivy felt the same way, but was simply better at hiding it than her older brother. Elara braced herself for an onslaught of torment, but to her surprise, there was no catastrophic bang, no violence-inducing enchantments, and Archer simply pondered her question quietly to himself.

'No, she misses him and wishes for our lives to be different,' he said quietly, finally breaking the silence, 'but I don't think she really understands the true impact of my father's choices.'

'Because she was young when it happened?'

Archer shook his head. 'Because I protected her. I didn't want her to see the nasty side of our mum, or the selfish side of dad. I'm her older brother, it's my job to take care of her.'

'Is she close with your mum?'

Archer laughed humourlessly; his gaze glued to the floor. 'No. No-one is. My mum likes me better because I take care of her. She doesn't have time for Ivy... doesn't understand her. My mum's mental health has always been poor. It got worse when my dad got his job. Every day she'd be a different person, her behaviour was so erratic... unpredictable. She wasn't fit to care for herself, let alone her children. My dad should've known that, and never left. But we needed the money more than we needed mental stability. But Ivy never saw the worst side of my mother. I locked her in her room when my mum was having a breakdown. Let her come out again when it was over. I'm sure she hated me for it, but it was better than the alternative.'

He said it so coolly, so detached. But Elara could feel the relentless tidal waves of weariness and abandonment that had taken up residence in his bones. The fear and neglect already deeply rooted into his mind, his heart. That was where the darkness came from, she knew it.

It made Elara think back to her own childhood. Though for many years she felt as though she ought to be pitied, she now realised how rich she had been. Though her family wasn't biological, they were so much more. They would've done anything within their power to protect her from the cruel hardships of human life.

'Are you sad that you lost your childhood? Became someone with so many burdens so young?'

Archer looked at her strangely, his arms folded across his chest. The sudden creasing of his brow and the heaviness that crept over his heart set Elara's teeth on edge, goosebumps spider-crawling down her arms.

He took a step towards her, seemingly growing in front of her eyes as Elara tried to take a step back, but found the counter behind trapping her in.

He took another step forward, placing his hands on the countertop on either side of Elara, his face close to hers. She held her breath, her heartrate pounding.

'I would do anything for my family, no matter what hardships they've cost me. I would die for them if I needed to. Perhaps one day, you'll understand that kind of loyalty, burner.'

Just like that, he was gone, invisible from view. All that was left was the lingering essence of him deep in Elara's core.

She hadn't realised she was holding her breath until it escaped out of her in a heavy whoosh.

CHAPTER THIRTY-ONE

Elara

The knock came very early the next morning. So early in fact that Valen wasn't scheduled to turn up for another couple of hours, and Elara was still dressed in the oversized shirt she slept in, her hair piled messily into a bun on top of her head.

She groggily made her way over to the bedroom door, squinting her eyes against the harsh beams of sunlight that were blaring through her windows.

'Why are witches such early risers?' she groaned, rubbing a hand across her face.

As she opened the door, there was no one to be found, but as she stepped out into the hallway, she banged her toe heavily against a wooden box.

'Because leaving it on the table next to my door would be too much to ask,' Elara huffed, glaring at the ruby end table that had appeared beside her door a week ago for Fleur to leave snacks on, so that Elara didn't have to take even a MOMENT away from studying. When Darya said that she had reminded Elara quite disconcertingly of her academia obsessed mother back at home.

Elara hopped on one foot as she reached down to pick up the box. It was a shiny oak wood, and heavier than she'd expected. She glanced down the corridor, but there was no one to be found, so she ducked back under her bedroom door and set the box down on the bed, sitting cross legged behind it.

The golden clasp was intricate, and it took a moment of puzzle-solving for Elara to figure out the correct levers to push. But the box sprung open on well-oiled hinges, almost glowing from within. There was a square of paper balanced on top of the tissue paper, it simply read 'A touch of home - A.'

Elara felt her breath catch in her throat; her stomach tight. He had followed through on his promise and then some. He hadn't fetched her grotty old tote bag from home that was saturated with paint and filled with grimy brushes... he'd bought her a whole new kit.

Elara unfurled the tissue paper gently, careful not to disrupt any of the precious gifts underneath. Trays and trays of new paints were stacked on top of each other, pastel colours and oil paints, pans that were almost neon and watercolours that would wash the page with an opaque hue.

There was also a leather wallet with an 'E' embossed onto the front that glinted in the light. Elara's heart pounded harder. It was stuffed to the brim with paintbrushes of every shape and size. Their bristles so soft that running her finger along them felt like air.

It was possibly the most thoughtful gift she'd ever received, from someone who barely knew her.

Elara's cheeks flushed a happy pink as she settled herself at her desk and began to paint.

CHAPTER THIRTY-TWO

Elara

Darya had had Elara and Archer practising their dance twice a day since Tuesday, adding in complex steps, fast sequences and winning smiles. Though the chemistry from that first time was certainly different, Elara could hardly bear to look Archer in the eye. She'd not even managed to thank him for her gift, for fear of that embarrassing red flush covering her cheeks and blowing her careless cover.

'Elara? Did you hear what I said?'

Elara snapped out of her daydream, finding herself looking at her reflection in the mirror, Darya stood behind her. She shook her head.

'Do you want your hair up or down?' Darya asked, running the long light locks of hair through her fingertips.

Elara hesitated, she guessed there was a correct answer here.

'Um, up?'

Darya smiled proudly. 'I agree. You'll look so elegant!'

She began curling her hair with a strange, twisted tool that Elara hadn't seen before that she kept hot over a ceramic bowl of tealights. Evidently, Felicia was a little behind Earth with its beauty products.

As Darya began to pin sections of hair into a messy updo, Elara took a moment to admire her makeup. She had to admit that Darya was incredibly talented with a makeup brush. Somehow, her eyes were now shaped like a cats, and widened dramatically, dusted with shimmering glitter. Her lips were curved in a perfect bow, and not a smudge of ruby gloss was out of place.

'There. Perfect.'

Darya placed her gloved hands on Elara's shoulders, meeting her gaze in the mirror and smiling widely. In those few short seconds, Elara's hair was immaculately curled with most of it pulled and teased away from her face, twisted into a perfectly messy spiral. Intricate plaits were threaded throughout, and deliberate curls were pulled out to frame her face and neck. As she turned to take it all in, tiny diamonds shone in the dim light, sparkling delicately amongst her blonde waves.

'And we can't forget the finishing touch!'

Darya turned away for a moment, pulling from a small round box a glittering tiara. Golden vines twisted into a point with three flashy emeralds suspended in the centre. It fit perfectly as Darya fastened it into her hair, the weight of it on her head was somewhat comforting.

'Dazzling,' she breathed, as Elara looked up at her in the mirror. She searched her witchy-mother's face, looking for any ounce of resemblance between them. She turned back to her own reflection when she found none.

'Stand up, let me see you in all your glory.'

As she complied, she caught a glance of herself in the full length mirror and did a double-take when she hardly recognised the figure before her. Gone were the t-shirts and joggers of her weeks of confinement and in their place, was possibly the most gorgeous dress Elara had ever seen. An off-the-shoulder emerald green ballgown with stunning lace appliqué all over the corseted boddice. Tiny sequins had been handsewn into the folds of the skirt, done in such a way that in the correct lighting, it looked as though the dress itself was creating its own source of light. Specially chosen rings had been bestowed upon each of Elara's fingers, and when she walked, the tips of her heeled sandals were just visible below the hem of her dress.

'I know these past few weeks have been hard, Elara,' Darya interrupted as she brushed imaginary specs of dust away from her own dress. 'But your father and I are so proud of you. You have truly become the witch we always hoped you would. So much talent and hard-work, it's hard to believe you're ours.'

Elara felt her skin begin to prickle, but nowadays she knew how to rein in the magic.

'Now, the hard work isn't over yet. This evening will be difficult, but I know you can do it. Plus, your father and I and your Guardians will be right by your side.'

Elara nodded silently, taking a shaky breath. She'd never been in a room with so many witches before, yes, she'd learnt about the customs and history, but was that really going to help her now?

Osmond was waiting outside the front door to lead her to the same huge lecture hall as before, where all the important journalists and members of the press would be waiting. He walked quickly and she struggled to keep up in her heels, she dropped even further behind when she could hear all the commotion from the other side of the door.

He turned when he heard her footsteps stop, a worried crease between his eyebrows.

'I can't do this Osmond, there's too much pressure on me.'

Her eyes were already beginning to sting with tears, and in an instant Osmond was by her side, a gentle hand on her arm.

'Miss Anderson, I have watched you grow for 15 years now. I've seen the incredibly resilient woman you have become with so much to offer the world. I promise you; you can do this. If you don't know what to say, someone will fill in for you. Just smile and be your lovely self, you'll win them over in a heartbeat.'

His smile was so genuine it almost made her bawl. She might have been upset with him lately, but he was the closest thing to home in this strange world, and that meant more to her than anything else.

'Now I'll open the doors for you, and Archer will be stood by the stairs to help you to your seat. Ivy will be on the front row, and your parents are already sat on the podium, I will go and sit next to Ivy. There will be approximately two dozen members of the press, and of course Forneus will be there with the rest of the council, and his private detail of Defenders. I think that's everything, but is there anything else that will settle your mind?'

Elara loved that he knew exactly how to reassure her, he was giving her the knowledge to face this ordeal, the unspoken message lingered between them of where to turn if it all went downhill.

'Are you ready?'

Elara straightened her tiara and smoothed out her dress, before lifting her chin and walking as confidently as she could manage through the mahogany doors.

As promised, the first person Elara saw as the room went silent was Ivy. She was smiling so encouragingly that Elara couldn't help but smile back, desperate to go over and hug her friend, suddenly guilty that she'd been avoiding her for the last couple of days. Elara turned quickly back towards the podium as cameras began to flash, blinding her instantly.

Archer was stood exactly where Osmond said he would be. Elara couldn't help but admit to herself how breath-taking he looked, but immediately her heart sank as Xander's warm smiling face popped into her mind.

But Archer was watching her intently. She tried her hardest not to blush as his eyes quickly darted down the length of her dress, then back up to her face. His eyes narrowed for a second, before reaching out his hand for her to take. His suit was perfectly tailored and as black as the night, with a tie that matched the colour and material of her dress exactly. The black waves that usually flopped messily across his forehead were styled neatly and gleaming in the light, and his midnight blue eyes were as clear as a starry night, the closer she got, the more flecks of violet she saw strewn throughout them that she hadn't noticed before. He was terrifyingly handsome, even without the shadows dancing menacingly across his skin. In heels, she only just reached his shoulder and as he looked down at her she could smell the rich forest notes of his aftershave.

'Don't let me fall,' she whispered as she haltingly placed her hand on his, doing everything she could to not look directly in his eyes.

'Never,' he murmured back as the cameras clicked and flashed even faster.

Darya and Dritan stood as she passed, greeting her with a kiss on each cheek as her hand remained firmly gripped in Archer's. The perfect picture of a united family front. Elara went to take her seat, and as she did Archer turned to walk back down the stairs to join the other Defenders, but she caught his wrist before he could take a step.

'Please don't leave.'

She half expected him to brush her off and disappear down the staircase in a flash, but her voice was panicked enough that he turned around in surprise. He hesitated a moment before nodding silently and instead quickly positioned himself behind her chair. Elara felt a sigh of relief escape her lungs at the comforting shield of his tall stature, her shoulders uncoiling from their rigid stance.

Out of the corner of her eye, Elara saw a witch with dark hair and bright eyes watching her intently, her face was achingly beautiful, but her expression was cold, unfaltering. Elara knew she'd seen her around the Council before, glued to Forneus' side, but for some reason every time she tried to grasp the image of the woman in her mind, she slipped further away... like a memory.

Suddenly, Forneus was giving a slight nod of his head to a witch hovering in the corner of the room, who in return lifted a single finger towards the crowd. Instantly a flood of hands went up into the air and a hush descended on everyone in the room. Elara could feel the static electricity of pure curiosity darting from chair to chair, it was exhausting and exhilarating at the same time.

A young looking witch from the centre of the room stood up from her seat, her hair was so long it almost swept the floor, and her eyes were completely black, even from this distance.

'Elara, is it true you remember nothing of your life from before you entered the human world?'

Elara shifted uncomfortably, the witch's voice was so high-pitched she sounded like a windchime, and the feather quill in her hand was held in such a death grip, Elara was surprised it hadn't snapped.

'Yes, that is true.'

Gentle murmurings began weaving throughout the crowd and harsh hushes weren't far behind as the witch sat contentedly back in her seat.

'Miss Anderson, do you have family and friend relations in the human world?'

Elara thought this a strange question, how would she have got by for 15 years without friends and family?

'Yes. I have a family that loves me and very good friends.'

She expected the witch who'd asked the question to sit back down, but he remained stood up from his seat looking at her expectantly, his dark skin glowing abnormally brightly.

'It doesn't feel unnatural to you when they care for you, or come within close proximity, or vice versa?'

His voice was genuine, but Elara felt her cheeks flare an angry red. She caught sight of Ivy and Osmond looking nervous on the front row and sensed the shift in Darya and Dritan's emotions as they glanced across at her. Even Forneus' cool demeanour seemed to shift slightly, indicating that this was not a pre-approved question.

She closed her eyes for a moment and took a deep breath, before meeting the gaze of the witch in the crowd once more.

'I love my human family as much as anyone in this room loves theirs. To the extent of my knowledge, I was raised a human, and we saw each other no differently. There was no hatred or animosity there from times gone by. There was respect and acceptance, and I look forward to the day when I can see them again, and I will see them just the same when I return. They will still be my family, my friends and just because I now know I am a witch won't make me love them any less.'

Elara was surprised at how little her voice shook when she spoke, it rang out clear and melodically in the space and she willed confidence to ooze from her answer. From the look on the man's face, something had worked. She snuck a glance back to Archer behind her, he didn't meet her eyes but there was a tug of a smile on his lips, an amused glint in his eye.

'Do you believe you will succeed as a witch within Felicia, despite having missed out on so many years?'

Elara pondered this question for a moment, she knew the answer Forneus, and her parents would want her to give, she just wasn't sure she agreed with it.

'With a tutor as talented as Valen I think I will learn plenty, I could probably pass any exam thrown my way on the history of Felicia, or social etiquette. However, opinion-wise I'm not sure I'll ever succeed. I won't lie and say I agree with all of your customs, and there are many that I will struggle to conform to, they're so different from my human norms. But perhaps that is something that will be up for debate in future, or something I will learn to live with. Either way, yes, I will succeed as a witch, just perhaps not the witch you expect me to be.'

She glanced over at Osmond who was smiling at her like a proud parent. His head was nodding so enthusiastically she was worried it might fall off, but he was hanging on her every word, and that made her fill up with warmth. Maybe she wasn't doing so badly after all.

'One last thing, Miss Anderson,' the witch continued, his dark eyes sparkling, 'where do you feel our species belongs? Here in Felicia? Or on Earth. Where do you belong, Elara?'

It felt as though everyone in the room had vanished and Elara was sat in solitude in the darkness. As though he had known exactly what to say to get into her head and under her skin.

Though she'd refused to acknowledge it, that exact question had been engulfing her mind since the moment she had entered Felicia. In fact, it had been at the back of her mind ever since she was a child.

An uncomfortable quiet had descended on the crowd, and a painful prickle was working its way gradually down Elara's arms.

She could feel as Osmond's gaze bore down on her, Ivy's, Darya's and Dritan's too. It was almost unbearable.

Her muscles were beginning to ache with how tightly she gripped the arms of her chair, her knuckles pressing white against her skin. Her jaw felt glued shut, and she'd never felt less like herself.

Until a soft fingertip brushed the nape of her neck. So ice cold it sent shivers down her spine and shocked her mind back into motion. The sensation was gone far too quickly, but she could hear Archer's breathing behind her. That's how she knew she hadn't imagined it.

'Can we get the next ques-'

'I've never felt as though I belonged,' Elara interrupted Forneus, earning horrified glares from her parents. 'In London, Scotland, or Felicia. The only time I have felt truly myself, is when I'm around those who see me for who I am, who accept me for who I am, and don't try to change me. I know that I have my faults, as does every warlock in this room and every human on Earth. I'm not perfect and I never will be. In London, I wasn't pretty enough, or smart enough, or mature enough. In Scotland I didn't dress the way the other girls did; I had a funny accent and couldn't keep my thoughts to myself. I'll never be studious like my adoptive mother, or spontaneous like my father. I'm far too dramatic, and I hold people at arm's length for fear of getting hurt. But most of all, the only place I have really belonged? Is to myself. I'm the only one who can truly forgive me for my faults and wrong-doings.

I know it's different in Felicia. You need hope because your people are starving and desperate… but please don't base the choices you make on age-old battles. I can't comment on where I believe witches should live, I don't know all the facts. But I honestly believe that if you accept my experiment as a success and make the leap to Earth, they will make room for you. For those of you that accept and belong to yourselves and aren't controlled by the restraints of your past. I don't belong anywhere. I deserve to be where I am happy and at peace, just the same as every one of you.'

CHAPTER THIRTY-THREE

Elara

'You didn't do half as bad as I thought you would, burner,' Archer murmured as they stood outside the doors to the main hall, waiting for their names to be called.

Elara smirked. 'I don't think I took a breath the entire time.'

'I could tell.'

Elara looked at him out of the corner of her eye, he was smiling to himself.

'At least you spent so much time worrying about the questions and the readings that you didn't even have time to think about the dance.'

'I did not enjoy the reading,' Elara huffed, 'there was absolutely no need to go into that much detail about my life, and why so many photographs?'

'For 15 years you lived peacefully alongside humans, had genuine relationships and happy memories, and nobody even questioned it. You weren't despised or ridiculed, and you could return to Felicia with little to no problems at all. This is a huge step towards witches and humans co-existing once more. Plus I think your little speech moved quite a few hearts.'

Elara rolled her eyes. 'But no one knew I was a witch, Archer. Not even me! I think if everyone would have known, it all would have played out differently. There was nothing to distinguish me as different.'

Archer looked sceptical. 'I don't know about that one, especially with some of your particular gifts.' He cleared his throat meaningfully. 'I bet if you were to tell your family now that you're a witch, they wouldn't be surprised in the slightest. Witches of all gifts have a certain effect on humans, but especially those with Ardent blood. Surely, you've noticed when people have clicked with you so easily, they've felt like an extension of your body, or those that have struggled to be near you at all. That's a witchy thing in general, it's just heightened with your Ardent gifts.'

'So, what do you mean, they sense something is different about me, even if they can't tell what it is?'

'Put it this way, think back to that first time I dropped you off at your house. Your parents and friends instantly trusted me, had a connection with me, felt as though I was familiar and safe. Your boyfriend, however, could almost see through the elixir we gave him, because he felt so strongly that I wasn't someone he should be around. All witches have a similar kind of effect on humans, no one really knows why, but it doesn't happen with other witches. That's just true hard work and friendship, or genuine dislike… unless you're an Ardent with the ability to deliberately alter someone's emotions. Whereas a human would never be able to explain why they feel the way they do about us. It's almost as though they're reflecting what we're feeling back to us, feeding off us, but we can't control it. It'll be twice as potent with you because of your Ardent abilities.'

He explained it so matter-of-factly, but it left one burning question bouncing around in Elara's brain. Did anyone truly like her for her, or were their feelings towards her just a reflection of how she felt about them? She thought back to the party at Natalia's, it felt like a lifetime ago. She'd been so angry at that guy, felt as though she could've punched him, but then Xander came in and did it for her. He'd said outside that it felt like someone had taken over, that in that moment he would have done anything to protect her. Was he just taking on her emotions and using them to fuel his own?

She didn't have much time to think about it, as suddenly the doors in front of them swung open silently revealing a huge ballroom at the bottom of the most exquisite staircase Elara had ever seen. Dozens of beautifully dressed witches turned to face them, as a lone piano melody began twinkling in the corner.

'May I pronounce our esteemed guest, Miss Elara Hazel Anderson, escorted by her Primary Defender, Mr Archer Corbin Levett.'

Elara exchanged a quick nervous glance with Archer as she linked her arm through his, and they began making their descent down the stairs to a round of deafening applause. She gripped his arm as tight as she could, desperate not to fall to her death in the long skirt. She could feel the muscles flexing in the top of his arm, and she tried to slow her breathing to match each step they took, a smile forced on her face all the while.

'Okay, go and mingle, your parents will introduce you to anyone they deem important, I have to go stand with the other Defenders now,' Archer whispered in her ear as they reached the bottom of the staircase.

'I swear to God if you walk away Archer Levett,' she hissed, but he turned smoothly with a smile, and instantly a flock of witches descended on her, offering out their hands in greeting.

'Elara honey, there are some people I'd like you to meet!' Darya called out from somewhere in amongst the crowd as Elara forced herself inwardly not to roll her eyes.

Darya led her towards two incredibly elegant looking witches. A woman who must have been at least seven feet tall with flaming red hair and bright yellow eyes, and a man not much taller than Elara with characteristically pointed ears.

'Elara, these are my good friends, Pearl and Maverick. They've been so excited to meet you,' Darya beamed and pushed her daughter towards the couple with a pointed finger.

Elara gazed up at the woman, her name couldn't have suited her any less, though she was adorned in jewellery with every colour and shape of pearl imaginable.

'Hi, nice to meet you,' Elara said as politely as she could manage, as the couple continued to stare at her.

'Are you both Ardent witches too?' she asked.

They looked confused for a moment before bursting into howling laughter, tears streaming down their faces. Elara took an uncertain step back.

'Oh, dear girl! How amusing you are. I doubt we would have been invited to this event if we didn't have Ardent blood! Unless we look like staff to you!' Pearl cackled as Maverick snorted in a very snobbish fashion.

'Sweetheart, all guests here are Ardent witches, any others are here strictly on duty, apart from Ivara. We allowed her entry as a special guest.' Darya said it proudly, as though she was granting Ivy a wish and Elara felt irritation begin to brew in her stomach. She looked around the room, searching for her friend, and eventually found her tucked away from the crowds in quiet corner. Stood beside her was Osmond, and in place of the beautiful and bright gowns of the rest of the party, were their typical working jumpsuits. Where usually they blended in seamlessly, here they stuck out like sore thumbs so clearly Inchoate and certainly not feeling comfortable.

Elara smiled a goodbye at Darya's strange friends and started making her way over to Ivy, ignoring anyone who tried to stop her to say hello, until suddenly a witch with platinum blonde hair pulled severely away from her face stood directly in her path, stopping her from going any further.

'Oh, sorry excuse me,' Elara smiled, trying to dodge around, but the young woman stepped to the side, blocking her path once more.

'Elara Headley, it's a pleasure to meet you,' the woman cooed, holding out an elegant, gloved hand.

'Um, it's Anderson.'

The woman narrowed her eyes and smiled sarcastically, dropping her hand back to her side. Her dress slinky dress was black and simple, forgettable in comparison to the garish gowns of the other guests.

'My apologies. That was quite an entrance you made there,' she said, nodding to the staircase.

'Trust me, I'd rather of snook in the back.'

'Your Guardian seems to be incredibly invested in his job.' The woman glanced to the other side of the room. 'He hasn't taken his eyes off you since you walked in.'

Elara turned to follow her gaze, finding Archer stood with a crowd of Defenders in their usual uniform. Just as she said, he was watching their interaction intently, directing a slight nod of his head at Elara as their eyes met. Even from across the room she could see shadows beginning to creep over his shoulders, tightening around his neck.

Elara turned back to the woman who continued to stare over her shoulder.

'I'm not to leave his sight, Forneus's orders,' Elara said as confidently as she could manage, straightening her posture. 'I'm sorry I didn't get your name.'

The woman snapped back to attention; Elara felt even more uncomfortable now that her icy glare was trained on her.

'Pardon my manners. I'm Cal. I knew you as a young child, before you were taken away to the human world.'

Her answer took Elara by surprise, she wasn't expecting to have met this woman before, especially with how peculiarly she was looking at her.

'Well, it's nice to meet you again, Cal. I'm sure we'll cross paths again someday.' She turned to begin walking towards Archer, unsettled by the interaction.

'I should've seen that there was something different about you,' Cal blurted out, grasping Elara's arm with such force she almost pulled her over. 'No... not different. Familiar.' Her voice was panicked, her words rushed, and in an instant Archer was pushing across the dance floor, almost flattening guests in his haste.

'You need to watch who you trust Elara, don't let anyone know your secret, they'll use it against you.'

Elara's Guardians were descending on them from all corners of the room. She could sense Archer's anger, Osmond's fear as they neared.

'Elara, are you listening? Don't trust anyone. Not even your Guardians. Nobody here is who they seem.' Cal's voice had dropped to a hushed whisper, the look in her green eyes was enough to make Elara's stomach turn. Her arm was growing achy from Cal's tight grip as she tried to shake herself free, but to no avail.

'I need you to look out for yourself Elara, I need you to be safe. I'll find you again, just be careful... promise me that?'

In a sudden flurry of motion, Cal disappeared as if into thin air, leaving only a darkening bruise around the top of Elara's arm, with snaking light purple lines that etched from her shoulder all the way to the tips of her fingers. It looked like a storm cloud and lightening had been painted across her skin. Elara's heart was racing faster than she'd ever felt it, when suddenly she felt Archer's firm hand at the base of her spine, pulling her away from the crowd.

'Are you alright?' he murmured, his gaze darting around the room, searching for Cal.

'Yeah, yeah I think so,' she said shakily, looking down at her arm where the lines were turning a deep, royal purple.

'What did she say to you? Did she tell you her name? What did she want?'

His flurry of questions was aimed at Elara, but he was still desperately searching the room. Elara watched in fascination as the rest of the Defenders began to swarm out amongst the startled crowd.

'Elara, what did she say?' Archer insisted, shaking her shoulder.

'Her name was Cal; she told me not to trust anyone... not even you,' Elara whispered, looking up at an increasingly angry Archer who looked ten seconds away from ripping the whole of the Council apart in search of the mysterious blonde witch.

'Shit,' he hissed, running a hand through his carefully styled hair, then glaring at the gel on his fingertips. 'Okay, did you guys see her?' There was a flurry of nods from the crowd, 'she's wearing a black dress, approximately 5'9, Ardent-'

'No, no she's not Ardent,' Elara blurted out, to her own surprise.

'What do you mean? What is she then?'

Elara looked around for a moment, trying to figure out who was watching them and who would hear what she was about to say.

'She was like me.'

Archer's expression immediately changed as the muscles in his jaw flexed back and forth. He hesitated for a moment, before taking a deep breath and squeezing his eyes shut.

'She's Ardent, her name is Cal. Find her.' His voice was surprisingly strong, his tone stern.

Elara wasn't sure how the other Fenders had heard him, but they nodded in unison and immediately spread out into the crowd.

'Fender magic, an enchantment that allows us to communicate from up to a mile away. Helps us stay in contact.'

It was then that Archer caught sight of her arm, his face turning deathly pale.

'What the hell is that? Does it hurt?' Archer grabbed her arm, turning it back and forth to survey the damage. 'Why didn't you tell me?'

'It's fine Archer, it's not that bad. I've had worse,' she joked, but Archer wasn't smiling.

'Come on, maybe Ivy will know what it is.'

He took her wrist and began dragging her over to the side of the room where Ivy had been stood watching the scene unfold.

'Hey, Elara are you alright?' Ivy asked, genuine concern colouring her voice.

'Yeah, I'm okay. She just had a crazy death grip,' she laughed to herself, though Ivy's brow was still furrowed as she studied Elara's arm.

'She knew something, didn't she? She was like you.'

Elara nodded as Archer opened a small box that had been hidden in his jacket pocket. Inside was a collection of tiny vials, each with different colour liquid. He selected one filled with what looked like green gloop and pulled out the stopper with a pop.

'Before I fix this, do you have any idea what the mark means, Ivy? Why do the lines do that? It almost looks deliberate.'

Ivy shook her head, her forehead creased. 'I have no idea. It looks familiar, but I can't for the life of me figure out why.'

Archer frowned, studying the lines for a moment longer.

'I can't leave it, we don't have time for it to heal naturally.' He poured a generous amount of the liquid onto a small cloth. 'This might sting a little,' he said, without an ounce of sympathy in his voice.

He instantly pressed it to Elara's skin and Ivy looked worried for a moment and in a split second, Elara found out why. Her skin was on fire, burning heat radiating down to her hand and up across her shoulder.

'Jesus Christ, what is that?' she panted, prickles of pain beginning to worm through her skin. She tried to move away from Archer's grip, but he kept the cloth pressed firmly to her arm against the storm-cloud bruise.

'Stay still, or I can't do the enchantment.'

Elara began grinding her teeth together as the feeling grew more and more uncomfortable.

'Well could you do it quick, it hurts!'

Archer smirked to himself, holding the cloth there for a moment longer than he needed to before removing it. 'Recreo,' he murmured under his breath, and instantly the pain subsided, and her skin cleared, the murky bruise faded into her skin.

'It just sped up your natural healing process, yours is already faster than the average, that's why it burnt so bad.'

'Lovely,' Elara cleared her throat, blinking away the tears that had formed in the corner of her eyes.

'Sorry,' Archer conceded, a slight smile on his face. 'Looks as good as new though, just in time for our opening dance.'

Elara looked down at her arm, it still felt a little tingly and as she turned it into the light, she could just about see faint snaking white lines etched deep into her skin. Almost like scars. Archer didn't seem to notice though, so she turned her gaze to the dance floor which had now cleared, Darya and Dritan were stood at the edge, waiting expectantly.

'You ready?'

'As ready as I'll ever be.'

Archer took her hand and led her to the dance floor, she tried to avoid the gaze of a hundred witches that followed her there.

'Could you at least try smiling? You're making it look like I'm holding you hostage.' Archer grumbled as the music began to play. Elara immediately switched her smile on, a huge Cheshire cat grin that made her cheeks ache. Archer looked comically alarmed.

'Okay never mind, the frown was better.'

Elara rolled her eyes, her feet beginning to step in time to the music.

'Keep your eyes peeled for Cal though, there's something off about her.'

Elara tried her hardest not to snort with laughter.

'You don't say.'

Archer glared at her for a moment, before pushing her out into the first spin of the routine. Despite their practises, Elara had never been in a floor length gown and heels before, and the weight of the fabric was a whole new challenge to consider. Her foot slipped momentarily on the wooden floor, but Archer's arm was around her waist in an instant, holding her steady.

'I've got you,' he murmured.

Their eyes met and Elara felt her cheeks flame pink, she could tell from the look on Archer's face that he'd caught her expression.

She cleared her throat and spun out of his arms again, her skirt flaring out around her.

The steps had been difficult only yesterday, but as soon as she accommodated for her new clothing, she flew through them with ease. Her arms extended gracefully, and her toes pointed as elegantly as she could manage. Her audience melted away, leaving her and Archer enraptured in the music. As the piano melody grew faster and faster, she couldn't tell which was making her breathless; the exhilarating dance, or the fact that Archer never once dropped her gaze. The energy between them was exhausting and uncertain, nothing like the comforting buzz she felt with Xander.

The music began to subside, so Elara tried to slow her breathing, not wanting to appear too dishevelled. She could see Archer biting the inside of his cheek to hide his smug grin, so she deliberately turned into him, smiling as her heeled sandal crunched down into his left foot, and he grunted angrily in pain.

She suspected she'd broken at least one of his toes from his response, but thanks to his Fender magic it would heal quickly.

'You'll pay for that,' he murmured in her ear as she suddenly felt the ground rushing up to meet her. She braced herself for impact when at the last possible second, Archer caught her in mid-air, the loose curls in her hair brushing the floor. The audience gasped and was silent for a second before erupting into deafening applause.

'Careful,' he whispered, before swinging her back up onto her feet, his hand on the small of her back holding her so close that she swore she could feel his heartbeat.

'Careful isn't my style.' Her voice was so hushed she was surprised he heard it, but finally he dropped his hand and she stepped away, her chest heaving with heavy breaths.

CHAPTER THIRTY-FOUR

Ivy

'You trying to drink yourself into an early grave?' Ivy laughed as she sidled up to Elara, who was surrounded by empty shot glasses.

'I can't believe you're permitted to buy your own alcohol at 13!' Elara gasped dramatically. 'You have to be 18 at home.'

Ivy stifled a laugh; it was strange to see her friend so at ease. She was no Ardent witch, but there had been an air of tension around Elara since the moment she stepped foot in Felicia. She glanced around the bar for a second, she couldn't see any present bartenders, so with a final check over her shoulder, she hopped over the bar, landing gracefully on the other side. She turned back around to find a surprised looking Elara; her eyebrows raised suspiciously.

'You know, I'm not sure you're supposed to do that.'

Her voice was judgemental but Ivy just grinned, beginning to line up glasses and ingredients along the workstation.

'Please, as long as I'm not trying to join in the dancing, no one will bat an eyelid.'

Elara frowned.

'Yeah, I don't like that,' the blonde witch grumbled as she leant against the bar.

'I don't mind. Means I can do stuff like this.'

She flipped a glass high into the air, and caught it skilfully behind her back, rimming it with lemon all in a fluid motion.

She began crushing up herbs with a pestle and mortar, watching Elara carefully who was beginning to sway.

'So why are you back here, drinking yourself half to death. This ball is for you, you know.'

Elara rolled her eyes, finally slouching down onto one of the bar stools.

'I don't need reminding,' she huffed, dropping her head into her hands. 'I can't stand all those people fawning over me, pretending they're my friends. I don't have a clue who any of them are, and to be honest I'm not sure I want to. They're all so full of themselves.'

Ivy laughed, tossing her crushed herbs into the cocktail shaker with a cup of water. She considered for a second before grabbing the bottle of vodka from the shelf and pouring a shots worth in.

'That's Ardent witches for you, I told you they're like royalty.'

'Royally annoying that's for sure,' Elara grumbled, eyeing up the glass that Ivy had placed in front of her. The liquid was murky green and garnished with leaves of basil and lemon wedges.

'I'm not trying to poison you, drink up.'

She smirked as Elara lifted the glass and held it up to the light, when she gave it an experimental swirl, drops of liquid flew out around them, Ivy ducked out of the way, narrowly missing the shower.

She cleared her throat meaningfully.

'Sorry,' Elara said sheepishly, before taking a quick sip.

'Oh! It's nice!' She sounded surprised. 'What is it?'

Ivy dried her hands on a tea towel whilst she pondered.

'Let's just call it the Ultimate Hangover Cure Cocktail. Works every time,' she winked.

Elara took another sip and pulled a face.

'And the vodka?'

'Well I didn't say you needed to be sober.'

Elara tutted her tongue against her teeth, a thoughtful expression on her face.

'Lavender and… fennel?"

'You catch on quick.'

'I thought only Alchemists and Greenies worked with herbs.'

Ivy smiled to herself as Elara drained the last of the drink and held the empty glass out.

'Greenies can sense herbs and they're better at growing them, and Alchemists know their properties to mix elixirs, but anyone can learn about their uses. One of my closest friends is an Alchemist, I learnt from her.'

She placed another full glass down in front of a confused looking Elara.

'You have friends?' Elara asked sincerely as Ivy struggled to choke back a laugh.

'I'll try not to take that too personally. Yes Elara, I am a normal person and I do have friends. Though to be honest, that friend wasn't always just a friend, she's actually an ex-girlfriend, but you keep that between us,' she said with a wink as she mopped down the surface with the tea-towel.

Elara's eyebrows shot up as she leaned in closer, 'Ivy Levett! You dated outside of your class?' Her tone was overly dramatic, her eyes bright with laughter. 'The scandal!'

Ivy poured herself a quick drink before swinging back over the bar, standing with her back to the doors leading to the dance floor.

'You're more interested in the fact that I dated an Alchemist than you are that I dated a girl?' She tried to mask the surprise in her voice, but to no avail.

Elara snorted and rolled her eyes. 'Have you seen you?'
'What's that supposed to mean?'
Elara frowned as she put her glass back on the bar, turning fully to face her.

'Let me guess, you dated boys until you were about 15, of course dressed super feminine with lots of pink and purple, but you always questioned that something was different. Then as soon as you turned 16 and developed some independence you cut your hair, got tattoos and found yourself a girlfriend, but you had to keep it on the downlow until you guys inevitably broke up from the stress of dating outside your class. I presume you've remained super good friends, but there's always that hint of sexual tension and what could have been.' She paused for a moment. 'Am I right?'

Ivy was silent, she tried to stop her cheeks from turning red, which would prove that the amateur witch had just read her like a book.

'Is that an Ardent thing?'

Elara laughed, 'it's a human thing. You're an excellent example of every lesbian I've ever known. Could tell from the moment I met you.'

'That seems very stereotypical,' Ivy mumbled.

'Maybe it is, and you're right I shouldn't judge. However, it's been fool-proof so far.'

Elara looked far too smug for her liking, so she gave her a light shove, smirking as her friend struggled to regain her balance on the small stool.

'Touché,' Elara slurred, taking another sip of her drink.

'Alright, maybe that's enough.'

She plucked the glass out of Elara's hand and knocked it back herself in one large gulp.

'Speak for yourself, I fleel fine… fleel fine. Jesus Christ, I feel fine.'

Elara was turning paler by the moment, her head looking dangerously light on her neck.

'Okay, definitely enough. Right, you stay here and I'm gonna go grab my stuff. I'll be two minutes, please try and avoid your parents, they will not be happy with all… this.' She gestured at Elara's pasty complexion and the impressive collection of empty glasses.

'Mmm, bring some snacks from the buffet,' Elara mumbled, resting her head on the bar, her tiara clinking melodically against the metal.

Ivy hurried quickly across the dance floor, not wanting to leave her less-than-sober friend for any longer than necessary. Over the years of living within the Council, she'd learnt to ignore the dirty looks of the Ardent witches. The way they saw her as so clearly beneath them. But tonight they were downright nasty, they stared at her as she passed, looking her up and down repeatedly as they curled their lips. Their bright eyes flashing with distain and disapproval as they took note of her plain working jumpsuit, choppily cut hair and patchwork tattoos. She stared back at them until they looked away uncomfortably and continued their meaningless conversations. It was one of the reasons she'd become so fond of Elara, her lack of judgement. Though she knew her friend would find it even more difficult to be exposed to Felicia as a whole, with its segregated society.

As she headed towards the direction of her bags, a hulking figure appeared in front of her, blocking her path.

'Where is she?'

It was Archer, his brow furrowed in its usual mix of anger and irritation.

'She's just over there, I'm getting my stuff and taking her home.'

Archer glanced around the room for a moment, his eyes narrowed.

'I don't see her.'

'Look harder then, she's right there,' Ivy said, turning around and pointing at the empty seat that Elara had occupied only moments before.

'Shit,' she murmured.

'Are you fucking kidding me, Ivy? How could you leave her by herself with that psycho on the loose?' His hands were tight on her shoulders, his eyes flaring angrily.

'You know she's your Protectant, not mine. Maybe you should've been watching her instead of chatting up the help,' she spat, nodding her head towards the pretty Broomie witch who had been sweeping the same corner for the last 20 minutes, eyeing up her brother from beneath lowered lashes.

'Don't start. Let's just find her before dad notices she's missing. Or her parents for that matter.'

He ducked out of sight for a moment and returned with her bag and jacket, before storming ahead through the crowd, quickly scanning the room.

'Oh, one other thing,' she whispered as she hurried behind, 'she's had a little too much to drink, that's why I was taking her home.'

He didn't even need to turn around this time for Ivy to see his frown.

CHAPTER THIRTY-FIVE

Elara

'Oh, for the love of Hecate,' Archer groaned as he found Elara sprawled on the bathroom floor, her cheek resting on the cool ceramic of the toilet seat.

'Go away, Archer,' she said, closing her eyes against the light that flooded in through the door.

'I thought you'd been bloody kidnapped or something,' he laughed as he stepped into the small room, pulling the door semi-closed behind him with a final glance down the corridor.

'I think this is worse,' she groaned; her eyes still closed.

'You're so dramatic,' he chuckled gruffly. 'I'm guessing you're not too well-rehearsed in the world of alcohol then?'

'Why would I be? I'm seventeen.'

'Oh yeah, I've heard the rules are different in Scotland. You've got to be eighteen, right?'

'Mmm,' she murmured softly in response as she finally opened her eyes to look at him.

His tie was tucked loosely into the pocket of his trousers, and he'd unbuttoned his shirt down to the centre of his chest, revealing the tanned, toned skin underneath.

She averted her gaze quickly when he caught her staring and shifted her position on the floor to sit up properly, but the movement made her stomach turn and she retched back over the toilet bowl. In an instant, Archer was crouched behind her. He didn't reach out to her, but she could feel the heat radiating off him from the close proximity of his skin.

Thankfully, to save her from embarrassment, nothing came up into the toilet, and she collapsed back against the wall, unable to stop a tear escaping down her face.

'The sickness will pass soon,' Archer said gruffly, misunderstanding.

'It's not the sickness that's bothering me,' she sighed, leaning her head against the wall.

Archer waited silently for her to carry on. She avoided his gaze, unsure of what to say next.

'My life is confusing at the moment; I never have a clue what's going on and it's exhausting.'

He looked puzzled. 'What do you have to be confused about?'

Elara choked back a laugh, raising an eyebrow at him.

'Did you not hear me in the interview? Everything! Do I belong here, or at home? Which of my friends like me for me, and which are controlled by my witchy emotions? Will the people here ever accept me, or will they just use me for their own gain? I'd also love to know what's truly going on with my parental situation.' She looked at him pointedly. When he quickly looked away from her face, his cheeks colouring, she smiled to herself knowing she'd hit a nerve.

'I don't know what you mean,' he said quietly, looking down at his hands.

'I'm sure.' Her tone was sarcastic, but she didn't bother to fix it and instead heaved herself up off the floor, trying not to sway in the process.

'Where are you going?' He hurried up after her as she pushed out of the bathroom.

'There's a little file I'd like you to see.'

The file had been tucked between the wardrobe and her wall for days now. Each night she took it out and studied it from cover to cover, the same images looked back at her, and the same names remained etched into the paper.

As she thumbed through to the page she wanted, she yanked the tiara from her hair. It suddenly felt as though it was digging its tiny metallic prongs into her scalp, and it clattered uselessly to the floor. She didn't feel anything like the royal Ardents who swanned around like they owned the place; she didn't need the physical reminder.

'Esmé and Gabriel Sylvaine.' She held the opened file out towards Archer, watching to see his expression. She felt in the base of her stomach as his nerves heightened, an uncomfortable flutter that tightened up his spine and made his jaw clench.

'Why are those names there? It doesn't make any sense!' she asked innocently, widening her eyes naïvely at her Guardian. He rolled his eyes and dropped the file onto the desk with a bang, before sitting down on the desk chair, leaning back against it lazily.

'We'll get through this much quicker if you stop dancing around the point, and just tell me what you know.' He laced his fingers behind his head, his posture much more relaxed than his heartrate would indicate.

'I heard you and Osmond talking a few nights ago in the corridor. You were arguing when Ivy came out and joined you. Do you remember what she said?'

Archer remained silent, studying her carefully.

'She said, 'she's not theirs'. I didn't have much to go off, but I found the most plausible explanation had already been rattling around in my head for weeks now. I knew you wouldn't help me, so I took matters into my own hands and broke into Dritan's office one night. There were thousands of pictures, files and letters in there, but this one caught my attention the most because of the adoption certificate. My parents had the same one framed in the living room my entire life, but birthparents had never been listed. So, it would seem rather strange that on this copy, not only are my biological parents listed, but they don't even share the names of the people whose house I'm currently residing in. I mean I personally think that that's a tad suspicious, but PLEASE do tell me if you disagree.'

Elara hadn't even noticed that her voice had raised angrily until she stopped talking to catch her breath. Archer's cheeks were red, his emotions hard to read.

As soon as he was sure she was done, he leant forward in the chair, looking up at her as her chest heaved with painful breaths.

'I promise you; I knew nothing about any of this until that night. I wanted to tell you, truly I did, but there was nothing really to tell. I didn't have any solid information, and anything that Ivy or my father knew, they weren't willing to share with me. I thought it would only upset you more if I brought it up, I knew you weren't settling here so I wanted to give you the best chance.'

He stood up, his emotions fizzing chaotically beneath the heat of his skin.

'I don't understand. Why am I here with Darya and Dritan if even they aren't my real parents? They talk as if they are, they have countless photographs with me, and they've never mentioned anyone else. I just don't understand.'

She was surprised when her voice cracked, but even more surprised when Archer carefully reached a hand out towards her, his fingertips just barely grazing her cheek. His eyes were clear of the darkness that usually enveloped him. She stiffened, it was the last thing she'd expected him to do, and stood completely still, unsure of how to react. For a moment, just a second, his features were awash with peace, his usually tense jaw was soft, his brow even. And then it was gone, so quickly that Elara was certain she'd imagined it, though the goosebumps that were tingling up and down her arms indicated otherwise.

Finally, after what could've been an eternity, his hand dropped limply back to his side, his expression guarded once more.

'Today you spoke with such truthfulness, such openness, not the sarcasm or anger I've come to know so well. I know we don't really see eye to eye, but I'm not sure I've quite understood anyone as well as I understood you on that stage. I think a lot of the other witches felt the same. I know this isn't your world, and I am truly sorry that you have been thrust so carelessly into it. I know if it had been me in your position, I definitely couldn't have handled it with as much grace.'

Elara nodded silently, not trusting herself to speak as stinging tears welled behind her eyes. Half the time she was certain she hated him and his ebony temper. The rest of the time, there was a lingering understanding between them that wrecked her stomach with nerves and guilt. Her mind flooded with images of Xander, but her racing heartrate betrayed her.

Archer opened his mouth as if to say something else but suddenly the front door creaked open, and Elara stiffened once more expecting the angry calls of Darya and Dritan. Instead, Ivy's hushed whisper could be heard from the other room.

'Elara? Where the hell are you? I don't get paid enough for stints like this!'

Elara looked up at Archer, waiting to see if she was supposed to answer. He was clearly weighing up his options, if they emerged from her room together after she had left the party clearly drunk and his shirt was still gaping open, it wasn't going to look particularly innocent for either of them.

'You go back to the ball with her, I'll follow you out in a few minutes,' he mouthed and stepped away, wincing as the floor creaked loudly.

'Elara is that you?' Ivy whisper-called.

Archer nodded towards the door, fastening a couple of his shirt buttons.

Elara took a deep breath and straightened her dress. 'Is my makeup smudged?'

Archer studied her face for a moment before stepping forward and cupping her chin with one hand and swiping away a smudge of mascara with the other. She held her breath, his face was so close to hers she could count every eyelash, join his freckles into constellations. He wiped the corner of her eye a couple more times until he was satisfied with the outcome, and Elara expected him to let go of her face straight away, but he didn't. She could feel his cool breath across her cheeks, the way his gaze held hers made a fire burn within her core. Every cell in her body was telling her to pull away, that this was wrong, but she couldn't move a muscle. The chemistry that buzzed between them was electric, she could almost taste it.

For the briefest of moments, she imagined what it would be like to kiss him. As if he'd heard her thoughts his gaze dropped quickly to her lips and then back up to her eyes. Her heart was pounding painfully in her chest, and she could feel the knot of confusion in his stomach. She bit her lip painfully to distract herself from the feeling, to break the spell between them. Any minute now, Ivy was going to walk through the door and find them like this, and there would be no plausible explanation.

As though he could read her mind, the look in his eyes shifted back to iciness as he looked up and focussed on something behind her, before grazing his lips ever so gently across her forehead, his hand still cradling her jaw.

He stepped away from her silently, still not meeting her gaze, so without a word she stepped around him, and walked out of the bedroom door. It took every drop of willpower she had not to turn around and drink him in one last time, as she headed towards her friend who looked incredibly relieved to see her.

CHAPTER THIRTY-SIX

Elara

The ball had finally ended well into the early morning. Already reports were flooding in from all corners of Felicia about how much the people had appreciated Elara's honesty... and her sense of style, much to Elara's dismay. One of the top fashion designers in the Southern district had already come up with an emerald green ballgown of her own that would be hitting the high street on Monday.

'This is simply wonderful news, darling,' Darya had cooed as she began unwinding her hair from her tight top-knot. 'Forneus' plan has worked like a charm. Everyone is focussed on how dazzling you were instead of the controversies surrounding the experiment! Don't get me wrong, the people will still be wary, but I heard rumours that you and Archer are the new 'it' couple! Though maybe don't encourage that one, what with his lower class and all,' she chuckled as Elara glared, her teeth grinding together.

'That's fine by me, considering I have a boyfriend,' she hissed, one hand on her hip.

'A human boyfriend. That won't last when you move back to Felicia full time though sweetie. My friend Lilith has a son the same age as you, he's wonderful Elara. I'll organise-'

Elara didn't stick around to hear what else Darya had to say, she slammed her bedroom door with enough force that one of her stacks of books toppled to the ground, sprawling out on the floor.

Not two minutes later, there was a light knock at the door.

'What?' Elara asked sharply, swinging the door open with a scowl on her face to find a startled looking Osmond, looking ready to run back down the hallway.

'I'm sorry miss, I know it's late.'

Elara sighed, opening the door open fully and slouching down at her desk, exhaustion winning the battle against her heavy eyelids.

'I'm sorry Osmond, I thought you were Darya.'

Osmond smiled sadly before taking a step into the room, carrying a large box.

'Please don't tell me that's more jewellery, I really don't need or want anymore.'

Osmond shook his head, a sparkle in his eye. 'Sent by Olive, she said you'd been missing your human delicacies.'

Hidden in the box were three vanilla cupcakes lathered in strawberry frosting. 'Well done, Elara' was written out across the top in expert gold calligraphy.

'You did so fantastically, Miss Anderson. I think you truly won over the nation's hearts.'

Osmond beamed at her as he sat down on the bed across from her, unwrapping one of the cupcakes and licking the buttercream experimentally.

'They only liked me because Forneus had me dressed up like a doll and put on display. They want entertainment, a distraction. That's all.'

Osmond pondered for a moment. 'Perhaps. But even if that's the case, it is a useful part to play, Elara. Felicia has been struggling for so many years, the people could use a bit of vibrancy in their difficult lives. You don't see much of it in the Council, Forneus is excellent at throwing a ball, distracting his court from the real world. By broadcasting you to every corner of Felicia, he's binding the two together. Creating trust and most importantly, hope. You might just be a pretty face now, but I think you have the potential to be so much more than that, to say things that really matter. Like today at the conference.'

'It just doesn't sit right with me Osmond. I wish I didn't have to play the part just for people to take notice of me. All those stuck-up witches were looking at me like I belonged, they couldn't have been more wrong.'

Osmond shrugged with a chuckle. 'Sorry, love. I'm sure your mother would've loved seeing you all dressed up though.'

Elara snorted, it was true, her mother had loved dressing her up like a princess as a little girl. As soon as she'd been old enough to fight her corner, she'd ripped her princess dresses to shreds, favouring her wellies and muddy walks.

'I'm not sure she would've recognised me tonight. Dancing and socialising in a tiara.'

'She would've been proud of you for speaking your mind, sweetheart. That's the woman she raised, no matter what outfit you do it in.'

In an instant, Elara had crossed the room and was hugging Osmond tightly. He stiffened for a moment before hugging her back. His cupcake forgotten in the box. His silver hair tickled her cheek, his cloak scratchy against her chin.

'Thank you,' she whispered, tears welling in her eyes.

Suddenly there was a sharp rap on the door, Elara turned to find Archer leaning against it, back in his usual uniform.

'I didn't mean to interrupt,' he said flatly.

'You're not interrupting at all; I was just leaving.' Osmond stood up quickly, plucking his half-finished cupcake from the box with a wink at Elara. He stroked his thumb against her chin momentarily before pressing a quick kiss to her forehead. 'Goodnight, sweetheart. Sleep well.'

Elara beamed at him as he crossed the room. He stopped briefly in front of Archer, giving him a quick nod before disappearing down the corridor, leaving crumbs of vanilla cupcake in his wake.

'I just came to let you know my watch is starting soon, so I'll be outside if you need me.'

'I never expected to hear those words come out of your mouth,' she taunted, resting back on the bed to kick off her heeled sandals.

'Things change,' he shrugged, tucking his hands into his pockets.

'You want a cupcake?' she asked, holding out the box towards him.

He hesitated for a moment before he saw the expression on her face. 'Sure.'

He inspected the cake, a frown on his face.

'It's strawberry frosting, not poison,' she teased.

He scooped a generous helping onto his finger, tasting it tentatively. Surprise registered on his face before he took a large bite, paper and all.

'You're supposed to take the casing off first,' Elara laughed, bounding up from the bed to stop him before he could take another bite.

She took it gently from his hands, peeling away the paper with a shake of her head.

'This isn't edible,' she smiled, holding it up before dropping it to her desk and sitting down at the chair.

'Blighted burner food,' he mumbled, before polishing off the rest of the cupcake.

'Do you need anything else before I go?'

'Actually, could you undo the back of my dress? I can't do the corset myself, I needed two Broomies to help me earlier.'

Archer looked dumbfounded for a moment before snapping to attention, wiping the crumbs off his hands onto the material of his trousers.

'Can't say I'll be much help,' he mumbled, gesturing for her to stand up.

They stood in silence for a minute, Elara held her loose curls out of the way as he moved methodically down her back, loosening the ribbons.

'Did you have a good time tonight?' she asked finally, turning to see him out of the corner of her eye. She stifled a smirk when she found his brow furrowed in confusion.

'Other than babysitting you whilst you retched over the toilet bowl, can't really complain.'

Elara dropped her head into her hands, her cheeks flushed. 'Ugh don't remind me,' she cringed, dispersing the fog of embarrassment from her brain with a shake of her head.

'Lightweight,' he murmured. She could hear the smile in his voice. 'You know, I really didn't think you'd make it through tonight. Even at the ball you fit in surprisingly well.'

He pulled the last lattice of ribbon free, and Elara turned to face him, a scowl darkening her light features.

'Never say that again. I don't want to fit in with those entitled Ardents. They could stand to learn a thing or two about common courtesies.'

Archer ducked his head down to his chest to hide his smile. 'I could've said the same thing about you when we first met.'

Elara scrunched her nose at him, her lips a little pouty. 'You were rude to me; I was rude back. If you would have given me the time of day, you would have seen that I'm actually a delight.'

Archer laughed properly now, a deep rumble from his chest. 'Is that so? Miss Anderson. You certainly think highly of yourself.'

'Someone has to be my number one fan,' she said with a shrug.

'I think my father has that job covered,' Archer replied, his voice suddenly quiet.

Elara tried to meet his gaze, but he was suddenly fixated on staring at the wall behind her desk where she'd begun pinning her paintings.

'You did these?' he asked, taking a step towards them.

Elara nodded, moving towards her wardrobe to find something more comfortable to sleep in, holding her heavy dress against her body with one arm.

'They're incredible,' he breathed, running one fingertip along the paintwork. Elara stopped and watched him, his expression was soft, his body language relaxed, his hair pushed casually away from his face in waves as dark as the night. He was free of the shadows that usually clung to him so tirelessly, his starry eyes bright.

In weeks gone by, Elara would've said that her and Archer couldn't have been more different. In fact, in this moment, he felt like the opposite side to her coin. It made her heart equally race and ache as the pounding of her pulse seemed to scream Xander, Xander, Xander.

'You painted me?' he asked suddenly, his finger landing on a page full of darkness and turmoil. Heavy brushstrokes and dark outlines, beautifully terrifying, just like he had been the night she almost died.

'I couldn't get it quite right,' she murmured. It was true, she couldn't. Nothing she did could match the force that had radiated from him that night. She'd been half tempted to paint over the whole thing in black and call it a day.

He stared at it for a moment longer before finally prying his eyes away, his gaze still soft.

'You know, I don't think I've ever seen my dad show such genuine care towards someone before. It's nice to know he still can,' he said softly and immediately Elara's heart plummeted.

'Archer... I-'

'Don't, it's okay. I know what you're going to say. I truly am glad you have somebody here who cares for you so deeply. We all deserve that.'

Before Elara could talk herself out of it, she'd crossed the room and wrapped her arms around his neck, her face pressed into his shoulder. He stiffened, it wouldn't have come as a surprise if he'd peeled her off him and disappeared into the night. But instead, he tentatively wrapped his arms around her waist, his cool hands brushing the bare skin of her back. His fingertips were so icy that she flinched. She heard an almost imperceptible 'sorry' in her ear.

'Thank you for not just being my Fender, but for being my friend,' she whispered against the material of his jacket, willing the tears in her eyes to stay put.

He was silent, a stoic pillar of determination and austerity, when finally he said, 'thank you for understanding me.'

His lips just barely brushed the bare skin of her shoulder, his breath tickling the side of her neck when in a shadow of darkness, he was gone. The heat in Elara's chest gone with him.

CHAPTER THIRTY-SEVEN

Elara

She was surrounded by bags and suitcases, a stark improvement to the bin bags she arrived with. Though she'd tried to avoid them, she'd been forced to say goodbye to Darya and Dritan who had spent the morning in tears, showering her with leaving gifts and too-tight hugs. She'd expected Archer to appear mysteriously at some point during the morning for a gruff goodbye, but he never came. Instead, Ivy arrived alone at her door, more emotional than Elara would have expected, though she hid it well with a smile and a final cup of rosemary coffee sent specially by Olive.

'Do you know when you'll be back?'

Elara shook her head. No one had told her what the next part of the plan was, she was unsure if anyone actually knew what was to come of her future. She had a horrible feeling she was about to spend another few months with her parents, not hearing a word from Osmond with only her memories of her time here at the Council. The thought of not returning hit her harder than she anticipated, an uncomfortable lonely swirl growing by the minute in her chest.

'Have you seen Archer this morning?' she asked Ivy, begging her cheeks not to colour with guilt.

'No, not since last night. He hasn't been by?'

Elara shook her head silently, Ivy narrowed her eyes suspiciously, trying to read between the lines of Elara's body language.

'I'm sure he'll stop by before you leave. I'll speak with my father to try and figure out when you'll be back, I'm sure they won't keep you away as long this time. If they do, I might just have to kick up a fuss myself.'

Ivy winked, making Elara giggle, despite the tears beginning to form in her eyes. She'd grown incredibly fond of Ivy. Her couldn't-care-less attitude, her intelligence and her loyalty. Elara knew better than to let her go, she would be an incredible friend to her over the years. She pulled Ivy in for a quick tight hug, pressing her cheek against her shoulder, then laughing when she had to wipe a smudge of makeup from the black material.

'Sorry,' she grinned, pressing a quick kiss to her friend's cheek, before wiping the tears away from her own.

Ivy scrunched her nose at her, smiling kindly.

'I'll see you again soon.'

'I hope so.'

When it came to the time for Osmond to collect her, the sun had disappeared completely in the sky and Elara had been left alone with her thoughts for plenty of hours. She was counting down the minutes until she could see her family and Xander again, but she hated to admit that she was also dreading the time when she would be escorted through those gates without the promise of a return.

A sharp knock at the door startled Elara to her feet. Darya and Dritan had left about an hour ago, deciding it would be too difficult to say goodbye again, so Elara was alone in the house, trusted to let herself out.

She opened the door, expecting Osmond with a crowd of witches to carry her bags, but a lone figure stood in the doorway. Archer.

'Hey.'

Elara stared at him, there were deep bags beneath his eyes that hadn't been there yesterday. She couldn't identify how he was feeling, it was unsettling.

'Hi.'

'Take a walk with me. The Fenders will come for your bags.'

Elara gathered it was an order rather than a question as he rested his hand against the top of the door frame and leaned in slightly, looking around the living room.

'Um, sure,' Elara said hesitantly, dropping her bag off her shoulder and onto the floor. 'Where are we going?'

Archer smirked as he pulled the door closed behind them and set off down the corridor.

'That's for me to know and you to find out.'

'Are you sure I should be up here? I thought I wasn't allowed to leave the Northern Quarter,' Elara stated, unable to hide the concern in her voice as Archer began leading her up a gentle incline through a forest behind the Council.

Archer turned to make sure she was keeping up. 'The secret's out, the experiment's over, you don't have to be kept hidden away anymore.'

Elara smiled to herself in the dim light, trying to look around for any indication as to where they were going, but to no avail.

The cool evening air was incredibly refreshing, and Elara was surprised at how easy she was finding it to climb the hill, evidently all her training had been paying off.

As they emerged out of the tree line onto a pebble path, a large meadow lay out before them, laden with exotic looking flowers that lit up and turned to face them as they passed

'They're beautiful,' Elara breathed as she stopped to get a closer look at one, the light glowing from its centre bathing her in gentle heat.

'They're the seeds of the dead. When a witch dies, we bring their aura here and it blooms into a magical flower. Each possesses a unique gift that can be extracted from the pollen, so don't touch them.'

Elara gazed into the flower, it did seem almost alive with power, drawing her in closer, but eventually she tore her eyes away and began following Archer down the path.

A large tree came into view before them, standing proudly at the highest point of the hill. The path led straight up to it, then abruptly ended leaving the tree posed in all its glory. Between the cracks of the bark, glowing orange lines snaked along the thin latticed trunk and up into the branches. It almost glistened in the light, and the leaves were tinged a deep crimson. As Elara neared it almost seemed to hum with noise, she was desperate to get closer to it, feel the energy running under its bark. She watched in fascination as Archer did exactly that, he placed the palms of his hands on one of the thicker branches and closed his eyes. The orange trails of light immediately traced onto his skin, working along his arms, up his neck and into his hair. It was breathtakingly terrifying, but Elara couldn't resist the pull any longer, so she reached out a hand and watched in fascination as the veins under her skin began glowing orange, and her mind was filled with white noise.

It sounded like whispers or singing, but she struggled to make out any words.

'What is it?' she breathed when she finally found the strength to tear her hand away and turn towards Archer who looked as relaxed as she felt.

He motioned with his head for her to follow him down to the edge of the hillside, where they could see the lights of Felicia against the night sky, and the twinkle of the river running through its centre.

They sat together on the soft grass, carefully avoiding the flowers. Elara shivered slightly in the crisp January air, so without a word Archer took off his uniform jacket and draped it over her shoulders. She turned to look over her shoulder back at the tree to hide her smile.

'Hundreds of years ago, witches and humans lived peacefully in harmony,' Archer said. His voice was soothing, so Elara closed her eyes and lent tentatively against his arm, the bowman on his forearm spared her a quick, mocking glance before firing a perfect bullseye.

'The witches were simple beings, they had a way with nature, made salves and mixtures out of herbs and fruits, and had excellent intuition. Humans gravitated towards them and benefited greatly from their unique gifts. But gradually over the years, the witches began to develop new powers, ones that meant they could control the elements or bring justice to those who had done them wrong, and the humans did not like this shift in power. They had felt for hundreds of years as though the witches were there to serve them and make their lives easier, but now the witches were fighting back, forming impenetrable groups with immense power.

Humans decided that witches were no longer servants of nature and instead that they had agreed to a deal with the devil which had granted them their strong magic. They decided that the witch population should be eradicated completely from Earth to protect humanity. They began burning us at the stake, drowning us on ducking stools and parading our private lives on cucking stools. Women and children were the most targeted, as humans were savage and shallow creatures that judged witchcraft on appearance, bad behaviour and sexual promiscuity. They murdered as many of their own as they did our ancestors. Instant karma if you ask me,' he chuckled sadly.

'They burned hundreds of witches alive, but simultaneously we were finding our own way to fight back.

There were four incredibly powerful witches at that time. Each of them possessed the ability to control an element. Nowadays we would know them as Inchoate witches, though of course that term wasn't around back then. There was Armel, he could control the Earth, Nerida who had ownership over the seas, and twins Tempest and Coro who could manipulate fire and air. They formed a plan to create a land where the witches would be safe from humans and live their lives peacefully. It took years of work and religious study of enchantments, but eventually Felicia was formed, with a portal that only allowed those with warlock blood to pass through. Any human that tried to enter would need to be granted authority from one of the big four themselves, or a direct descendant. Once the remaining witches were safely in Felicia, they decided they would never return to Earth and destroyed the portal, a final act of freedom that would eventually cause more problems than it solved. It was the nail in the coffin of segregation.'

He took a deep breath and looked down at Elara, she felt the shift in his emotions as she met his gaze, and he continued the story.

'The four witches were regarded as royalty in Felicia. They had saved so many, but whilst they all played equal parts in Felicia's creation, Armel was crowned the King and trusted to rule over the people. He was a very intelligent and charming man, he could get anything he wanted, and his people loved him dearly, though feared him just as equally. He was well-known for his short bursts of anger that often resulted in catastrophe. One thing he always made very clear was his love for Nerida, the witch who could control water. He wished for them to rule together, as King and Queen, and create the strongest, most pure magical bloodline. Little did he know, Nerida was madly in love with Tempest, Coro's sister. Of course, the world was a little different then, and for two women to be in love was simply unacceptable, so they never told anyone, until the day Armel asked Nerida to marry him.'

Elara felt her heart begin to pound; this was sounding all too familiar.

'Nerida declined his proposal, declaring her love for Tempest, and in a fit of rage Armel killed Tempest with the root of a tree through her abdomen, whilst Nerida watched.'

A tear soundlessly slipped down Elara's cheek.

'Nerida was so devastated by Tempest's death that she created a river through Felicia with her tears, one designed to divide the two halves. On one side was Armel's castle and his cult of devout followers and on the other was the tower in which Nerida and Tempest had lived in together. But the segregation wasn't enough to keep Armel away, he chased and hunted her, if he couldn't have her willingly, he would take her forcefully, so Nerida took matters into her own hands and accessed a very unique stream of magic. Some would say it was cursed Shade Magic, others would say she was simply the most talented, brave and intelligent witch to ever have lived. The spell she performed she knew would kill her, but she felt as though she was ready to die and be reunited with Tempest, so she took one last chance at defeating Armel forever.

She found a way to bind the essence of her soul into a wand which was made from the wood of the tree that had killed Tempest. As she lay dying, she gifted the wand to Coro, who was instructed to kill Armel with it when he deemed it to be time. That way, all four of their souls would be combined within the wood of the wand, two out of murder and two out of sacrifice. Nerida sacrificed her life, whilst Coro sacrificed his innocence and freedom, becoming the man to murder the first King of Felicia.

Coro left it many years after the death of Nerida before he felt the time was right to kill Armel. The King, meanwhile, had his fun with his leadership. It will come as no surprise to you that every leader of Felicia has been a direct descendant of Armel himself. You can see it in their power-hungry greed, I'm sure you felt it from somewhere within Forneus. They were the original family to create the divide between the magical streams, desperate to keep their gift pure and laws were put in place to ensure the other witches followed suit.

But eventually, Coro had had enough of his King's reckless reign, and murdered him one night whilst he slept, bonding each of their souls into the wand.

Nerida had then instructed Coro himself to gift the wand to someone he deemed trustworthy, of any magical stream. She knew Coro was nothing like Armel and would fulfil his task to the best of his ability. It was never recorded who the wand was gifted to, as Coro was quickly exiled to Helabasus by Armel's son, though it was believed to be his wife, a woman named Aeni. But whoever that person was, it gave them the power to bear a child who would contain all streams of magic, therefore that child would be the most powerful witch in the whole of Felicia, an Omnia witch, and rightful heir to the throne. Now not all children in this family would bear the gift, only those who were pure in heart and mind, a condition of Nerida's sacrifice.

The children who bore this gift were misunderstood, however. They lacked the training to control their gifts and were seen as powerful and dangerous. They were exiled from society and grew resentful of the people who turned their backs on them and with their emotions fuelling their powers, and they became uncontrollable. The people of Felicia decided that all children in this family were infected with Shade Magic and sought to murder them the second they were born to protect themselves. The remaining members of the family were banned from procreating and exiled to Helabasus to live their lives in isolation. The witches believed they had solved their problem, as for a hundred years no Omnia witches made themselves known. Of course, some must have slipped through the cracks, as here you are.'

Archer smiled down at her, her eyes were wide with intrigue at the information that had been bestowed upon her. It was more fantastical than she could ever have imagined.

'And that tree over there? That was a final act from Coro before he was exiled. The hazel tree was a favourite of his sisters, due to some old myths and legends that they were told as children. There is much folklore surrounding hazel trees, they've always been quite magical.

From signifying wisdom and beauty to rods made of the branches used to find water and buried treasure… but the one that Tempest liked was about making your wishes come true. The custom stated that if you made and wore a 'wishing cap' of intertwined hazel twigs, your wishes would come true, and you would be gifted protection from things you could not foresee. She was known for carrying a twig of hazel wherever she went, and it was reported that this was what made her such a successful warrior. It also just so happened that the day she was killed, she had forgotten her hazel.'

'So, Coro planted this tree,' he gestured behind them to the figure that seemed to be hanging off his every word, listening to the story just as intently as Elara was, 'as a tribute to his sister. Whilst we plant the auras of the dead into the flowers, their essence goes into the tree, it's what makes it glow and lets them rest peacefully. The hum you can hear is their collective conscience, there's an awful lot of energy in there.

My mother used to say that if you placed both palms on the tree and waited with patience, if the witches felt you deserved it, they would drop a leaf to give you good fortune in whatever was troubling you. I've only heard of it happening twice in my lifetime. Once was when you were due to enter the human world, they brought you here to the tree and sure enough a leaf fell, I believe they tucked it into your cot to send with you.'

Elara couldn't even try and control the tears streaming down her face now. Ugly, hard sobs that shook her core and ached in her throat.

Archer said nothing, instead just wrapped a cautious arm around her shoulders and held her whilst she wept.

As she finally came to, a thought crossed her mind

'How do you know all of this? Why didn't you tell me before?'

Archer smiled. 'Ivy wasn't the only one to spend her childhood in the restricted section,' he chuckled.

Something about his response bit away at Elara's mind, though she couldn't figure out what it was that was bugging her.

'So Esmé and Gabriel, they must have been the descendants of Nerida's sacrifice?'

Archer nodded. 'One of them will have been, yes.'

'This all makes so much sense,' Elara sighed, thinking back to her nightmares and the memories that had practically torn her apart with emotion.

'So how did I end up with Darya and Dritan?'

Archer pondered for a moment, chewing on his lip. 'That's still something I'm trying to figure out. I'll get back to you on it.'

Elara was silent for a moment, there was a question echoing around in her brain, it was driving her mad. He seemed to notice her expression.

'Go on, spit it out. You're not usually one to hold back,' he smirked.

'When will I be seeing you again?' she asked, avoiding his gaze.

'Whenever my father allows you to return to Felicia, I guess.'

Elara frowned at his seemingly unbothered tone. 'What, you aren't even gonna come visit me?'

She could feel the amusement bubbling in his throat.

'Is that something you would want?'

There was a daring glint in his eye that made her heart race.

'Maybe,' she replied.

'Could've fooled me,' he drawled, stretching out his legs and leaning back on his elbows.

Elara chewed on her bottom lip. The moonlight was casting shadows across his face, but not like his own darkness that emerged from his skin. Light, caressing shadows that deepened the caverns of his cheekbones and set his eyes alight with a haunting fire. His dark hair ruffled in a soundless breeze, his shoulders tense against the ice cold chill of the night.

Elara had never felt more plain cocooned up by his side. Her eyes were no doubt puffy from crying, her cheeks pinched crimson from the cold, her hair knotted from the wind.

'I'll come and see you in February,' he said finally, breaking his gaze away from the view in front of them, his eyes settling on her face.

'Why February?' she frowned.

'My birthday is in February, I got you a gift, I'm expecting one in return.'

'You expect too highly of me. There is a 98% chance that I'll forget to get you one.'

'Three weeks together, burner, and I'm still not at the forefront of your mind.'

It was such a strange tightrope they balanced on, the thin line between hatred, friendship and flirtation.

She rolled her eyes and batted his arm lightly. 'How old will you be?'

'Nineteen.'

She tried to hide her shocked expression; it clearly didn't work. He laughed up at the sky, his throat bobbing.

'Are you suggesting I look middle-aged?' he tried to force a frown onto his face.

'No! Not at all. You just act so much older, and you've already been working for Forneus for what, five years? I assumed you would be at least, like, 22.'

Archer sat up proudly. 'I told you I was the best in my class, I was enlisted to work for Forneus at fourteen, the youngest they'd had.'

Elara tutted disapprovingly. 'Show off,' she muttered under her breath.

'What did you call me?' There was a mischievous twinkle in his eye.

'Nothing,' she grinned, shrugging off his jacket so that she could stand up.

'Oh no you don't. Not so fast.'

He grabbed her arm under the jacket as she passed it to him and pulled her back to the floor with a squeal.

Just before she could hit the ground, he caught her with a strong arm, pulling her close to his chest, her knees supporting her weight on the soft grass. Her arms were pinned to her chest, unable to flail away as she laughed, the cold rush of the breeze swept through her hair and tickled her neck as the night suddenly seemed to fall silent.

As her laugh quietened, she realised how closely Archer was holding her, coiled up against his chest. The heat of his skin was seeping through his thin T-shirt, and she could feel his heart beating underneath her hands. His gaze was so intense it took the air out of her lungs, and as she took deep breaths in, she could feel her ribcage expanding against the muscles in his arms, which was not helping at all.

'I-' she started but didn't get any further as in an instant his lips were on hers. They were confident and certain, everything that Elara was suddenly sure she'd never felt. He was gentle at first, but then his hands were on her face, around her waist, pulling her closer to him. She tried to fight it for a second but kissing him back seemed to come more naturally than breathing. She gripped his shirt, pulling herself fully onto his lap as his fingers tangled deep into her hair, she shivered as his cold hands brushed against the sensitive skin on the back of her neck. She could taste the salt from her tears on his lips, and the smell of the forest behind them heightened her senses even more. Each of his emotions seemed to be rushing under his skin, barely below the surface and tingling under her fingertips. It was exhilarating, so she pushed a little harder, desperate to be a part of them. She felt lost in time, as though she was hurtling through space at a thousand miles an hour, when suddenly she crashed through the atmosphere with a bang.

Xander.

It took every ounce of willpower to muster the strength to push Archer away. She held him back as his hands remained firmly gripped around her waist. She turned away, those betraying tears pooling once more in her eyes. For weeks now, her heart had ached for Xander. His warmth and comfort, his truthfulness and loyalty. Yet in front of her was the only person who she would never have expected any of that from, but with one kiss he seemed to have mended her broken heart, filled a hole she didn't even know was there. It was too much. She couldn't do this to Xander. She loved him; Archer was practically a stranger.

Without meeting his gaze, she quickly stood up and ran back towards the path, dragging the heels of her hands fiercely across her eyes. She bit the inside of her cheek until she could taste blood to jolt her back to reality and stop her from crying out to Archer to fix the mess he'd just made.

She'd almost reached the treeline before she heard Archer running behind her.

'NO, stop! Don't you dare leave now,' he yelled; she knew he could outrun her but that wasn't going to stop her from trying.

'Elara, I swear to the hounds of Helabasus you can't do that then just leave me here!' He was still shouting, but there was a softness to his voice, he was hurt.

She gradually came to a stop, her cheeks burning from the cold air.

'I can't do this, Archer,' she cried, 'Please don't make me do this, you're going to ruin everything. You hated me up until two days ago.'

'Turn around,' he whispered, the night turned still.

'I didn't do this. You kissed me.'

'YOU KISSED ME BACK!' he roared, the trees seemed to quake in his anger, the rolling hills threatening to toss them over the cliff and into the night. She turned, barely able to look at him.

He took a second to register her expression, before dropping onto the balls of his feet, his head in his hands.

'I'm sorry, I shouldn't have yelled.' His voice was quiet, gentle in a way she hadn't heard it before.

'I have to go, Archer,' she whispered, turning to walk back through the forest.

'No! Wait!' he begged, darting forward to catch her wrist.

He was stood so close behind her she could feel him breathing, she untwisted her arm from his grasp, like a vine uncoiling from a tree trunk.

'You can't leave now, please Elara,' he whispered, 'let's just talk about this. I'm sorry.'

Her heart felt on the brink of shattering into a thousand pieces, but with one last surge of strength she turned to face him, finding herself against his chest once more.

'I have to go home, Archer. I made a mistake and this- this is too much. I-... I love Xander.'

There it was. Any last thread of hopefulness plummeted down into his stomach like a bullet and pieces of her heart pierced their way through her lungs, each breath becoming torturous.

'But even if I didn't, this isn't about me choosing you or Xander. It's me doing what's best for me and I need to go home to be with my family. I've been in Felicia too long; I need my parents and my home and my friends. Can you understand?' Her voice shook and cracked every other word, but she was proud of herself for getting it out, even if it wasn't entirely truthful.

He wouldn't meet her gaze, that familiar weighted blackness beginning to form a barrier between them. It's near constant presence had become somewhat reassuring in passing days, but now it was oppressive, buzzing with sparks of turmoil and guilt. She could feel it shoving her away, pushing on her chest with an insistence she couldn't ignore.

She turned to make her way back to the Council, but at the last second, he jumped in front of her, his hands cupped her jaw roughly and he kissed her one last time. This kiss wasn't exciting and new, it was a point to prove. A flood of hollow understanding and nightmarish defeat.

But just like that, he was gone. It was all she could do not to drop to the pebbled ground and scream out to the hazel tree for a leaf of good fortune. God knew she could use one.

CHAPTER THIRTY-EIGHT

Elara

Osmond had met her at the gate without question. He didn't comment on her smudged makeup, the clear tear-tracks down her cheeks, or her bedraggled hair. He didn't even complain that she was an hour late.

He simply took a lace handkerchief from his pocket and dusted it over her face, wiping away any traces of her guilt. He flattened down her hair with the care of a doting father and pulled her in for a quick, warm hug. He smelled like moss and greenery, a winter's night. The gesture almost made her start crying all over again.

'Are you ready to go home, Miss Anderson?'

She nodded silently, not trusting the words that were desperate to flood out of her lips.

They walked most of the way in silence. Every now and then, Osmond would dart a glance over at her, before staring hard at the pavement before them. The sun was just dipping below the horizon in Scotland, revealing a deep indigo sky. Elara had received a text from Xander just a few minutes after she passed through the gate, that he was waiting for her at her parent's, and most of her bags had already been dropped off by the 'trip-staff' whoever that was supposed to entail.

When they reached the corner before Elara's road, she found herself hanging back.

'How am I supposed to do this?' she whispered.

Osmond smiled down at her sadly, 'tell them what you need to, Elara. If that is the truth, then so be it. If you trust them, then I trust them. You earned my respect long ago, but I am certain that you've earned a little bit more from the rest of the Council. Plus, I'm good at keeping secrets,' he said with a wink.

Elara gripped his arm tightly, suddenly desperate for him not to leave. 'Will I see you again soon?'

He stroked a gentle thumb across her face, a gentle but sad smile awash his features. 'Of course, my dear. Though I daresay you would do just fine on your own nowadays. However, I'm not sure I could say the same for myself,' he chuckled. 'You are destined to do such great things, Elara Anderson. Whether that's in Felicia, or here on Earth. Try not to worry so much, dear.'

She nodded graciously, desperately trying to pull in the tears that threatened to fall. She was incredibly surprised she had any left at this point.

'There's one more thing, Osmond.'

She took a deep breath, unsure of how he would react to what she was about to say.

'I need to know more about Esmé and Gabriel Sylvaine, my parents. If I'm going to do anything for Felicia, I deserve to know my heritage.'

His eyes held a look of understanding, though he said nothing and instead turned and walked away with all the grace of a wise warlock, his silver hair gleaming in the last dregs of sunlight.

Elara let out the breath that had been uncomfortably pressing down on her chest out and watched as he disappeared into the shadows, before turning back towards her home.

She rounded the corner and waiting there on the street for her as promised, were her parents and Xander stood waving madly, surrounded by her suitcases.

She couldn't help but break into a run as she neared, so desperate to be close to them.

She crashed into her parent's arms at full force, almost taking them down with her speed as they laughed.

'Hi sweetheart! Looks like you missed us then!' Pete joked as he stroked his daughter's hair and littered kisses on her forehead.

'I missed you so much,' she whispered into her mother's shoulder, breathing in her familiar scent.

'Oh, love! We missed you more than anything in the world. You're never going away for that long again!' her mother sobbed, squeezing her so tight she could hardly breathe.

'Come on sweetheart, let's get inside, get you a nice hot drink and we want to hear every single detail.'

Elara nodded, still not letting go of her mum, even though she was getting splashed with mascara stained tears. It felt suddenly as though the last three weeks had been spent in an ice-cold box, starved of love and affection. Now suddenly, in blinding colour and overwhelming sensation was everything that she had so desperately yearned for.

'What are they like!' Pete joked to Xander who had been stood waiting patiently for his turn.

'Come on Rose, let's give them a moment,' Elara's dad said with a wink as he finally dragged his wife into the house.

That was all it took for Elara to throw herself into Xander's arms, her legs around his waist and her arms around his neck.

'Hi, El,' he whispered into her hair. 'I would say I missed you too, but I feel like that line's been used already,' he said with a grin.

She pulled back and studied him for a moment. Here he was, finally in all his beautiful warmth. The golden-flecked hair, the kind eyes that seemed to hold every emotion all at once, the cheeky grin that made her heart melt. Her heart raced back to long days hidden away in the Council, tucked away in nooks and crannies for just a chance to hear his voice. All the time away was worth it just for this moment. She kissed him with every ounce of love she could muster, slowly but surely pushing the image of Archer down into one of the boxes in her mind. She couldn't seal it all the way, but it was a start.

'Damn, you can go away more often if that's how you're gonna come back!' he joked hoarsely, his accent lilting in the most sing-songy fashion.

She put a finger on his lips to shush him, a wide grin on her face.

'Xander? I love you so much,' she whispered.

His eyes widened and answered for her, before kissing her again, spinning them both around in circles until she squealed.

He laughed as he finally set her down, keeping his arms tight around her waist in a bone-crushing hug that she returned with all her might, breathing in his familiar scent.

'Oh God, I have so much to tell you,' she whispered in his ear, 'you're not even gonna believe the last few weeks I've had.' She giggled as he finally released her from the tight hug and lent down to rest his forehead on hers.

'I can't wait to hear it,' he smiled, before pressing a gentle kiss to the tip of her nose.

'Come on, I can spare another twenty minutes or so away from my parents, but this can't wait.'

She grabbed his hand, starting to drag him away towards the cliffside.

'Oh God, should I be worried?' he joked.

'Probably,' she called back over her shoulder.

'Did you turn into some kind of Welsh dragon whilst you were there?'

'Not far off,' she whispered to herself.

She felt a tug on her hand as Xander had stopped walking with her. She turned to find him looking equally worried and confused.

'Come on, I promise I'll tell you everything. You just have to swear you'll keep an open mind.'

She grinned as his eyebrows shot up and his eyes widened dramatically. She reached up on her tiptoes to kiss him one more time. Revelling in the familiarity, the softness and sureness of his lips, the smell that she'd dreamt of ever since arriving in Felicia. As she pulled away, he brushed her cheek softly, his expression gentle.

She turned to continue her path to the cliffside, when suddenly at the edge of the clearing behind her house, she saw a tall, shadowed figure standing as still as a statue, clearly watching their every move. She couldn't see their face, but it was impossible to mistake the quick swish of a wooden wand before the figure disappeared into the shadows. She stared at the spot a moment longer, wondering if her mind was playing tricks on her.

'What is it?' Xander asked, turning to follow her gaze.

She was silent for a beat longer, waiting to see if the figure returned.

'Nothing. Don't worry. Come on, let's go,' she said after a second, taking Xander's hand once more and leading him deep into the forest.

'Well, Mr Levett. Were you planning on informing Forneus of Miss Anderson's unusual gifts?'

The dagger was pressed so tightly to his throat, he didn't dare speak for fear of his jugular being sliced clean open. Instead, he stared unflinching at his captor, his jaw clenched.

'Not that that matters now of course. You've committed treason, Mr Levett. You know the punishment for treason, don't you?' The pressure against his throat heightened, he felt the skin begin to split.

'Tell me the TRUTH about Elara. You knew what she was, didn't you Mr Levett? You kept the information from Forneus… disobeying the oath you took when YOU WERE 14!' the captor bellowed, grasping his gloved hand around Archer's jaw with bruising force.

'ANSWER ME!' he roared, pushing Archer's head back to expose more of his throat.

Archer's breathing was heavy, his nostrils flared as sweat dripped down his spine.

'My oath was to Elara. To HER safety. Forneus had nothing to do with it,' Archer hissed under his breath, his skin pulling painfully taught against the metal blade

'You know what they'll do to her, Mr Levett. If you tell me everything now, I'll protect her. Watch out for her. Perhaps I'll even persuade Forneus to lessen her punishment. That's what you want, isn't it? For her to be safe?'

His breath was hot and sticky in Archer's ear. Every Fender bone in his body was desperate to confess, begging him to trust the promise of Elara's safety. But he knew it was a trick. Anything he said would be used against them both, against his family and Elara's. There was only one thing he could do, and their captor needed to die.

Printed in Great Britain
by Amazon